MISSING LYNX

THE LYNX SERIES

FIONA QUINN

MISSING

Lynx

FIONA QUINN

THE WORLD OF INIQUUS

Ubicumque, Quoties. Quidquid

Iniquus - /i'ni/kwus/ our strength is unequalled, our tactics unfair – we stretch the law to its breaking point. We do whatever is necessary to bring the enemy down.

THE LYNX SERIES

Weakest Lynx

Missing Lynx

Chain Lynx

Cuff Lynx

Gulf Lynx

Hyper Lynx

MARRIAGE LYNX

STRIKE FORCE

In Too DEEP

JACK Be Quick

InstiGATOR

UNCOMMON ENEMIES
Wasp

Relic

Deadlock

Thorn

FBI JOINT TASK FORCE
Open Secret

Cold Red

Even Odds

KATE HAMILTON MYSTERIES
Mine

Yours

Ours

CERBERUS TACTICAL K9 TEAM ALPHA
Survival Instinct

Protective Instinct

Defender's Instinct

DELTA FORCE ECHO
Danger Signs

Danger Zone

Danger Close

This list was created in 2021. For an up-to-date list, please visit FionaQuinnBooks.com

If you prefer to read the Iniquus World in chronological order you will find a full list at the end of this book.

1

I strained against the seat belt, leaning forward with impatience as if by weight and will, I could get us there faster. My fingers drummed anxiously on the car door. I wanted to be at the airport now; I had waited more than a year to see my mentor, Spyder McGraw, and hear his rolling thunder laugh.

Striker slid his eyes toward me then refocused on the road. A little smile played across his lips. "You think that screaming like a Hellhound through Washington is going to get Spyder off his plane any faster?"

Striker Rheas took up a lot of space. His silken rusty-brown hair with its tight military cut brushed the roof; his shoulders — powerfully built from his days in Special Ops Forces — spread wide against the seatback. His bearing was always calm and capable — sometimes too much so. And while I obviously amused him right now, he was pissing me off. I answered him with my best withering stare and turned to the window as he drove sedately through the city streets.

The snow outside fell in big fluffy flakes, powdering the trees and cars, making the road shiny and slick. DC traffic was non-existent this morning. Everything had shut down for Christmas.

Striker pulled into Reagan International Airport's parking deck and set the brake. I narrowed my eyes so he would know not to hedge. "At least give me a hint. What kind of assignment are we going to be working on?"

There it was again, the glimmer of amusement. "I've told you everything I've got. I'll be finding out the same time you do."

"Okay, then where's Spyder coming in from?"

Striker released his seatbelt and swiveled toward me. "He flew his last leg from Dallas — DC" He held up his hands. "I swear that's all the information I know."

"This is a little surreal." I pushed a blonde curl behind my ear. "One minute, I'm starting new classes at the University, and the next, you're handing me my gear to take down some bad-guy. I had a plan."

"Plans change. Seems serendipitous — Spyder reappearing just as you wanted to head out the door." He flashed a smile. I loved Striker's smiles — slightly crooked, the hint of dimples, straight white teeth. His smiles started in his warm green eyes where the flecks of gold danced. They disarmed me, but I wanted my armor up.

I arched a brow. "I think perhaps you used more bullying and less serendipity to change my heart. Maybe a little bribery?"

"Incentivizing, Lynx. You wouldn't pass up an opportunity to serve your country — and, of course, to work with Spyderman."

I got out of the car. The wind whipped the skirt of my Christmas-red cocktail dress around my legs. I was still in my party dress from last night.

After the guests left, Striker surprised me with the news about Spyder coming home. Since my parents had passed away,

Spyder took on a bigger role than playing my mentor; he became my other dad. Spyder's homecoming was the best Christmas gift ever. Well, that and the beautiful gold brooch Striker gave me under the mistletoe — along with the kind of kiss that should end every great romance novel. The kind that promises a happily-ever-after.

I sighed.

Ah, if life were only that simple. I didn't need a fairytale ending. Right now, I just wanted to regain my balance. And truth be told, Striker wasn't looking for fairytales, either.

I wasn't sure what he meant by that kiss. Striker was his job. He was a highly effective operator dedicated to protecting national security. Everything was secondary. Everyone was secondary. Would I change that? No. Could I live with it? Hmmm. I tried before with Angel, and that ended about as badly as anything could end. If Striker wanted a relationship with me, he'd want it on his own terms. He hadn't articulated his parameters to me. Probably because he knew I wouldn't like them.

I tightened the belt around my short wool coat as Striker walked over to my side. His eyes caught mine. He tilted his head with that assessing look of his. "That's a curious expression, Lynx. What were you just thinking?"

I smiled up at him. "That the décolleté on this party dress might be a little inappropriate for Christmas morning."

Striker grinned. "You're probably right, but I'm not complaining. I think you're beautiful." He planted a light kiss at my hairline, entwined his fingers with mine, and we walked toward the terminal.

Even in my heels, Striker's six-foot-three frame towered above me. His Irish cable knit sweater and pair of 501s accentuated everything a girl could want to be accentuated. His assets weren't lost on the woman passing us, pulling her carry-on behind her. She turned to give his rear an appreciative glance, clearly enjoying the view. Pretty tactless — the man was holding my hand, and she didn't know we weren't a couple.

In the waiting area, I shed my coat and paced in front of our seats, wringing my hands. Impatience and excitement made me hot and twitchy.

"If you get any warmer, there isn't much left to shed, Lynx." Striker stretched out his long legs and slouched back in the hard plastic chair.

"It's Lexi. I don't use my call name when I'm off the clock."

Striker's eyes moved over my dress. The low cut bodice showed off my full breasts and cinched tight at the waist like a starlet from the fifties. I'd felt flirtatious and sexy when I'd danced at the party. The skirt had ballooned out as I'd spun around, showing off legs toned from years of running and martial arts.

"What if he's late? Did you check and make sure he made his flight?" I pulled my hair back into a ponytail to get it out of my face. "I should take another peek at the board. Maybe there's been a delay."

"That's fine. You go do that."

I focused down the hall where the flight board stood. "I can't." I plopped down beside him. "My feet hurt too badly."

"I will never understand why a woman does that to herself."

"You think my high-heels are sexy, don't you?" I straightened my leg for him to see.

"Definitely."

"And that's why I wear them." I kicked off my shoes. The cold floor eased the ache. I didn't care too much about propriety since we were almost the only people at the airport. "They make my legs long and my butt perky. I like dressing girly and pretty." Actually, looking young, cute, and approachable made my job a whole lot easier. Being discounted as a piece of fluff let me go places and do things that would normally set off alarms.

Striker wrapped his arm around my shoulders, pulling me to him. "I totally agree with the girly and pretty part, Chica," he whispered into my hair.

I pushed Striker off me and jumped to my feet. "Oh God, he needs our help."

"Who does?" Striker rose beside me, his eyes scanning the room for a threat. "What are you talking about?"

I hopped on one foot, cramming my shoe onto the other one. Striker cupped my elbow to hold me steady.

"Spyder. I heard him say it in my head." I tapped my finger to my temple as I came upright.

Striker's body shifted. His muscles tightened, and the laughter left his eyes. "You heard this ESP-wise?"

A disembodied voice over the loudspeaker announced Spyder's flight was deplaning.

I didn't bother answering Striker. Of course, ESP-wise. Why else would I hear voices in my head?

I grabbed up my coat and purse and ran toward the security gate. The passengers coming up looked rumpled and droopy-eyed. I, on the other hand, was chomping at the bit, eagerly searching the crowd.

Normally, Spyder McGraw stood flag-pole tall and thin. The contrast between his white teeth and midnight, blue-black skin was startling, and it was the only distinctive thing about him. He shaved his head and wore non-descript clothes. Spyder liked to blend.

There! The last one off. His tall frame loomed in the back behind the swarm. His shoulders bowed uncharacteristically as he moved forward zombie-like.

With my focus glued to Spyder's face, I pushed through the

crush of travelers leaving the security gate. The guards jumped up from their posts — my actions drawing their attention, but I didn't care. I had to help Spyder. One guard grabbed at my arm. His other hand popped the snap on his holster. Striker brandished his Iniquus ID, and the guards fell back.

I swam forward against the current of travelers until I could reach Spyder. The deadly strong arms, that I knew so well, hung lifelessly by his sides. I pulled him into a hug. Sweat glistened his face, and his body trembled against mine. I reached up and touched his head; the heat wavered off his skin in almost visible pulses.

"I need a wheelchair," I commanded the guards whom I caught in my peripheral vision. They had braced for action mere inches away. My focus never left Spyder's face. "Spyder, you're burning up."

He mouthed, "Malaria," and keeled over.

Striker lunged for him but couldn't get a good hold from over my shoulder. I dropped to the ground to protect Spyder's head from the tile floor.

The guards pushed passengers out of the way.

"Call an ambulance!" I shouted and struggled out from underneath Spyder.

He was conscious, but his eyes were glassy and his pupils unfixed. I patted his face and called his name. He didn't even try to respond or focus on me. Striker loosened Spyder's clothes at the neck and waist.

Grabbing my purse, I upended it, searching frantically through the debris to find the extra diabetic supply kit I carried for when I babysat my neighbor's little girl, Jilly-bean.

With shaking hands, I grasped Spyder's finger. I have done blood checks about a thousand times as a volunteer EMT, but my training whispered from deep in my brain — muffled by the storm clouds of my emotions. Memories of the night my dad and I were in the car accident swamped my mind. I knelt exactly like this, on the side of the road, holding my dad's head and praying the same prayer, "Please be okay, please be okay," even though it was obviously too late for him.

The number on the meter came up low. Way too low. Verge of coma low. "Think," I commanded myself as I reached blindly for the glucose gel from my purse jumble.

"Striker, hold him still." My EMT voice sounded focused and in charge. Where did that come from? I felt everything but professional; I felt gelatinous. "When I give Spyder this glucose, he won't understand what's going on. He'll fight for his life."

Striker fastened down on Spyderman's wrists. Straddling him, Striker used his weight as leverage.

Kneeling, my thighs clamped like a vice by Spyder's ears to restrain him and protect his head. His chest didn't rise or fall. Horror jetted through my veins. I put my cheek toward his face to reassure myself that he was still breathing. Spyder's exhale whispered against my skin. My breath blew as thinly as his. My legs and feet burned and tingled from lack of oxygen. "Breathe deeper!" I ordered as much for Spyder as for myself.

By muscle memory and not from conscious thought, I held Spyder's nose until he unclenched his teeth and parted his lips. I stuck the tube into his mouth and squirted the glucose down his throat. I used all of my leg strength to protect his head and to keep him in place while I squeezed the gungy gel. As he fought, glucose smeared everywhere.

Striker wrestled Spyderman down like they were on the Olympic mats, going for a gold medal. I knew Striker would have to. Once, I watched Spyder lift a man twice his weight and throw him like a rag doll. Spyder had long thin limbs made of steel.

I had tunnel vision. Nothing existed but Striker, me, Spyder, and the red goo. As I worked, I chanted my mantra. Each inhale was a "Please." Each exhales, "Be okay." "Please, be okay." Like the Little Engine-Who-Could, cheerleading itself through the crisis. "Please, be okay."

I startled when the security guard crouched beside me.

"The rescue squad's in the building, ma'am. They'll be here in a minute."

"Grab more gel and pop the top off for me." I pointed at the tube with my chin. The guard put it in my hand and waited for further instructions.

"Hold his legs down."

The security guard looked dubious but did as I said.

I was squirting the second tube of glucose into Spyder's mouth as the paramedics rushed over with a gurney. I knew one of the guys, Chuck; I recognized him from my volunteer-training. The sight of him buoyed me. We had resources now and trained support. I put on a costume of competence. My teeth stopped chattering; my hands stopped shaking.

"What've you got here, Lexi?" Chuck asked, setting his equipment bag beside me.

"Forty-five-year-old male, with no history of heart problems, weak vitals, reporting a recurrence of malaria. High fever. Exhibiting signs of hypoglycemia. I checked with a meter I had. It read 29. I have most of one tube of gel in, and I'm working on the second one. If you've got any more, we could probably use it."

Chuck opened his case, grabbed a tube, and pulled off the plastic top. He laid it beside me and took out his official blood glucose meter. He swabbed Spyderman's finger, with Striker's help.

"22. He's not coming up yet. He's thrashing too much to try

to run a line with dextrose. We may want to use a Glucagon shot." Chuck rummaged in his supply kit.

I caught Chuck's eye. "Since he's not unconscious yet, let's see if I can get enough gel in to calm him down, then we can put him on the gurney and strap him down for the IV."

He nodded. "We'll work your plan. Let me get more gels out. He's spitting most of it on you." Chuck pulled a handful of tubes from his kit.

I was covered in the gel.

Spyder was covered in gel.

It took every single tube the paramedics had brought with them to get Spyder stable.

While Spyder became lucid, the EMTs wiped him off and loaded him onto the gurney. I sat on the floor and watched — nerves vibrating.

Chuck tapped his pen against the clipboard. "Malaria. How'd you know to check for hypoglycemia, Lex?"

Spyder had contracted malaria when he was in Africa, supporting a DEVGRU operation. It was Striker who carried him out of the jungle to safety. When Spyder returned home to recover, I made sure that I knew everything I could about the disease. I wasn't about to lose another loved one. Not if I could help it. "I don't know," I said. "I must have read something about it along the way. Quinine and hypoglycemia…"

Chuck nodded. "Do you have a name and address?"

"His name is…" And I stopped. I didn't know his name. He was like a father to me, but the only name I've ever associated with him was his call name, Spyder — or as Iniquus baptized him "Spyderman" since Striker and Spyder sound the same over the airwaves. I had no idea what his legal name was. I searched out Striker's eyes, and he shrugged.

"His name is Mr. McGraw. He's just back in the country. I don't know where he traveled in from. He'll be living with me." I gave Chuck my contact information.

"Are you following us to the hospital?" Chuck placed a kit between Spyder's legs on the gurney. His partner attached the IV bag of dextrose and saline onto a support arm.

"Yes," I said from my place on the floor.

"Okay, he's packaged for transport, so we're going to head on out. We're taking him to Suburban. Dispatch says they have a pathologist on call this morning. I'll catch up with you at Emergency. It's good to see you again, Lexi. I'm sorry it's under these circumstances."

I slowly gathered the contents of my purse back together. Striker helped me to my feet and held me steady until I caught my balance.

"You're sticky." He moved his hands out and away so as not to spread the goop any farther.

"Yeah, let's wash up, and then we can go," I said.

The shock my body was processing pushed me beyond exhaustion. I shambled into the ladies' room and stood in front of the mirror. Not girly. Not pretty. Not even approachable. I was one big fat mess. Red slime in my hair, on my dress, up and down my arms. My mascara had run with the tears down my cheeks, leaving black rivulets. I did my best to wash off, took a deep breath, and headed back to the car with Striker. He opened the passenger-side door for me. I sat down but couldn't swing my legs in. I stopped for a minute.

"You okay?" Striker crouched beside me.

"Ha! My legs are shaking from that workout. Spyder fought like a madman."

Striker put his warm hands on my thighs and slowly massaged them up and down. I reached out and grabbed his wrists, his hands caught under my skirt. I swirled with emotions — too many feelings in one big rush; they made my head spin. "Please don't." The last wayward tear slid past my lashes and got stuck beside my nose.

"Lynx, I was trying to help — I wasn't thinking," Striker said earnestly.

"Not your fault. I'm just — it's too much. My emotions have been doing cart-wheels since the party."

"It's been a hell of a morning for you." Striker looked deeply into my eyes. His calm confidence steadied me. "Okay, Chica?"

I nodded.

Striker slowly brushed a stray lock of hair back, kissed the tear from beside my lips, and walked around to the driver's side.

I hauled the door shut with the last of my energy. "I'm exhausted."

Striker slid under the wheel. "It was a hell of a fight for first thing in the morning."

"What I want to know is why Spyder would chance traveling in that condition. You spoke to him — he said nothing about his being on death's door-step?"

"All he said was, 'I'm coming in for Christmas, gear up, I need help beheading the Hydra."

"Wow!"

"My thought exactly." Striker warmed me with a smile, pulled his belt across his chest, and steered down the early morning streets with his normal calm — which, as usual, drove me absolutely crazy.

At Suburban, Striker hadn't even shifted into park before I jumped out the door and sprinted across the parking deck. I thundered down the stairs, not waiting for the elevator, and ran full out to the emergency department entrance. Frozen slush splashed up my hose, leaving mud sprays on my legs. I clattered down the hall, arriving just as they raced Spyder's gurney through the automatic doors and out of my reach.

Chuck handed his paperwork to the intake nurse at the desk and headed over to where I stood, open-mouthed and bewildered, outside the locked corridor.

"They aren't going to let you in. Immediate family only until he can say otherwise."

An exasperated huff escaped my lungs as I spun in place. "This sucks. Can you tell me anything?"

"You know it's against HIPAA to talk to friends about his status, but I think I can get away with discussing the case as one attending EMS member to another." Chuck maneuvered me to an alcove. "Lexi, your friend is in bad shape. He should never have been on that plane."

"How bad?" I gnawed at my lower lip.

Chuck put his hands on his hips and shook his head. "I can't say. His vitals went south. We bagged him most of the way. I'm not sure we got him here in time. I'm sorry."

My eyes felt wild in my head. My eyebrows stretched to my hairline, my lids unblinking. I couldn't wrap my brain around his words.

Chuck took my elbows. "Lexi, are you going to pass out? Do you need to puke?"

I glanced down to find my fingers entwined in Chuck's sleeves and forced myself to unclench my grip. I shook my head to line up my thoughts. "It's important that I know — did he say anything to you on the ride in?"

Chuck glanced over his shoulder, waited for a couple to pass, and dropped his voice. "Does 'Sylanos' mean anything to you?"

"Yes, Sylanos."

"He came around briefly and said, "Sylanos became a Hydra, tell Alex.' Then he took his nose dive. Do you know an Alex?"

"Yes, I'll pass the message. Think again. Anything else? Anything at all?"

"Um. He said Alex…and Hydra… I guess he muttered some other stuff, but it sounded like a foreign language."

Chuck didn't have anything more for me, so I thanked him for his kindness and said good-bye. Disbelief blanketed me as he and his teammate went out through the double glass doors. I turned my focus to where Striker leaned against the wall across from me with his arms folded over his chest.

Striker pushed off and walked over. "And?"

"Chuck doesn't think things look good for Spyder." I sucked in a gulp of air like I had been underwater for way too long.

Striker pulled me into a hug and kissed the top of my head. "I'm so sorry."

Standing in Striker's arms grounded me like nothing else ever has. It was like being able to slam a door shut on all of the bad things raging on the other side. I rested for a minute before I leaned my head back to see his eyes. "Spyder said Sylanos is the Hydra."

"No shit?" He pulled out his phone. "Command is going to be interested to hear that."

"Who are you calling? It's Christmas morning."

"Iniquus. They should have someone from human resources who can come in. Fill out Spyderman's paperwork, handle the insurance."

"Even today?" I asked.

"I hope so. Someone's usually available when an operator's unconscious." Striker pressed a button and held the phone to his ear.

"This happens often enough that they assign someone?" I pinched at the skin on my neck.

"Precaution. We're all required to leave a directive so the doctors can talk to someone, otherwise—"

"HIPAA — got it. We're in the dark."

Striker held up a finger and turned his body while he spoke to Headquarters.

My phone buzzed in my coat pocket. I checked the screen. It was Dave Murphy, my across-the-street neighbor.

"Lexi, you're not at home."

"Nope, I had a friend rushed to Suburban Hospital. I'm just getting here myself."

"You're at Suburban now? Good. Hey, tell Mrs. Nelson Cathy's going to come up to the hospital later this morning and bring her communion, and ask what else she needs."

"Okay." I put a finger in my ear and turned toward the wall as a noisy group moved past. "You didn't call me about Mrs.

Nelson, though." I raised my voice over the din.

"The boys want to show you what Santa brought. I let them go over and ring your bell. They heard the dogs bark, your car's parked outside, but you didn't answer. I thought I'd check-in and make sure everything's all right."

"Thanks. Let them know I'll stop by later. Okay?"

"Yeah, hey, did you know we're getting new neighbors?" Dave asked.

As he said the word "neighbors," a thought leaped through my mind like a white leopard. I reached out to grasp the tail so I could pull her back and understand the meaning, but she slipped silkily through my fingers and slinked under the brush, too quick for me to grab hold. A shiver tingled down my spine.

"I spotted the SOLD sign up. So Detective Dave, what's the skinny?" I asked.

"No idea. I haven't noticed anyone hanging around. Hey, Cathy's calling me. Gotta go."

"Merry Christmas."

Striker raised a questioning brow as I dropped my phone back in my purse.

"Dave called. The little old lady on the other side of my duplex had a stroke a couple of days ago. She's here, too."

"Is her family with her?"

"She doesn't have a family. She just has us neighbors. What did Headquarters say?" I asked.

"You're listed as next-of-kin. They're on their way with the papers."

"They can't fax them over?"

"Protocol. The information is classified."

I exhaled my frustration at the rules and hurdles standing between Spyder and me.

Striker reached for my hand. "Let's get you something warm

to drink and some food. The doctors are doing their work. Iniquus is on the way to get the papers straight. Then we'll make a plan."

I wiggled frozen toes in my sopping wet shoes. How could Striker run through a freaking winter storm and stay immaculate, and I looked more like something a dog chewed on? Dogs. I slapped my hand to my forehead and glanced down at my watch. "This is a little complicated because of Christmas."

"Why? What's going on?" Striker used his body to shield me from another big family group moving through with presents and "It's a Boy!" balloons.

"Right now, I'm thinking about Beetle and Bella. They need to be fed and walked. They're probably pacing at the door."

"Gator's on duty at Iniquus this morning. He can go to your place if you want. I'm sure he'd jump at a chance to eat the party leftovers." Striker stooped to pick up a little girl's bunny she had dropped and handed it off to someone else in her family.

Gator was one of seven men on our team at Iniquus, lead by Striker. Last fall, they were assigned to safeguard me after Travis Wilson's attack had me rushed to this very hospital. I stared up the hall with tightly sealed lips—bad memories.

The doctors here glued and bandaged me back together, then the Iniquus team slipped me out in the middle of the night to hide me in a safe house and protect me while they hunted for Wilson.

Six women. Six. All with husbands or fathers in law enforcement — all killed. I was supposed to be number seven. My survival turned out to be a skin-of-the-teeth miracle. I lived because Spyder had trained me well. God, please make this okay. Make Spyder better. I needed to thank him. And I needed to ask him… No one could figure out how I got caught in Wilson's crosshairs. When they were alive, my dad had been a mechanic, and my husband had been a Ranger over in Afghanistan — not in law enforcement.

While tucked away at the safe house, I explained how I actually had a long-standing relationship with Iniquus through Spyder. We had guessed that it was this association — well, my connection to Spyder more specifically — that made me Wilson's last target. Now that Wilson was dead, Spyder was probably the only one with an answer to the puzzle of why I was stalked and attacked.

Well, the silver lining to this mess was that the puzzling skills I demonstrated at the safe house caught the attention of Iniquus Command; I was offered a job here. And voila! Mostly I loved my job; I certainly loved my team — especially Gator Aid.

I took off my coat, tucking it over my arm. "I thought Gator was with Amy."

"Amy wanted Gator to go home to North Carolina to meet her family and spend a couple of days visiting. In Gator's book, spending Christmas with a girlfriend's family is just shy of getting engaged. Gator isn't as committed to the relationship as Amy's feeling. He asked for duty, so he'd have an excuse to stay put and not rock the boat."

"Maybe Gator should be clear with her about his commitment level." *And maybe you should be clear with me, Striker Rheas.*

"Gator tried. He's told her, on more than one occasion, he's married to the job and not interested in a serious relationship right now."

"And, Amy said what?"

"He'd change his mind because she's the best thing that's ever happened to him."

"Huh. So what do you think Gator's doing?"

"He's probably still hunkered down at the barracks on-call. Iniquus only runs a light crew on Christmas. Though if there was an emergency, we'd all get pulled in, no matter where we were or what we were doing."

I cocked my head to the side. "Did I sign up for that part of the Iniquus pledge?"

"Nope. You're special. You get your own set of rules."

That made me smile. "I like having my own set of rules."

"I thought you would." Striker put his hand on the small of my back and steered me toward the doors.

"Wait, I need to call Gator before we go in."

3

It wasn't quite seven o'clock when we joined the blurry-eyed nurses and doctors in the cafeteria breakfast line. I certainly won the prize for the fanciest dress. The cashier stood open-mouthed, his eyes directed down my cleavage.

Striker cracked his knuckles.

The guy refocused and rang up our trays.

I took a sip of coffee and swirled my fork in my scrambled eggs. I couldn't get my brain to rest on a single subject. My thoughts kaleidoscoped in my head. Striker watched me over the top of his coffee cup with that quiet assessing look of his and let me have my mental space to process this turbulent day.

When we went back to Emergency, we found that the doctors had moved Spyder into level four isolation until they determined his diagnosis. They had confirmed the recurrence of malaria, but I guess that was only part of the picture. I wrung my hands and listened to the nurse explain that Spyder was still unconscious, and we should just go home for the time being. It might be days before we were allowed any contact with him.

We took the elevator up to the fourth floor to check on Mrs. Nelson. I hobbled like Quasimodo, grimacing with each step. "Darned shoes!"

"Not feeling pretty and girly?"

"Oh yeah, nothing says sexy like spaghetti legs and aching feet. I think between wrestling with Spyder and tottering around on these heels, my legs are ready for a nice, long hot bath."

Striker's eyes grew dark and intense when I said that.

"Stop," I warned as we stepped out of the elevator.

"I can stop the action, Chica, but I can't stop the thought behind it."

I cared for Mrs. Nelson, but to be perfectly honest, I wasn't up for chit-chat.

I peeked in her room and was relieved to find her still asleep. I left a message with the nurse and headed home.

When we parked, I found my stairs and walk neatly shoveled. Gator's black Vibram-soled boots stood at attention on my porch by the door. I headed back toward the kitchen, where I heard the microwave beeping.

My dogs lay sopping wet at Gator's feet on the cool kitchen floor, their chests heaving and their tongues lolling out. They must have gone long and hard on their morning run.

Gator grinned at me from behind a plate piled high with food. Gator was in his early twenties. He had sun-bleached blond hair — even in the winter — deep brown eyes, and a smattering of freckles across his nose, which seemed at odds with his Iniquus uniform — gray-camo fatigues, and a long-sleeved, charcoal-gray compression shirt, showing off his massive arm muscles and washboard stomach. It was a rare thing for Gator to be dressed in anything else, though.

"Good timing." He set his plate on the counter. "Much later, and I cain't for sure say there'd be anything left."

We sat down to eat. Striker filled Gator in on the morning's happenings.

"You still don't know how Spyderman's doing? Or where he come in from?" Gator asked in between bites.

"Right now, it's all classified, and I'm not privy." Striker dunked his shrimp into the cocktail sauce. "Later this evening, we'll call over and find out if the doctors made any progress. Lynx has vamp-shoe-itis and needs to take a bath and a nap."

"Yeah, I saw her limping in here, but I weren't gonna say nothin'. I know how ladies get all pissy if you point out something like that when they're all gussied up." Gator popped an egg roll into his mouth.

Striker focused down at his plate.

"What are you grinning at, Striker? I'd like you to try walking in these heels as long as I have and still be able to stand up. You know what they say about Fred Astaire and Ginger Rogers, don't you?"

"No, what?" Striker reached for one of Gator's egg rolls.

"Fred was a good dancer, but Ginger could do the same things he could only in four-inch heels and backward."

"True," Striker paused to take a bite of egg roll, "but at night, she couldn't walk any better than you can now."

Gator snorted. I rolled my eyes at them, took my tea, and headed upstairs to the bath.

When I came back down, the kitchen was clean. Striker had his shoes off and was lying on the couch in front of a football game. I hate football, but I stretched out with him, anyway. Striker cuddled me into him, flipped a blanket over both of us, and curled me into his arms. As good as it felt to lay here with Striker, I couldn't throw off all of my scared-for-Spyder thoughts, all of my holy-shit-Sylanos-became-a-Hydra thoughts. And all the thoughts that had me wondering who the hell was moving in that would make me think of predators?

4

The phone buzzed near my head — it took me a minute to realize what was making that noise. It sounded like the swarm of mosquitos tormenting me in my dream as I hacked my way through the jungle, searching for Spyder. I put the phone to my ear. The sky shone periwinkle through my window — what time was it?

"Striker here. You awake?"

"Is it Spyder? Is he okay?" My hand clutched the sheet up to my throat.

"No, sorry, Lexi, I don't have any new information from the hospital."

My muscles released their protective clench. I glanced at the clock — 4:37 — ugh. "So what's up?" I scratched my nails over my scalp to rev my brain and swung my feet out from under the covers.

"Sorry to do this to you. We need you in the Puzzle Room. Now."

"Okay, Give me thirty minutes."

I grabbed my jeans and turtleneck from the chair — not my

usual professional outfit, but now means now, and this would have to do — and ran to the bathroom. What had them pulling me out of bed so early? It must be serious. I wished Striker had at least given me a heads up about what clues I'd find on my table when I got to headquarters.

I put the dogs into the back seat of my new car, a Lexis Rx400, charcoal-gray, just like Striker's. Command gave it to me as a Christmas bonus — probably "bribe" was a better description. They didn't want me to leave Iniquus? Fine, if I was going to stay on, at least I wrangled a cool car out of the deal. I slid behind the wheel and headed to Headquarters.

As I drove through the sleeping neighborhoods toward the highway, I called over to the hospital. No change in Spyder's status — test results not in, no visitors allowed. He was alive. I had to pin that thought to the front of all of the other thoughts pinging around in my brain, vying for my attention. Every time one of those wayward, worse-case-scenario thoughts rushed to my frontal lobe, I pushed it back with my new mantra: "He's alive."

The work-crisis was a good thing. If I could do nothing for Spyder — not even hold his hand — then I needed to keep myself busy with something else, or I would go absolutely nutso.

I took the elevator up to the top floor and tramped to my office with snow clinging to my boots. Last fall, when I solved a crime that put a lot of very bad men away for a long time, I got my Puzzle Room as a reward. A designer created the space for efficiency and clear thought. Three tables lined up like soldiers in the large square room — plenty of surface area for spreading out the files and pictures — the flotsam and jetsam my team gathered in the field. I had a whiteboard across one wall and a corkboard across the other. A cosmetic magnifying glass sat on my desk next to a top-of-the-line computer system with some very kick-ass software — I even had a predictive algorithm to guess who would commit crimes in the future or estimate where they lived once the crime had been committed. The designer even thought to include beds and feeding dishes for my dogs because they were almost always with me. On the far wall, a little walkway led to a full bathroom off to the right and a closet to the left.

My job here at Iniquus was challenging and interesting — and all the more so because I got to wear two hats. Working out a recognizable picture from the random puzzle pieces my team handed me was job one. Sometimes I went undercover in the field. I planted transmitters, did sleight-of-hand work; I cracked a safe every once in a while, stuff like that. I've only officially worked for Iniquus for a couple of months now. But they know I've tucked a few years of experience under my belt. I started working for Spyder when I turned eighteen — and soon I'd be twenty-one.

Under Spyder's tutelage, I was a shadow. No one here had even known I existed. After surviving Travis Wilson, my identity and background were exposed to management. Now that I worked out of Headquarters, Command wasn't quite sure how to classify me. I mostly winged it.

While the President of Iniquus himself was the only one who could order me around, I always worked with the same seven men. The guys on our team: Axel, Randy, Blaze, Gator, Jack, and Deep, along with Striker—the men's commander, and me—as an attachment, are collectively known as Strike Force.

"Hey, I'm here. What's up?" I sauntered in. My pups, Beetle and Bella, headed straight to their beds and plunked down. The whole team had gathered except for Randy and Axel, who were out in the field. Bad guys didn't take a Christmas holiday, apparently.

"We blew a case. We set up a sting with a German executive, Hans Schumann, who has his dirty little fingers in a bunch of get-rich pies. This is Schumann." Striker handed me a corporate head-shot of a man with blond hair and watery blue eyes. The man wore a designer suit and square Gucci glasses that seemed a little off on his round face. "Our operator planned to meet him this morning. Schumann was supposed to trade us South African diamonds for US military contract information. Earlier, we picked up a conversation on surveillance — there's a new player. This guy, whose name sounds like 'almonds,' hacked our clients' system and stole the intelligence we were going to trade."

"So cyber espionage?"

"Partially. We were lucky enough to get a heads-up. We faked the reports before the hacker got hold of the real data. We may not be so lucky next time. Schumann needs to be stopped before he can do actual damage to American companies competing for defense contracts."

"What role am I playing here?" I pulled my hair back and quickly knotted it into a braid, wrapping the end with an elastic band I had on my wrist. I liked it out of my face when I needed to think.

"We'd have a pretty solid case against Schumann if we had the diamonds. The diamonds, unfortunately, are the lynchpin."

"The almond-guy got paid instead of our operator. He has the jewels?"

"Right."

"Why did Schumann switch horses mid-stream?"

Striker shrugged. "I'd guess something spooked him, and he went with Plan B."

"Can't you fake the diamonds, substitute some in?" I asked, putting a knee on my chair as I stretched out for the file box.

"These are specific diamonds stolen from a diamond rep

leaving Johannesburg. Thirty-seven, flawless, colorless diamonds, each one weighing from three to five carats," Jack said. Jack was our team's second-in-command. He stood like a mountain with black hair and husky blue eyes.

"Wow! Those diamonds must be worth a fortune!"

Jack nodded. "Over a million. If we can't find the diamonds, our mark is going to walk. Finding the diamonds will implicate Schumann in crimes on three continents. It'll take him off the playing field for a very long time."

"So, how can I help?"

"We haven't got a bead on the guy with the rocks. Where would he go if he were trying to get rid of the diamonds in a hurry? Listening to him, we're pretty sure he's an American computer geek trying to cash in and not a player," Jack said. "He probably doesn't know what he's got or have the connections to fence them."

"Most people would sit on them or take them to South America somewhere." I set the photo down.

Deep shook his head. "We're confident this guy's going to dump and run. We've brought in everything: pictures, files, tapes. We're hoping you can make some connections and make them fast." Deep came from Long Island, and his accent was lightly flavored by his Italian background. Built on a smaller frame than Striker and Jack, he stood maybe six feet? Hard muscled, without the bulk, he had the kind of smile that could melt a girl's heart and will power.

"Hmm." I rubbed at my lower lip with my index finger. "The fast part's going to depend on the quality of the information, but I'll give it my best shot."

"That's what we need from you, Lynx." Deep pulled out a chair to my right and sat down. His chocolate brown eyes lost their usual mirth as he focused.

I sorted through the stack of evidence. I asked questions as I went. The men maintained perfect silence until I spoke to them — a pattern we quickly fell into once I joined the team. Puzzling, for me, was a meditative and often intuitive progression. If something pulled me out of my thought process, I might lose the tiny thread of understanding I had started to spin and weave.

"This is everything?" I glanced up from the empty box.

"Unfortunately." Deep moved the box under the table.

"Okay, I'd better get to work."

"What can we do to help?" Jack stood — feet wide, arms crossed over his chest. I had to smile. Standing that way, he looked like a prototype for a Marvel Comics hero.

"I missed breakfast. Could someone call down to the cafeteria for an egg and cheese sandwich and put a pot of coffee on? I'd really appreciate it." I stood with a file held up in each hand. "And can someone help me with computer searches? That might speed things up a bit."

"That would be me." Deep rolled over to sit behind my monitor, shook out his hands like a concert pianist preparing for a performance, and booted up.

I pushed my sleeves up to my elbows. As the conversations played on the recorder, I leafed through police reports and case notes.

Food showed up. Gator took my dogs out and brought them back. Without a window in my office, it was easy to lose the concept of time — not that it mattered. Immediate threat meant immediate action—no rest for the weary.

Striker came in and looked over my shoulder at the lists printed neatly in different colored pens on my whiteboard.

"Still working?" He moved around me to rest his knuckles on the table, reading the board. "Where's Deep?"

"I sent him home around three this morning." I yawned

loudly and stretched. "I didn't need any more computer support. I'm reviewing, but it's a little bit like throwing a dart blindfolded. Honestly, there's not much here." I shoved the files to the side and rested a hip on the table. I gestured toward my whiteboard. "I've narrowed my guesses down to these four strategies. If Command is serious about making this capture, and money's not a problem, I'd put a team on each of these scenarios. If I had funding and manpower for a single shot, this would be my door number one." I pointed to the list written in green marker. "It's all speculative, though. A lot of the records I need are classified with the client, so they're not even in-house. What data we've got is weak."

"Understood. What are these addresses? What is Slaybourgh Jewelers?" Striker read down the list.

"The first address is for a Jamal Omondas. Does his name mean anything to you?"

"Nada." Striker turned as Jack came through my door.

"I think he might be the guy with the diamonds in his pocket. Slaybourgh Jewelers is my best guess for where he might try to unload them fast. Jessup Slaybourgh and Jamal Omondas have a long, reckless history." I sat down and laid my forehead on the table. "My brain's fried."

"Criminally reckless?" Jack stood behind Striker, reading the board.

"Sort of? Here's my theory why I think this is the right route — the Defense Department let Omondas go on Friday morning for 'failure to follow protocol.' I'd guess it's code for 'he was sniffing around where he didn't belong,' and someone in his division clued into his odd behavior. Omondas worked on cybersecurity. I agree with you. This was probably Schumann's Plan B and seemed like the safer path. Omondas seems easily manipulated, so easier to hold in check, and I wouldn't doubt that Schumann had plans for retrieving those diamonds once the deal was done. Schumann's not stupid. He wouldn't go after the diamonds himself, so if you've got a tail on Schumann, that won't get you what you need."

"Agreed." Striker poured a cup of coffee from my machine. He held the mug out to me, and I shook my head. Striker drank it black — yuck.

"You said Omondas and Slaybourgh have a past?"

I rubbed at my eyes. "They went to MIT together. They were in the same class, same fraternity, and lived at the same address for two years after school. They had a few brushes with the law together during their college days: drunk and disorderly, public nudity, mostly young guys-gone-wild on campus sort of stuff."

"That's everything on their record? Some college pranks?"

"Nope. They both got arrested for hacking into the Pentagon computer system. The charges were dropped, and Omondas got hired by Defense the same day. They hired Slaybourgh, too, but he quit within the month to open his jewelry shop."

"And the other lists?" Striker gestured toward my whiteboard.

"Defense personnel — so they'd have access — whose names vaguely sound like 'almonds.'"

"Got it." Striker caught Jack's eye. Jack copied down the information from the whiteboard.

"I came across the file on Johannesburg." I turned to face Striker. My hands went to my hips. "You and Jack were down-range that week. Was it you?"

"Classified."

"I read between the lines. A hell of a mission, Striker."

Striker didn't answer. Which confirmed what I was saying. Even though this happened a month ago, fear for them ran through my body, making me shiver. Unprofessional emotions pressed behind my eyes. I was trying to develop a stoic exterior, like the guys on my team — mostly without success. "God, I feel puny standing in your shadows."

Jack glanced up. "We've each got our talents, Lynx. You're on our team for this." He waved the paper at me, turned, and left.

Striker eased me toward the door and called Beetle and Bella to follow.

"Where am I going?" I asked.

"To bed. I can either drive you home, or you can bunk in my guest room at the barracks."

I checked my watch — five-thirty. "Maybe your place for a couple of hours. I want to get to the hospital by nine and find out if they have any news about Spyder. Maybe they'll let me check in on him for a minute."

"Okay, but I'm driving you. I don't want you behind the wheel until you've had a good night's sleep. It's been a long couple of days for you."

I nodded—what a gross understatement.

When I walked into Striker's apartment, calm enveloped me. A panoramic view of Washington DC filled a whole wall of his great room, while a stone fireplace scaled another wall from floor-to-vaulted-ceiling, flanked by bookshelves. The other walls were neutral shades and showed off oil paintings that Striker had painted for relaxation — huge modern seascapes in cobalt, indigo, and violet. He chose manly and substantial furnishings made from natural materials: leather, marble, granite, mahogany. It was gorgeous and luxurious, urban, maybe a touch of Zen quietude.

I slogged into the guest room. My dogs trailed behind me and plopped on the floor by the bed. Here, the walls were painted a rich teal. I flung myself face-first on to the winter-white linens.

Striker followed me in and handed me one of his T-shirts. "Here. You won't get any rest bunched up in your street clothes. I'm taking the girls for a run, okay?"

"Yes, thank you." The pillow muffled my words. I pulled myself back up and yanked off my boots and socks—Mazel tov for wanting to run in the snow. I thought the girls would be just as happy on the treadmill in the gym downstairs.

I heard Striker in his room changing into jogging clothes while I climbed under the covers. He came back in and gave me a kiss on the forehead and turned out my lights, softly calling the pups to go with him.

I burrowed under the covers and shut my eyes. I liked being in Striker's apartment; it felt like Striker to me.

Striker made me feel good.

Mostly.

Sometimes I felt compressed by him, uncomfortably wedged into an odd posture. Our relationship was both years old and brand new.

Striker and I had met on many occasions. But when I was Spyder's sidekick, Striker didn't even know I had girl parts. He thought I was a teenaged boy named Alex.

It was a shock when Striker walked into my hospital room after Wilson's attack and introduced himself. Striker Rheas was to play knight in shining armor to my damsel in distress. My teenaged fantasy, in the flesh, acting itself out. Okay, well, there was no dragon, but Wilson made a fair approximation.

While Wilson acted as an external dragon, Striker could slay, fighting the internal dragon that roiled up the sediment of my past desperation for Striker's attention belonged to me alone. I thought those fantasies would lie dormant after I met my husband, Angel. But there they were, all of those Striker emotions, clouding my perception of my husband and of my marriage. Though I never acted unfaithfully while Angel was alive, I wasn't without sin. Was it so different to think things a faithful wife shouldn't?

Guilt poisoned me as Striker, and I wove ourselves more tightly together.

While Striker has never talked to me about where he thought all this was going, his feelings hung in the air, palpable at times, thick like a Tar-Baby catching and holding me tight. Not to say that Striker was ever outwardly anything less than a gentleman, anything less than professional.

Gah! Where is this going?

We were friends and co-workers… And then Christmas, and the mistletoe, and that kiss. I have never been kissed that way before. When I think about it, I can still taste him, his soft lips against mine asking for more. Not demanding more. Asking. And as I complied, he asked for still more until my head swam drunkenly with him…

I took my muddled emotions into my sleep with me. Strange dreams danced in my brain. At one point, I was spinning around until I fell just to get up and do it again and again. I was relieved when Beetle and Bella prodded me awake with their wet noses.

Striker stood over me, breathing heavily from his workout. "I'm getting in the shower. Are you sure you want to get up now?"

"I'd better, or my sleep patterns will be all off. I'll be fine. Are you going to the hospital with me?" I pulled his T-shirt down modestly before I threw off the blanket.

Twenty minutes later, Striker steered an Iniquus Hummer onto the highway. I stared out the window at the mountains of black snow shoved aside by the plows to let the bumper-to-bumper traffic pass.

"Lynx, I know you're exhausted, and your mind's on fast forward, but I'm going to throw something else into the mix," Striker said. I twisted my body around to face him and waited.

"I got a call from Lynda yesterday." This got my attention. Striker's sister, Lynda, and his three-year-old niece, Cammy, narrowly escaped from a drug lord's rage back in October. They beat Lynda until she was all but dead, suffering a dozen broken bones. Iniquus saved them with sliver-thin timing. Now Lynda was learning to walk again with extensive medical treatments.

"Is Lynda doing any better?" My eyes scanned over Striker. His body seemed relaxed. He looked his usual calm self except for the tightening at his jaw and the tension under his eyes.

"She's doing better than expected. It's still a long road. She's moved back down to Miami with my dad and stepmother. Mimi and Dad are taking care of Cammy." Striker took a sip from his coffee and set it back in the cup-holder. He shot me a glance. "Lynda is hoping you and I would come down to celebrate Cammy's fourth birthday."

"Oh?" The invitation surprised me.

"Cammy's been talking about you since you rescued her, and Lynda thinks it would be good for her to see you."

"I can't believe Cammy has any kind of memory of that night, especially of me."

Striker looked over at me; a funny kind of emotion flickered in his eyes — it came and went too quickly for me to figure out what it could mean.

"What did you tell her?" I asked.

"I said I'd be there, and I'd invite you."

"When is this?" I picked at some imaginary lint on my pant

leg. I didn't want to go. I didn't want to see Lynda. I knew I'd end up re-living the horror of that night in my head.

"Cammy's party is on New Year's Day. We could fly down and celebrate New Year's Eve in the city with some of my old friends, and go to Cammy's party on the first. We'd fly back that evening."

"Do you think it's important for me to see Cammy?" I was stalling for time to think. "I'm not sure I understand my invitation."

"Cammy's having some trouble separating reality and fantasy right now. She believes you're a fairy godmother. She's wondering why you aren't showing up to help her anymore." Striker flicked on his signal and slid in front of the semi. "But you've got a lot of responsibilities here with Spyder and Mrs. Nelson in the hospital." He was giving me an easy out.

"…Yeah, well." I felt like a coward for not saying yes right away. I pushed my hair behind my ears and leaned back, looking up at the gray headliner fabric while I tried to balance all my obligations in my mind and come up with a plan. I breathed out and refocused on Striker. "Okay, I'll go if at all possible. I can't promise to go to the party until I know more about Spyder. I will promise if I can't go for Cammy's birthday, I'll go as soon as I can."

"Thank you." Striker's voice was gruff. He has always treated his niece like a daughter since Cammy's biological father never stood in the picture. This must be incredibly hard on him, but he wasn't going to talk to me about it. Striker had gone into stoic-mode; I was locked out. Which I hated.

Miami. Huh. I rubbed my thumb into my palm and looked out the window. What role would I play in Miami? Co-worker? Friend of the family? Girlfriend…? How all this would unravel might just prove enlightening.

5

Striker and I arrived at the hospital and headed straight to Isolation to check if the nurse had an update. She told us that Mr. McGraw had been moved to the step-down unit on the sixth floor. Step-down unit? What did that mean? She didn't have any further information on his status. Up on the sixth floor, Spyder was getting vitals checked. Someone would come to get us when he was ready for us.

I rested my hip against the nurse's station outside of Spyder's room, wringing my hands. Worry for him made my palms sweat. Striker leaned against the wall and watched me from across the way; his face was relaxed, but his eyes smiled with warmth. My anxiety charmed him. I turned my shoulder to the wall and looked in the other direction.

Growing up unschooled — that's homeschooling on steroids — had its advantages and its disadvantages. My parents were pretty avant-garde; they followed Leonardo da Vinci's philosophy: "Study without desire spoils the memory, and retains nothing it takes in." Far be it for my parents to spoil my memory with the drudgery of rote memorization. A smile tickled my lips.

Yup. I got to follow my heart's desire when it came to learning. And fortunately, I ended up being mentored by Spyder McGraw.

Of all my mentors, I was most enthusiastic about studying under Spyder. I had this fantasy of growing up to be a modern-day Nancy Drew. I wanted nothing more than to spend my life puzzling out crimes, which was exactly what Spyder trained me to do with computer simulations, brain exercises, and a little sleight-of-hand thrown in for good measure. God, I loved it. I absolutely loved everything he taught me.

And I loved him—my second dad.

Tears stung the corners of my eyes.

Last September, a little over a year ago, when Spyder got called off-grid, he took off to go save our world as we know it. Left me hanging in the wind like wet laundry. I had no more partner, no more crimes to solve. I floundered; I re-thought everything. Maybe my life was too crazy — Mom was dying — Spyder was gone. Things kept changing. I desperately needed the Earth to stop spinning so fast; it made me dizzy.

I shifted around against the wall, remembering vividly the overwhelming emotions of last year, still alive, though muted now, in my body. Yes. I could almost taste the engulfing bleakness from when I ended up all alone. Everyone left me in one way or another. My neighbors dispersed from the fire that destroyed my apartment building, my parents dead, my husband at war, Spyder…

I wasn't built to be alone. By nature, I wanted to run with a pack. Thank goodness for Iniquus and my team. I worked hard every day to prove I belonged and was up to their standards — which was a lift of monumental proportions.

I scowled. I had almost left. Did I really think quitting would calm my world, and I'd get to lead a normal life? Something. Something tickled in my brain. The white leopard. I recognized her from when Dave told me about the new neighbor. She peeked out from under the bush, watching me with shining onyx eyes, baring her razor-sharp teeth with a low throated growl. Fear prickled my nerve endings. Shit! What sparked that?

A cart rolling past roused me. I shifted my purse strap on my shoulder as the nurse gave us the all-clear. I offered Striker a weak smile, and we went in. Spyder was thinner than I remembered him, and Spyder was always a rail. The sight of him shocked me — in the bed with his arms full of IV tubing, wrapped in a hospital gown. This man seemed antithetical to everything Spyder. He jostled my spirit and left it dangling at an odd angle.

Spyder folded into a hundred-degree angle. The huge pile of pillows at his back forced him to lean slightly forward, his torso sandwiched between more pillows stacked on his lap. I knelt down beside the bed, so I could see his face, and he could see mine. His breathing was labored and obviously painful. I waited. We just stared at each other.

"I missed you fiercely, Lexicon." Spyder's accent, slow and golden-rich like maple syrup, filled my homesick heart.

I nodded solemnly. "I'm so happy you're back."

"Good thing Striker brought you to the airport. Had we waited for the surprise... They tell me your quick action saved my life."

"Please don't, Spyder. I can't think those kinds of thoughts." My words stuck in my throat, and I had to force them out. Striker sat on the chair behind me with his hands supportive on my shoulders.

"Striker. You're looking fit."

"Yes, sir. Glad you're home."

"We have much to talk about in the days and weeks ahead. Right now, remember — walls can hear, and the things I will tell you from my travels must wait." Spyder's words floated lightly in the air, then made him cough.

"Spyder, what's going on with your health?" I reached out for his hand. His skin felt papery.

"Many tests. I don't expect answers for a few days." He coughed, turning his head toward the wall. We waited while he caught his breath. Spyder turned back to me. "Striker told me you followed my advice and sought help from him. Since then, you've become the first Iniquus Puzzler. You must have performed brilliantly to gain such an accolade."

"Did Striker tell you any of our stories?"

"No, Lexicon, he said he would leave those for you. Let's start at the beginning. I have been much concerned with your mother's health. How does she fare these days?"

"Mom passed away just weeks after you left." My voice sounded rusty and seemed to stick and squeak as I tried to push it forward. "Mom had your dogs by her side, and they brought her comfort at the end."

"I am sorrowful to hear of your loss, my girl. And yet, I am much relieved. Your mother was exhausted from her fight and in a great deal of pain." Spyder's head rested on the pillow. His breathing seemed to be easing. The pinch of his face smoothed.

"Yes, sir, her passing was a blessing. Though I miss her every day."

"Of course you do, my dear." Spyder patted my hand. "Striker says you've made many changes in your life. I need to catch up. Tell me some of your news."

I cleared my throat. "Well, in September of last year, Mom died. I finished my classes over at the community college and graduated with an Associates in Criminology. I planned to start my bachelor's degree this semester, but Striker told me I needed to take a break while we teamed up on a special project."

Spyder squeezed my hand. "Indeed, an extremely important project."

"At the end of last January, almost a year ago, a fire at my apartment building burned it to the ground. Everyone relocated. Some around the city. Some far away. Nona Sophia is up in New York City, and Abuela Rosa went back to Puerto Rico." I took a deep breath. "And I got married."

He lifted my hand with a smile. "When did you and Striker wed, Mrs. Rheas?" Spyder asked, twisting my wedding and engagement rings on my finger.

"We're not married, Spyder. We're just..." I turned toward Striker, confused, and stopped. I wasn't sure what 'we just' were. Striker waited for me to finish the sentence. How would I define our relationship? My mind went completely blank.

"I don't understand," Spyder said. "Striker, I can clearly see in your eyes that you are in love with my Lexicon. Am I correct?"

"Yes, sir. I am very much in love with Lexi."

"And Lexi?" Spyder asked, turning to me.

My head whirled. Striker had never said anything to me about his feelings. Ever. And now he was saying 'I am very much in love,' like this was a known fact. A given?

My gaze swung back and forth between Striker and Spyder without a clear thought visible.

Finally, Striker spared me — "Lexi's new surname is Sobado, sir. She married an Army Ranger, Angel Sobado, last February. He deployed to Afghanistan. Unfortunately, at Thanksgiving, his truck hit an IED. He didn't survive, sir. Lexi is in mourning for her late husband."

"Lexicon. I am grieved to hear this." Spyder gazed deeply into my eyes.

I couldn't stand the intensity of the emotions that he radiated. I lowered my lashes to shield myself from his pity and nodded. "Thank you, sir. I need to excuse myself. Spyder, I'll come by tomorrow, okay?" I gave him a kiss on the cheek, too distracted to say anything more. Spyder nodded but said nothing to me while I gathered my things and hustled out the door.

I all but ran down the hallway to the exit. I hid in the empty stairwell, grateful for the cool darkness, sitting on a stair supported by the green cinderblock wall. I breathed deeply for a few minutes, trying to get my whirling emotions under control.

The door creaked open. I glanced over my shoulder; Striker stood framed by the hall lights. I turned my back to him, leaning my forehead against the wall.

He came and sat next to me. "This was not the way I meant for you to hear that I'm in love with you, Chica. I imagined better timing and a different setting." He kept his hands to himself. "Though I'm sure you're not surprised, I imagine hearing it said out loud so abruptly is what has you upset."

I shook my head. I wanted him to go away.

"This wasn't the right time," he pressed on, "but Spyderman asked me a direct question, and you told me you think of him as your second father. I respect him too much. He needed to hear my intentions are honorable. I needed to be clear with him."

I sat in silence, staring at the green wall. Numb.

"There's no pressure on you. I mean...you don't have to love me back. I'm not asking anything from you."

I turned to him. "Striker, I need to get out of here," I said under my breath.

"Okay. Sure."

We walked in silence to the parking garage. Striker opened the car door for me and walked around to the driver's side. He started the engine and sat with his hands on the wheel. "Chica,

I'd really like you to say something. Are you okay? You don't look okay."

I took a deep breath in and let the air hiss back out. "I never saw his body."

Striker stilled.

"Do you know how weird that is? Here we are in December. Angel left me at the end of February last year, and I knew I wouldn't see him again for a long time. I steeled myself for the long haul." I swallowed and rubbed my thumb into my palm. "At first, we got to talk and pass messages sporadically. Then he went on a mission. He was gone for months with no communication. Every day I imagined where he went — what he did."

Striker's unwavering gaze warmed me with his concern.

"Then two men in uniforms stood with their hats in their hands and their damned expert, low-toned voices telling me Angel was dead. Blown up by an IED. In nine months, I went from 'I do' to 'death do us part.'" My thumb worked convulsively, kneading into my hand, trying to smooth the lifeline on my palm. An apt metaphor, I'd like my lifeline to run smoother. I took a few deep breaths; I felt dizzy and nauseated. "They sent me a pine box, and they said my husband was in the box. I guess I have to take them at their word since it was sealed; his remains 'unrecognizable,' they said. Identified by his tags and dental records."

"You'd have better closure had you seen Angel's body."

I nodded. "Cognitive dissonance. My brain is playing me."

"I can't even imagine."

I twisted my wedding ring around my finger. "Striker? When did you know you were in love with me?"

"Honestly?" Striker started to reach for me, then pulled his hand back and laid it on his thigh.

Good. I wasn't ready to be touched.

"I felt a pull right from the beginning when I met you in the hospital after the Wilson attack. I felt it a little bit more each day we had you holed up in the safe house," he said. "I guess the thing that sent me over the edge was when you told me the story about your special un-schooling studies with the hooker."

"Chablis? That's what did it for you?" I felt the pink creep up my face.

"The whole scene did it for me. The story about how you got married and your one-night honeymoon went to hell-in-a-hand-basket, and you ended up still a virgin with your husband gone to war. And as a teen, you wanted to make sure the man of your future would be happy. So much so that you thought getting lessons from a hooker and practicing on a purple dildo was just a normal thing to do." Striker looked like he was working hard to keep from smiling. "All of it. You were such a dichotomy of innocence and femme fatale. I was completely charmed and fell completely in love."

"Has this been hard on you?" I whispered, wide-eyed.

"My feelings for you have been inappropriate, and I've tried to control them. But being around you…" He stopped and cleared his throat. "Figuring out the boundaries is awkward. I never wanted anything to happen to Angel."

"No. Of course, you didn't." I took a minute to gather up some bravery. "You know, Spyder was darned impressed with you. He told me so many stories of your exploits before I even met you, I had a huge case of hero worship."

"And when you met me, you found out I wasn't a hero at all."

"That's an opinion."

"Right. I guess hero is in the eye of the beholder."

"Mmmm. Here's the thing, I met you lots of times while I worked for Spyder, only you weren't meeting me." I turned in my seat and leaned my head back against the side window. "I was a boy named Alex with an ingénue's mad crush on the mythical Striker Rheas." Striker opened his mouth to say something. I could see his mind working hard. I held up my hand to stop him; I needed to get through this. "I had these adolescent fantasies about saving the day. I'd take a bullet and be lying on the ground. You'd rip open my T-shirt to stop my bleeding only to discover I was really a girl, and you'd tell me I was awesome and brave and strong. You'd fall in love with me, and we'd live happily ever after." I laughed at how ridiculous this all sounded.

"I don't know what to say. I had no idea, you know. I really had no idea you weren't who Spyderman said you were."

"Yeah. But I need you to understand this is more complicated in my head than boy-meets-girl, and Angel isn't the only reason."

"Chica, there isn't one damned thing about you that isn't surprising or complicated. I've learned to let the wilding river flow." Striker shot me a teasing grin, wanting me to laugh.

I couldn't give him what he wanted.

Striker seemed to realize this because he dropped the smile and said, "Lexi, you don't need to burden yourself trying to figure out how I fit into your life right now."

"What about you? What do you want from me?"

"Nothing you're not willing to give."

"I guess it's also a question of what you're willing to give and how you think this will play out."

"Yeah." He took a deep breath in. "You're right. I don't have an answer for you," he said on the exhale.

"We'll go slow and figure this out?" I asked.

"We'll go slow."

6

A FedEx waited for me on the porch when I got back to my house. I picked it up and opened the door to the joyous cacophony of Beetle and Bella. Deep had brought them home for me. "Hey, sweet girls, let's get you something to eat."

"Lexi, why don't I feed the dogs? I'll take them for a walk while you relax in a hot bath. You look done in."

"Okay, thanks. I'll take you up on that." I gestured toward the kitchen, "I set a cassoulet in the fridge to defrost, and you'll find some bakery rolls in the bread box. When I'm out of the tub, I'll just make a salad. You're going to stay for lunch, aren't you?"

"Yes, thanks." His cell phone vibrated. He held up a finger for me to wait. "What've you got?" Striker listened for a minute, then glanced over at me. "Are you up to Gator coming for lunch? He needs to go over some things with us about the Schumann case."

"Yeah, sure, that's fine. I'd like to hear how it's going." I glanced at my watch. "Tell him to come at twelve-thirty-ish. The food should be ready by then." Striker finished his conversation and headed for the kitchen with the girls prancing after him.

Twelve-thirty on the dot, the doorbell rang, and I opened it to Gator's smiling face. "Ma'am, I can smell your good cooking all the way out on the sidewalk. What Kitchen Granny are we doing today?"

When I was an un-schooler, one of my mentors, Snow Bird Wang, decided that if I were to have a worthy husband, I would need to develop honorable wife skills. Snow Bird rallied the other grandmothers in my apartment building to step forward and help. Five women signed on as my Kitchen Grandmothers, each adopting me for one day of the workweek. While the idea was old-fashioned, Mom decided this would be a wonderful opportunity for me to learn about many cultures and traditions. From the time I turned twelve, I learned whatever that day's grandma thought I needed to know. I still cook in my Kitchen Grandmother pattern.

Monday was Jada's day; she came from Turkey. Tuesday belonged to Biji. She was from Punjab, India. "It's Wednesday: tonight is Nana Kate," I told Gator. Nana Kate hailed from the mid-west. She taught me how to make the old fashioned, American, rib-sticking meals of her childhood… with a dollop of Julia Child thrown in for good measure.

"Well, God bless Nana Kate." Gator shucked off his jacket and hung it in my hall closet.

Gator went back to the kitchen, where Striker banged around in the cupboards. I picked up my FedEx and followed behind. Striker had the dishes set out and the food on the table. The guys were familiar with my house, having spent a lot of time here when they were doing stakeout duty, trying to capture Travis Wilson.

I sat down with my envelope and pulled out a letter from

Bryant and Kimber, Attorneys at Law. I wrinkled my brow as I read it through. "Wow," I said.

"What?" asked Striker.

"It's from Mrs. Nelson's lawyers. She's decided not to come home. She's going to move straight from the hospital center to Brandenburg Assisted Living."

"Why are the lawyers informing you about it with a FedEx?" Striker buttered a roll.

"She's invoking my first right of refusal on her side of the duplex. They need to know within the week whether or not I want to buy her house."

"You gonna do it?" Gator filled his plate with beans and sausage.

"I locked in the price before they did the upgrades I bartered for with Manny, so it's a really good deal."

"Manny, across-the-street-Manny? What was he bartering?" Gator forked up a bite.

"Yes, my neighbor. He inherited his house, and it was uninhabitable. His grandparents were hoarders. I cleaned out his dump, and he played poker for me. He won the services of the people who came over and fixed things up over here. My house was border-line condemned when I bought it."

Striker glanced around. "Hard to believe this place was in bad shape."

My home was gorgeous now if I do say so myself.

"Okay, enough about that." I shoved the papers back in the envelope and tossed them on the table. "Let's talk diamonds. Was the prize hiding behind one of my doors?"

Gator finished chewing his bread and swiped his mouth with his napkin. "Behind door number one, ma'am. My team found Omondas by staking out Slaybourgh Jewelers. Omondas headed up there before opening. He had the rocks on him. We watched him pulling them out to show to Jessup Slaybourgh. They tossed around some heated words, and Jessup physically threw Omondas outa the store." Gator grinned broadly at the memory. "Since we were waiting for signatures on our warrants, we followed Omondas to his house. He went inside for twenty minutes. By the time he come out, our paperwork had cleared, and we moved in for the capture. He didn't have the diamonds on him when we took him in hand."

"The diamonds are in his house?" Striker asked.

"They should be, sir. Our client searched Omondas's car, and they weren't able to find them," Gator took his bowl to the sink.

I pushed my plate to the side to make room for my elbows as I leaned forward. "Have you searched the house yet?"

"No, ma'am. We figured you'd want first dibs before we moved anything around," Gator said.

"All right. Shall we go now?" I turned to Striker for confirmation.

"Fine with me," he said.

Gator parked the Humvee across the street from a seventies-style tri-level. I sat in the car, trying to imagine Omondas living here. It seemed incongruous. Too domestic for a single guy his age.

Gator interrupted my thoughts. "Hey Lynx, would you mind walking me through how you find something in the clients' houses? I'd like to be able to do that."

"Sure. I guess the Marines didn't teach search-and-find?"

"Yeah, sure, if you lost something in a swamp."

I laughed and jumped down from the Humvee. Gator showed me how Omondas parked his car and walked to the porch. We followed the same path. Striker stood to the side, on the phone with Command.

I stopped at the door. "Gator, stand here for a second and look."

The house was sparsely decorated with brand-new, low-range, bachelor-type furniture. He sunk a lot of money in electronics. Huge speaker systems, flat-screen TV, and gaming systems were visible from the door.

"What do you think?" I asked.

Gator had one hand on his hip, and with the other, he rubbed his chin with his thumb. "Young. Male. Military neat."

"He's not military. So what else could be in play here?"

"Good cleaning service? A granny?"

"A granny?" I stared incredulously at Gator. He shrugged.

"So the three thoughts that came to me were — One, he's never here. He moved in and stays somewhere else. Two, he has an excellent cleaning service," I said.

Gator bumped me. "Got one."

I shook my head at him. "Or three, he's O.C.D. So let's check the kitchen."

"Why the kitchen?"

I pulled on a pair of latex gloves, opened the fridge door, and pointed. "Because of this." A mess of open jars greeted me, along with dripping spills and half-eaten take-out containers. "The fridge answers which of my three initial hypotheses was correct. The first one is out. Obviously, he's here all the time, eating take-out. The third one is out. He's clearly not OCD; there's a biology experiment going on in here. And he's not neat by nature. It must be number two. He has a good service. Hey, keep an eye open for their business card. I might like some help around my house from time-to-time."

"You didn't rule out his having a granny."

I rolled my eyes and pulled open the freezer. "Sure I did," I said, peering in. "A granny would have this fridge clean and filled with either healthy foods or delicious treats, but not cartons of crusty Kung Pao Chicken." The freezer desperately needed defrosting, but nothing jumped out at me. "Okay, Gator, now we're going to walk through the house and get a sense of it. See what we can discover. Don't touch anything. Okay?"

As we walked up the stairs, I asked, "Tell me again, how long did Omondas stay in here?"

"Twenty minutes, ma'am."

"And, what time of the day was this?"

"Zero-Nine-thirty."

The first bedroom stood completely empty. The second held a bed, a dresser, and a nightstand. I opened the closet and drawers. "Not much in the way of clothing. Jeans and T-shirts, khakis and work-polos, tighty-whities. Nothing personally expressive, no photos, no books, no newspapers, no papers by the computer." I threw my hands in the air. "Nothing, period. He probably eats and sleeps in the house, and that's all." We walked into the bathroom. Other than the wet towel behind the door, he kept everything here neat. I opened the medicine cabinet.

"No tampons," Gator said with a grin. When I first did a puzzle for the team, I told them to look for a flash-drive in the suspect's tampon box. Now it was a running joke.

"Right, no tampon box, also no condoms, so I doubt there's a girlfriend."

I headed back down the stairs… Something's wrong. I went back into the kitchen. Striker was off the phone, and both men followed me over to the fridge.

"I'm scanning, Gator. I can't put my finger on it. Something's poking at me. Do you notice anything wrong here?" I leaned into the fridge.

Gator looked over my shoulder. "There's a whole lot of wrong here."

"Crime wise." I crouched down and pulled open the veggie drawer that held some moldy cheese. I stood up and opened the freezer, and it stood out immediately. I lifted my watch — fourteen-hundred, five hours since Omondas had been in the house.

"What's the first thing you would tell yourself about this freezer, Gator?"

"I'd say the frost is pretty thick. Omondas needs to de-ice and do a better job of shutting the door."

"Right. Everything is covered in frost and look — it's hard. It's been this way for a while. Everything is covered in the frost except …"

"Except for the ice cube trays, ma'am."

I took out the three ice cube trays stacked up in the very back. I corkscrewed them to release their cubes, dumped them into a bowl, and started running hot water over them.

Striker and Gator came over to the sink to watch me. No one said a word. Soon a plink, plink, plink rang as the diamonds fell to the bottom of the glass bowl. When the ice had all melted, I carefully scooped the diamonds onto a dishtowel, and we counted them.

I grinned at Striker. "All present and accounted for, sir."

"Now that there's crazy." Gator flashed an endearingly boyish grin.

"Not crazy — methodical. I felt like the kitchen was the place this guy spends most of his time. You saw for yourself. Like I said, he probably eats and sleeps in the house, and that's probably all."

"So you focused in on the kitchen?" Gator leaned back against the counter, his arms crossed over his chest.

"Usually, people will hide things in the rooms they hang out in the most. The room they feel most comfortable with."

"Is that how you do it every time, ma'am?"

"I've developed different techniques I use. I try one, and if I don't get anything, I test out another. It's usually a matter of perseverance. I keep trying until I get something."

"Say he hadn't left his freezer open and gotten all that frost. Would you still have ended up looking in the ice?" Striker held a diamond up to the light.

"Yes. Actually, that would probably have been one of the first places I would have checked."

Striker's eyes were keen on me. "Because...?"

"In the tapes you guys handed me, Omondas used 'ice' as a synonym for diamonds. If I used serendipity to find the diamonds, I would check for ice."

"The discovery of something fortunate? I'm not following." Striker put the diamond back on the towel and leaned a hip into the counter.

"It's my puzzling version of Jung. Carl Jung says that serendipity is awareness. If you think about something, you kind of prime your brain. Like doing a word search. There are lots of words hidden in a box of letters. Once a word is read off of the list, the brain can search more effectively. Once you think a thought, then your brain will find ways to reinforce those thoughts."

"Can you give me another example?" asked Striker.

"Sure, if you find out your best friend is pregnant, then when you're out and about, you'll find pregnant women everywhere. Or, if you tell yourself you're a lucky person, then each time you hit a green light, you think, 'Wow, lucky me.' If you stop at a red light and your phone rings, you think, 'I'm a lucky person. I wanted to get this call, and here I had a red light and could answer safely.' Do you get what I mean?"

"Yes. I understand that. What I don't understand is how using the synonym ice for diamonds would fit."

"Omondas was thinking 'ice.' He was under a great deal of stress. He would have acted on serendipity, that is, the thing he had primed his brain to reinforce. The thing making his conscious actions reflect his subconscious mind — 'diamonds are ice.' Hmm. it's a little complicated to explain." I bit at my lip. "Let's say that words have power, and under stress, words often become action. The word as action here is taking the 'ice' — diamonds, and making them ice — in the freezer."

"Got it. Interesting. I like it," Striker said.

"Good thing they were in the ice, though. I was afraid he might try to bread them."

"Bread them, ma'am?" Gator had moved to a barstool next to Striker.

"Yeah, you know, like the women in World War II. When the Jewish women from the ghettos were taken to the concentration camps, they tried to save the family gemstones to use as money if they were to survive. When they knew the Gestapo was coming, they would wrap the stones in bread and swallow them. Later, they'd search for their gems in their feces."

"Couldn't that rip a hole in their intestines?" Gator asked.

"Sometimes it did, though I imagine the gems those women swallowed were smaller than the diamonds on the counter."

"You think Omondas would know about breading?" Striker asked.

"He might have read about someone being a drug mule and swallowing deflated balloons with cocaine in them. Same scenario. He could have made the leap. If he had breaded the diamonds, it would have created issues with the fourth amendment and due process. If we really thought he had breaded them, we'd have to arrest him and hold him long enough for his natural due process to occur. Believe me, that search is no fun." I grimaced.

"Believe you? You've searched someone's feces before?" Striker's lips curled in disgust.

I laughed. "Yeah, well, did I ever tell you about my internship at the National Zoo helping with the primates?"

"Nope." Striker went over to the sink and scrubbed his hands with soap and hot water.

"Let's just say I'm not willing to do that kind of work ever again. I'd insist on a peon taking over the task. What do we do with the diamonds?"

Striker's phone buzzed on his hip. "I call over to the client and get an agent over here to collect them as evidence." Striker grinned. "Then, we celebrate our success."

Striker walked out of the room to take his phone call. When he came back in, a hint of stress hardened the corners of his mouth.

"Who called?" I asked.

"Command. Schumann's in a body bag."

"What? Dead?" I spread my arms wide. "This was all for naught?"

"We retrieved the diamonds and captured Omondas. Not a complete waste of time. Just not the outcome that's going to pay the big paycheck. Command says we're a day late and a dollar short."

7

"I'll catch up with you at the office tomorrow." I gave Striker a quick peck on the cheek. I was disappointed in myself and sulking. If only I had puzzled out the Omondas thing quicker, we could have arrested Schumann before the killer got to him. We would have won.

Striker grabbed my arm as I got out. He peered at me over the rims of his sunglasses. "Hey, I need you in by six, and I need you to dress corporate. We've got an assignment. We'll be in the field."

"Okay. How far up the ladder am I? Is this a Chanel suit kind of day?"

"Definitely. You'll be rubbing elbows with the top execs and probably a board member or two."

"You going to give me a clue what this is about?"

"Nope. It's classified until the briefing." Striker released my arm.

I wanted some shut-eye. Well, that was my thought, anyway. Anxiety wrung my stomach. I was still fairly new at Iniquus, and I couldn't go around failing, or I'd be out on my butt. Tomorrow I'd play my A-game and show Command what I was made of. Sleep? Impossible. I thought about Spyder's health. I thought about the mystery assignment. I thought about how Sylanos could possibly have turned into a Hydra after all the work I did to make sure Iniquus took him down. Surely, Sylanos should be in someone's prison cell by now. Okay, truth be told, I thought about Striker.

After tossing and turning most of the night, I gave up and threw on a jogging outfit to go run with the girls. I'd let a few days slide since I'd gotten any exercise. It felt good to work some of the tension out of my muscles. I arrived home around three in the morning. Still riled, I headed to the basement to lift weights and de-stress in the steam room before turning on my brewer.

Coffee in hand, I scrounged through my closet for a good disguise. I picked out a power suit — a hand-me-down from my friend Celia — some hose and heels, and a briefcase.

Spyder drilled the refrain into my head: when out in public, alter your appearance; anonymity is a safety net. *"Yes, sir,"* I thought as I went to the bathroom to shower and use temporary coloring to tint my hair strawberry blond. I did my makeup with corals to accentuate the red in my hair, painting myself in a more sophisticated manner than usual. I popped in brown contacts and scrutinized my reflection in the mirror. I wouldn't recognize myself in a photo. Good.

The slender cut of my skirt had some spandex for easy movement. The boxy jacket hid some of my curves as well as my shoulder holster. I carried a Ruger today. Low profile. I dropped an extra magazine into my pocket. The gun served as a precaution and could help me make a point — more for show than action. Though I seriously doubted, I would show it to anyone today. I've only shot one person in my life, Wilson, and that was really enough for me.

I drank down a breakfast shake, jumped into my car, and headed into the office.

I was idling in front of Missy's house, where a moving van took up half the street, waiting for the men to negotiate a large, brown, over-stuffed sofa out the back. The sky glowed a soft pink and butter yellow. These guys got an early start.

I decided to take a minute to call up to the hospital and check on Spyder. I heard a woman's voice. "Suburban Hospital, how may I…" Holy cow. As the movers turned the sofa, I saw the white leopard rocked back on her haunches. Still. Glaring. Ready to pounce on her prey. I reflexively reached out my left hand and hit the lock button on my door — the blood drained from my cheeks. The movers must have heard the snap of the locks because they shot scowls in my direction.

Danger is moving in.

Ever since I was little, I had what I called "knowings" — thoughts flashed through my mind, unbidden. These words felt illuminated and special. They were usually silly little things like Johnny was about to fall; it was so-and-so's anniversary, or my dad had a fever. These thoughts came to me of their own volition and sometimes acted as a heads-up that something of significance was happening or soon to happen. Right now, the words weren't just illuminated: they flashed a red warning light. Never have I felt a "knowing" so viscerally. Never did a warning come to me accompanied by a …what? Illusion? Vision? What in the hell was going on? My body convulsed, bringing me back to my senses. The men juggled the sofa's weight up the new neighbor's front steps, and I inched my way around the truck.

I sat in my puzzle room, doodling leopards on a pad of paper, wondering what I should do with my "knowing." I decided my best option would be to go over this with Spyder. I'd run by and check on him tonight after work. That thought seemed to settle my apprehensions; I smiled up at the men as they filed into my office.

Jack — dressed for Iniquus right down to his black, Vibram-soled, military-style boots — had deeply chiseled features, making him seem unapproachable, but that would be a wrong impression. Warm, fun, and incredibly loyal were much better descriptors. But if he gave off the impression that he was rugged and formidable? Well, yeah, that one was right.

Today, Deep and Striker were out of uniform and had dressed in impeccably tailored suits with silk ties and Italian leather shoes.

The men sat with me around the table. Striker passed each of us a file with pictures and layouts. Our assignment was to infiltrate Burdock and Associates. The V.P. for International Affairs, Joseph Richy (nicknamed Seph), and two targets had a meeting planned for this afternoon. They needed me to get to the contents of Richy's briefcase, photograph the documents, and return everything without his knowledge. Meanwhile, Deep would hack into the computer system and plant spyware to keep an eye on the company's cash flow. Striker would have eyes and ears on the players. Jack would serve as the backup. Striker gave the operation a four-hour window, and then we'd need to exit.

We reviewed the photos, names, and titles of different employees whom we'd run into along the way. Next, we studied the floor plans, so we knew who worked in which office and where the exits were located. While we discussed possible scenarios, this was going to be a seat-of-the-pants operation.

Striker stood. "Rallying point at eleven-hundred." The men shuffled out. Striker steered me through the door with his hand under my elbow.

"We're heading to Treasury now?" I asked.

"Yup. We have a client meeting at nine-thirty. I have an appointment with a new team this morning, two guys transferring in from New York. They need Iniquus to intervene, and I'm making the initial contact. I want you along to see what you think."

"Okay, but can we run by Starbucks on the way? I didn't get to drink my coffee."

I twisted my wedding ring around my finger and stared out the window at a nanny pushing a stroller as we passed down the side street.

"You look like you're brooding," Striker said at the stoplight.

I turned to him. "I was thinking about a dream I had last night again."

"Again? That's intriguing. Care to share?"

"I spent the nanosecond of sleep I got last night fighting a ginormous demon rat. Once I finally had it trapped, I called over to animal control to come to kill it," I said.

"But instead, they put a tracking collar on it and released it back out to see where it would go." Striker finished for me.

"I've told you this one before."

"A few times," Striker said. "Does it mean anything to you? Is this one of your psychic fortune-telling things? And why did you only sleep a nanosecond?"

"My psychic what? No. I don't know. Maybe? Look, I started having this dream right after I showed you the Sylanos-puzzle when I was at the safe house. I originally puzzled through the Sylanos crime cartel and handed my findings over to Spyder sixteen months ago. Sixteen. Okay, then Spyder goes off-grid the same day I passed his answers to him. Weird huh? And then you never got that file. That's strange, too, because this was a huge deal to Spyder. Huge. But no one at Iniquus was acting on my intel — for over a year. Because what? Spyder forgot to hand them the file? That's crazy. Spyder must have decided to keep the intel to himself."

"Okay." The light turned green, and Striker eased his car into traffic.

"Okay? You said you and Spyder were on the same team, right?"

"Correct."

"Spyder left you with nada — left you flapping in the wind. You only got the answers because I happened to be under your protection at the safe house, and you asked me about the case. It didn't strike me as odd then. It sure strikes me that way now. So I gave you the answer to the puzzle last October and started to dream about rats."

"Which means what exactly?"

"I guess it means I'm not done. I think the rat is Sylanos. So tell me, what happened to the information after you took it to Headquarters? Did they act on it? Obviously, Sylanos is out and about, not in a cell somewhere, because why else would Spyder say that Sylanos became a Hydra?"

"I don't know what they did with your data — I wasn't delegated to that case anymore. It got re-assigned when Spyder left. I can call Command to find out if they're willing to share."

"Spyder probably has a better idea of what's going on. I'll talk to him about it tonight."

Striker shot me a glance full of...something. What in the world was that?

Before I could ask, Striker whipped the car into an open parking space and jumped out. *Huh. I'm not so easily put off a subject, Striker.* I'd bide my time and bring this up later.

We parked about a mile away from the Treasury satellite office. Parking was always a bitch in the city — and I was seriously rethinking my pointy-toed heels. They looked great, but boy, were they torturous on the cold cement. I had my coat pulled tight against the wind. I could smell snow in the air.

Once we arrived at the building, we flashed our credentials for the security guard and went through the metal detector. Our weapons were locked in the glove compartment of Striker's Lexus RX400.

In the conference room, two men stood by the window in deep conversation. They wore cheap, brown, badly tailored suits. And the word "dirt" came to mind — bland, uninteresting, unremarkable, just like dirt. It would be hard to describe these guys two seconds after meeting them. It occurred to me that I used my appearance to my advantage, and I wondered for a minute whether these guys did the same. Perhaps "dirt" actually meant "dirty" — as in not to be trusted. Hmmm.

"Ken MacNamaly." Dirt-Guy One held out his hand.

"Striker Rheas." Striker reached for the handshake. The dirt brothers' eyes met, just for a second, in silent, intense communication. I didn't like them. MacNamaly turned to me, his hand jutting out.

"Alex," I said as I shook his hand.

Striker lifted his chin in the slightest of nods. Alex was code. Whenever I introduced myself as Alex, Striker knew I'd be disappearing from the scene, so I could watch unobserved à la Master Wang.

Master Wang was one of my earliest and most beloved, un-schooling mentors. He taught me the martial arts that he had used as an elite soldier in China. I studied with him from the time I turned five until I was sixteen, and he moved away to Chicago. One of my favorite lessons was "shadow walking."

When I became a shadow, my goal was to disappear from sight, to be the proverbial fly on the wall, to vanish from a would-be attacker.

Shadow walking was a fairly easy technique in theory — it took loads of practice to make it work in reality. I stayed in the recesses and shadows and kept the light in my opponent's eye. The glare gave me an excellent cover. I used everything in my environment to disguise my presence. Movement had to be sloth-like. Even my breath became shallow and imperceptible. I colored my thoughts with the textures and colors around me, playing human chameleon. If I were standing in front of a tree, I used my imagination to project the rough texture, the grays, and the browns of the bark out in front of me.

The masters of this technique — like in the Japanese Ninjitsu training — could disappear from sight. I was a few levels below mastery, but still. . .

As a child, I practiced shadow walking all the time. I reigned as the hide-and-go-seek champion, and I got out of many a chore, and many a punishment, by perfecting this skill. When my parents told Master Wang about my antics, he would reprove me, but I always sensed a twinkle of amusement in his eye. Shadow walking served as an important arrow in my operator's quiver; it got used frequently. And it impressed Striker — always a bonus.

It looked like I was going to get to test those skills today.

"Alex, would you go out and find me some coffee?" Striker didn't really want coffee; we had just finished our Starbucks. He wanted to make me his subordinate, ensuring that the Dirts didn't think of me as a threat.

"Yes, sir." I did my best "I'm a piece of fluff — don't pay any attention to me" impersonation as I blinked vacantly at MacNamaly.

"There's a kitchen to the left, down the hall. I'll take one, too. I drink mine black."

"Yes, sir." I Mona Lisa smiled at Dirt Number Two.

"Yeah, black," he said.

I hustled down the hall, grabbed the three mugs of coffee, and hurried back with a tray. When I got to the conference room door, I tapped lightly and entered quietly, putting a mug and napkin in front of each of the men. I made sure to go around the table in such a way that I ended up close to the window. When I laid down the last mug and the tray, Striker coughed loudly to create a distraction. I simply took in a deep breath and slid seamlessly into the shadow. My breathing slowed. My mind conjured up the industrial-blue, dimpled texture of the walls. I used my imagination to project this out in front of me, just like Master Wang taught me to, and settled in to wait.

Right away, the Dirts forgot I ever existed. They never looked around for me. Striker had them focused. As the Dirts told their story, under the table, they tapped their feet and swiped their palms down their pants, trying to hide their nervousness from Striker. And, they were lying.

Forty-five tedious, uncomfortable minutes of dry information went by before Striker stood up to go to the men's room. I used the distraction of his movements to turn on my digital recorder and went still.

As soon as the door shut, the Dirts exhaled loudly. MacNamaly pulled a handkerchief from his pants pocket and mopped at his face.

"Fucking hell! They sent us Striker Rheas as our contact? What the fuck are we going to do now?" MacNamaly demanded.

"We're going to follow the plan. Get your shit together. You look like you're headed for a heart attack."

"Fuck that. I think we should bail. Rheas. Fuck. Why do you think they sent in their A-Team? Do you think they know?"

"They don't know shit. They sent in Rheas because we're making first contact. Rheas isn't gonna keep this case. He's gonna go back to the office and assign it to some low-level newbie who'll bumble through and do exactly what we want him to do."

"Man, you'd better be right. You'd better be right about this, man. I'm not gonna spend my life in no jail cell. I'm fucking ready to bail," MacNamaly whisper-shouted, wiping his face some more and shoving the handkerchief back in his pants' pocket.

"We've passed them the bait. They're going to go after this like a dog on a steak bone. Iniquus will be marching home in victory, and we'll be there to catch them red-handed. They'll be implicated in the crime, take the fall, and we come off like heroes and retire with our bags of money. Easy peezy."

"Easy peezy, you shithead, unless we don't get the newbie, and we get Rheas. Then what?" asked MacNamaly.

"Then, we come up with Plan B. Plan B might not be too good for Rheas' longevity, if you know what I mean."

Striker opened the door. I turned off the recorder and stepped to the side. I was visible. Striker focused over at me. I gave him a nod.

"Alex, did anything interesting happen while I was gone?"

"Little bit." The Dirts whipped their heads around to look at me. I gave them a little finger wave and walked toward Striker. The men turned their heads, following me. Their mouths gaping like trout.

"How long have you been here?" MacNamaly growled.

"I never left. I've been here since I brought you coffee. Maybe I should give Commander Rheas a blow-by-blow of what transpired, so he's up to speed."

Both men stammered incoherently. They had no way to protect themselves, as I repeated their conversation verbatim.

"Your secretary is out of bounds, Rheas. Get her under control." MacNamaly was all but foaming at the mouth.

I waved my recorder at them, and MacNamaly lunged. I jumped out of his reach. Striker had his face down. Dirt Bag Two got up and made for the door. He stopped when he heard the ratcheting sound of me chambering a bullet. He reached for his weapon only to find an empty holster.

"Before I joined Iniquus, I aspired to be a Vegas magician." I smiled, aiming his gun at his center mass.

The Dirts were handcuffed and taken into custody. Treasury could handle the case from this point. Striker shook his head on the elevator ride down. "Lynx, you've got to start making this look harder. I'm telling you."

Ha! That'll show Command what I'm made of. "You want to know what's hard?" I asked, looking down at my feet. "Walking a mile in pointy-toed shoes. Can you go get the car without me? Maybe pick me up out front?" I glanced at my watch. "We need to head right over to Burdock. The team is probably taking up their positions."

8

Striker pulled into the underground garage of the Mason Building. The enormous glass skyscraper loomed above us with its marble front steps. Ralph Lauren clad executives passed each other on the sidewalk with curt nods.

Thoughts of leopards filled my head. "After the mission, do you want to go with me to visit Spyder?" I asked.

"No." Striker shot me a glance then followed the car ahead of us through the ticket gate.

That seemed abrupt. I frowned at his tone. "Okay, I'll go myself, then."

"I'm sorry, Lynx, but no," Commander Striker Rheas said in his full-on I'm-in-charge-so-don't-mess-with-me voice. "I planned to tell you about this after we're done with today. Command says Spyder's no-contact until he can be debriefed."

"What? But I haven't spent any time with him. I need to talk to him. And what about Sylanos?"

"Exactly. Spyder's bringing in highly classified intel, and he needs to be no-profile until he's safe. Command is running covert surveillance. They don't want anyone associated with Iniquus anywhere near that hospital, calling attention."

"Why didn't you tell me this before?" I worked to keep my lower lip from pouting.

"I didn't want you emotional. Your full attention has to be on the target. This is one of Command's pet projects, so they'll be watching the outcome with a microscope. No room for error." He swiveled to back the car into a spot near the elevator. "You need your head in the game."

"You don't think I know how to focus?"

"Precaution."

"Mrs. Nelson's up at Suburban."

"I told them. Command says to keep it to a minimum and don't go *anywhere* near Spyder. You'll put more than the mission in jeopardy."

"But…" I thought the honed edge on the look he sent me was unduly sharp.

"Seriously, you aren't to whip out the shadow walking or anything else from your bag of tricks. Command gets wind that you're ignoring a direct order, and I won't be able to help you. You've got to wait until Spyder's stabilized and back at headquarters, then you can have your reunion. Got it?"

"Yes, sir." I gave him a sarcastic salute.

He released his seat belt and popped open the car door. His gaze slid over to me. When I raised a sardonic brow, he seemed to re-think what he was going to say and got out. Smart boy, he knows when to leave me the hell alone.

Striker took the elevator. I stomped out of the garage and around to the front of the Mason Building, which housed Burdock and Associates on the top three floors. It ticked me off when Striker treated me like a child. Head in the game. I'll show him head in the game.

I gave myself a shake, lifted my chin in a corporate-confident way, clacked up the stairs, and pushed through the revolving door to the UBT National Bank that took up the ground floor. As I walked across the lobby, I felt insects crawling over my skin and too many eyes on me. I scanned the space for anything out of place, but everything looked the way I would expect. The heebie-jeebies — my personal-warning system — made me want to turn around and run. Huh. That didn't bode well. I forced my feet in the direction of the elevator bank and rode up to the executive floor.

When I stepped out, the receptionist glanced up at me with cheerful professionalism. Before she could ask me my business, I gave a terse, "Good Morning, Andrea," and checked my watch. "I'm running a little late. Did Seph beat me in?"

Andrea seemed confused. She nodded. "Yes, ma'am. He came in ten minutes ago."

I slipped into Richy's office. His briefcase and coat lay on his desk.

Richy himself was nowhere to be found. I examined the briefcase lock — keyless, the kind where you rolled in a PIN. I'd have to figure out the numbers, but breaking the combination would take time. I shrank back into the shadowy corner behind an enormous jade plant. The blinding sunlight streaming through the window would help protect me from detection. I hoped Richy would spin the numbers for me to read.

Seph Richy launched himself into his office and flung his coat across the side table. He took a seat in his leather chair behind the massive, carved ebony desk and watched the door expectantly. Moments later, a tall, well-endowed brunette followed him in. She eased the door shut behind her and leaned vampishly against it, batting her eyelashes. With a satisfied grin, she turned the lock and slithered her way over to Richy.

Seph Richy wasn't an attractive man by anyone's standards. He was fat and bald with a skin condition. A road map of broken capillaries crisscrossed his bulbous red and purple nose. But that didn't stop him from chuckling and trying to look sexy for this woman.

"I've missed you, Daddy," the brunette cooed and postured.

"Come here and show Daddy how much." He wiggled a fat sausage finger in a come-hither gesture. Brunette slinked over, slid her pencil skirt up to her hips, and sat her fanny on his desk. She planted her high-heeled shoes on the arms of his executive chair like she would on a gyno exam table. Richy reached over and pressed a button on his phone.

"May I help you, sir?" a crisp voice asked.

"Hold my calls. I'm not to be disturbed."

"Yes, sir," the voice replied.

Richy turned his attention back to Brunette. "You are a very naughty little girl. You're not wearing panties today."

"No." Brunette licked her lips and fluttered her lashes. "I heard the rumor that you were back in town, Daddy, and the thought of being with you made me so hot, I couldn't bear to wear them."

Oh, gag me. This was horrible — like watching a Grade C porn-flick, bad dialogue and all.

Richy rubbed his hands on her thighs and played with her nether regions. Brunette laid back on Richy's desk and let him do his thing, groaning and writhing.

Richy chuckled. "Shhh," he said and went back to the task at hand. Brunette couldn't seem to help herself, though. She took up her moaning again.

I had to fight hard not to get sick to my stomach. I sank deeper into the shadows and planned strategies for getting into his briefcase instead of focusing on what was playing out in front of me.

Richy stopped and sat up, "I said shhh. You naughty girl. You know what happens to bad little girls."

Brunette got off the desk. With her skirt hiked up around her waist, she leaned over Richy's lap and got a spanking. Richy didn't hold back, either. He left big red welts across her fanny. I was horrified. I couldn't believe this could happen at eleven o'clock in the morning. This seemed like something that should transpire at night. After a lot of drinks. When everyone else had gone home for the day. Especially me!

Brunette knelt on the floor with red-rimmed eyes. "I'm sorry, Daddy, what can I do to make you happy again?"

"Get my lolly."

And she did. She pulled his wanger right out of his pants. It was tiny and thin and nauseatingly ugly, but she went to town on it anyway. Seph's face turned an alarming shade of purple. I became genuinely afraid that he was about to have a stroke. Then what would I do?

He pushed Brunette onto all fours and came up behind her to finish off the deed. Thankfully, they pointed away from me, and I didn't have to watch too much more.

They cleaned up with some tissues, giggling with satisfaction, and stuffed themselves back into their clothes. I think I deserved a raise for having to witness that. That seemed above and beyond the call of duty. *Honestly*.

Richy pulled his briefcase out, set it on his desk, whirled the number, and popped the locks. I did a mental victory dance and crossed my fingers that I'd get a chance to read the PIN. He pulled out a little blue Tiffany box and handed it to Brunette, who squealed and clapped her hands. She opened it to find a pair of gold and diamond earrings.

"Welcome home, Daddy." She kissed him on the cheek, put the box in her pocket, and walked out of the office.

Richy closed his briefcase and secured the latches. My heart stopped as I waited for him to roll the tumbler on his lock — then I'd be shit-out-of-luck. Before he did, a knock sounded at his door. Richy went to open it for a short, corporate drone of a man, who stood waiting. The flunky stretched his head up and whispered something in Richy's ear. I leaned out of my shadow, read the combination off the tumbler, and glided back to my place.

Richy whirled the tumbler, put the case back on the floor, and clunked his heels up on the desk, where Brunette had been displaying her bare rump just minutes before. He relaxed back for a little recuperative snooze. I couldn't move. I was stuck. I was pretty sure he'd wake up if I opened his office door. Minutes dragged toward the second hour. The rendezvous time quickly approached. The light coming in through the window had shifted, making my location more visible. Nerves made my skin prickle. My stomach growled; my knees ached from kneeling on the carpeting. I needed to use the bathroom badly, and all I could do was huddle deeper into the plant's shadow.

Finally, Richy roused himself and made some phone calls. At one o'clock on the dot, a crisp knock announced a matronly woman, who stepped in with a lunch tray and set it on his desk. Shit. Was this man ever going to leave his office? I struggled to maintain my focus on shadow walking for so long without relief. Richy got up and headed out of the room. I guessed he was heading toward the men's room — hopefully, to wash his hands before he ate.

I jumped from my place, spun the combination lock, pulled out the contents of his case and put them in my briefcase, clipped the toggles shut, leaving the combo in place for easy access, and replaced it under Richy's desk. I walked confidently out of Richy's office. A man sauntered up the hall. He eyed me curiously. I flashed him my most winning smile, "Hi, Paul." He nodded back at me. I could tell he was trying to place my face; he offered up a weak smile and moved on. I made a bee-line for the girls' bathroom.

Holed up in the handicapped stall on the end, I sat down with my briefcase balanced on my lap. I flicked the clasps open and ran my scanner, sending the images on to Jack, positioned outside. After each page, I waited for a confirmation buzz on my communicator. One buzz for good reception, the data came in legibly, continue; two for resend. It took me a long time to go through the contents.

A woman banged on the other side of the stall door. Irritation and impatience colored her voice. "Are you almost done in there?"

I bent to peek under the door and saw wheels. Shit. I groaned as if I were in pain. "So sorry. I'm not feeling at all well. Please try another floor."

The woman went into a tirade about handicapped bathrooms being reserved for handicapped people for a reason. She continued on and on as she wheeled herself out of the bathroom. She had a point. I'd make an effort not to hide in the big stalls anymore. I finished up and got the okay from Jack.

The hands on my watch seemed to spiral forward. Gah! I hurriedly tucked the files into the waistband of the back of my skirt for easy access. I wasn't quite sure how to replace these documents in Richy's briefcase. I didn't even know Richy's loca-tion. I came out of the women's room and headed back toward his office when I spied him, briefcase and all, heading for the elevator bank—finally, some luck.

I rushed over to stick my foot into the closing door and pressed myself sardine-like into the crush. People around me grumbled and sent me nasty looks. Sorry!

Even with my sleight of hand skills, I couldn't get the papers transferred, squished up the way we were. The doors opened two floors down, and the rest of the people got off, leaving just me and Richy. I set my briefcase on the floor next to Richy's feet and turned to him.

"Seph?"

As he focused on me, his mind scrambled for a connection.

"Seph, I can't believe it. It's so good to run into you. Hey, you've got some lipstick on your cheek." I rubbed his jowl with my thumb. "Can't let you go home like that, or you'd get in trouble with the Mrs." Richy set his briefcase down and let me rub him. "Are you going to be in town for long?" I asked.

"Just through the weekend," he said.

"Maybe we could…get together, do something fun?" I gave him a friendly smile.

Richy obviously thought this was an invitation; he started pressing up against me. Whoa, stud-muffin. You'd think Brunette would have worn you out for the day. She had clearly made him delusional about his appeal. If Richy got any closer, he wouldn't be feeling smooth curves, though. He'd be brushing up against my gun.

The doors opened, and a man in a pin-striped suit stepped on.

"This is my floor." I bent over to pick up his briefcase, smiled, and blew him a kiss. Dashing off the elevator, I ran for the stairwell, popped open the case, and transferred his papers back in, trying to make them look like I had found them. I clicked the toggles, rolled the lock, and ran back to the elevator bank. The ride to the ground floor was excruciatingly slow. As I jumped off the elevator, I searched for Richy through the plate glass windows and found him walking toward his limo.

"Seph! Seph!" I hurried after him. He turned to search for the person calling his name, saw me waving, and stopped.

"Whew!" I panted as I came to a stop next to him. "Seph, this isn't my case." I held up his briefcase, and he glanced down at the one in his hand.

"And this one isn't mine." He chuckled and exchanged the two. "Thanks."

Waving, I walked back toward the building, using the reflection on the glass wall to monitor Richy. He didn't seem to think anything odd was happening; he simply climbed into the back-seat of his car before it motored away.

I pushed the button on my communicator. "Lynx. Over." I was still getting used to using a call name in the field. It was weird.

Jack's voice crackled over my wire. "Jack. We have what we need from you. Striker and Deep are still in the office. Deep is having some trouble. Find him and run interference."

"Roger Wilco. Do you have a location?"

"He's in Neaman's office."

"Lynx. I'm heading there now."

I walked back into the office building and up the elevators to the top floor. As I got off the elevator, the receptionist glanced up at me. I gave her a nod and headed back.

In Neaman's office, I found Deep busily tapping away at the keyboard. He looked suave and intelligent in his fake horn-rimmed glasses. Deep glanced up as I walked in.

"This office is Grand Central." He plugged a new flash drive into the computer.

"Are you finding what you need?"

"Some of it. They have security on top of security."

I sat in a chair in front of Deep to give him a break from the interruptions. A knock sounded at the door. As it swung open, I grabbed a file and peeked around at the man standing in the door frame.

"Where's Neaman?" He squinted at us.

"Not sure. We expected him fifteen minutes ago." I scribbled an agitated pen across the papers. The man backed out. Deep tapped furiously on the keyboard.

The door opened again; a woman stuck her head in. "Where's Neaman?"

"Wish I knew." I glanced at my watch. "He's late, again."

She blew out an exasperated sigh and shut the door.

Another knock at the door. "Come in," I called—mail delivery. I accepted the envelopes with a vague "thank you" and focused back at the file. As soon as the door shut, I rifled through the pile. Nothing seemed helpful, so I laid it on the desk out of Deep's way.

"Holy Cazolli." Deep thrust a victory fist in the air. I went around to see what got him so excited. Numbers flashed across the screen. Deep sat back with his hands behind his head, watching data fly onto the flash drive. The door opened; I caught my breath. A man stood with his hand on the knob; he called to someone down the hall. Shit. Milton, Vice President of Accounting. Deep and I both recognized him from his picture. This was bad.

I pitched myself into Deep's lap. Covering the sides of his face with my hands, I pulled him into a passionate kiss. He bent over me, acting the full part — one hand supporting my body, the other caressing over my fanny.

I heard, "Whoops! Sorry, Neaman." And the door clicked shut.

I jumped from Deep's lap, cleared my throat, and straightened my skirt, then slid back onto my chair. "Sorry, Deep."

"All in the line of duty, Lynx." He focused back on the computer with a shit-eating grin.

Deep's communicator buzzed. "Deep, you've got to get out of there pronto. Board meeting's concluded. They're heading to the elevator," Striker said.

Deep pressed his button. "Roger. Wilco."

I snuck out while Deep finished his download and headed toward the elevators. As my hand reached for the down button, a gunshot concussion ripped the air. I balanced on the balls of my feet, hands wide, like a tennis player waiting for a service, then I had the good sense to duck behind a marble column. My heart beat wildly. *Holy cow*.

Where is Striker?

Why would someone shoot at him?

I couldn't think of another possible reason for a gunshot here. I waited for someone to come on the wire and tell me how to help.

Worker bees flew out of their offices, trying to figure out what was going on. Striker's voice, thank God, came over my communicator. "Lynx?"

"Here."

"You and Deep okay?"

"Fine, you?" My lips vibrated from the adrenaline surge.

"The shot came from downstairs. I'm going to investigate. You two sit tight."

"Roger." I slunk back to Neaman's office. "Striker said to sit tight."

"Yeah, but not in here. Let's head closer to an exit and find cover."

People milled around, their cell phones in their hands,

making 911 calls for information, not sure what to do. Deep and I stood behind a column. I ran my sweat-dampened hands down the back of my skirt; I still needed to pee. *Why didn't I do that when I was holed up in the handicapped stall?*

Striker burst out of the stairwell, sharply focused. His whole Captain America persona told me this was bad. He was in hero-mode.

He scanned the room, then moved over to us. "There's a robbery in progress at the bank on the ground floor. I counted four tangoes. They're grabbing hostages. Flak jackets and semis. Their tactics are professional and rehearsed. We need to get people out of here. Lynx, I need you to disengage the alarm on the fire exit."

"Do you know where the electrical box is?"

"Jack checked the schematics; he says there should be one in the utility room on the third floor. Three taps on the communicator will tell us you've succeeded, and we can get people out quietly. Be cautious with communication. People won't know we're the good guys, and we don't want anyone playing linebacker."

"What do you need me to do?" Deep pulled off his fake glasses and slipped them into his jacket pocket.

"I'll send people down with their shoes in their hands. Deep you take the next floor, and we'll clear everyone out. Jack's communicating with SWAT. He'll run us from the outside."

"And after I have the alarm off?" I worked to hide the quiver in my voice.

"Go to the ground-floor exit and make sure everyone leaves silently, and they don't put on their shoes until they clear the building."

In my mind, I was back playing one of Spyder's computer games during training. Hard to believe this was real. I ran down the stairwell on my toes to avoid the clatter. When I reached the third floor, it took me a minute to get my bearings. The hall stood empty, all the doors shut. I skated into the utility room, over to the large electrical panel on the wall, and found the circuit breaker label that identified the stairwell and rear exit— time for a contingency plan. I couldn't throw this breaker. A group of terrified people going downstairs in pitch black created a recipe for disaster.

I rifled through the desk drawer, found a set of keys, and moved cautiously toward the exit. A fire exit alarm key and an elevator operations key look similar. Their small size makes them easy to spot. It didn't take long to figure out how to turn off the alarm. I depressed my call button three times.

"Striker. Over."

"Lynx. Alarm's off. I have a set of custodial keys if they're helpful."

"You have an elevator key?"

"Affirmative."

"I need you to shut down the elevators—work from the third floor. And be careful. Your weapon needs to be in hand when those doors open. We don't know how many hostiles are working the building."

"Roger."

With the elevator task checked off my list, I made my way down to help with the exiting. I stopped on the second floor when I heard shouts. See? This was what I got for ignoring my heebie-jeebies. When my feet said run, I should just let them. Now I had to deal with this crapola.

I cracked the door to see what was happening.

A hall full of people.

A man, dressed in black with a bullet-resistant vest, waving a Glock. "Lie the fuck down and shut the hell up."

The crowd, obviously in shock, failed to register the words. The robber seethed frustration. He aimed randomly — first at one person, then another — using the gun to bolster his authority, trying to get them to comply.

I patted my pocket to reassure myself I had an extra magazine and slid through the door. Ruger aimed, I pushed my shoulder up to the wall and slunk along, maneuvering myself close enough to relieve this asshole of his gun — when goddamned it! A woman screamed and pointed at me.

As the robber turned his head to look, he made a stupid mistake and dropped the sight on his Glock toward the floor. I had a split-second window. Trapping the top-slide of his gun with my left hand, forcing it back so he couldn't fire, I aimed the pointed toe of my high heel and clipped him full-force between the legs.

He sucked wind and collapsed to the floor, rolling over in a fetal position to vomit.

I kicked the Glock out of reach. The people in the hall cowered into balls with their arms protectively circling their heads.

I used the robber's handcuffs from his utility belt to manacle his hands together, then used his duct tape on his ankles. I circled the tape several times around his mouth and head to keep him from shouting for back-up.

I had been gagged like this once; it was terrifying and dangerous.

The guy's face glowed bright red; he floundered around like a freshly caught fish lying in the sun. I was pissed off and glad he was suffering. I reached for the robber's gun — extended magazine, 40-caliber jacketed hollow points. This team wasn't playing around. I dropped his magazine and put it in my pocket. I popped his chambered bullet out and whispered to the people in front of me, "Take off your shoes and crawl toward the stairs. Help each other. You need to exit in complete silence."

As those closest to me heard and followed my commands, others got the idea and did the same.

A man crawled toward me on his elbows and told me he was ex-military. What could he do to help? I had him and his buddy drag the robber into the nearest office and secure him to a chair.

The robber's radio signaled. *Shit. Shit.* The call went out once, twice.

I shoved the Ruger to the guy's temple. "Behave or die." My conviction echoed in my voice. Good. Using my knife, I sliced through the tape, then roughly tore the gag off the guy's mouth, and prodded him with my gun.

"I got me twenty-two hostages holed up here in the conference room."

"Excellent!" came the response. "Start collecting their IDs and get the names of their next of kin."

I decompressed his radio button and told my prisoner he was to make his partners think the radio was malfunctioning. I moved my gun from his temple to the middle of his forehead, right between his eyes, so he had a visual, visceral threat.

I compressed his radio button again.

"This damned r…'s n…wor…f…shit. Do…y…me?" He acted it out well. I yanked the old wad of tape from his head, tufts of hair coming with it, and gagged him again with more circles of tape. His eyes still streamed from the kick. He blew mucus globs out of his nostrils with force to keep his nose clear enough to breathe.

I left the phlegm dangling from his chin. I couldn't be a nice-guy now. "As long as you behave, I'll keep checking you have an airway. You give me grief? You can suffocate in your own snot." I hoped the threat would be enough.

My helpers stood in front of me. Panting from adrenaline. Waiting for their next directive.

"You guys get out," I ordered.

"But ma'am…" Soldier-boy stammered — reluctant to leave. I bet it was my high heels and lipstick — these guys thought they needed to protect me.

I thought they were a liability.

"That's an order, soldier." I used Striker's commander-voice and got the result I wanted.

Military guy saluted and crawled out on his belly. His buddy tried to follow suit but wasn't nearly as coordinated.

What now?

I edged out into the corridor to the railing that overlooked the main lobby and lay flat against the balusters, wanting to give SWAT some intel.

Suddenly, a robber ran toward a withered old woman — the only hostage on her feet. He ripped her cane from her hand and threw it, clattering across the pink marble floor.

Thrust bodily up against the glass door, gun to her temple, I watched as she peed a wide yellow puddle.

A bright burst of sound exploded.

Brains sprayed out the side of the woman's head, spattering the glass, leaving wet smears running down the pane with long strands of gray hair and bone fragments visible even from my distance.

He let the woman's lifeless body collapse like a heap of dirty laundry into the pool of urine. I never saw anyone shot in the head in front of me before. It was horrifying, and suddenly this was all too real — not a computer simulation. *Real*.

I rolled into the nearest office and shut the door so no one could hear as I vomited up this morning's coffee and a good amount of stomach bile. Squatting in the corner, I wiped my mouth on the sleeve of my jacket. I wasn't supposed to be on assignments with a high risk-factor. I was the Puzzler, a sleight-of-hand girl who planted transmitters.

This was way above my pay grade.

I didn't think there was a pay grade high enough for me to want to be here.

"Lynx," I whispered into my communicator. A vibration came in response. They were listening but didn't want to put me in danger by speaking. "One hostage fatality. Three tangoes visible in the lobby. I have one in custody on the second floor. Over." The robbers were talking over my prisoner's radio; I let my team listen. I counted voices. I heard five. I had visual on three in the lobby; I had one who wasn't functioning, so there had originally been at least six — bad odds for Striker, Deep, and me.

Huh. Well, one way to figure this out...

I crawled back to my prisoner. He wasn't doing well. He was definitely low on oxygen; his skin was blue and clammy.

"Now's the time to cooperate." I sliced, then yanked the tape roughly from his mouth, the Ruger pushed to his temple, my thumb on my communicator. "How many of you in the building?"

"Eight." He gasped, opening his mouth wide, desperately searching for oxygen. Blood dripped from his raw lips.

"Where are they?"

"Three are on the first floor with the hostages, two emptying the security boxes, I'm here, and two drifting — making sure everything's going according to plan."

"Are they all dressed like you?"

"No, only the ones who are in charge of the hostages and the boxes — the drifters are dressed in suits."

"How can we recognize them?"

He paused, so I moved the Ruger under his chin. "You won't be able to," he said. "Except they're wearing bullet-resistant vests."

I focused on not letting my hands shake. "What's the end game here?"

"Rob the bank safety deposit boxes of precious metals, coins, and jewelry, whatever we can get that's untraceable, get gold for the hostages, get flown to safety by taking hostages with us." His eyelids stretched wide, exposing the whites of his eyes. His focus swept from me to the tape on the desk.

"They shot an old woman." I pulled his attention back.

"They'll shoot one hostage every hour on the hour." His voice didn't hold the defiance I would have expected.

He sounded deflated.

I twisted around to see the wall clock — this took me a second — my mind was muted under gauzy layers of shock. "Out," I said into the communicator and got a confirmation buzz. "Okay, we're going to work together to keep you alive. I want you to blow your nose hard." I held tissues up for him to clear his nose. Disgusting. As I rewrapped his mouth and head with the tape, I noticed the pink color had returned to his skin. "Be good," I told him and edged back out to the overlook.

People, lying face down, peppered the bank lobby. I counted them off. From my vantage point, I got twenty-two. Many were crying. They lay in various protective positions, curled around themselves, covering their heads. A mother lay across her children, using her body as their last defense.

The same three robbers were visible. They stood in front of the glass walls of the bank lobby. I assumed since the SWAT snipers weren't taking these men out, that there was some kind of dire threat that had been communicated to the police.

Time froze. I sat with my prisoner, waiting for instructions, praying for Striker and Deep. Where were they?

A shriek sliced the air. I scuttled out to the baluster. I located all three robbers in the lobby. One stood in front of the door, holding a pregnant woman in front of him, his hand clamped on her jaw. The woman wrenched and snaked her head, trying to get away from the semi-automatic pushed up against her temple. Her sobs rose up toward me, grabbing at my throat, making it hard for me to breathe. Had an hour passed already? Certainly, if they were trying to make a point of their ruthlessness, killing a pregnant woman would do it.

I crouched back on my heel, posting one knee to use as a support for my gun hand. My Ruger felt slippery in my sweaty palms. I wanted to wipe my hands off on my skirt, but I couldn't take my aim off of the guy holding the woman. My mouth went completely dry. My lips stuck to my teeth.

I gazed down the gun barrel, lining up the sight window with the man's head. What the hell were the snipers thinking? Why hadn't they taken this guy out? I wasn't equipped for this — in any sense of the word.

Okay. I needed to think this through. A shot to his core was of no consequence. I traded my 9mm for my prisoner's Glock. I needed a one-and-done bullet if I was going to pull this off. This was a Hail Mary moment. I'd be foolish to take it. No. I wouldn't take it. This woman stood too close in height to the assailant. If she and her baby were going to die today, it wasn't going to be my hand that took their lives.

Loud phone negotiations carried up from the lobby, but I only caught a word or two. Things weren't going well. The robber jerked the woman this way and that to punctuate his demands. Wait. I recognized this scenario from one of Spyder's 3D computer teaching games.

Okay, if I could get a shot off on the one holding the pregnant woman, I'd have shock on my side. I'd have what? –About seven seconds where the other two robbers couldn't respond. I think that might be enough.

I shifted my attention to the other two bad guys. They weren't pointing their guns at anyone in particular. They were focused on what was going on outside the windows.

My gun sight glued to the center of the man's head by his ear.

The pregnant woman grabbed her belly and doubled over.

At that moment, I pulled the trigger. One, two, three, four, five-times I shot in quick succession.

The robber holding the woman went down immediately. So did the pregnant woman. I didn't know why. It couldn't have been me. Could it? She was on all fours now. The other bad guys sprawled on the ground, unmoving.

I yelled down at the hostages, "RUN. RUN. RUN."

A few of the hostages lifted themselves — zombie-like, in shock, and uncoordinated — they ran-stumbled toward the door. I watched them slipping on brain-matter and blood, grasping at each other as they climbed over the attacker's and the old lady's bodies that lay in their path.

My heart squeezed like a tight fist. I went tingly-numb from lack of blood circulation.

A man grabbed hold of the pregnant woman's arm and

dragged her behind him as she scrambled her legs under her, trying to stand up. Some of the hostages crawled in the direction of the door, some lay as if petrified — not yet able to move.

Shoes, bags, and coats were strewn everywhere.

A flash of Deep and Striker raced back toward the vault area. More shots blasted the air and echoed off the marble. I pinched my nostrils almost closed to stop myself from hyperventilating. Nothing. Silence. What? What?

Shivering, sweat-covered, ripped stockings, nose running, puke-stained, I crawled back into the office with my prisoner. The buzz of my communicator snapped me back to operator mode.

"Lynx here. Five shots fired, Three tangoes down. One tango in custody. Striker and Deep in the vaults. Additional shots fired. No further information."

This time Jack came over the line. "We're coming to get you. Sit tight. Out."

I sat tight. It was a miserable wait. I wouldn't let my mind go where it wanted to go. I had to stay professional. I'd allow myself all of the scary feelings later, in private.

My communicator buzzed. "We're outside your door coming at you. Out," Jack said.

I stood to one side of the door jamb and aimed my Ruger just to be sure. Jack opened the door slowly and walked in. He nodded at me. I lowered my weapon.

Jack dropped Striker and me off at my house. I went up, showered, and changed clothes to go back to Iniquus for our debriefing and mental health check. Apparently, I was the only one who needed a shower — no one else had puked. When I went down the stairs, my hair hung wet and back to blonde; my brown contacts were stowed in their case. Striker sat pensively on my couch.

"I want combat pay." I plopped into a chair beside him, rubbing my hair with a towel. "Daring deeds of do or die aren't part of my contract. As a matter of fact, I think it specifically says I don't do that."

"That was a random crime we happened on. You weren't acting as an Iniquus operator." Striker's tone was flat, his face unreadable.

I narrowed my eyes and looked at him sideways. I didn't like it when Striker acted impermeably. "Oh, yeah. You're right. Well, I don't want to happen on any more crimes. That sucked." I tried to smile, but my lips wouldn't cooperate.

"You ignored my order." He pitched his voice glacial and low.

"How do you mean?"

"I told you to get the people out the back door."

"Right." I considered him for a minute. I had curled up in my chair with my dogs at my feet — their eyes unwaveringly on Striker, on guard. I guessed I was too. When Striker brandished his hard edge, it was intimidating as hell. "I was following your order when I heard more people in the corridor. I hoped to get them moved out, as well," I said. "Unfortunately, a guy with a gun blocked their path. Once I had him secured, I found him useful for getting information. I stayed in constant communication, and I never got a subsequent order. Things change during a mission. Obviously."

We stared at each other. A long moment passed before either of us moved or spoke.

Striker exhaled, letting go of some of his tension. "I know this about you, Lynx — you're clever. Trained. Effective." He leaned back into the couch and crossed his arms over his chest, sticking one long leg out in front of him to resemble nonchalance.

I wasn't buying it.

"I remember vividly my first impression of you, well, my first impression when I met you as Lexi after the Wilson attack. Even though you were in bad shape, you were still level-headed and smart — you once told me that you use this sweet, girl-next-door looks, your girly, innocent-sexiness to your advantage. It confuses and disarms people. Sometimes, I forget who I'm dealing with."

We sat some more. I wasn't sure what reaction I was supposed to have here. I'm not really sure what this conversation was about. Striker was clearly working through something in his own mind.

"Sometimes, being with you is confusing." He shook his head as if he was trying to line up his thoughts. "I want to protect you, and you don't really need me to do that. It screws with my mind a little bit." Striker pursed his lips and cocked his head to the side, taking me in from a different angle. "Deep had a lipstick mark on his mouth and collar. It's your color."

"Are you jealous?" I batted my eyelashes.

"Curious is a better word."

I told him about the embrace in Neaman's office and how Deep had put up with my kiss as a sacrifice 'in the line of duty.' That got me a half-smile. Striker stood. "We had better head into the office. They'll have a team pulled together to assess us. How're you doing — you okay?"

"I saw a lot of gray matter and blood today. I think it might be a good idea to get some strategies for how to deal with that. I'd like to talk it over with Spyder, but you said that's off the table." I worked my jaw. It ticked me off that they were keeping me from Spyder, especially after I rearranged my life to saddle up for their mission.

"Completely off," Commander Striker said.

"I got it already," I shouted. I could hear the throaty leopard growl victoriously in my head. The thought brushed through my mind that Command might be keeping me away from Spyder for some reason other than his safety.

9

I curled up in front of my picture window with a steaming cup of ginger tea. Knee-deep snow blanketed the city last night, leaving my view crystalline. Serenity painted the scene as I watched the sun breaking through the clouds at dawn, but now the neighborhood kids, sausaged in their winter gear, waddled out to play. Soon, their calls and laughter punctuated the still and hush. Their feet churned up the smooth white perfection as they rolled out their snowmen and built their forts.

I woke up early this morning after a difficult night; adrenaline factored largely in my discomfort. My dreams weren't about gunshots, banks, and blood, though; they were about the rake of long, sharp claws down my back and gleaming white fangs.

The psychiatrist at Iniquus told me in our de-briefing that it might take a few days for me to get back on even kilter — if I had trouble, I should head in and have a chat. The person I needed to talk with, though, was off-limits to me. God, Spyder, get better already. Tell me what to do.

Manny headed around the corner of his house with a shovel in his hands. I opened my door and called him over. He stomped up my steps, kicking his boots to dislodge the snow.

"What's the word?" he asked.

"The word is 'winter' apparently. Can you come in for a coffee? I wanted to ask you about something."

"And get out of shoveling the walk a little longer? I'll gladly take a cup of joe."

Manny took off his coat by the door, and I went back to put a K-cup in the brewer. Manny stands about five-ten and stocky. And while his hair had started to recede, his eyebrows valiantly tried to make up for it. His dark eyes were always unreadable unless he was talking about his sons, then they filled with affection.

"You hungry?" I called from the kitchen.

"Nah, I just got done eating pancakes with the boys."

"How'd Christmas go with Gladys and her visitation?"

"She didn't show. I'm not sure she's even living in town no more. Her phone's been disconnected, and her dad said she isn't staying with him."

I handed Manny a coffee mug. "What are the boys saying about that?"

"They don't mention her, so I don't either. I'm gonna sit tight and see what happens. So, what's up? You wanted to talk to me about something?"

"Did you hear Mrs. Nelson's moving into an assisted living facility?"

"Yeah. Things are gonna be weird not having her right across the street. She's like an institution — the closest thing my boys got to a grandma."

"She won't be far. I'm sure she expects visits." I poured

myself another cup of tea while Manny checked his phone. When I had his attention again, I said, "I'm going to go ahead and buy her half of the duplex."

Manny whistled. "That'll be a chunk of change. So this conversation must be about poker?"

"It is."

"What's gotta get done? New bathrooms, kitchen, HVAC for sure. Anything else?" He cracked his knuckles.

"Paint and floor refinishing."

"Not a problem. I'll need babysitting when I go out. And I want food as barter."

"You want to spell that out?" I put another packet of Splenda in my mug and swirled my spoon around.

"Sure. Do you remember when you made the month of food all up in them plastic baggies, I stuck them in the freezer, and we just had to cook 'em up with your instructions?"

"Packaged meals are easy enough."

"Three-months-worth." He added — finger in the air.

"Okay. When do you think you can start?"

"Tonight. I gotta game, and I was gonna ask if you'd babysit. The guy who did your heating system is gonna be there, so this here is one of those happy coincidences."

"Can the boys spend the night with me?"

"That'd be good. I'll bring them over at bedtime." Manny set his mug on the table, went back to my living room, where he huffed into his coat. "Back to the salt mines." He smiled and went out whistling. *Wouldn't it be great if all of my problems were so easily handled?* I stood at the door and stared down the street at my new neighbor's house.

Manny's boys were tucked under the duvet in my guest room, completely zonked from their day of cold, fresh air. I pulled back the covers to climb into my own bed with my Kindle when my cell phone rang—Striker.

"Hey." I smiled widely, scooting myself down under my covers. "I was thinking about you."

"Good thoughts, I hope."

"Command gave me an update on Spyder." I clicked off my bedside lamp, and the moon sent a rivulet of light over my white comforter.

"And?" Striker sounded wary.

"No better, no worse. Still nothing in the way of test results. With him being incommunicado, there's no pressing reason to stop me from leaving over New Year's. So, I needed to figure out what kind of dress to wear to the party in Miami."

"Something sparkly, short, and dance-y."

"Sparkly and short, I can manage. What's dance-y?" I twisted my hand in the air, scattering moonlight through the diamonds in my rings--Angel's rings.

"I'll let you figure that out. Where are you right now?"

"Tucked in bed." The long silence following my response made me blush. I cleared my throat. "Um, I went to bed early. I'm tired. Did you need me for something?"

"Nope, just called to find out how your day went."

"It went fine, thank you. I made a deal with Manny about poker — food for upgrades at Mrs. Nelson's — so I've been food processing onions all day."

"Are you almost done?"

"Ha. I wish. Not even close. I hope it was okay that I stayed home from the office. They told me to take a few days off."

"You're doing exactly what you should be doing. I don't

want you back at Headquarters until after the New Year. Did you enjoy the snow?"

"There's something magical about a snow-covered morning. So beautiful. What did you do today?"

"Paperwork, briefings…"

"You didn't take a mental health day?" My brows drew together. I didn't want to be treated as if I were delicate. I needed to prove I belonged on the team.

"I didn't shoot anyone — it was business as usual for me."

"True, you didn't. For a second there, I felt like a wus for not showing up at the office."

"Nope, following orders. Are you going to be cooking all day tomorrow?"

"It shouldn't take the whole day. I need to take a break and go find a present for Cammy. Can you come with me?" I stifled a yawn.

"I'll pick you up around noon. We'll grab some lunch out — give your eyes a break from the onion fumes. I have to find something for Cammy, too.

"Okay. G'night."

"Sweet dreams, Chica."

I had a hard time hanging up. I was remembering the safe house and how every time I got creeped-out with the heebie-jeebies, I'd skitter to Striker's bed — the only place I found relief from my pervasive anxiety. Most nights, it was the only way I got any sleep at all. When I thought about it, I could still smell Striker lying next to me, fresh and warm from the shower, with the scent of soap and mint toothpaste. In his sleep, his arms would snake around my waist and pull me into him. I lay very still, pressed against his body. Our contours, like puzzle pieces fitting perfectly, seeming to belong together. And as I lay there, guilt swamped my senses.

Oh yeah. There it was…the guilt.

The Molinary boys sat at my kitchen table in their Batman jammies, hair ruffled from sleep, kicking their dangling feet in their warm slippers. They were six and almost eight and looked just like their dad minus the gut and over-active eyebrows. I stood at the stove, making pumpkin pancakes, when Beetle and Bella gave warning barks followed by the doorbell. I went to let Manny in.

"Goodness, get in here. It's freezing."

Manny stomped in, shucked his coat, and toed off his boots. "No kidding, I crossed the street, and my face is numb."

"Come back here. The kitchen is warm. Do you want hot cocoa or coffee?"

"Coffee, please." We moved toward the back of my house. "Hey, guys! How was your night? Were you good boys for Aunt Lexi?"

"Yes, sir," they chimed, as they shoveled pancake into their mouths, dripping syrup down their chins.

"How about you?" I set a plate of pancakes and a mug of coffee in front of Manny. "Any success?"

"Mixed bag. The HVAC guy stood us up. His wife got pissy about something. He's gonna be at a game tonight, though. I did get your bathrooms and kitchen. We can mark those off the list. I didn't win big enough for top-a-the-line like in here, but I made sure you got good, lasting quality. I'll take some measurements today, and we can check their web site for styles. They'll start the install on the second unless you need me to push the job out later because of your closing date."

"The second should be fine. You need me to babysit again tonight?" I asked, dropping into the chair across from Manny.

"Yup."

"I'm leaving tomorrow around lunchtime for Miami, though." I curled one leg underneath me as I leaned in for a warming sip of coffee. "I won't be back until late on the first."

"Okay. I'll be over bright and early to get the boys. Who's taking care of Beetle and Bella?"

Good question. I drummed my fingers on the table. "This all just came up, and I haven't made any plans for them. They're okay here on their own if you wouldn't mind feeding them and making sure they get let out in my backyard to potty."

"We can handle it. We'll make a stop in when we take care of old Mrs. Spritzer's dog."

By the time Striker let himself in my front door, I was dusted in flour and splotched with pumpkin. Egg smudges dappled my apron.

Striker leaned against the door jam, dressed in civilian clothes. Yummy. I liked how his moss-green sweater hung on his broad shoulders and how his jeans tightened around his thigh muscles. And I liked the way his eyes traveled over me with that slow smile of his. It made me hungry — but not for food.

"This looks like a cooking circus. I can't decide whether to give you a kiss or lick you."

Color rose in my cheeks. "Ha! You'd better stand well back. This is definitely a mess." I grinned over at him.

"Are you going to be able to go now? Or should we do this later?"

"Now's fine. I was expecting you. Can I get you anything to drink? I need to run upstairs and shower real quick, then we can get going."

10

In and out of the bathroom. I tugged my hair back into a long ponytail. I did the minimum with makeup, hurriedly pulled on jeans, snow boots, turtleneck, and thick wool sweater, and clomped down the stairs.

As we headed out, Striker grabbed my hand.

Good thing, too. I slipped and slid over the re-frozen ground to a charcoal-gray, Iniquus Humvee with chains on the wheels parked across the street.

"Striker, I need to sneak by the hospital. Mrs. Nelson has her list ready for me."

"What's the list about?" He wrapped his hands around my waist and hoisted me up to the front passenger seat.

"She can only take so much with her to her suite in the assisted living facility. The rest goes to Missy next door."

"Mrs. Nelson can't tell you over the phone?" Annoyance hardened Striker's jaw.

"She can barely talk after her stroke. You said Command would let me visit her."

"Her," he said sternly and narrowed his eyes at me.

I batted my lids innocently at him. "Who else would I be going to see?"

Striker shook his head at me. He moved gracefully around to the driver's side, slid under the wheel, and put the Hummer in motion. He was telling me a story from work, idling in front of Missy's house as Dave's kids, Colin and Fletcher, scrambled out of the road. Jilly and her brothers sat on their porch, laughing and throwing snowballs from their cache.

I wasn't paying attention to Striker anymore. Suddenly, my head swam with vertigo, and I refocused on the view outside the Hummer window as if the scene were playing out in slow motion on a silent screen. My gaze finally came to rest on a middle-aged woman, who looked Latin American, standing hands-on-hips in front of her new house, watching the goings-on.

The woman turned her head our way. Chills galloped down my spine as her feral eyes glittered darkly at me. I imagined a slow, menacing grimace, her baring sharp white teeth—the leopard.

Danger is moving in.

Holy crap, I knew her. And from the way she considered my face, I realized she recognized me too.

How?

Where?

My gymnastic mind did tumbles and flips, trying to find a memory to land on. My breath had caught in my throat. My hands went rigid with cold. I was a rabbit surprised to have found my way into the path of a rabid fox. My limbic system responded with petrified-stillness. I vaguely registered the fake smile the woman plastered across her face as she waved over at us. Before I could decide how to respond, we rolled past.

"Chica?" Striker reached over to rub my arm. "Hey, are you okay?"

My body shuddered as the spell broke. "What? Yeah, fine. Why?"

"I've been talking to you, and I don't think you have any idea what I've been saying, and when you saw the woman on the sidewalk, your face went completely blank like a plastic mask."

"I know her. I'm trying to figure out how. I definitely recognize her face…it's from a long time ago."

"You don't seem happy about this. What was your first impression when you saw her?"

I shrugged and turned to stare out the passenger window. *Danger is moving in.* I wanted that thought all to myself right now. I wasn't ready for Striker's intrusion.

Striker left me alone the rest of the drive as I tried to place this mystery woman. Her face had aged since I had seen her last. And maybe I hadn't even seen her. Maybe she had been in a photograph I saw a long time ago.

My head throbbed. When we sat down at the table, I opted for a cup of tea. Striker ordered the steak dinner. I sat silently, only vaguely aware of the clink of glasses and the murmur of voices. The server startled me out of my reverie when he put a plate down in front of Striker.

Striker took a sip from his water glass. "Are you ready to talk?"

I nodded, not sure I could.

His jaw was tight, his green eyes keen on me. He looked like a man ready to do battle. "What are you thinking about? It seems serious."

"Yes. It feels serious."

"And?"

"Why do you guys stay in the barracks? Is it because people would be attacking you left and right if you tried to live with the regular populace?"

My question seemed to surprise Striker. He contemplated me before answering. I guess he was trying to figure out why I took a new angle. "Is this about the Mason Building attack? That was a random crime that. . ."

"No. It's not." My voice dripped vehemence.

"Spyderman, then? I understand you're upset about the no-contact deal," he concluded, wrongly.

I said nothing.

Striker leaned back in his chair and folded his arms across his chest, his eyes speculative. "We stay in the barracks because it's convenient to the job, and the job can be all-encompassing. Many of us have somewhere else that we live like I have my house on the water, and Jack has a place with Suz. Spyder stayed at his own house, off Iniquus Campus, before this last assignment. I'm not sure what he'll do now."

I glared at Striker — pissed, but for no good reason. Even though I certainly wasn't angry at Striker, my eyes basted him with rancor.

Striker studied at me for a long minute, and I guessed he realized he missed the mark. He tried again, leaning forward and lowering his voice. "So, when you say being attacked left and right," he said, "I'm assuming you're thinking about Travis Wilson." He paused, and I gave him a nod. Sure. Why not lay my panic at the feet of maiming-stalker-Wilson, since I didn't really have anywhere else to lay these emotions? Well, yes, they belong to leopard woman, but I couldn't tell Striker that.

"When Travis Wilson was stalking you, we were working on the assumption that he went after you because of your association with Spyderman and Iniquus." He balanced his elbows on the table as he leaned in to speak in tones that wouldn't carry to the other tables. "That was speculation. There's no proven connection between the two men."

"I'm well aware." My tea sent up curling ribbons of steam. I took a tentative sip as I tried to contain my insecurity. All I wanted to know was how to get safe and why a damned leopard came to live in my neighborhood.

"And with Wilson dead, we'll probably never get our questions answered. I did ask Spyderman about him, and he doesn't know of any correlation between Wilson and him." Striker's tone was serious, his gaze direct.

My eyes opened wide. My fist came down on the table, making the cutlery jump. "You asked him? When? Why do you get to talk with him and not me?" Striker glanced around. That came out a little bigger than I had planned. People had stopped eating and stared over at us.

"I went by last night after I talked to you on the phone. He sends his love. The rest is classified."

"Damn it, Striker." I groaned. "I just want to live a quiet suburban life. I keep trying. I wanted to take a little hiatus from my studies to help you and Spyder out, and then I was going to go right back to my plan."

Striker definitely seemed perplexed by my new tack. "This is the 'I'm your typical everyday suburbanite plan'?"

I leaned over the table and hissed, "Why can't I live a normal life?" I sat back and put up my hand. "Stop. Don't answer me. I don't want to hear your theories about my being a Ferrari driving only on Sundays. They're ridiculous. And on this one, you're wrong." I stared down at my napkin, trying to get control of my swirling emotions.

"Lexi, look at me." Striker waited until our eyes met. "Why

do I get the impression we aren't talking about Spyder or Wilson. What's going on here?"

I shook my head with a scowl. I didn't know. If I did, I could act. But not understanding — not having a plan — made me... "Endangered" was the only word I could fish out of my whirlpool of thoughts. I took a deep breath and tried to smile sweetly. Years of fluff-training came to my aid. Striker seemed to buy the change of pace — though, to me, the veneer of my smile was rice-paper thin. "Let's change the subject. You have something you needed to tell me?" I asked.

The warrior stance shifted to the background. Striker took a bite of his steak and chewed slowly. He wiped his mouth with a napkin. "When are you going to be able to rent out your duplex?"

"I close sometime around the 10th. Manny's getting the upgrade contracts together. Maybe by the third week of January if everything works like a charm. Why?"

"Gator wants to move in." He focused down at his plate and shoveled up another bite of steak. Something wasn't right here. Striker was fibbing.

I narrowed my eyes at him, my make-believe smile forgotten. "Oh, really? When did this come about?"

Striker offered up his boyish lopsided grin.

God, I loved his smiles.

"About ten minutes ago."

I waited for an explanation.

"I have to go out of the country on an assignment." His voice sounded nonchalant, but his posture was guarded, probably getting ready for my barrage of unanswerable questions.

"When?" The Johannesburg file flitted through my mind. Shit. He was going down-range. Tears prickled behind my eyes.

This is really too much for me to handle. Okay, I know — selfish as hell for me to be thinking of myself right now.

"I'm not sure. There are still a couple of key things Command needs to put in place. Soon, though." Striker's calm voice steadied me.

"Will I know you're leaving? You'll tell me before you go?" I unconsciously reached out my hand to cover his.

He laced his fingers with mine, gripping me tightly. Striker had a disturbing way of making me feel delicate and fragile, which was not how I normally thought of myself.

"Absolutely." He nodded for emphasis, our eyes locked.

"Do I get to know where?" My diaphragm vibrated, making me pant. I didn't blink. What was he doing to me? I was hypnotized. All I wanted at this moment was to crawl into his lap and snuggle my head into his shoulder with his arms tightly around me. I wanted to sink into his steadiness and calm and bathe in his warmth.

"Classified." He frowned slightly and tilted his head to the side. "What's going on, Chica?" His voice gently invited me to confide in him, have confidence in him.

"Do I get to know how long?"

"Undetermined — but this isn't like Spyderman's last mission. I'm hoping to get things wrapped up pretty quickly. I never really know, though." He watched me closely.

I shook my head and tried to unravel myself from his spell. "And this is why Gator wants to move in next to me?"

"To be honest with you, I'm concerned about what you just said. You're acting ..." His voice shifted perceptibly. "Are you keeping something from me?" Oh, Commander Striker was back.

Of course, I was. What could I possibly say to him? There's a leopard who keeps growling in my subconscious, baring her teeth and scaring the bejeezus out of me night and day? Or maybe I could explain how I had a "knowing," and the phrase *Danger is moving in* now pulsed ominously in my veins? He'd have me committed. I smiled my sweet veneer smile again and shook my head with a shrug.

"I wish you were living in the barracks. I'd like you to stay at my place while I'm gone." He raised a questioning eyebrow. "Would you consider a temporary move?"

Only while you're gone? Was that disappointment I registered? Where was that coming from? I loved my house. "That's kind of you. But you're right. I can't. I have people who need me to be involved right now. There is Mrs. Nelson and my new place, and I have to get Spyder set…"

Striker nodded. He disentangled our fingers to take a key out of his pocket and handed it to me. "You and the pups are welcome. It's available to you whenever you want. Even if you just need a nap."

I accepted the key and wound it onto my key chain. "Thank you. So go on. You're leaving town. You're concerned about me. And, you want me to have a Strike Force watchdog in position."

"That's pretty blunt and accurate. I'd be happier with the situation, and frankly, Gator would be overjoyed to eat you out of house and home."

I rolled the idea over while I poured a new cup of tea from the little pot. Striker knew me well enough to let me marinate. His leaving meant I'd be more vulnerable in every sense of the word. Those poor-delicate-me thoughts didn't sit well in my psyche. And then it flashed into my mind — a picture on Mrs. Agnew's desk.

Instantly, I was back in my childhood apartment building, standing in front of Mrs. Agnew's writing desk. Mrs. Agnew was connected to me by none other than Spyder freaking-still-incommunicado McGraw.

Mrs. Agnew and her two children moved into my apartment building when I was thirteen. At that time, Spyder approached my parents and offered his mentorship in exchange for my helping out with Mrs. Agnew's children. Mrs. Agnew worked at the hospital from seven at night until three in the morning. I was supposed to get the kids in bed on the fold-out in my living room, then in the morning, I'd get them up, breakfasted, and shuttled on to the school bus.

My dad had known Spyder McGraw for years, having done special adaptations on Spyder's work cars. So, when Spyder offered to barter, my parents were thrilled. They thought Spyder's mentorship was perfect for building bridges in my thinking processes and firing up my synapses. They accepted happily. And I learned from Spyder happily. No — hungrily. I craved the lessons and skills Spyder taught me.

What did I know about Mrs. Agnew? Next to nothing. I had no idea what Spyder's relationship was with her, but I didn't think it was romantic in nature. Mrs. Agnew wasn't the kind of woman that made me think about romance. She reminded me of an unmade bed. Hmmm. And then one day, she packed up and left so suddenly I didn't even get to tell the kids good-bye. She was just there one minute, and boom, gone the next. Okay, true — I didn't miss the babysitting. I was thrilled when her disappearance didn't stop Spyder from teaching me.

In my mind's eye, I stepped closer to the desk and picked up the photo of two couples. Yes — there on the left was the mystery woman, all right, and that couldn't be a coincidence, and it didn't seem like anything good.

I let my memory tickle and spark as I tried to recall the details of the photo. Mrs. Agnew and a younger, happier leopard-woman sat arm-in-arm on a deck, grinning broadly, swinging their legs. Huge palm trees made up the backdrop behind them, and two men, who stood equally carefree, framed the women. The cheery, relaxed photograph seemed completely antithetical to what I currently experienced from this woman.

Now, she was hungry, menacing.

And for some unknown reason, I was her prey.

11

I slid behind the giant framework of an obese man as he waddled out of the stairwell. Skimming seamlessly along the wall, using people and objects to obscure me, I shadow walked, scanning up the corridor for any obvious operator -eyes. I stole my way down the few doors to what I hoped was still Spyder's assigned room. Opening Spyder's door would change the lights; a camera would definitely pick up the contrast. If they were doing remote surveillance, this was my most vulnerable point. Iniquus didn't tell me what precautions they had taken to protect Spyder. I was winging it.

I stretched out my fingers to turn Spyder's doorknob when two hands caught my shirt, yanking me back and then releasing me, so I bounced against the green-tiled wall. I spun my head with a startled gasp—Striker.

"You aren't following orders." He trapped my wrists by my side.

Even though he was obviously furious, my breath rushed out in relief. "You saw me? And hid behind the towel cart?" He was unbelievable.

"Shadow walking is like a magic trick — once you've seen how it works, it's not hard to catch you in the act. What the hell are you doing here?" he growled. He actually growled at me.

When I tried to shake off his grip, he stretched my wrists down and moved my hands a few inches behind my back. I didn't know if he was trying to hide his clasp from the people strolling in the hallway or if he was making sure I had no leverage. This seemed somewhat playful — and yet...

I narrowed my eyes at him. "Let me go this minute."

"Lexi, what in the hell are you doing here? You're risking your job and now mine, not to mention Spyderman's damned safety."

Shit. He's right — I'm risking all of us. "I have to talk to Spyder. This has nothing to do with Sylanos or Iniquus. I need his help. I'm in danger." I twisted my wrists slightly to position them for a release. "Let. Me. Go."

Striker shifted my arms farther behind my back and pushed a knee between my legs, leaning into the wall. I was effectively trussed. Striker slowly shook his head "no."

"I can get out of this. You can't stop me." I wiggled against him, testing his hold. Why was I behaving this way? I should just explain. Striker was reasonable. He'd look the other way. But being in his grasp this way set something off in my brain I didn't recognize.

"Chica. We can go hand-to-hand right here in the hospital corridor. Then security will come, we'll both get kicked out, and Spyder will be left vulnerable."

There was a glint of something feral in Striker's eyes, inflating the sensations burning through me. I wanted... This was wrong. *Head in the game.* Stop it. Stop it now, Lexi. While my head might be playing one game, my body seemed to be playing by a different set of rules. And it was winning out. I couldn't seem to pry my attention north of Striker's belt. "That would only happen if you didn't let me go — or if you tattled." I had to get him off me.

The steely muscles of his leg flexed between my inner thighs.

"I'll scream." I tried on for size, but it came out husky and low pitched with zero conviction.

Striker's attention moved to my lips. "You could try," he said, not shifting his gaze.

Definitely a challenge.

I took in a deep breath and opened my mouth. I didn't really mean to scream. But a shriek danced up my throat. Before the sound hit the air, Striker's lips sealed mine in an open-mouthed kiss — a kiss very different from the tender one under the mistletoe. This kiss was jarring — slamming into me like a locomotive. It was its own emotional thunderstorm.

And all I wanted at that moment was for him to keep kissing me.

Spyder, Sylanos, and the creepy neighbor two-doors-down be damned.

I heard a wolf whistle followed by a "Get a room!"

Striker pulled away. His eyes were dilated to black. The vein on the side of his neck pulsed. I was dizzy and welcomed his constraining stance. It kept me from sliding down the wall.

Striker whispered in my ear, "You scream here, and I'll slap handcuffs on and put you under arrest."

"On what charges?" Handcuffs. Did I just bat my eyes at him?

He stalled. Then slowly shook his head "no" again. Leaning down, he whispered into my ear. "Idiocy."

I swayed; yeah, I'd say that summed this whole thing up.

With his hand still on my right wrist, Striker yanked me toward the stairwell, forcing me to run after him on wobbly legs.

When we were safely alone, he turned on me. "What do you mean you're in danger? Why didn't you tell me immediately?" he demanded, holding my arm up in front of me.

All I could do was stare at him. I was having trouble shifting gears. No words were forming in my brain.

He dropped my arm and gave my shoulders a shake. "What kind of danger?"

Something hummed just under his skin. Anger? Concern? I rubbed my bruised lips. "Because…" I stammered.

"Because what?"

"I'm not used to you." I took a step back from him. "I'm used to puzzling things out for myself."

"Lexi, I'm in love with you. I want to protect you. That's the role I'm supposed to be playing."

"I wasn't clear that we'd established a role for you in my life." I glared at him.

He scrutinized me, then his eyes hardened. "I'm Team Command of Strike Force. So if you need a clear position title, there it is." He still had me by the shoulders, and he gave me another shake.

"You know what I mean." My voice turned quiet with a dash of defeat.

Striker leaned down and touched his forehead to mine. "I know what you mean. Let's do one thing at a time. Why are you going to Spyder and not me."

"You don't have the answers I need. Spyder does. I was afraid if I went through Command, they would stop me before I could figure out what's going on."

Striker nodded. "You're right. You are absolutely barred until Spyderman's back at HQ. You don't have time to explain this to me now. I'm in charge of Spyder, but I only have fifteen minutes left on my watch. They'll have my relief coming in...you're going to have to make this fast."

Striker's the watchdog?

That explained his oversized T-shirt and 501s.

Holy cow, this must be serious if they're using Commanders as surveillance.

Why didn't he tell me?

Then I realized I wasn't exactly forthcoming with Striker either. Trust. Right? I'd lay my life down for him, just as he would for me. But the emotional stuff seemed so damned daunting.

Striker opened the door and scanned the hallway. Empty. "Quick," he ordered, pushing me behind him, using his body to shield mine. I scuttled up the hall, and we burst through Spyder's door.

"Spyder, I hope what I'm about to ask you isn't going to be stressful, but something happened today, and I need to know what to do." I dragged a chair over to his bed and sat, so we were eye-to-eye.

"Yes, Lexicon, what happened?" Spyder's voice was deeply resonant with an unusual accent. Even though Spyder was an American citizen, born in New York City, Spyder grew up somewhere else. I've asked him repeatedly where he learned his English, and he'd smiled his response. His accent was beautiful and rich and had a gentle formality about it. It made me think of a yoga bow — and the word namaste.

I reached out to smooth the blanket on his hospital bed. "I

got a new neighbor. I have a bad, bad feeling about this new neighbor. I had a 'knowing.'"

"What did you hear?" Spyder asked.

I bit my lip, not wanting to repeat the words out loud — making them whole and tangible instead of a pulse in my veins. Spyder gave me a stern look.

"Danger is moving in." I managed.

Spyder stilled. Oh, dear. Was this too much for him? Maybe I shouldn't have come.

"You have met this neighbor?" he asked.

Striker stood glaring at me from the end of Spyder's bed. I swallowed past the lump in my throat and refocused on Spyder. "No, sir. Not met. I saw her…and recognized her."

Spyder nodded slightly; I should continue. I worked my thumb into my palm. I took a deep breath in and met Spyder's gaze. "I never saw her in person before now. I remember her from a photo at Mrs. Agnew's."

"The couples honeymooning at the beach?" Spyder's hushed tone brushed the air.

"Yes, I believe so, two couples at the beach with trees in the background. My new neighbor is a Latina with black hair and deeply tanned olive skin. She's gained weight since the picture, especially around her waist, and her hair is short now. But I'm pretty sure I'm right."

"Maria Castillo," Spyder said under his breath before refocusing on me. "This is not good news." Spyder's eyes searched over the wall as he thought. "I'm afraid I cannot tell you much about my connection to Mrs. Agnew except that Agnew is not her real name — she was under my protection until she decided she would be safer outside of the United States. There is nothing more I can reveal at this juncture. You will treat this neighbor as an enemy."

The leopard in my head screamed as if burnt and slid under the bush to rumble her displeasure. A shiver racked my body.

Spyder stopped and studied me for a moment. "Listen to me closely. I came back to Washington because I needed you and Striker to help me with an assignment. We are to incapacitate a dangerous beast with many arms reaching in many directions. This is a case I have been working on for over a decade—one where you have already worked through several of the puzzles, Lexicon.

"It is remarkable that this woman comes to your neighborhood now. She has been but a barnacle on one of the monster's tentacles, yet she may prove dangerous to you, or me, or our mission. I can't imagine she could know of your capabilities. I presume they lost track of me over this last year and have sent her in to befriend you. I believe you might be in direct danger, and yet I am torn…"

While Spyder weighed options, Striker took a surreptitious glance at his watch. His lips tightened, and I knew our time was coming quickly to a close.

Spyder nodded his head. "Perhaps it is best for you to remain where you are so that you can watch her. An enemy is always more dangerous when masked. Keep an eye on your house and your vehicle — make sure no monitoring devices are planted. Striker, would you please do a sweep of Lexi's house and car?"

"Yes, sir, I'll call it in." Striker nodded but didn't make a move to leave. "I'll need to brief Command."

"Absolutely, they need to know about this new twist. Every precaution will be used to keep Lexi safe." The last words were barely audible. Spyder panted before continuing. "Lexicon, you will be careful not to let this woman know you have identified her. You will not spend time with her alone. Your conversations will always be brief and non-consequential. You will not speak with her in Spanish — guard your tongue. She is not to know you are bilingual. At some point, you may have the need for a safe house — if you believe she is pressing too hard."

"What will that look like, sir? How will I know?" I asked. Pressing too hard? Right now, it seemed as if she had perched on my chest, not allowing me any air. How much more "pressing too hard" could I take?

"You will trust your inner knowing, and you will act accordingly." Spyder smiled, though the smile didn't touch his eyes.

My inner knowing said run for the hills, do not pass go, do not collect two-hundred dollars, just run. *Run now.* "Yes, sir. Striker gave me a key to his place in the barracks."

Spyder shifted his focus to Striker. They stared hard into each other's eyes, the alpha dogs in silent communication.

I felt mildly left out. What was that all about?

After a minute, Spyder gave him a nod. "Thank you," he told Striker warmly. Their years of working together in the worst possible conditions made actual speech irrelevant, and I was jealous of their connection.

"I will need to be moved to a different hospital where I can be secured," Spyder continued. "Too much is at stake to allow them to take me out now. Obviously, I am in a vulnerable state. Striker, you will have Iniquus arrange this. Lexicon, with all of my heart, I am sorry to tell you that, once again, I will not be able to be in contact with you. It might endanger both of our lives, as well as many others. A mission would be at risk."

"I'm sorry, sir. Time is up. Lexi has to leave. Now," Striker commanded.

I jerked my focus over to him, startled. I needed more time. I wasn't ready to go. Pain filled my heart as I pushed reluctantly up from my seat. "I love you, Spyder. Please get better soon." I leaned down and gave him a kiss on the cheek, and I left.

Striker followed me out and told me to sit tight in Mrs. Nelson's room. I did as I was told, apprehensive about how this was all going to play out with Command — my disobeying direct orders... Striker facilitating my meeting with Spyder... Spyder's revelations...how would I keep my extra-sensory crap a secret from them? Right now, the only ones at Iniquus who knew about this were Spyder, Striker, and Jack.

When Striker came to collect me, he didn't speak — not a single word. He made me swap cars with him, and he followed me back to my house.

A Hummer sat out in front of my duplex, and we pulled in behind. Striker came over, opened the door, and jumped me down. We found Blaze and Gator inside, crouched on the floor playing with scanning equipment.

"Hey, Lynx." Blaze glanced up from his monitor. "It looks like your kitchen exploded." Blaze was usually soft-spoken, thoughtful, with bursts of bravado. He kept his bright auburn hair, shot with copper highlights, in a short military style, but it still tried to curl rebelliously. I thought that his coloring gave him the call name Blaze; it turns out his name came from his motto: "If I'm going out, it's going to be in a blaze of glory!"

"Manny's food. Shoot, Blaze. I completely forgot about my project." I ran back into the kitchen and grabbed an apron.

Blaze nodded, standing at the kitchen door frame, taking in the mess. His eyes were startlingly blue, like a clear October sky.

"I'm bagging up prepared dinners. They're my barter with Manny," I said by way of explanation. "Did you find anything?" I asked.

"Nope, all clean," Blaze said. "We think you should keep your car locked in your garage. Try not to park exposed when you drive. The best thing to do, though, is just to use an Iniquus car and trade it out every day. That way, they can't track you, and you can always leave with a clean vehicle, especially if you're headed anywhere that might be sensitive."

"Okay, I'd be willing to try. Thanks, Blaze. Gator, did Striker talk to you about my duplex?"

"Yes, ma'am, I'm looking forward to being duplex-mates with you." He grinned, picking up a slice of green apple and popping it in his mouth. "Striker said I should move in as soon as it's ready unless he's off, then I'll come no matter the state."

"If the house isn't ready next door, you can stay in my guest room until everything is nice. That is, unless Amy objects." I glanced over my shoulder at him from where I gathered ingredients.

"Yes, ma'am, that'll be fine. And Amy don't have no say in where I bunk."

"Lynx, what did you plan for the pups while we're in Miami?" Striker asked.

"Manny's going to feed them and let them potty. Why?"

"I think we should remove any obvious leverage until we get a better handle on what's going on. I think your dogs need to stay up at Iniquus unless they're directly with you."

"Yeah, you're right. Darn it — I just did this. I don't want to do this again." I blew out a huff of air. I hated being the focus of someone's craziness. First, Wilson and now a barnacle from a monster's tentacle?

Too much.

Especially with so little time to recover between the two events. I wondered how Striker did this as a SEAL — every day was hell-day filled with focused-on-him bad guys. That must be why SEALS carry those trees around — to build stamina. I needed to get back down to my gym — build more stamina of my own.

I gave an embarrassed smile. "Sorry. I needed to say that out loud. Blaze and Gator, can I impose on you two? If this interferes with your plans, I can drive my girls over to the Millers'."

"No problem. We can keep them." Blaze rubbed Bella's ears.

"Obviously, I'm going to follow Spyder's orders. I'd like to be proactive here and figure out why this woman is in the neighborhood. I mean, I can do some computer searches when I get back to work, but do you think she should be under surveillance? Should we bug her house? I don't want to hang out here in her crosshairs. I want to know why she's here and how to get her gone."

"Right." Striker checked his watch. "An extraction team is moving Spyderman as we speak. He'll be under an assumed name, and we don't know where in America he'll be moved. He's out of the chain as far as giving orders. I have a meeting with Command in an hour." He held his mouth in a grim line. "I'll find out what I can and get a game plan together — see what they want to do."

"Will getting warrants be a problem?" I scooped cranberry sauce into the bag in my hand.

"Not for Iniquus. Are you sure you don't want to pack up some things and move over to the barracks?" Striker's eyes bored into me. I tried to read the message there but got nothing.

I stalled over my work as I bit my lip. "No, I'm not sure." I zipped up a bag and added it to the box I was getting ready to walk over to Manny's. "Spyder wanted me here, though. Until I feel too pressured." I reached for the next packet.

"Okay, how about this," said Striker, "why don't I move back into your guest room, like when you were being bait for Wilson?"

My eyes locked on Striker's. When the Strike Force team and I had decided the best way to catch Travis Wilson was for me to move home and act as a lure, I had a teammate no more than an arms-length away at any given moment.

During the day, Gator usually filled the role.

At nighttime, I was under Striker's care. Things between us had drastically changed since last October; this wouldn't be the same dynamic. Did I need to think it over? My mouth ran faster than my brain. "Okay. Thanks," I said with a smile.

Striker left for his meeting and to pack his bags. He wasn't going to wait around for me to change my mind. Gator and Jack stayed; they were out on a jog with Beetle and Bella and would come back for dinner.

When I heard them walk through the front door, I called, "Hey guys, could you give me a hand with something?"

I pointed over to the coolers and boxes I had ready to go next door. "I need to get these across the street and down into the basement."

The guys took everything in one trip, with me slipping and sliding behind them. I knocked on Manny's door.

"Hallelujah!" Manny whooped and opened the door to his basement. We tromped on down, and the guys handed me the food packets so I could place them on the freezer shelves in rotating order.

As the guys and I walked back across the street, I let my gaze glide toward Leopard Woman's house. Maria Castillo stood in her front picture window, watching me. My foot slid out from under me on the ice, and I would have hit the road except for Gator reaching down and scooping me up. He carried me, cradled like a baby, back to my house, up the stairs, to stand in front of my couch.

"Are you going to let me down, Gator?"

"Huh? Oh, sorry." He set me on my feet. "Just like old times at the safe house."

Wilson had clocked me with his gun, and I had a lot of issues with vertigo while my brain recovered from the blow. Gator had had his work cut out for him, keeping me off the floor. "How about I show my gratitude for saving the knees of my favorite jeans by letting you pick the dinner menu. Come on back in the kitchen, and I'll give you some ideas."

Gator chose cheesy grits with sautéed onions and red peppers topped with Cajun shrimp. Good. That was quick and easy comfort food for a cold night. Striker came in as I was getting dinner going. He walked into the kitchen, wrapped his arms around me from behind, and gave me a smacking kiss on my head.

I was forgiven for my myriad of sins.

"Hey, good timing." I leaned back into his arms. "Blaze and Gator started a movie. I'll have dinner ready in about twenty minutes. Should we eat on trays in the living room?"

"Works for me." He put two six-packs of Corona in the fridge, took three bottles out, and walked them into the living room for the guys. He hadn't said a single word about what happened with Command. His body language gave nothing away. I took a deep breath in and scowled at my pots.

12

I hadn't asked Striker about our hotel plans for Miami. Surely, he would be a gentleman about our sleeping arrangements, but how was this going to play out? Standing naked in my closet, I rifled around until I pulled out a beautiful dress that I thought might work for the party. Thank you, Celia, and your over the top rule that you only wear a dress once, and thank you that I got to be the repository for your cast-offs.

I fingered the dress material. The light shade of blue could easily be mistaken for silver. Holding up the two thin spaghetti straps, I pursed my lips. I'd have to go without a bra, and it was designed to show some cleavage. Too much cleavage? I peeked inside and realized the lining was tailored to give shape and support. Good news. Stretching my arms over my head, I let the delicate fabric slide over me and adjusted it down so I could see if it flattered me in the mirror. The bias cut, metallic material clung to my figure and swished, but didn't fly up when I spun around. Cranking up the volume on my radio, I practiced dance moves in the reflection to make sure my fanny stayed covered. With the skirt hitting mid-thigh, I would have to be careful with dips, and anything other than a thong would show through the fabric. So, closed legs, bent knees, demure moves.

Now to pack for the rest of the trip, especially my meeting Cammy and Lynda for the first time. What I needed to wear for that introduction was some emotional armor.

I was twitchy about the plane ride. Striker glanced down at me curiously as we took our seats and buckled in, but thankfully he left me to my thoughts. My mind was all over the place — my emotions too, for that matter. The overlying feeling was trepidation. Not quite to the level of anxiety, but close. Striker's friends and family — would they like me? Would I fit in? And Lynda... Truth? I really didn't want to do this — any of it. I wished Striker had invited me on a date for New Year's for some fun that wasn't interlaced with all of the shit that went down last fall. I leaned my forehead against the little bubble window and watched the green quilt of pastures float underneath me. Sooner than I expected or wanted, we touched down in Miami.

"We're here," Striker said.

I found myself clasping his hand tightly in my lap.

He gently brought my fingers to his lips and kissed my knuckles. Without releasing me, he swiveled in his seat. He tipped my head back, ran his thumb along my jawline, and planted a kiss on my lips. "Hey, are you okay? You've been quiet."

I pushed the corners of my mouth into a smile. "First commercial plane trip. I was a little nervous. It's different than piloting a prop."

People jumped up and rushed for the door. I startled; was this normal?

Striker shrugged. "Claustrophobia. Let's let them pass. It'll take a few minutes for the crew to unload the luggage."

I nodded.

Now what?

As if able to read my mind, Striker said, "We'll take a cab to the hotel. I have reservations at the same place as the ball tonight. We won't have to worry about finding cabs or dodging drunk drivers. We can just relax and enjoy."

Well, you can relax, Striker. I, on the other hand... "Sounds great."

The hotel was opulent and unexpected. I had thought it would be...less. Like a movie scene from the 1940s, everything was marble and crystal and luxury. The valet opened my taxi door and handled the bags; a doorman bowed a welcome. I stood in the middle of the intricately mosaic-tiled entrance taking in all of the beautiful people milling around. I was overly-warm and a little dowdy in my jeans and turtleneck sweater. Yes, good quality thanks to Celia, but still. Striker gave my elbow a squeeze then sauntered to the desk to get our keycards. Singular? Plural? I blushed. I couldn't figure out what to hope for.

He ambled back to me with a full-force Striker grin, dimples and all, and my breath hitched. *God, he was beautiful.* And I wasn't the only one who thought so. As Striker moved by, the other women in the lobby perked up and took notice. Jeans were anything but dowdy on Striker. They were a visual dessert. Did that woman really just lick her lips? Incredible.

Striker draped a possessive arm around me, and I shot a look at the woman as we swept past. **Mine.** *Really? Really, Lexi? Are you sure? In what way exactly?* I shook my head. Those thoughts were too much for the close confines of the elevator. The bellhop pressed number twenty-five and took us to the top floor. He held one keycard in his white-gloved hand.

As I followed the bags through the door, I realized Striker had reserved a suite. My luggage went into the room on the right; Striker's case went into the room on the left. I stood in the middle of a lavish sitting area with a beautiful view as the focal point. I walked over to the French doors, out onto the balcony, and absorbed the sight. The water beneath us reflected the last rays of the sunset. Stunning. Striker came out to tell me there would be a fireworks display at midnight; we could watch from up here. That would be romantic; I smiled inwardly.

We ordered our dinner from room service and ate outside on our balcony. I was famished, and everything tasted so good and fresh. Watermelon, mint, and feta cheese. Who knew that would be so yummy? The sky had turned deep indigo and had a lushness I never experienced in DC. The evening so far was wonderfully low pressure. Striker, ever attentive and charming, steered the conversation to his memories of Miami, and away from the work-a-day world of Washington — away from his soldier-boy stiffness. My stress melted. What bliss to sit and relax together.

As the music from downstairs wafted up to us, we moved inside to get ready. My part didn't take much. I had very little to put on — just panties, dress, and strappy sandals. My hair hung in soft curls down my back and coiled over my breasts. I upped my makeup with long, black, Hollywood-star lashes, and cherry red lip stain with pink glitter gloss. My reflection showed a toothy smile and bright eyes. I felt pretty and flirtatious as I swayed out of my room to the sitting area where Striker waited for me. He wore a perfectly tailored black dress pants and a light as air white silk shirt, accentuating his Bowflex model's body. He made me want to lick my lips and purr.

"Wow," I gasped.

"Wow, yourself. You look like Titania, Queen of the fairies." Striker's phone vibrated noisily. He glanced at the screen. "Command," he mouthed and held up a finger as he took a step back to answer the call. Striker listened intently, disconnected, and put his phone back in the holder on his waist, squinting at me. "I can hear the cogs whirring, Chica. Care to share?"

"I was thinking if I were Titania, that would make you Oberon, and we'd be in a terrible relationship. In which case, I should be watching out for your Puck tonight. I don't want to fall under an enchantment where I wake up in love with a donkey. I haven't researched it, but I'm pretty sure there are bestiality laws here in Florida."

Striker threw his head back and gave a full-throated laugh. "Oh my God, I'm so sorry." He wiped tears from his eyes. "I was trying to compliment you, not get you arrested. I'll tell you what. Why don't you pick the fairy princess I should compare you to?" He stood close to me now, with his fingers circling my waist.

I had to arch back a little to see his face. "Hmm. Okay. How about Niamh?"

"Niamh. Who is she?" He reached up and traced a finger down my nose and along my jaw.

"An Irish fairy princess, the daughter of Manannán mac Lir. They lived in the Land Where Time Stands Still. Niamh set out on her horse one day to find Oisin, the greatest of all of the Fianna warriors. Those are the king's mightiest and best." As I spoke, Striker whispered little kisses from my eye down to where his fingers had woken my nerve endings along my jaw.

"So he was the best of the best?" he murmured, then continued his trail of kisses down my throat.

I couldn't answer him. I was barely breathing. My body sang, *yes, do that.*

He stopped and quirked a brow.

Oh, his question. "Absolutely," I said. "The best of the best. She invited him back to her realm to be her love." How was I supposed to have this silly conversation when my thoughts were so distracted?

"And did he go?" Striker whispered in my ear and caught my lobe between his teeth.

I wriggled deeper into his arms. "He did indeed, and they lived there happily for two hundred years."

Striker pulled back. "And what happened after two hundred years?"

"He got stupid, left, and died." I shrugged.

"Oh." Striker actually seemed disappointed.

"Two hundred years is a good run," I offered.

He reached out and ran his fingers through my hair, cocking his head to the side. "And Niamh was beautiful?"

"She's described as golden-haired and radiant."

"That will do it. Okay, rewind. You say 'Wow.'"

"Wow?" My brows knit together, not understanding his game.

"Wow, yourself. You look like Niamh the Princess of the Land Where Time Stands Still."

"Thank you." I smiled and twirled out from his arms. "You said short, sparkly, and dance-y."

"I did, and you are dazzling. Are we ready to head down?" Striker held out his hand.

13

We wandered into a ballroom filled with people dressed to be festive and fun in their flashiest outfits. As the band took a break, no one danced to the recorded music playing over the speaker system.

Striker scanned the room. "Hey, why don't you stand here for a sec? I'll go brave the crowd around the bar and grab us something to drink. When I get back, I'll introduce you to some of my old friends."

"Sounds like a plan." I smiled up at him.

Striker bent down to my ear and whispered, "A reminder, everyone here calls me Gavin." He planted a kiss on my shoulder and moved away.

I strolled over to the open window. The breeze floated over my skin. I took in the din of conversation, the clink of glasses, and the glitter of laughter. Lovely, and exactly what I needed after all — a night of relaxation, away from work, away from stress, away from leopard growls and flashing inner-warnings. A shiver ran through me. *She can't get you while you're here*, I reminded myself. I watched Striker join the crush of men jockeying for position by the bar. Damn, but he was one gorgeous, gorgeous man.

Striker in civilian clothes was always a shock to my system; somehow, he just seemed more at home in his camo-wear. Or maybe I had a better handle on who he was when he wore his uniform. This man, in his dress pants and silk shirt, was unfamiliar to me. But boy-oh-boy, I couldn't argue with his outfit, the way his pants hung from his hips and made his butt…

"That's Gavin Rheas." A girl in a black bugle-beaded dress leaned toward me, gesturing at Striker with her drink.

"Excuse me?"

"The guy whose buns you're checking out, his name is Gavin Rheas. Hi, I'm Rebecca."

"I'm Lexi." I grasped her outstretched hand in a friendly shake and turned my gaze back to Striker. "Do you know him well?"

"We grew up together. Hey, you guys. You came!" Rebecca smiled at two girls who danced their way up to us. They all gave smoochy air kisses. "This is Isabelle. This here's Tracy. And this is Lexi."

I shook their hands. "Nice to meet you." *Maybe*.

"We're checking out Gavin's buns," Rebecca said conspiratorially.

"They're worth checking out. He just seems to get better with time. But darned," Tracy, the newly arrived, winter-tanned, blonde-haired woman all but stomped the floor with a full pout on her lips, "I thought he'd be in uniform."

"Not anymore, remember?" Rebecca said.

"Who's Gavin? What uniform?" Isabelle, the voluptuous Latina, cast her doe-eyed gaze across the room.

Rebecca pointed over to Striker, who had just turned our way, and gave a smile and a wave.

"Oh, that's Gavin. Oh, he is yummy." Her face turned pink. I honestly think Striker took this girl's breath away.

"You don't know the half of it," Rebecca said. "He used to be a SEAL, and he had a chest full of medals."

"I bet he was a hottie in his uniform," Isabelle said. They turned in unison to study Striker — who slowly made his way closer to the bartender — probably imagining him in his Class A's. Group sigh. Good God, this was uncomfortable.

Isabelle bent in and whispered, "Is he on the market?"

I bristled. Was he? I didn't know myself. "I'm very much in love with you," he said. "We'll take it slow," he said… maybe too slow? Why didn't he stake a claim or something? Tell me what was going on in that head of his — well, his heart, his heart was really what I wanted to understand.

"I think so," Rebecca said. "He would have told me if he was dating someone special. His job's keeping him pretty busy, though. He goes out on dangerous operations and things."

He didn't tell them about me. Is that significant? Should I care? Hmm. Maybe I should introduce myself. As what? "I'm being escorted tonight by the hunky Gavin Rheas. Glad to meet you?" I didn't think so.

"Why? What does he do?" Isabelle asked.

"He's working up in DC for some government support group. Anti-terrorist stuff," Tracy said.

"No, not anti-terrorist stuff, military support stuff," said Rebecca, then she made a face. "Actually, he won't tell me what he does. He says his job is classified."

"That sounds dangerous," I offered. "You grew up together? Was he a dangerous kind of kid?"

"No, he was real responsible. That kind of got heaped on him, though," said Rebecca.

"Why do you think he's down here in Miami? Do you think he came for Falicia?" Tracy asked.

Falicia? Who is that? My antenna shot up.

"I think he probably flew down to check on Lynda and Cammy," Rebecca said.

"How's Lynda doing? Have you seen her since the operation?" Tracy asked Rebecca.

"Jeezus. What a nightmare. The doctors think they were able to fix her nose this time," Rebecca told her, then turned to Isabelle. "Lynda is Gavin's sister. These drug dealers attacked her, and she got beaten near to death. Gavin figured out she was in trouble; he found her in the nick-of-time before she bled to death. Saved her life."

Another group sigh, some eyeball rolling on my part. I shuffled my feet. Striker was a hero, but I was used to it, and this idol worship was a bit over the top — even for me.

As Rebecca swiped her lips with some gloss that smelled like Dr. Pepper, Tracy gave her a nudge. They turned in unison to focus on a beautiful woman, gracefully traveling across the floor. She wore a gold metallic backless dress that defied gravity. I'm not sure how it stayed on her or how it continued to cover her ample breasts since the neckline draped down to her navel. Skintight from the waist to a hem that barely covered her bottom, the men's eyes turned and followed her as she prowled by. She knew it too and lapped up their attention.

"Falicia. She's got her radar fixed," Rebecca hissed.

Oh, that's Falicia. Hmm, what has she got to do with Gavin? My lips compressed with displeasure.

"Of course she does. She's still holding out hopes," Tracy said.

"Hopes of what?" asked Isabelle. "What's on her radar screen?"

"Gavin. They dated all through high school. She thought they'd be married and have their 2.5 children and brick house with a garage by now."

"She's gorgeous." I managed to sound disinterested, which was a total lie.

"Oh, and don't she know it? The year we graduated, she was Cheer Captain, Prom Queen, and Homecoming Queen." Tracy ticked off on her fingers. "And after she graduated, she became a cheerleader for the Dolphins. The boobs are bigger than in high school," Tracy said speculatively. "She must have had them enhanced."

"All those multi-million-dollar football players around her, and she's still gunning for Gavin?" Isabelle asked.

"Just look at her." Rebecca gestured toward the bar. The gold dress now draped over Striker, who had a pink cocktail in one hand, and a soda glass in the other. A beer bottle dangled between his middle fingers. Dexterous. I watched as Falicia greeted Striker with great familiarity. She leaned seductively over the bar, the dress barely hanging in there, and got a beer for herself, clinking bottles with Striker. He moved out of the way to let the next guy up, and Falicia moved with him.

The next thing I knew, Falicia had Striker's face in her hands and planted a big kiss on his mouth. From this angle, I couldn't tell how he was responding other than to hold the drinks out on either side, to keep them from sloshing on their clothes.

Rebecca scowled. "Look at her. She's practically choking him with her tongue, the bitch."

Ditto that!

Tracy laughed. "You're just mad because Gavin hasn't fallen head-over-heels in love with you instead."

"And you're not?" Rebecca put her hands on her hips.

"Sure I am. Who in their right mind wouldn't be? But I'm

also realistic. I'm not in his league. Look, he's trying to head this way," Tracy said.

Rebecca adjusted her dress, fluffed at her hair, and licked her already glossy lips. Falicia had her hands around Striker's arm and walked possessively back with him. I gave him a little wave.

Tracy grabbed my hand and stared down at my rings. "Are you here with Gavin?" she asked.

"Yes." I smiled shyly.

"You're married? You and Gavin are married?" Tracy asked, her eyes wide in horror.

Whoops. Probably that introduction would have been a better way to have gone. I sighed. Couldn't do anything about it now.

"What? Gavin got married and didn't tell us?" Rebecca glared over at him and then scowled back at me.

"No, no. Gavin and I aren't married." I retrieved my hand. "I'm the widow of an Army Ranger. Gavin and I are… Gavin is my…"

Striker arrived just in time to hear me floundering to define his role in my life. He stood patiently, waiting to see what word bubbled up. "He's my transmission," I finally offered.

The four women who stood with us looked perplexed.

Striker gave me a slow nod. "Hey, I got all of the way up there and realized I hadn't asked you what you wanted to drink, so I ordered you a Cosmo and a Diet Coke." Striker smiled, full-on dimple action, holding both out to me. I took them from his hands. Felicia was still entwined with his arm.

"Thank you." I slapped on my perky face to cover up my annoyance.

Falicia, of the long black silky hair, beautifully and expensively cut and styled, was the high school girlfriend. Striker told me in the safe house he had no one of significance in his life, and he said he loved me.

So, what the hell was this nasty reaction making me want to slap this delusional vamp?

Jealousy?

No, that didn't fit.

Territoriality?

Bingo. She was draping on my turf. Hmm. Wasn't that an unexpected emotion? I put the Diet Coke down. Since no one carded me tonight, this might be a good time to try my first sip of alcohol. I tasted the Cosmo. Oh. Very nice.

"I see you've met Rebecca and Tracy. I've been friends with them since we were babies together. They're like sisters to me." He hugged them warmly, each in turn. Tracy and Rebecca visibly bristled. They didn't like being sequestered in the sister-corner — it was even farther away from dating than the friendship-corner. They had no chance.

"This is our friend, Isabelle," Rebecca introduced the girl standing next to me. Striker held out his hand, and Isabelle giggled like a child.

No one introduced Falicia.

"I'm Lexi Sobado." I extended my hand to her. I was the big girl here, being friendly. At least, that's what I told myself.

The reality was I wanted Miss Huge-Tatas to have to unravel her arms from Striker's.

"Nice to meet you." Falicia grasped my fingers in a dead-fish finger shake. "You know my Gavin?" She smiled possessively up at Striker and batted her false eyelashes. Striker cast a glance at her, then extricated his arm to hug yet another pretty girl who came squealing over to him, and then back to her date. Striker took the opportunity to stand farther away from Falicia, but Falicia worked her way back over again.

"Yes, Gavin invited me to the party." I smiled sweetly.

"How nice of him. I'm sure he told you all about me." She

brushed her boob against Striker's arm and glared pointedly at me. "I'm his Falicia."

"Oh?" I made my voice as saccharine as hers. "He never told me he had a Falicia." Rebecca, Tracy, and Isabelle tried to hide their snickers behind manicured fingernails. Falicia glanced their way, then back at me with narrowed eyes before she recovered.

"Cute dress." Falicia smirked. "Last year's Prada knock off?"

"Mm, maybe. A friend of mine gave this to me when she cleaned out her closets. Knowing her, it could very well be Prada. Good eye, Falicia." *Bitch.*

"So, how did you meet my Gavin?" she cooed as she flicked her hair over her shoulder and licked her full, red lips to pull Striker's attention.

"From work." I searched for an exit strategy. I was done here.

"Oh. Do you answer phones? Or are you the copy girl?"

I slammed my Cosmo. "Neither. I do entertainment."

"Like a stripper?" Falicia cast a critical eye over my length. Obviously, her idea of entertainment was fairly narrow.

"Mm, no. I'm a magician — I pull rabbits out of hats. I entertain when they have clients they want to impress."

"So you're impressive? Why don't you show us some magic then?"

Striker shot me a look, telling me he didn't find this very fun, but I was warming to it.

"Do you have a business card?" I asked.

"Sure." Falicia reached into the evening bag hanging from a thin gold chain over her shoulder. She pulled out a business card holder and handed me her Dolphin's cheerleader card.

"I don't suppose you have a pen in there?" I asked.

"I don't suppose I do," she replied.

I smiled at the other women. "Anyone?"

Isabelle dug one out of her purse and handed it to me, then cast a moony gaze over at Striker to see if she would get some approval. But Striker was dividing his attention between Falicia and me.

I handed the pen to Falicia. "Can I have your autograph? I've never met a real, live, celebrity cheerleader before." Falicia didn't pick up on my sarcasm; she took the pen from me with a superior smile and signed her name with a flourish. Striker took the opportunity to squeeze my elbow, a warning of some kind.

Whatever.

Falicia handed me back the card then took a swig from her beer bottle.

I asked, "Have any of you ever seen anything disappear before your eyes?" No one replied — guess they haven't. I tore the top right-hand corner off Falicia's business card and handed it to Rebecca. Then I ripped up the rest of Falicia's card into tiny, satisfying pieces.

Falicia narrowed her eyes at me, and the other girls did a little intake of breath. Maybe they thought I was insulting Falicia.

Maybe I was.

After I'd torn the card into the tiniest pieces I could, I showed them to everyone and fisted them in my left palm. I raised my fist to my lips and blew. As I blew into my fist, I opened my fingers; the pieces of paper had vanished.

"That's it?" Falicia's tone was pure boredom.

"Yup, tada!" I said.

Falicia gave a sardonic laugh and raised her beer bottle to her lips.

Rebecca's finger came up and pointed at Falicia's bottle first; her mouth hung open.

Everyone focused where Rebecca pointed. Falicia's beer

bottle was now empty of beer and in its place was a single un-bent, un-shredded business card with Falicia's loopy signature prominently scrawled across it, showing through the dark glass. The upper right-hand corner was missing.

Rebecca held the corner, which I had handed to her earlier, up to the business card in the bottle. The pieces clearly matched together.

Tracy brought her hands to her cheeks, and Isabelle gripped at her as if too frightened to stand alone.

Falicia gaped at the bottle, trying to wrap her mind around what just happened.

Striker leaned down and whispered in my ear, "Hey, want to dance? This might be a good time to make an exit." I let him pull me to the dance floor, where the band had started up a slow song that had couples cuddling up and swaying.

"You pull rabbits from hats?" Striker drew me into his arms, putting his palm at the base of my spine, holding my hips tightly to him. I pillowed my head on his chest. "That was pretty good. Pretty accurate, too. Sorry about Falicia. I think she's knocked back a few already," Striker said.

"Really? That wasn't my impression at all. I think she genuinely believes you're her destiny, Gavin Rheas." I arched my back so I could see his eyes.

"Yeah? Well, that sentiment is very much unrequited." His feet moved to the rumba. He was smooth and easy to follow.

He spun me out.

"Did it used to be otherwise?" I asked as he collected me back in his arms.

"No. She was a nice girl in high school, pretty, fun. I never saw her as part of my future, though. She's not the kind of girl I'd want to spend my life with. I think I've seen into all of her corners, and there's never anything new. She doesn't grow. It's all been done, and I've moved on. Actually, I moved on about seven years ago, when I graduated high school. I feel a little sorry for her."

I nodded. She was pitiful. But hearing this didn't make me any happier about her being here. "Okay," I said.

Dip — careful. He held me there, arched backward, hair brushing the ground. "Okay, what?"

"Okay, let's not talk about her — a new subject, please."

He pulled me up and pressed me to him again. "I have one. The girls thought we were married?"

"They have huge crushes on you."

"Please don't tell me that. They're old friends, and I don't want to be uncomfortable around them."

"Okay, I won't tell you then, nor will I mention how jealous they got when they thought we had tied the knot. I don't know what to do about my rings. I don't like people asking about them, and I'm not ready to take them off."

Striker moved my hand down from his shoulder and examined my rings, twisting them and angling them. "I could design a ring for you, using all of your stones. I have a friend who's a jeweler — does custom work. He made the brooch I designed for your Christmas present. We could use your gold and have him reset the diamonds and sapphires. Angel got you those to match your eyes, didn't he?"

I rolled my lips in and nodded. Angel. When would I let this guilt go? When would I stop feeling disloyal?

"If you had your rings re-made, you could put the new piece on your left or right hand. You would appreciate the significance, but it wouldn't seem marital, so no one would ask you uncomfortable questions."

"Oh, that's a really good idea. Let me sit with it a little bit."

Striker nodded and gave me a spin. When he pulled me back into his arms, he chuckled. "So, I'm your transmission?"

It sounded stupid hearing that parroted back. I felt my face warming.

"Are you the engine in this metaphor?" he asked.

I nodded, surprised that he had worked his way that far into my logic.

"A transmission is pretty important to an engine's ability to move forward."

"Exactly!" I leaned back and looked him in the eye. "You understood me!"

"I'm learning, Chica. I'm learning."

The music picked up, and Striker proved that men from Miami knew how to sway to a Latin beat. We danced and laughed until the five-minute warning sounded.

The waiters passed out the champagne.

I took a glass and sipped it cautiously. The bubbles tickled my nose. It didn't taste anything like I'd imagined. I thought it would be like ginger ale. But no. I sipped some more, trying to figure out how I would describe the taste. Striker held out his glass and waited for me to focus on his eyes. "Chica, may this year be filled with raspberry moments, abundantly fresh and sweet."

A smile played across my lips. "Thank you." I stretched up to my tip-toes to kiss him. His mouth was soft and tender against mine. As the room counted down the seconds to the New Year, and the horns and noisemakers erupted, Striker pulled me up against him. His mouth deepened the kiss. It was all tongue and desire. I melted my body into him like icing on cake.

He kissed me dizzy.

14

Striker took my hand and tugged me toward the door. "Let's go watch the fireworks from our balcony."

I nodded my agreement; I didn't trust my voice. My body hummed with anticipation. On the way out of the ballroom, Striker grabbed a bottle of champagne and two glasses from a waiter, pulled me toward the elevator, and pressed the floor button.

At our suite, Striker swiped the key and pushed the door open. With his hand on my back, he shepherded me over the threshold, across the room, and out onto the balcony—Good God, what he could do to me.

My body vibrated with need.

The wind, as we stood on the balcony, floated my hair around my face. Striker stood solidly behind me with his protective arms encircling my shoulders, keeping me warm. We watched the beautiful fireworks overhead and mirrored below in the water.

Striker moved my hair over my shoulder. He bent his head and kissed the nape of my neck, eliciting a deep purr from my throat. The humming in my body took over my senses. I spun around and leaned my head back. Striker's lips voraciously found mine with tongue and heat. His fingers played along my sides. When he unzipped my dress, I slid the spaghetti straps from my shoulders, letting the glittering material pool at my feet.

Striker held my hands and stepped back to look at me. I stood naked except for a lacy white thong and my rhinestone sandals. His eyes moved slowly, appreciatively down my body. That look did things to me deep inside.

I stepped out of my dress, and Striker twirled me slowly around. When his eyes found mine, he gently pulled me back into the suite. "You are so beautiful." His voice was pitched gruff and low. Striker danced me backward until my bottom pressed against the cool wall. "I love you," he said. And I felt his words catch me, entangle me, hold me. His lips butterfly kissed down my neck, and I groaned deep in my throat.

My fingers deftly unbuttoned his shirt, and I pulled the silk over his shoulders. Leaning forward to kiss him — my breasts pressed into his chest. His skin was hot against mine, his heart beating a fast tattoo.

With his hand cradling my head, he leaned in, trapping me against the wall. I felt womanly and powerful and full of want. I moved one leg between his, so I could feel him aroused. Striker groaned against my mouth.

I reached for his belt buckle, pulling it out of the loops like a whip. His hands cupped my breasts; his thumbs gently circled my hard nipples. He bent his head and whispered in my ear, "I am so in love with you, Lexi. So beautiful. So soft." He ran his hands down my sides to my hips. "Satin and luxury."

I gasped when his fingers traced across the top of my panties.

Boldly, my fingers undid the top clasp of his slacks and moved his zipper down... I startled when Striker used one hand to stop my progress; his other hand rested on my hip. Striker lay his head against the wall to the side of mine. "Lexi, stop," came his voice husky and thick.

"What? Why? No!" I was panting and oh-so-ready. This sudden brake...what had I done wrong?

"We have to stop," he whispered.

"I don't want to stop. I want you inside me." Frantically, I reached again for his clasp.

Striker's whole body strained. "Jesus Christ," he breathed out. "Lexi, please stop. I don't have any protection."

"Could we get some?" I asked with the tiniest bit of a slur.

Striker moved to sweep me with his assessing look. "Have you ever had alcohol before?" He tipped my head up and tried to get me to focus on him. "Have you ever had champagne?"

"No." I pouted. Why did he care?

"Chica, I can't do this when you're tipsy."

"I want to do this," I whispered under my breath.

Striker picked up his shirt and dressed me in it, slowly buttoning it up. "I am fighting every cell in my body. Believe me, I want to do this too. If we were already lovers, I wouldn't stop for anything short of a nuclear explosion. But your first time, I need you to make the choice, not let the alcohol choose for you." He led me by the hand back to the couch, and we sat down.

"You're being a good guy." I was beyond miffed. I was melting from the fire he started inside me, and there he sat, solid and calm.

How the hell did he do that?

I squirmed uncomfortably, pushing my thighs together, trying to find relief.

Striker focused on me. His eyes, black as coal, glittered with intensity.

Okay, maybe not so calm.

"I don't want you to be a good guy," I whispered. "I want you to take advantage of me."

He pulled me onto his lap. "How are you doing?"

I sat with that for a minute before I replied. "I'm frustrated as hell...my nose is numb...and my stomach's a little ishy."

Striker gave a low chuckle. "I'm frustrated as hell, too," he whispered and pressed a kiss onto my temple. His nose rubbed against my hair, and he breathed me in.

After a minute, he reached over and called room service to bring us up some food.

We ate in silence, then Striker took me by the hand and walked me into his room. He took his dress shirt off of me, replacing it with a T-shirt that came nearly to my knees. As I sat on his bed, he knelt at my feet to unbuckle my high heels. I felt incredibly sexy as he rubbed a hand up my calf.

Don't stop! Don't stop now.

A little groan escaped my lips, and he stilled.

He shook his head slowly, "no," and stood to take off his dress pants. He was still hard.

Another wave of lust rushed through me, and I watched with disappointment as he pulled on a pair of sweatpants. He drew me under the covers with him.

We cuddled and kissed and spooned, and I fell asleep feeling lonely.

15

I woke up to sticky eyeballs. My head clanged. My stomach churned. Striker lay beside me, bare-chested. He reached out and traced a finger down the side of my face, tucking a loose tendril behind my ear. "Feeling rough this morning?" His voice was all concern.

As Striker waited for my answer, my mind scrambled to last night and how I ended up in his bed.

I lifted the sheets to see what I was wearing.

"Nothing happened," Striker reassured me.

"Oh yeah, now I remember." I blew out a long breath. As my head fell back to the pillow, I squinched my lids tight and threw an arm over my face to hide. "How embarrassed should I be right now?"

Striker chuckled, lifting my arm so he could see me. "Not at all embarrassed. You are a very sexy drunk, but a complete lightweight."

"I feel awful."

"I bet. Let's get you fixed up." Striker climbed over me and brought back some Tylenol and a nasty fizzy drink. I had to hold my nose to get the mess down, but I improved dramatically as soon as I did. Striker went off to take a shower. I wished my head wasn't stuffed full of cotton; I'd like to join him. Still beyond frustrated from last night, I would've loved to have his big calloused hands soaping my body—damned champagne.

I needed to get myself together. This was the day I'd be meeting Lynda and Cammy. I wasn't going to be able to handle it feeling like this. While Striker showered, I put my hands to my head and performed Reiki. Reiki was healing energy. Ki meant energy in Japanese, like the chi in Tai Chi I did with Master Wang, or pranayama in yoga I did with my Kitchen Grandmother, Biji. I first became aware that people used healing energy when my mom was in hospice care. Our lead nurse, Kim, did several different energy techniques, and she taught them to me, so I could bring my mom comfort at the end of her life. I've used Reiki almost daily since then; it just became part of who I was.

Sadly for me, it worked far better helping those around me than curing myself. I've heard other practitioners say the same thing. I thought there was something intrinsically soothing in just putting hands on someone in a caring way and giving them attention.

Striker came and sat on the bed. "Reiki?"

"Yup."

"Are you doing any better?"

"Mmm."

"When you Reiki yourself, do your hands get hot and vibrate like they do when you work on me?"

"Yup." I held out my hand to him. Striker brought my palm up to his cheek. "It's like a heating pad."

"Yeah. My headache's gone, but my teeth are still fuzzy, and I'm seasick. I should teach you how to do this, so you can help me when I'm injured or ill. Not that I'm planning to need help for a hangover ever again. I think once is enough. Been there. Done that. Never again."

Striker laughed. "I've heard that one before."

"Not from me, you haven't."

Someone knocked at our door. Striker went to answer and came back in with a tray. "Here, Chica, I need you to eat this. It'll help settle your stomach."

"Is this what you eat when you get a hangover?" I cut into my steak and nibbled a bite of scrambled eggs with salsa.

Striker sat at the end of the bed with a plate balanced on his knee. "I don't get hangovers. I pace myself."

"Where did you learn this trick?"

Striker looked at me, weighing his words.

"That's all right. You don't have to tell me about all the women who have tumbled into your bed, with or without the need for morning remedies. You especially don't have to tell me about Falicia." Oh, jealousy had a painful bite.

"I have a past, Chica. If you ever need to know something to make you more comfortable, just ask, and I'll tell you. Though right now, I'm enjoying your green-eyed monster act." His teasing just added salt to the wound.

"Hmm. I think the only green-eyed monster around here is living in my stomach as a result of you plying me with champagne, Commander Rheas," I pronounced with slitty eyes.

Striker threw back his head and laughed heartily. "I knew it! The whole 'I entertain when they want to impress,' and the show-off scene with the card in the bottle. Brilliant!"

I smiled warmly back at him in between bites. I probably should be ticked at him mocking me, but he had such an honest, wholehearted laugh, and to be truthful, he was right.

"Okay, Chica, time for you to get up and take a shower."

Striker moved my tray to the side table. "I put your robe in my bathroom. You have thirty minutes until we need to leave." He lifted back the covers. During the night, his T-shirt had worked its way up past my waist, and I lay there splay-legged in my little lace panties. Striker froze with the blanket in his hand. His eyes settled on the bit of lace and crystals I wore. His eyes moved slowly up my body with a question in his eyes.

I pushed myself out of bed, pulling the T-shirt down. "All this time, I thought you were a good Boy Scout. What happened, huh?" I stalked toward the bathroom.

"What do you mean?" Striker followed closely behind.

"I thought their motto was to 'always be prepared.' You still don't have any protection." I gripped the knob.

"I can get some, Chica. I can be back in five minutes flat — just leave the bathroom door unlocked." His hand blocked me from closing the door all the way.

"Uh-uh. You missed your opportunity. Now, I've got thirty minutes to get ready for Cammy's party." I pushed his hand out of the way, shut the door, and turned the lock.

"Are you punishing me?" Striker called.

"You feel like I'm punishing you?" I shouted as I adjusted the water temperature.

"A little, yes."

"Well, you're wrong."

"Lexi, you know, I never was in the Boy Scouts, but you'd better believe I'll be living up to their motto from here on out," he hollered through the door.

A grin played over my mouth.

I stood under the warm water for a long time. We'd be late, and to tell the truth, I was glad. I wasn't looking forward to this at all.

Once I stood under the shower, I realized probably only a little bit of my nausea came from last night's drinking. It was mostly nerves. A whopper of an anxiety attack doubled me over and had me panting with my hands resting on my knees like I just ran a marathon. Lynda would surely be asking me questions about the night I helped to save her and Cammy. I didn't want to remember, and I didn't want to talk about going behind the Veil.

Back when I was unschooled, one of the mentors who expanded my perception of reality the most was Miriam Laugherty, an honest-to-goodness Extrasensory Criminal Investigator. She worked up and down the East Coast for various law enforcement agencies. When Miriam learned about my natural ESP experiences, she took me under her wing.

I had made up my own vocabulary to try to describe what I called "going behind the Veil," separating from my body and existing on a different plane. Apparently, Miriam started the same way. She said she'd like to train me as a potential partner. Miriam needed someone who could work with her and help her lighten her caseload and increase her solve rate. I studied with Miriam to find out what it was like, and figure out if I even had the talent to do this kind of work.

After a great deal of study and practice, I performed some basic searches for Miriam. But unlike Miriam, I made brutally painful physical and mental connections with the victims, and I decided I couldn't do that kind of work. I stayed away — far away — from anything remotely associated with "walking behind the Veil." That was until I lived in the safe house.

One awful night, Gator and Jack came in covered in mud and blood. They'd been ambushed. I performed Reiki on them, waiting for transportation to get there and take the men to the hospital. While I worked, the healing energy turned into something else, something I didn't recognize. I tried to talk it out with Striker and told him all about my ESP, but this tread so far from his understanding of the world that all he could do was offer to serve as my sounding board.

The next day was one of anguish. I had never endured those sensations before — like I wanted to take off my skin and lay it neatly on the chair; like my lungs had no capacity for breath; like blue electrical charges moving in my veins instead of red blood cells. Something called me from behind the Veil, and this time my experience came from a direction I'd never experienced before. This call came at the behest of a group of women in Africa.

The images offered to me told me that Striker had done something extraordinary for their village. I knew these women sang and did rituals daily, including Striker in their protective rites. They sensed my attachment to Striker and realized I had power, so they called to me. Their magic was strong. But not strong enough to stop the madness half a world away in America. They wanted to work through me and with me. I needed to stand between Striker's sister and niece and the unknown threat.

Relief only came when Striker burst through the door at the safe house, pictures of his family in hand. I took the photos from him and flew out of my body for a hell-filled night.

I merged with his sister, Lynda, trying to figure out who had kidnapped them and where they were taken. I became one with Lynda when they dragged her into a hunting shack and beat her to within an inch of her life. Iniquus men, not far behind, followed my instructions as I passed them on to Striker. They found Lynda, just this side of dead, and raced her to the hospital.

The drug lord still held Cammy, hoping to coerce information from her Uncle Juan. I joined with Cammy. Her little three-year-old body had been shot full of drugs to keep her quiet, and they were too much for her. Her system was shutting down. Her breathing became shallow, and her blood pressure had dropped too low. I had never experienced trying to save someone through the Veil, but I had to try.

I followed my instincts, expanding and contracting her lungs to help her breathe. I floated on the chants of the tribal women as I helped Cammy's heart to beat. The Iniquus cars screamed through the night as Striker and the men tried to reach Cammy and save her life.

Just like the last time I went behind the Veil when I was working with Miriam, I came back to my body but fell into a deep recuperative trance. This time, I needed more than a week and an intravenous bag of blood to recover from my wounds and to gather myself together and become whole again.

I don't regret helping.

Realizing Cammy had seen and heard me while she was drugged was truly amazing since I wasn't literally there. I was being not so safe, in the safe house, miles away. I had only sent my spirit out to her. Yes. That concept even stretched the boundaries of my imagination, and I had always thought my boundaries were pretty darned elastic.

Okay. I was wigged out. To tell the honest truth, I never wanted to meet Lynda and Cammy. I would rather let the images of that night lay in my past. I didn't want to see the destruction wreaked upon Lynda's body or know Cammy had physical substance.

What almost happened to that little girl was so horrific.

I'd rather all of this remain a nightmare from which I awoke and not reality.

But what I would rather have happen seemed irrelevant.

16

Our cab threaded through the city. The wind blew hard, making the palm trees sway. I smoothed down the full skirt of my 1950s-style raw silk dress. The beautiful, deep, indigo blue reminded me of ocean water; I hoped the color would evoke a sense of peace in me today. I slid my feet nervously in and out of my patent leather kitten pumps. Anxious and twitchy, I spun Angel's rings around my finger.

"What?" Striker's brows knit together as he studied me, puzzled.

"They know we're not married?"

"I haven't talked with them about our relationship. We're a little undefined right now."

I nodded and twisted my rings some more. I pulled them off of my left hand and moved them to my right hand. I stared out the window as we pulled up to the community center.

The number of cars parked in the lot astonished me.

My eyes stretched wide as I turned to Striker. "Are all of these people here for Cammy's party?" My words came out all breath and no voice.

"My extended family usually does a gathering on January first each year because getting everyone together at Christmas is hard. Since Cammy's birthday is on the 5th, we celebrate her at our annual party. Didn't I explain this to you?"

"No. No, you didn't." I measured my words to hide my distress.

"Is this okay? I wouldn't have thought this would faze you." Striker put a hand on my knee, quietening my twitchiness.

"I'm just nervous, I guess." I pressed a hand to my heart to stop the runaway galloping beat as I opened the door to get out. Striker reached out to stop me. I slid past his hand and walked over to the tree to breathe for a minute while he paid the cabby.

"Can we talk about this?" Striker asked when he walked over.

"What do you want me to say?"

"I don't want to put words in your mouth, Chica. I'm hoping you'll help me understand what's stressing you." His patient voice invited my confidence.

"I don't know. I just needed a minute, I guess," I tried, vaguely.

He stood there, waiting.

"I'm fine now." I hoped I sounded like I had some conviction behind my words.

He still stood there.

"Striker? Are we going in?"

"This is complicated, isn't it? The more I think the situation through, the more I realize what a complicated thing I've asked you to do. I thought I was asking you to come down and have some fun with me on New Year's Eve and help Cammy out by letting her understand you're…"

"I'm what?" I slit my eyes.

"I was going to say that you're just a regular girl." He

laughed and gestured a wide arc with his arm. "But *that's* absurd."

We stood there.

"Do you want me to take you back to the hotel?" he asked quietly.

"No, I told you. I'm fine. Let's go in."

Striker watched me, thinking. "This was a bad idea. I shouldn't introduce you to Cammy and Lynda in public. I shouldn't even have introduced you to my family and friends yet. I'll tell you what, I'll go get Lynda and Cammy and bring them out here. Why don't you sit in one of those chairs under the tree over there? We'll ease into this. Play it by ear. And leave the second you want to."

I nodded and walked over to the live oak, where the low branches cut most of the wind and sat down in a bright orange Adirondack chair. I set the gift bag with Cammy's present down beside me and watched Striker move gracefully away on his long legs.

Soon, Striker came around the corner carrying a little girl who had her hands covering her eyes. Dressed like a princess in a pink sparkly dress and party shoes, her hair was a mass of silky black ringlets held out of her face with little ribbon-covered barrettes. She wore an expectant smile.

Behind Striker, a young woman dragged her body forward on a walker. The bandage covering her nose glared white against her purple and green bruises and swollen eyes. The devastation this woman had suffered shocked me.

I stayed seated. Striker walked over and stood in front of me. "Cammy, are you ready for your birthday surprise?" he asked.

Cammy bobbed her head up and down as she smiled widely with expectation.

"Okay, this year as your gift, I brought someone to meet you.

When I say three, you can open your eyes. One, two..." Cammy couldn't wait; she peeked through her little fingers. When she saw me, the smile disappeared, and her mouth dropped open. Nobody moved. Finally, I spread my arms wide, and she squirmed from Striker onto my lap, where I tucked her in and held her tight. Cammy's little hands gripped into the fabric of my dress and hugged me closely. Striker helped Lynda get to the chair next to me.

I let Cammy cling and burrow. The healing energy of Reiki flowed from my hands. Cammy snuggled up against me, and I felt long-held stress leave her body. I'd let Cammy set the pace and decide how this should play out. So, there we were—all of us sitting in silence.

"Mommy says you're not a fairy godmother," came Cammy's sweet voice, as she played with my hair.

"Isn't that too bad? I'd like to be one. I'd wear a pretty crown and have a magic wand with a glittery star on the end. I think it would be fun."

Cammy smiled and put her hands on either side of my face, patting my cheeks.

"If you could have a magical power, Cammy, what would you choose?"

"I'd be strong as the Hulk, and I'd find bad guys and smash them."

"How awesome would that be? I don't have a power as awesome as turning into the Hulk and smashing bad guys, though I do have one magical power. Sometimes someone gets into trouble, and if they are loved like you and your mommy are, then my magical power tells me you are in trouble and need help. Not a little bit of trouble, like you've been caught being naughty, or when someone at preschool is bothering you, it has to be bad trouble. Do you remember when you and your mommy had bad trouble?" I asked Cammy.

She nodded, her velvety black eyes held wide.

"Uncle Gavin needed my help to protect you. And, because things were very bad, I was able to find you. Do you remember that?" I kissed the top of her head.

"We stood by our car, and the man gave me a shot, and Mommy was screaming."

"That's right. When I found you, I told Uncle Gavin to send help. I didn't go in the car to find you. I stayed at my house. With my magical power, I can help, but not with my body. It's just my love I send out. Did you feel me loving you?"

"I sat in your lap in the car. Your hair wasn't curly like this." She picked up a lock of my windblown hair. "And then I woke up, and the man pulled me out of the car. When I opened my eyes, you got mad, and you yelled at me to go back to sleep. Then I got another shot."

"Cammy, I was never mad at you. I just didn't want you to wake up. I knew the man might give you more of the bad medicine. You were a good girl, and you did nothing wrong. Not one thing. I tried my best to keep you safe, sweetheart. I'm happy I got to help you," I said. "But Cammy, I don't always know when something bad is happening. I don't get to send my love to help every time. You can't think I will always be able to do that. Though I will always try to help you if I know you need me. It was special that I could help you, with my magical powers, on that night. Do you understand?"

"Yes," she said.

"Uncle Gavin and I brought you a present. Would you like to open it?" I reached for the bag.

A smile lit her face.

Striker and I spent time playing with Cammy, wrapping the

silky dress-up fabrics around her, making her turbans and cloaks and togas. Lynda watched us with sad eyes. Some of the other kids came out to play on the jungle gym near us, and Cammy went over to join them.

"Thank you," Lynda said.

"You're welcome." I smoothed my skirt with nervous hands. "I heard from Rebecca last night that you had surgery on your nose, and they were able to fix it?"

"I hope so. The surgeon seems confident."

Striker sat on the arm of Lynda's chair; he rubbed his hand up and down her back. "You're walking better," he said.

"I like the physical therapist who's working with me. I think he's good," she told him and then turned back to me. "Would it be okay if I asked you about your experience?"

"Sure." *No, it wasn't okay.*

"What happened? I mean, you gave Cammy a nice little explanation, it satisfied her, and that's why I asked you to come. But I'd like to understand. Gavin says you're a psychic, and when you held our pictures, you figured out where they took me and what they were doing. Then you told him to send the men and the ambulances. You saved Cammy's and my life."

I cleared my throat. "I, uhm… Well, the process is called by different names like 'remote searches' or 'remote recovery.' I trained with a police investigator." I fidgeted with the folds of my skirt. "Did you tell anyone how you were rescued?"

"No." She shook her head, emphatically. "Absolutely not. Gavin told me you'd want to keep that private. No. I will take your secret to the grave with me, and Cammy will only understand that you and Uncle Gavin loved her enough to go look for her and help her. Gavin says you supported Cammy's breathing and pumped her heart to save her. The doctors didn't know how she survived until she got to the hospital. How did you do that?"

I could feel the moisture forming under my arms and on my belly as my anxiety ramped. A dull thud started behind my left eye. "I don't have a logical way of sorting out what happens when I'm on the other side of the Veil."

"My brother said you got badly hurt while you helped me."

"I'm fine," I said way too abruptly. My eyes flickered away — in reading body language, they called this a "tell" — I was lying. I glanced at Striker; he didn't seem to notice.

"If you did this remotely — how could you get hurt?"

Flashes of the night and her beating zipped across my memory, fiercely powerful. My anxiety ramped, crushing my ribs together, so I had no room to expand my lungs. I pushed a fist into my chest and shook my head. Striker saw.

"Lynda." Striker softly rubbed her back again. "Lexi went through hell, trying to help us. She put herself in a great deal of danger and pain. You aren't to press her," he warned.

"No, of course not." Lynda smiled with her mouth; her gaze remained sad and haunted. "Of course not."

A group walked toward us. Striker changed the subject to tell Lynda about some of the people he'd seen at the party last night. After a while, the guys finished up at the grill and brought huge platters to the tables.

Cammy made her way back over to us. She curled up in my lap to take a nap and didn't wake up until Striker brought us plates filled with aromatic food.

Disengaged, I pushed my meal around, un-tasted. I didn't have much to say. Striker fielded all the questions his family asked.

Someone brought out his guitar and struck up a sing-along. Everyone was convivial — having a great time dancing, teasing, and playing. Normally, I would have joined in, but today I wasn't in the mood. Being physically near Lynda was an ongoing struggle.

Finally, Striker told his family we needed to get our luggage from the hotel and head to the airport. They protested loudly, his dad asked him to stay and get a flight out in the morning. I could tell how much his family loved and respected Striker. That was nice. I was so glad for him that he had these roots. My roots had been yanked up when my parents died. I have no family at all. No — that's not right. I have my neighbors, and I have my team. I wasn't completely alone.

Striker didn't talk in the cab. He held me close. He briefly left me in the car while he ran in to get our bags from the concierge; when he got back in the cab, he tucked me right back into his arms. I realized it wasn't just for my benefit; Striker needed me right now, too.

The wind storm had picked up and caused some problems with loading and unloading, delaying our flight. We sat holding hands, each of us with our own thoughts. We both startled when his phone buzzed.

"Striker," he said into his cell. He listened for a minute. "Yes, sir. I'm heading back into Washington from Miami. I'm at the airport now… Wind delays. I'm not sure what time we'll set down… Yes, sir… Yes, sir… I'm on it." He listened for a while and ended with a final, "Understood."

"You're on what?" I asked when he slid his cell into his pocket.

"That was Command. I'll need to head out again as soon as we get into DC tonight."

"Is this the assignment you told me about?" Apprehension rose in my throat.

"No, this is something else. I'll be out of the country for a few days at least. I need to know where you're going to stay. Your house or mine? I prefer mine."

"I know you do, and I don't want to be a distraction, but I need to be at my place because of Mrs. Nelson. Can I try to find someone from the team to babysit me? If no one will come, I'll do what I have to during the day and spend my nights at the barracks."

Striker pulled his phone out again and speed-dialed Gator.

Gator planned to meet us at the airport and take me home. A watchdog would be with me whenever I went near my neighborhood.

Command decided to keep leopard woman under surveillance.

They were motivated to find out who she was and how she fit into a high-stakes puzzle that they had been working on for almost a decade, but they offered no other information about the history of the case.

Striker told me all of this, pushed up to the wall behind a potted tree, whispering in my ear in between kisses.

"Why are you telling me this way? We could walk over someplace private." I giggled as he nibbled at my ear.

"Nope, this is more fun. I like playing spy with you."

Gator, Deep, and Jack waited at the gate for us when we finally touched down. Jack had already packed a fresh suitcase for Striker and handed him his passport and ticket. Jack would be

Striker's swim buddy on this assignment. Gator and Deep took me to baggage claim to get Striker's and my bags.

"Where are you bunking tonight, ma'am?" Gator asked.

"Where are my girls?"

"Back at my place in the barracks."

Good, I thought, *Leopard woman could wait until tomorrow.* I needed a little respite as I transitioned from one high-stress, angst-filled event to the next.

17

It felt weird letting myself into Striker's apartment, with no Striker around, using my own key on my keychain. Deep brought in my bags while Gator collected Beetle and Bella.

"Lynx, I don't know if you've been updated."

Deep had my full attention.

"Iniquus provided Spyderman with a false identification and moved him to an undisclosed hospital for his protection. His condition is stable, and he's receiving the care he needs." Deep set the bags in the hall by the bedrooms. "We've set up surveillance equipment on your neighbor. She's calling herself Consuela Hervas. We put a copy of her file and what background information we're allowed on your desk. We figured you'd want to read it over." He stood in front of me, unzipping his coat. "The case starting all this is classified until Spyderman is back at Headquarters. Command won't release any details to us or to you."

"That means it's about some deep doo-doo." I crossed my arms over my chest.

"Yup. I think that's the classification stamped on the file."
Deep grinned at me, rocking back on his heels.

"Were you ever assigned to this case before, Deep? Is there
anything you can tell me?" I perched on the stool and leaned an
elbow onto the countertop.

"No. Sorry. From what I understand, you came into the
picture seven, eight years ago. I was at Parris Island doing boot
camp then, not even with Iniquus. Command said you were
around thirteen when you started working for Mrs. Agnew." He
examined me with curious eyes. "I'm amazed you remember
Hervas from a picture that long ago."

"Do you know anyone else assigned to the case?" Someone's
darned well got to know something — someone besides freaking
off-grid-again Spyder. Maybe I should have insisted on going
with him. I snorted to myself, yeah, like I had that kind of power.

"Only Spyderman," Deep said. "I'm assuming whatever this
woman wants with you has to be tied into him. Command says
right now, everything's on a need-to-know basis. However," he
pointed his finger at me for emphasis, "Command also said if
any clues present themselves to you, and you are able to puzzle
any of this out, they would appreciate your sharing."

"I don't like driving on one-way streets. Did they offer up a
plan?"

"They want you to go about your normal everyday life with
watchdog support. Gator's assigned as top dog. He's charged
with your safety until Striker's back from his mission. Gator'll
do overnights when you aren't in the barracks, as you'd already
planned."

"Understood." I slid off the stool and circled the marble
breakfast bar to get a glass of juice. "Do you want some, Deep?"
I asked, holding up the jug.

"Yes, thanks. Listen, Lynx, Command doesn't want you to

engage with this woman. Follow Spyderman's advice to you — act as you normally would, but keep any contact superficial and always in the company of others." Deep reached for the glass I held out to him. "Apparently, Command is surprised Hervas resurfaced. They're hoping your presence will trigger some sort of information that will help us to understand what's going on. There's no way anyone outside of Iniquus knew you and Striker were tapped for this new assignment with Spyder. But Striker explained to you how the Schumann case tied into Sylanos, so I'm curious to see where this goes."

I took a step backward, completely floored. No. As a matter of fact, Striker didn't explain the Schuman/Sylanos connection to me. How would Schumann from Germany with diamonds from Johannesburg possibly have anything to do with the Sylanos case? Sylanos became a Hydra. Yowza.

"When did you get this intel?" I stammered. "How come I wasn't informed?" I went from cold disbelief to red-hot fury in five-seconds flat.

Deep held up his hands in front of him, protectively. "Hell, the team only found out Spyderman was coming in when he took a dive at the airport. The Schumann thing... Shit. I shouldn't have said anything. I found out when I was doing computer work for Striker. I assumed you knew."

"Exactly when did you figure this out?" I asked, burying my unprofessional anger.

"A couple of days ago." Deep shrugged.

"Just before Spyder went incommunicado at the hospital?"

"Exactly."

I busied myself in the fridge, waiting for my emotions to calm. I needed to work on my whole stoic-work-face. "Everything else is classified," Striker had said. Really? *Really, Striker?*

I thought we were teammates on this one. I was going to get to the bottom of this. No matter what.

Deep must have seen a glint of that in my eye when I faced him again because he said, "Command wants me to remind you you're our Puzzler, Lynx. You're not a trained combat operator, so please act accordingly."

"Aye aye, Captain." I snapped to attention with a stiff-armed salute.

"Okay, funny girl, what're your plans for tomorrow?" Deep turned his focus to the door as Gator walked in with my dogs.

"Training in earnest, just in case. I think I'll take the girls for a run in the morning, hit the gym to lift some weights. I'll probably go by the range and do quick draw and target practice. Either of you want to go at it on the mats?"

"I will," said Deep, "but Gator's got to tag team with me if you're pulling out your Kung Fu moves."

"She's pulling out Kung Fu moves?" Gator asked, moving farther into the apartment.

"Pretend she's the ten-footer that gave you your name, and you might have a chance of pinning her."

Most of my stress left my body as I strained under the weights in the gym, where I worked up a good sweat. Ten o'clock already, I had to get going to the office. I showered hurriedly and dressed in a pair of jeans and a turtleneck from my suitcase. I borrowed a jacket from Striker's closet.

Blaze brought my car to the barracks for me last night. I was supposed to drive a different Iniquus car each day. I don't like driving the Humvees, though, and I didn't want Gator parking one out front of my house, either. I thought they seemed too conspicuous. Gator and I both ended up with Nissan Xterras today. Charcoal-gray, of course.

I spent the morning reviewing the Hervas file. The data was thin; Command didn't give me much to work with. I made notes on different directions I could follow to continue the search.

Spyder had given me a huge present in the hospital.

He had told me Hervas' real name, Maria Castillo. Sometimes when Spyder and I worked together, he had to pass me sensitive information out in the open. Information that shouldn't be dangling in the middle of public discourse. We've found the safest way to do this was to front-end-load it into the conversation. Give the datum first, making it sound like a passing thought or something of no consequence. Then, add information that seemed more significant, or better yet, ask a question to get the other person's mind headed in a different direction — it was a verbal sleight-of-hand trick. Get the opponent refocused on something else. The technique worked like a charm. Spyder was able to pass me Maria's name right in front of Striker. Spyder must have wanted me to keep that intel quiet, though. And it must have been pretty darned important.

18

The rest of the week didn't give me much satisfaction. I spent most of my time listening to the Hervas surveillance tapes and massaging my throbbing temples. I was frustrated by the lack of useful information she offered up. If Consuela Hervas was linked into the Hydra, so far, she's been careful to stay no-contact with anyone at all.

I plugged away at uncovering her background.

She'd assumed a false persona, Spyder confirmed as much in the hospital, but usually, people will create their new identity on aspects that are vaguely familiar to them, so they are conversant enough not to blow their cover. Mostly all I got from my research was a great big goose egg. And a stress headache.

I also worked with the name Spyder offered me, Maria Castillo. Maria Castillo was here in America illegally. She wasn't a US citizen, and she didn't have a current green card or visa; they had both expired. I felt confident I was researching the right person, though; I had found photographs and documentation in both the Iniquus and Consular databases that made that clear.

I was able to pick up on her housing background from nine years ago, and I worked on following the scant trail. I pieced together tidbits here and there up until the September before last. It occurred to me at the edges of my thought process that this was the time period when Spyder went off-grid. Curious. Something to be aware of — not something to hone in on. I don't want to miss the forest for the trees, and while curious, it could also be coincidental.

On Friday night, I found myself trailing behind Gator as he plowed through the grocery store. He piled the cart full like he was preparing for Armageddon. Good gracious, but this man knew how to eat — though there wasn't an ounce of fat on him. I wondered how hard he pushed himself — how far he went on his early morning runs. He's been taking the girls out and bringing them home with their tongues hanging out of their mouths, sides heaving, exhausted. They never did that after a run with me. Hmm, maybe I was slacking off. Gator never seemed drained. Amazing.

I'd been a wimp the past week, avoiding any possible Consuela interactions by doing my cardio in my basement gym. Gator came down, and we'd lift. I moved the sofa out of the way and rolled up the carpet to make way for the gym mats so we could spar. Gator was trying to show me some of his grappling moves. Since he has me by about half a foot and eighty pounds of muscle, I've had to resort to some of Master Wang's pressure point moves. Gator hated that — he said I was cheating.

"Gator, what are the plans for this weekend? Surely they don't keep you on duty seven days a week."

"Well, ma'am, this is sorta semi-duty. They told me if I want to go do something else, I should call in relief."

"Who's on this weekend?"

"Deep's gonna come by tonight. I have a date planned out with Amy, and I'll probably end up staying over at her place. She's going to her cousin's wedding Saturday, though, so I'll be back at your place then."

"Are weddings like Christmas in your book? A little too much like a commitment?"

"It ain't like that for me, ma'am. Amy's got all these plans for us, and I don't want to be leading her on. Right now, my heart's with my job."

I meant to tease him, but Gator's response sounded so earnest that I changed the subject. "Okay, but I should warn you, things are going to be pretty crazy over at my house tomorrow night."

"How come?" Gator reached way down in the meat chest and came up with an armful of steaks. I stood wide-eyed as he dumped them into the little remaining room in his cart.

Why not buy a whole cow while you were at it, Gator?

"One Saturday each month, all of the kids on my block come spend the night with me. We bake cookies, build forts, and watch Disney movies."

"Why?" Gator asked, with a look that told me he thought I'd gone crazy.

"You know my neighbors are like family to me. The parents in my neighborhood have small budgets. They can rarely afford babysitters. I give them one night a month to go out and relax and then go home and have some undistracted adult time. If I choose one dependable night a month, then they can make plans, the kids and I look forward to it, and I don't have to divide my time between the families. It's a win-win."

"How many come over?" Gator reached for a twenty-pound turkey.

"Eleven, but three are babies, so they go to sleep pretty early."

"Three babies and eight little kids?" Gator rolled his eyes. "Okay. You cain't never tell Amy I missed her cousin's wedding to stay home with a passel of younguns. I'd never hear the end of it."

"I won't lie, but I can't imagine this coming up in conversation. What do you want me to make, cupcakes to decorate? Or cookies?"

"Cookies — peanut butter with them Hershey's kisses."

I pinched my lower lip. "Shoot, Gator. Is this a good idea? Do you think having the kiddos at my place will put them in danger?"

"Well, ma'am, Spyder wanted you to keep to your normal routine. I think dodging out on the whole neighborhood might get some gossip going. We've got eyes and ears on Consuela. I'll give the surveillance monitor a heads up. But honestly? Between you, me, the dogs, and your alarm system, those kids couldn't be safer."

"Okay, but would you mind running an infrared alarm around my perimeter for a better heads-up?"

"Not a problem," Gator said.

Describing Saturday night as lively would be a gross understatement. Gator was just a big kid, and I have to say, he was the instigator of much of the hoo-ha.

When Alice and Andy came over, their infant twins were both howling. I handed them off to Gator, who put one up on each of his burly shoulders and patted their tiny bottoms. Alice raised her eyebrows when she saw this but didn't say a word when she handed over the diaper bag and went to put the babies' bottles in the fridge. As she headed out of the kitchen, she saw her twins lying quietly, content with their little fists curled into Gator's T-shirt. Alice patted him on the arm and smiled over to me with a knowing wink.

"Not what you're thinking, Alice. Gator is my dear friend and colleague. He's my housemate for now, and he's going to be living in the duplex as soon as Manny's got everything fixed up."

"Okay, well, thanks you two for keeping the babies tonight. We'll see you in the morning."

Sarah showed up with Mike, a rough and tumble eight-year-old with crazy hair, a bazillion freckles, and an infectious smile, and his baby sister, Ruby. Ruby had just turned one. Her auburn ringlets framed a porcelain face; she was as close to a living doll as I have ever seen — with rosebud lips and chubby pink cheeks. She was like a tonic to me. When I held Ruby, all of the bad melted away.

The bell sounded again; Missy stood on my porch with her two boys and Jilly. Poor Jilly didn't have any girls in the neighborhood to play with. I had hoped a nice family with lots of little girls would move in next to her, but instead, we got Maria/Barnacle-on-a-monster/leopard-woman, and Jilly still didn't have a playmate.

Jilly's brothers came in and went over to the TV to search through the stack of kiddy DVDs I had put out. They started fighting immediately. Jilly sighed and went and sat on the couch.

"Jilly's blood glucose numbers have been pretty stable today. She was real excited to come over here, though, which always drops her sugar levels, so you may want to do a few extra checks." Missy handed me Jilly's diabetic paraphernalia in her purple backpack.

"What are you doing tonight, Missy? Got a hot date?"

"No, but if you know anyone…" Her voice trailed off as she sent Gator a speculative look. "I wouldn't mind a blind date. Tonight, Consuela and I are going to drink wine and watch sad movies. I bought extra tissues and dark chocolate to go with." Missy made a face that had me laughing, though; I knew she felt lonely for someone special in her life. "Have you met Consuela yet?" she asked. "You'll like her — she's real friendly. And she particularly wants to meet you. She's been asking lots of questions."

"Oh? Why's that?" A frisson of anxiety rippled through me.

Missy tilted her head. "She didn't say." Her statement sounded like a question. Maybe my tone gave away my disquiet. I smiled and rubbed Missy's arm. "Well, I hope you two have a good time, er, cry — whatever."

Manny and his crew showed up last — coming in right behind Dave and Cathy with their twins, Fletcher and Colin. Cathy's eyes grew wide when she spotted Gator with babies in each arm. She glanced over at me and gave me a nod. Apparently, she approved of this one. I went through the whole 'this is my colleague' spiel again, but Cathy seemed unconvinced. Gator seemed oblivious, so I guessed it didn't matter. And there we were: three babies, eight kids.

I put Ruby on the floor, with Jilly in charge, and I went back to the kitchen to warm bottles. Gator and I fed the twins, Hannah and Zack, first. Gator was either a natural, or he'd had babies in his arms many times before. I decided not to ask — it might ruin his tough-guy persona.

After they were burped and snuggled, we took the babies up to my second guest room, where I'd set up portable cribs.

I went down to get Ruby and start all over again; Gator said he'd watch the others. Watch them, ha. Gator decided to play war with them. I stepped down into a full out battle scene — kids were diving behind my furniture, screaming in pain, writhing on the floor, and giggling madly. There were bombs exploding and bodies dying and being revived to die again. Beetle and Bella got in the mix, leaping about. I sat on the stairs, away from the havoc, and laughed.

When the smoke cleared, there were nine tired soldiers lying around. I popped the Balto DVD into the player. Everyone settled in and cuddled up to Gator, draping over his lap, peeking around his legs. His long arms reached to snuggle them closer and rub their heads affectionately—what a softy.

I went to the kitchen and made cookies and warm milk, then brought our snack into the living room for a picnic. Gator helped the kids build forts and spread out their sleeping bags. They all lined up to potty and brush their teeth, and then we tucked them in. Once the lights went out, Gator sat on the floor with a flash-light under his chin, and he spun them some tall tales until the warm milk took its effect, and they fell off to sleep.

I checked Jilly-bean's blood. 150. That felt like a safe number, but I'd set my alarm to check her during the night. I put Beetle at the back door on guard duty, and Bella was at the front. Gator and I surveyed the house to make sure we were locked up tight, and the alarm was on.

"Missy's hanging out with Consuela tonight?" Gator asked as we climbed the stairs.

"Apparently, my new neighbor is friendly, interested in meeting me, and asking questions."

"You gonna pick Missy's brain tomorrow?"

"That's the plan. Though, I may need something to barter. You got any friends who'd like to go on a blind date?"

19

I made a big breakfast in the morning, setting the food out buffet-style as the parents started trickling in around seven. We filled our plates and sat wherever, untying the sheets and blankets from last night's forts to uncover chairs.

The kids were still in their PJs; the adults looked like they wished they could still be in theirs.

Gator was out running with Beetle and Bella. He'd eat when they got back.

My phone rang as I loaded the dishwasher. Judy Miller wanted me to come up to the farm later today; Beetle and Bella's mom, Dagger, was in labor. Oh, fun. New puppies. I said I'd drive over after I had straightened around.

Cathy tapped me on the arm. "Hey, let me do that. You go get ready and head on."

I smiled appreciatively and headed up the stairs to don camo-gear and combat boots. I wanted to get to the farm to watch the puppies being born and maybe take my girls through the firearms obstacle course. It had been a while since I had been to the

Millers'. Too long. I hadn't been up there since before Angel died.

I clomped down the stairs to find my house empty except for Gator, who was warming his plate of food in the microwave. "What's the plan now that the invading army has retreated? Why are you dressed for battle?" he asked.

"Jilly left her supply bag here. I need to take it back over to her house, then I'm heading over to the Millers' to run Beetle and Bella through the agility course. I don't think I need a watchdog if you want to go do something else besides hang with me."

"Nah, I got nothing planned. I'd like to see Beetle and Bella in action, though." Gator didn't need to change; he was always dressed for battle in his Iniquus uniform. He called over to the barracks; Blaze and Deep wanted to come, too. They headed over with a van so we could all fit in together.

Meanwhile, Gator and I walked up to Missy's house with my pups in tow. As soon as we stepped onto the porch, the girls' ears flattened. They growled low in the backs of their throats. Hackles raised. Danger. I scanned to find a reason.

"It must be me," the leopard woman sprang from behind the holly tree. I gave a start, and Gator slid between us. How did I miss her? Why was she there? "Dogs and I don't get along." She chuckled.

Consuela moved onto the porch and extended her hand.

Gator reflexively angled his body to stay between us. "I'm new to the neighborhood. I think I waved to you the day I moved in. You were in a Hummer?"

I ignored her question and stepped from behind the cement

wall Gator had formed. I was in full-out "cute-girlie-next-door" mode. *"Innocence is your best defense, Lexicon. Never tip your hand. The enemy should always underestimate your capabilities."* Spyder's words rang in my head. No fear — just fluff.

"I'm Lexi, and this is my housemate, Gator."

"Gator? Nice to meet you both." Her accent was heavy, not Mexican, not Puerto Rican... Hmm. I wondered if we could get a linguist to identify her country of origin. I'd ask over at Iniquus when I went back into the office.

Jilly opened the door.

"I hear we have some things in common," Consuela said.

"Oh?" I asked blankly. I turned my attention to Jilly-bean and handed over her bag. "This is too important to leave behind, baby doll." I gave her a friendly wink.

"Yes, ma'am." Jilly hugged the backpack to her.

"I'm told you like to cook. Jilly says you make wonderful burritos, and you speak Spanish," Consuela pushed on.

Friendly, vacant smile, Lexi. "Ha. No. I know some basic phrases. My husband was from Puerto Rico. He's the one who spoke Spanish, and his aunt is the one who taught me to cook burritos. I'm sorry, but we're running a little late. Beetle. Bella," I called, stepping off the porch. Consuela jostled us as we passed by, and there was a moment of confusion and re-balancing, then we were down the walkway onto the sidewalk.

"Good thing you have command of your pups," Gator started. I squeezed his arm and gave him a death glare. He stared down at me, confused. Deep and Blaze waited in the van for us; I signaled them into my house.

As soon as we were inside, I turned to the three guys with my finger to my lips to signal for quiet. "I think our hostess likes chocolate cake. I'll whip one up, and then we can go over after lunch."

Gator cocked his head to the side, trying to figure out what he should do. I opened my eyes wide and nodded at him, willing him to respond affirmatively.

"Yes, ma'am. I think she'd really like one of your chocolate cakes," he said brightly. We walked to the kitchen, where I took off my coat and searched it thoroughly. While I banged around with pots and pans in one hand, I patted down all my clothing with the other. The way she shoved past us felt too deliberate. I hummed loudly to myself as I wiggled out of my boots. Then I pulled off my pants. I was glad I had on my demure black cotton panties today. The men had seen me in all states of dress and undress; they didn't seem fazed by my stripping down in front of them. I found the transmitter adhered to the inside of my waist-band. I held the gizmo up triumphantly. Tada!

I was actually relieved to find something, or this would have taken a lot more explaining. I pointed at Gator, who followed my actions.

He found a monitor in his pants as well.

I made a lot of racket, then, "Ahhhh! Gator! Look what you did. I had everything ready to go in the oven, and now we're covered with batter."

"I'm sure sorry, ma'am," Gator said, standing in his boxer-briefs. I tried very hard to keep my eyes on his face.

"Here, let's get these clothes into the washing machine so they don't stain." I trounced down the stairs, opened the lid, and put the GSM bugs in with the load of towels already in there. I ran the washer on hot water — heavy soil. I'd dispose of the bugs when I returned.

Back in the kitchen, we gave ourselves another once over, checked the dogs, put on our clothes, and left.

"Was that woman's intuition?" asked Deep, once we were safely in the van.

"No. That was a pathetically amateur attempt to bug us. I can't believe anyone could be so bad at it."

"Only because you're so good, ma'am. I didn't realize what she was doing. I thought she was clumsy. But now I know to strip down to my skivvies if I ever get bumped like that again." Gator grinned.

"The van is clean? We're sure there are no GPS units stuck to the undercarriage?"

"I just gave it another scan. We're good to go," Blaze said.

"Yeah, it won't help, though. I told Missy that we're headed for the Millers', and she won't know to keep my location quiet." I sighed.

"Do you think it'll matter?" Blaze asked.

"Beats me. I don't know what this woman wants from me."

20

Nona Sophia Alfonz was my Kitchen Grandmother from Italy. Every night her apartment would fill with noise and family, family, and noise. Sometimes the noise was light-hearted and teasing. Sometimes someone broke out in song. Many times they broke out into fights.

Deep came from this background — born and raised on Staten Island. He missed it. Joseph-Pasquale, his mother called him — Joey to the rest of his family. I still don't know why we called him Deep. A "Deep" dark secret, I giggled to myself, popping the garlic bread into the oven. Tonight he was bringing a new girl — Ghianna — to dinner. Honestly, he goes through girls like I go through a bag of potato chips.

Deep rang the bell right on time; I turned the burner under the sauce to off and headed to the door. Deep always showed up at my house for dinner on Thursdays — didn't even bother to ask. He'd call to check on the time and to see if I needed anything besides the bottle or two of good, red Italian wine he always brought. I'm not supposed to drink any until my birthday, March third, when I'd turn twenty-one. But I liked to have them to set on the table for whoever showed up for my weekly Italian dinner. Deep and I had started a tradition, and it was pretty much open door night — anyone who was hungry or wanted a little *famiglia Italia* was welcome.

Okay, almost everyone. Tonight, not so much. As Manny and his boys burst through the front door, I spotted Consuela trailing them in. I quickly ducked into the kitchen and flattened against the wall. Holy cow.

Manny's Italian comes from his father's side, and Manny liked to eat. Manny and his boys coming for Thursday dinner was a given. But how in the world did Consuela glom on to Manny's crew? Was she making inroads with the neighbors? First Missy, now Manny? What were they telling her about me? What did they know?

The neighbors all thought I did data entry for Iniquus. They've run into my team from time to time, but I introduced them as my friends, which they are. Manny knows I shoot and do martial arts — I wracked my brain for any other information that would benefit Consuela. I didn't think any of them knew I spoke anything but a little Italian… Shit. I hated this.

Think. Think. Tonight I had a full house. Good. That might help. Gator, Amy, Amy's friend, Nicki, Deep, Ghianna, Manny, his two boys, and now Consuela. How can I get rid of her? I stirred my sauce manically, sloshing the tomatoes up the sides of the pot and splattering the wall.

Amy and Gator appeared in the kitchen, interrupting my thoughts. "Hey, do you need any help in here?" Gator asked.

"Yes, thanks. Can you open the wine and put the bottles on the table? Amy, would you grab some of the platters?" Amy picked up the antipasti and serving forks and moved to the dining room.

"You hiding out in here?" Gator whispered in my ear as he twisted the corkscrew into the bottle.

"For as long as possible." My hand trembled as I reached for the pasta pot. Why was I so unsteady? My brows drew together. What could she possibly do to me in a house full of people? My rational mind scolded my limbic system. The leopard purred arrogantly and swished a long lazy tail.

"Can you seat everyone and make sure you and Deep are on either side of Consuela at the far end of the table? Put the little boys up near me on the stools. They'll make enough noise that I can seem distracted."

"Wilco." Gator popped the cork out of the second bottle and headed into the dining room.

I swirled my food on my plate. My stomach refused even a single bite, though the night seemed to be passing drama-free. Deep and Gator deflected the conversation into ankle-deep, banal waters whenever Consuela tried to take a plunge into some aspect of my life. She seemed especially intent on bringing up my homeschool days — my neighbors apparently had been talking. She wanted to chat about my teachers and where I got my dogs. Both of these things connected me to Spyder. Luckily, my neighbors didn't know anything about him — well, that wasn't true. Dave Murphy did. But he also knew how to keep his mouth shut.

Consuela spent the night annoying me by speaking in Spanish. I had to be cognizant of which language she spoke, so I wouldn't respond either by word or facial expression to anything Spanish, as Spyder instructed. It was a lot of work and irritating as hell. Good God, but I've been swearing a lot lately. Stress... I couldn't for the life of me figure out why Consuela was baiting me. What did it matter if I spoke Spanish or not?

Finally, Deep looked over at Consuela and asked, "Why do you keep talking to everyone in English but Lexi? She doesn't know how to speak Spanish. Lexi's second language is kitchen Italian. And if you ask me, she speaks it very well."

"Hear, hear!" Manny raised his wine glass. "A toast to Lexi's kitchen Italian!"

On that, I smiled and escaped to the kitchen to get the cannoli and coffee.

"Okay, all clear. Table tidied. Guests gone. You can stop hiding out in your kitchen now." Amy burst through the door with a platter in her hand and a smile on her face.

I put a finger to my lips and shook my head.

Gator must have been thinking my same thoughts. He walked into the kitchen, holding up the Tektronix to sweep for surveillance equipment.

I gave him the thumbs-up, and he went to work in the dining room.

As I turned on the dishwasher, Gator walked in with a little gizmo resting on his palm. After showing me, he opened the dishwasher door, threw it in, and adjusted the setting to disinfect.

"That's all of them?" I leaned my hips against the counter with a big exhale.

He glanced at the dishwasher. "You're clean."

For some reason, this struck me as wildly funny, and I bent over laughing.

"Y'all are weird." Amy shook her head with exasperation and went to get her coat from my hall closet.

"In Honduras?" I doodled leopard ears on my pad. I was talking on the phone with a linguistics professor who specialized in Latin American accents. "You're sure she's originally from Honduras? Okay, I'm taking notes…and the capital Tegucigalpa, specifically?" I asked.

I sent this guy declassified tapes three days ago with a bonus check if he prioritized my project. Maybe I had a starting point, or maybe he just wanted his money — hard to tell from his voice alone. I should have Skyped. Well, at least I knew how I'd spend the rest of the day. I'd be searching Honduran vital records. Huh. Honduras. Sylanos was Columbian…

I lied in bed, lonely, and wondering what Striker was doing.

My mind went to dark, dangerous places as I remembered the tales Spyder had told me about their down-range assignments. I decided my own disaster was easier to deal with than thoughts of Striker in peril, or hurt, or… *Don't you dare go there!*

I derailed my Striker's-in-mortal-danger thoughts with grim determination and locked onto today's discoveries. According to Honduran Vital Statistics, Maria Castillo was born in the capital. Kudos to the professor; I have to say that was impressive. She had married there, too. Her husband's last name was Rodriguez. Julio Rodriguez. Now that name was familiar to me. I'd researched Julio in the past — in connection with the Marcos Sylanos case. Excitement bubbled in my veins. I had a new name to look for in American files, Maria Castillo Rodriguez; a new line to fish for information.

The piece of the Sylanos case I worked on had to do with illegal arms distribution out of Colombia. Hmm. I needed information from the source, Spyder, but he was recuperating undercover in Somewhere, America. I could try to find him, but that might endanger both of us. I also thought about the high-security storage unit where I stowed Spyder's things when he took off on an assignment.

I cosigned the contract, so I had the key.

Surely, the files I puzzled for him were still boxed up.

If that didn't work, I'd try to get hold of the file Striker brought to the safe house—just two little problems. First, Striker didn't have a complete file; Spyder's information proved much more comprehensive. Second, there was a good chance Iniquus had classified the file, and I hadn't been read into that program. Come to think of it, Striker never told me what happened after I broke the case. I had never heard anything about Sylanos being taken down — surely that would have made the newspapers. So he didn't get off on a technicality; he didn't go to trial... I remembered my rat dream, where they collared the beast and let the humongo thing go.

Holy cow — they watched while Sylanos morphed into a Hydra. Anger and frustration vied for my attention — the battle of emotions raged loudly in my head.

21

"What's the plan today, Lynx?" Gator asked as we finished our coffees.

"We're going to get dusty. I'm working on the Hervas case. I need to go over to Spyder's storage unit and do a little digging. I'll probably need your brawn to move a bunch of stuff around."

"I'm game. Are you going to tell me what we're looking for?"

"Sure. I want to see if I can find the files I was working on when Spyder took off."

Gator stalled with his breakfast burrito seemingly forgotten in his hand. "Marcos Sylanos? You're kidding. You're thinking this Consuela girl's caught up in all that? That's bad juju."

"Very bad juju. She's married to one of the key players."

"How'd you figure?" Gator asked.

I smiled smugly.

"Damn, girl."

Pawing through the boxes in Spyder's storage unit, I wished Striker were here with me. I liked that his calm and steady played antithetically to my bristly and electric. He was like a metronome set to four-four time while I danced an emotion-filled fandango around him.

Gator was a great guy, and I loved him dearly. It's just our relationship was different. I couldn't show my soft underbelly around Gator. I was his teammate, and I wasn't about to be seen by my team as a weak link.

Gator and I hefted and sorted, rubbed dust into our clothes, and sneezed violently. Now we were sitting on the cold cement with our backs to the wall, stacks of files at our feet.

"Hey now. Looky here!" Gator waved a thick manila folder at me.

I reached for the file and looked hungrily down. Boom. Page one, a photograph of the spider web of string leading from name to name stuck to my bedroom floor back at my old apartment. Life was very different at the time of this photo. Mom was alive, Spyder and I were partnered, I hadn't met Angel yet. He was still alive, too. I was so innocent then. It wasn't long ago, a year and a half, but it doesn't take long for life to swing wildly out of control. My life certainly proved the point.

"Good job." Sadness colored my voice, and Gator cast a perplexed look at me.

I offered him an artificial smile. "I'll have to look at these in the Puzzle Room for security. But, listen, Gator, I would really appreciate it if you didn't mention our outing to anyone. You know — that I have this." I waved the file at him.

Gator's expression clouded. "Do you mean Striker?"

"Um." Did I mean Striker? I thought for a minute — I'd never ask Gator to hide something from his Team Lead. "No. I mean anyone outside of the team. I have to play this close to the vest. I need this information to puzzle with, and I'm afraid Command would take this data away from me if they found out I had it." I wasn't sure I understood all of this "on a need to know basis" business. They were using me to draw out information, which made me bait, and quite frankly, that meant I needed to know.

Gator looked uncomfortable. "Is that an order, ma'am?"

Surprise shot my eyebrows up to my hairline. "Do I have that authority?"

"While Striker's gone, yes, ma'am. You're Team Lead on this case."

Shoot, who knew? "Well then, yes, it's an order."

In my office, I verified Julio Rodriguez as the guy I thought he was — definitely in Sylanos's inner-circle, and I even found information on Maria. Her name in the file was Castillo; that must be why Spyder had said Maria Castillo and not Maria Rodriguez. Okay. One mystery solved.

Julio seemed to be attached to Sylanos through his shipping route in some way, and yes, indeed, when I reviewed the shipping information, I found triangular stops — Columbia, US, Honduras.

But some of Julio's information didn't fit...seemed strange. Julio was an educated man with a Master's degree in computer software design from the University of California. Why in the world would he get involved in shipping a Colombian weapons dealer's merchandise from East Coast ports down to Honduras and then to Colombia? Hmmm, "curiouser and curiouser," as Striker liked to say.

As I flipped through the file, I came upon the picture from

Mrs. Agnew's desk. On the back, someone had written in black pen. "Honeymoon in Costa Rica, Julio and Maria" — with a heart around drawn around the names — "with our new friends, Amando and Beth Sylanos." A shiver ran through me. Amando Sylanos? Was he related to Marcos? I needed to do some more research — this time in the Colombian vital stats. But exhaustion weighed heavily on my shoulders. I needed to go home.

I called over to the barracks. "Gator?"

"Yeah?" His voice rumbled, thick with sleep.

"It's zero-one-thirty. I had no idea I had worked so late. I'm going to bed down in the barracks tonight. Go back to sleep."

"K." He hung up.

My mind played on fast forward. I lay in bed, tossing around, trying to find a position that made my body feel restful, hoping my brain would get the hint and let me fall asleep.

Around three in the morning, the girls popped their heads up, but they weren't barking, then the door opened and softly closed. Striker must be home. I let go of my stress with a big sigh. A giddy smile tickled my lips as he walked softly to the bathroom to brush his teeth. He came into the guest room where I was snuggled under the covers, and he burrowed in beside me, pulling me into his bare arms. The smattering of his chest hair tickled my back. His sweatpants rasped my thighs.

"Hey, welcome home. How did everything go?" I rolled toward him and could just make out his smile in the dim light from the Cheshire Cat moon outside my window.

"Pretty well. Things are moving in the right direction. I'm bringing in some data that needs to be puzzled. I'm afraid I have to get you to put your other cases on hold while you focus on

this. It's time-sensitive and serious. We've got competition, too."
He kissed me lightly.

"Who?" I reached up and traced his full lips with my finger.
He had beautiful lips.

"Bunch of the agencies. Everyone's stepping on everyone's
toes."

I moved my hand to his hair. Mmm. Silky. I kissed him
sweetly; he tasted like mint toothpaste. He smiled against my
lips.

"It's pretty fierce — you'd think they'd get themselves
together and cooperate," he kissed the tip of my nose, "...then
they could pull it off. But then Iniquus wouldn't have a mission."
His mouth moved to my neck just below my ear.

I giggled. "Do I need to go over now?"

"No, first thing tomorrow will be fine." He moved his kisses
to my throat down to the v of my clavicle. I angled my head to
give him better access. "We can't move until we get an updated
file, and the info isn't coming in until eight," he murmured, his
words tickling my skin, making me squirm. He gathered me in
his arms and pulled me tight against him.

"So, why are you climbing in bed with me?" I whispered into
his ear.

"I have the heebie-jeebies." He chuckled, rolling me onto my
back and hovering above me.

"Cute." I breathed in the clean smell of his body wash — just
like in bed at the safe house. But at the safe house, I had to fight
against desire and here...now...

"It worked for you." Striker kissed my lips softly as he
adjusted his knees underneath him. His hand explored down the
length of my body. Edging my silk camisole up fractionally to
expose my belly, he lay soft kisses in a tantalizing line across the
top of my panties. I groaned and arched toward his mouth.

Striker stilled, and I felt him smile against my skin and the heat of his chest against my thighs.

He gathered my camisole in his hands and slowly lifted the pink silk up and off. His fingers trailed down my breasts. My nipples hardened as he rolled them between his fingers and then with his tongue. I needed more of him and tried to pull him to me, but Striker was not to be rushed.

Very slowly, he dragged his fingers lightly over my skin, waking up my sense of touch, making me tremble. "Please." I gasped my need. His mouth found mine, his kisses serious and demanding, our tongues dancing and exploring. His thigh moved between my legs, his erection pressed against me. *He wants me.* The thought worked as a powerful aphrodisiac. He eased his other leg between mine, and my knees came naturally up on his sides, opening me to him. My body hummed — greedy for his attention.

Somehow he was naked. His silken erection brushed down my inner thigh as he moved over me, tormenting me.

"Please." I gasped. His fingers hooked my panties, easing them slowly, slowly down my hips and off...

"Striker?" My voice sounded small and quivery. He moved back up; hovering over me, he looked down into my eyes and waited. I gulped. "I love you touching me," I said on the exhale.

He smiled and kissed me.

"Striker?"

He opened his eyes to look at me again.

"I want you to make love to me...but..."

When I said 'but' he lowered his forehead to mine. He had to regroup, shift gears.

So did I.

Oh my God, I can't believe I'm such a freaking prick tease!

But could I do this?

My body and mind were in full out battle.

"But what, Lexi? Tell me." His voice had the gruff and lusty quality to it, like in Miami.

"If we make love, we'll keep making love. We'll be lovers."

"Yes." He smiled. He seemed to like the idea.

"And that means we'll be in a relationship."

"Chica, we are in a relationship, just an unusual, undefined relationship."

"Being lovers would define us. We'd be a couple. I'm not there, Striker. I'm not ready to be in a new defined-couple relationship yet." There it was — my truth — no matter how my body longed for him, I wasn't ready.

"So, being in bed with me leaves us undefined. Making love defines us. You're okay with me sleeping with you. The line comes with making love?" Mirth shone in his eyes along with... wariness? Frustration?

"I guess so." Guilt, love, loneliness, contentment, deprivation... I was full to overflowing with clashing emotions. "I'm sorry. I don't know what else to do. I can't just be your lover. I'm not wired like Amy. I don't want to be your Amy." My voice rose with conviction.

"Amy? What has she got to do with us?" he asked, quietly brushing my hair from my face, looking down into my eyes in the moonlight.

"Well, here she is wishing for a relationship, and she gets sex and Gator's emotional leftovers instead." I lifted my hand to caress the beginnings of his morning stubble. God, but Striker was breathtaking. He was everything — everything I ever wanted, but I wanted it all. Not scraps. My thumb outlined his lips, hoping the right words would come out of his mouth — whatever they were...

"I'm not asking you to be my Amy, Chica."

Oh? "Then what exactly are you asking me to be?" I held my breath and mentally crossed my fingers.

Striker paused for a long time. I didn't say anything. I understood my question was a complex one, and if he'd had a response readily at hand, he'd already have shared it with me.

"I can't answer you. I'm sorry. My love for you doesn't seem complicated until I try to think in practical terms."

"What a mess," I whispered, softly running my fingers along the planes of his face.

He brought my hand to his lips, pressing a kiss into the pulse point on my wrist, then laying my palm on his heart. "No, not a mess, Chica. Everything's all right." Striker lay flat on top of me then rolled to his side with me still in his arms. "We'll figure this out. And until then, I'm trying to understand your sleeping parameters." I pillowed my head on his bicep. He nuzzled against my ear. "Can you tell me how far I'm allowed to go?" He ran his warm hand along my naked side, fingers grazing my breast. I loved how the roughness of his callouses made me feel ultra-feminine. "Is this no actual intercourse, but maybe a little fooling around kind of sleeping?" His hand slid between my thighs and rested lightly. He nipped my shoulder playfully.

"One would kind of lead toward the other, wouldn't it?" I asked. "I'm feeling guilty here about saying no to you, and that adds some pressure."

"I'm the transmission. All you need to say is, 'shift gears' or 'back up,' and I will. No pressure, Chica. Really. None."

His reassuring kiss was light, friendly, warm — definitely no pressure, I noted with a little disappointment.

"Can I sleep with you tonight?" he asked.

"All right." I sighed. "But if you snore, I'm going to get Beetle and Bella involved." When I said their names, my girls stuck their noses up over the bed to see if a command would follow, and when it didn't, they plopped back down on the floor.

"I missed you," Striker whispered as he tucked his knees up to spoon.

"I missed you, too," I whispered back.

With another kiss, he settled the covers over us and fell asleep, his arms holding me possessively against him.

He deserves better than me.

22

A few hours later, the team assembled in the Puzzle Room, waiting for Jack and Striker to brief us on the case and give us our assignments.

"Gentlemen and Lynx, we are up against a short time frame. Tomorrow evening, at twenty hundred, a plane will leave Reagan International for Abu Dhabi carrying Andrew Brennon and two of his associates. Once he's on the plane, we will have lost our opportunity to bring him to justice. Our job is to put together a strong enough case to keep him on American soil. He's wealthy. He's well-connected. He has a pile of get-out-of-jail-free cards in his pocket. We have to craft a solid, irrefutable case."

"What charges are we looking at?" Deep pulled out a chair and sat down at the evidence table with his coffee mug.

"Espionage, cyber-terrorism, and blackmail for starters, and anything else we can possibly pin on him." Jack handed out photos of Brennon.

Striker continued, "We believe his first attack was a test balloon — a five-second computer anomaly interrupted a single Wall Street purchasing algorithm. It seems simple, but in that five seconds, there was what they call a 'flash crash,' and 9% of the Dow disappeared. Intel indicates Brennon recently uncovered another hole that opens the door for a second attack. His intent, according to our sources, is to play games with the stock market, undermining US financial security. He's a megalomaniac after the triumvirate — power, money, and prestige on the world terrorism stage."

We sat stone-faced, focused.

Striker continued, "…highly intelligent and vicious. Pretty heinous things happen to people who stand in his way. If you're out in the field, you'll take every precaution. Lynx, you'll obviously be here puzzling. Jack and I will be working with you, explaining everything we have from the other agencies. I don't mean to add any pressure here, but this is a huge deal. Our various clients are all taking a stab at this. We want to be the ones who take him down."

"Understood." I crossed a foot underneath me and leaned forward to study the photo. *Good God, this was intense. Breathe. You're a professional — act the part.*

"Deep, you'll be on the computer. Gator and Blaze are Alpha Team. Axel and Randy make up Bravo. We need to have eyes on this guy until we get him, or he gets on the plane, so we're borrowing Clay and Bonz to give us a third surveillance team. They're Charlie. Remember, there are a lot of government runners in this race, so try not to step on any toes. We don't want to get yanked off the field after all our efforts. We'll do five-hour shifts. Brennon deplaned at Kennedy at zero-seven hundred, Charlie took the first shift. Axel and Randy, you'll relieve them at 1200, then Alpha will take over at 1700. You will continue this rotation. Make sure you've been fed and had adequate rest between rotations," Striker directed.

"Yes, sir," the men replied in unison. The surveillance teams headed out. Deep moved to the seat in front of my computer and entered his codes.

Nervous energy made my palms sweat and my toes tap the floor. I don't work well under pressure. And last time we had been on a time crunch, with the Schumann case, I failed, and he wound up dead — you can't get much worse than that.

Striker and Jack pulled out a box with files in it. They went through the cyber-attack that had already crazied up Wall Street last week.

I squinted at Jack. "Did he launch the attack from the United States?"

"No, Pakistan," Jack answered without glancing up from the map in his hands.

"Is that where you two were?"

"Classified," Jack said.

"It's not part of this case? Or you don't think I should be privy?"

"Classified, Lynx. Move on."

I slit my eyes at Jack. If he wouldn't share, I couldn't puzzle. "Okay. Did he come in from Pakistan this morning?"

"Abu Dhabi."

"And that's where he's going tomorrow?"

"Correct."

"Does he have a return ticket? What about family? Are they scheduled to head out with him?"

And so went the day. I asked billions of questions, and Jack and Striker patiently answered — when they had data. Deep searched our massive data banks to fill in the holes. We listed everything on the whiteboard that still needed fleshing out.

Command sent meals in. Coffee comprised a major food group. Progress was measured in millimeters. Frustration. I saw no clear lines of reasoning in the copious data spread out in front of me. Truth be told, this was darned complicated and probably needed weeks or months instead of hours.

After dinner, I went into the bathroom off my office and took a long hot shower until my skin turned red and pruney. I let my muscles relax. I dressed in yoga pants and a tank top, snagging my hair in the zipper as I pulled a fleece jacket over my head. I stayed barefoot, so I could think better. I always thought better barefooted. I slogged into Striker's office and spent twenty of our precious minutes meditating — freeing up my mind, letting the myriad facts percolate.

I re-approached my mound of clues, making piles, making lists, asking questions, drawing possible connection charts…and so it went through the day, through the night, and back through the day again. Crimes were obviously being committed, but I couldn't find the smallest shred of evidence to implicate this guy. Everything was indirect and circumstantial. I might even have chosen to venture down a different route, along a different set of clues, if Striker and Jack weren't absolutely convinced that Brennon was at the top of this food chain. *Arr*.

Working a puzzle under time-pressure, and no sleep made me feel overwhelmed.

I really couldn't speed up the process. My brain didn't work that way, and the team knew it. I felt them trying to be patient, but this was a big deal. This really bad guy had the potential to do a lot of harm to our economy, and the hourglass was draining quickly. Striker realized the stress was getting to me, shutting down my ability to gather a strand of understanding from here and there and spin them together. Even though time was precious, he ordered me outside to run. He and my dogs jogged beside me. I breathed in the frigid air. I tried to unknot my muscles and relax, so inspiration would bloom, and I could save the day.

As we headed back around the trail, Striker's phone buzzed. He listened and told the caller we'd be right there.

"What?" I asked.

"Gator's coming in from his surveillance shift and brought you photos. He doesn't think they'll be very helpful. But then, we don't think the way you do. I need to get you back and let you take a look at them."

"Who's watching Brennon now?"

"Axel and Randy are on. Charlie Team's racked out before their next op. The rest of the team is in the Puzzle Room, waiting for instruction. Why don't you head back? I'll take Beetle and Bella over to the barracks for now."

"Okay, I'll see you in a minute." I jogged off toward head-quarters.

When I reached my office, the team was bent over the photographs laid out on my table. They had coffee mugs in their hands. Gator held one out to me.

I shook my head. "No, thanks. Give me a second, and I'll come see what you've got." I went into the bathroom and washed the sweat from my face, and swiped on some deodorant. "All right, what's the story?" I walked over to them.

"Ma'am, Blaze and me were out on surveillance today, and I c'ain't say we got much of anything," Gator said.

He handed over the pile of photos. I looked down and gasped. The energy radiating from them was overpowering. There was the bad guy, Andrew Brennon — average good looks, about five foot ten, a hundred-and-seventy pounds, with straight, black hair, hazel eyes, thin lips on an over-wide mouth. He was with his family: his wife, Naomi — who looked like a Scandinavian model. The two didn't visually fit together even if he was rich and powerful — his two little girls, who would grow up to look like their mother, and…

When I looked at the other woman in the photograph, it was as if I was punched in the stomach. I couldn't inhale.

This woman was frantic, hopeless. This woman had the answers we needed.

I felt the tug and familiar pull, a call from behind the Veil. I was teetering between two planes. I had a choice to make. The Veil was open to me. If I wanted to, I could walk behind it now and merge with this woman — maybe get the answers we needed, maybe find something to implicate Brennon and keep him on American soil. In an American prison. *Should I go?* The call lured my awareness behind the Veil. It sounded familiar to me — "Come. Come," chanted the African women who helped me save Striker's family. "Come," they sang. I trusted these women. Yes. I'd go.

I dragged my eyes up from the photographs and found Jack staring at me. "Jack, I have to go help her." I pointed at the woman in the photo. "You know the rules."

Jack didn't usually wear his emotions on his sleeve. He was a huge man whose carved features lent themselves well to stoicism, but right now, it was easy to read the anguish in his eyes.

I put him through hell last time — when I went behind the Veil to save Lynda and Cammy.

"Yes, ma'am." His voice was tight. "I will not leave beginning to end. I will not touch you. I will not allow anyone else to touch you. No one else will come in… What about Striker? I don't think I can keep him out once he knows what you're doing."

I nodded my consent. Now that I had made my decision, any interaction in the here and now was a monumental effort.

Jack continued, "I will not allow you to leave until you are able to walk out on your own two feet. Please, Lynx, we should wait for Striker. This isn't a good idea."

"She needs me now, Jack. I'm so sorry…"

The Veil pulled at my consciousness.

Jack got on his phone. "Striker, Code Red. Puzzle Room."

I sat down, with the photos, but I barely felt the chair. I was already on my way out of my body. I looked at the photo in my hand. I didn't pay the least bit of attention to the Brennons; they made my stomach heave, but they wouldn't be the ones to tell me what was going on.

This girl would.

I sat with the photo. She was my age — maybe nineteen? Twenty? In the photo, the wind had caught her raven black hair and whipped it across her high cheekbones. Her dress was chic, if extremely modest. The dark blue wool outlined her rounded breasts and cinched in at her tiny waist. She was model-beautiful. Especially her eyes.

I focused on her eyes. *Tell me.*

Her eyes were tormented, staggering, mesmerizing. She was in hell. I waited as a name formed in my mouth.

"Anna, Anya, Anushka. She is Anushka," I said out loud, pointing to the photo.

"Yes." Blaze looked quickly over at Jack to see if he should have responded.

Jack and Striker had never told the team about this talent of mine. They had protected my secret at their own expense. This meant that Blaze, Deep, and Gator were in the dark right now, watching something very peculiar transpire.

Striker burst into the room. He looked over at me, and then Jack. "She's gone behind the Veil? Why?" Striker sounded like a commander, but there was a frantic tinge to his voice, belying his control. He knew I was going somewhere where he had no power and no way of helping me.

I heard Jack. "She said she had to go."

Striker turned away from me to address the team. "Men, this will be explained later. There will be silence unless you can corroborate a fact. The only words you will use are 'confirmed' or 'refuted.' You will under no circumstance, and I mean NONE, touch Lynx. She's on a mission."

"Yes, sir," they replied.

I looked at the pictures again. Brennon and his wife were too distracting. I tore the picture, so only Anushka stared back at me with her hollow gaze. She was incomplete. There was something important missing. I felt empty arms—unbearable grief. There was someone missing from this picture — a baby. I drew a baby on a piece of paper and cast about for a name.

Two names came to me in layers. Both belonged to the same child, yet both did not belong to the child. I didn't understand.

"Anastasia," I mouthed. "Olivia." I looked up for confirmation; the men stared at me blankly. "Can you confirm an infant? A baby less than one year of age?"

"No, Lynx," Blaze said. "I can neither confirm nor refute. We haven't seen any babies and no other children other than the Brennan's children in the photo."

"The names Anastasia and Olivia mean nothing to you?" I mumbled rhetorically.

I breathed in, waiting for Anushka to speak to me.

Volcanic heat enveloped me.

My skin prickled from fear sweat.

My center dragged forward as I merged with Anushka. Oh my God, the heat. I jerked off my fleece hoodie. Even in my sleeveless jogging tank, I sweltered.

My forearms rested on the arms of my chair, and now to my

horror, I couldn't lift them. I was held in place by panic and some kind of leather binding.

I glanced around a windowless room lit dimly from above. Cement walls, unfinished ceiling beams. A basement? A desk sat on my left and bookcases to my right.

Andrew loomed above me, naked from the waist up. His black suit pants were unbuttoned and sliding down his hips. His psychopathic face was purplish-red and transformed, hideous with anger and evil.

Dear God, what is he doing?

He leaned in — inches from my face. His breath was ragged with excitement and stank of salami and cigarettes. His eyes were bloodshot, glowing red with anticipation. He licked his lips, and I cowered the best I could given my restraints.

"I am your lord god. I will do whatever the fuck I want to you, and you will thank me."

"Thank you, Master," I bleated and cringed.

"If you make a single noise — just one, I will strip your flesh from your bones," he hissed.

I pushed my lips together tightly, curling them in to hold them in place with my teeth, and nodded my understanding. Anushka's eyes were screwed tightly shut — I couldn't see what Brennon was doing, but I felt it. Oh dear God in Heaven, deliver me from this hell.

I felt tiny points of blood spring up from the soft skin of my inner arms as Brennon stabbed something into me with quick staccato thrusts. My muscles convulsed as I yanked against the restraints trying to escape.

A song sung in a foreign language, in a thin off-key voice pushed against reality. Anushka tried to force a lullaby between her soul and her physical self. She struggled — wavering and reclaiming — using the song as a barricade. I tried to focus on her voice. Something. Anything to distract me from the searing pain.

I sucked air in hard through my clenched teeth and exhaled through nostrils that flared and dripped. Tears leaped to my eyes and pushed through the dam of my lids. I fisted my hands against the pain. That's all there was — pain — like fireworks bursting against me, light and color and soul-shaking sound.

Andrew bellowed like a crazed animal, then joy filled his voice as he caressed the plots he hatched and revealed, explaining how he was going to hurt me next.

"Open your eyes, Anushka." Andrew's voice was sing-song and silky as he swept the hair, hanging damp across her cheek, back behind her ear with gentle fingers. He planted kisses near her lips — still curled in and caught between her teeth. "Open," he said.

Anushka forced wild, unblinking eyes onto Brennon's face. His slow smile seemed benevolent as he slid his signet ring from his finger. He reached into his pocket, pulling out a lighter, and before our eyes, he heated it, twisting the gold in the yellow flame.

Oh, like a fairy. Sunlight on glittering water. No. No. — *Baby, baby-mine, Mommy will save you — protect you. Do you know what Mommy does to protect you?* I saw a sweet infant's face wrapped in a pink blanket, peacefully asleep. Anushka pushed the lullaby forward again.

"You. Are. Mine. And I will brand you as such." Brennon's smile turned to a snarl, and Anyuska's eyes clamped shut. She screamed the lullaby in her mind as the ring pressed into her inner thigh.

She draped her body against the chair. We were held in place — as she slipped in and out of consciousness — by the bindings. Black, red, and orange. Baby cries and the lullaby…

I was roused from the stupor by the sharp bite of a whip. My eyes were wide and fixed.

"I am your master. I control you!"

A moan escaped my lips.

"Quiet!" The whip rained down across my shoulders, licking hotly across my breasts. I focused on clenching my teeth and not allowing my lips to part, not allowing any sound to emit from my throat. Andrew held complete control, and he commanded silence.

I slipped limply in my chair, exhausted from bracing taut muscles against the onslaught. He stood beside her, panting with his gentle hand on her head, rubbing Anushka behind the ears like she was a dog. "Good slave," he whispered carnally.

My pants were sodden and sticky from the blood.

In the Brennons' basement, Anushka sat naked. Dark red ran down her legs to pool on the floor.

I had sensed my teammates' strong emotions brewing and swelling like a thunderstorm around me, as Anushka's welts, bruises, and burns appeared on my arms and chest, visible above the low scoop-neck of my top.

A clock chimed above me for a second time. I knew this had been going on for over an hour. Andrew's erection bounced free as he stripped off his pants and boxers. He rubbed himself up against my wounds and groaned with pleasure. He slowly released her restraints — first the ankles and knees, then the wrists and elbows. My feet and hands were numb from lack of circulation.

Anushka's head fell forward, and Brennon wrapped her hair onto his wrist. He dragged her from the chair, laughing perversely. With what thoughts I could gather, I wondered what he would do next with his sex-slave fantasies. I was on all fours, being pulled forward by my hair, crawling toward a bed.

The phone rang on the table beside him. A lick of hope flickered in my chest. He kicked her in the gut, sending me flying. Anushka landed under the desk; I hit against the wall. My head stopped with a solid thud. The wind was knocked out of me. I needed to puke — my diaphragm and stomach muscles convulsed in opposition, so I garnered no relief from oxygen or vomit.

Anushka floated in and out of consciousness — the basement scene coming in and out of focus. I heard Andrew on the speakerphone. His wife, with great apprehension, announced a car had arrived; the men waited outside.

Andrew hung up without a word to his wife. He went through a door — the bathroom, maybe. We lay there, blinking, minds as numb as our limbs. When he emerged, he was dressed — the lines on his face were smooth, his eyes warm and intelligent; he was a well-groomed, fairly handsome, businessman. I heard his tread on the staircase.

I took a minute to catch my breath, then dragged myself back to the table, up into my chair. Picking up the photo. I asked Anushka to tell me what was happening. Her story filled my head. "I am an unwed mother from the Czech Republic. Like many girls, I dreamed of coming to America to improve my English, so I could get a good job in the city back home. Or perhaps maybe I would fall in love and marry an American man and make a happy family for my Anastasia.

"Naomi hired me as a nanny for her two daughters. She told me it was fine to bring my new baby. She said her girls loved to play with babies. Within days of coming to Washington, I woke up with Andrew standing over me, his red face contorted like a crazed bull. He told me he gave Anastasia to another family. Her new name is Olivia. He said the only way I could keep her alive is to be a very, very good slave. If I ever cried out or tried to escape or to get help, then Anastasia would be killed."

I got the image of an empty crib with a rumpled pink blanket in the corner.

Dread. Engulfing bleakness. Panic.

"I asked Naomi what was happening. Naomi looked at me with hard eyes. She said someone had to take her husband's torture and sadistic sex. She said Andrew promised her that if she found him a slave he liked, then Naomi would be safe. She would be his wife, and the slave would take care of his needs. She said this, and she walked out the door." I related all of this out loud so my team would hear the story.

I saw the image of a well-appointed office. The Brennons, another couple I didn't recognize, a man…maybe a lawyer? I sat in a leather chair, and they handed me a contract — papers stapled across the top, rimmed by the blue cover. English words danced but didn't make much sense to me. Struggling for breath, I focused on not fainting. I wanted to wail and wring my hands, but I remembered what Brennon told me about saving my baby. The lawyer — yes, he must be a lawyer — pointed out lines, and I signed my name with a pen that shook so hard that no one would be able to read my signature.

"I would do anything to keep my baby alive. God help me, I will survive to protect her." Anushka's soft voice lamented in my head.

Holding the picture I had drawn of the baby, I asked Anastasia/Olivia where she was living. I put my pen to the map and let my hand be free as it drew a line from our headquarters and followed the highway into the part of Washington where the rich and well-connected had their mansions. Jack moved a computer in front of me, with Google Maps on the screen, showing the area I had pointed out on the map. I searched from house to house until I found the one connected to the baby.

I was devoid of personal feelings. Personal thought. I was being used as a vessel — an inanimate object. Robotically, I looked at Striker. "Confirm the address. The family's name is Hildebrandt. Confirm the adoption of Olivia Hildebrandt on March 15th last year." I repeated the information I saw on the contract at the lawyer's office. My voice was the staccato drumbeat of a funeral march. "Confirm the work visas and entry into the US of Anushka Vlamnisch accompanied by her infant daughter, February 23rd."

Striker was on the phone asking for computer searches. While we waited for the confirmations, Striker quietly worked on assembling three teams to make apprehensions, and one team included medics to rescue Anushka.

I sat like a plastic doll, unblinking, unfeeling, a void.

Suddenly, I bent over the trashcan and vomited. I lowered myself back to the floor to rest. Awareness slowly returned along with physical pain. Ah, there was a feeling that belonged to me — exhaustion. I moaned, knowing now I could; Brennon wouldn't hear me and punish me.

"Can you be touched? Can we help you?" Jack crouched down beside me.

"Not until Anushka is safe. I have to keep the Veil open. This is my only opportunity…"

Jack hovered beside me.

I clung to the picture of Anushka.

She had crawled behind a wall Brennon had been built to hide her. This was where she recovered unseen, so the Brennon girls would not stumble upon her while her bloody wounds were visible. We rested together.

The phone rang again. "Confirmed, Anushka Vlamnisch

entered the US on February 23rd with an infant girl named Anastasia. Also confirmed, Anastasia Vlamnisch, from the Czech Republic, was adopted on March 15th by Eric and Tesla Hildebrandt. Her new name is Olivia Clair Hildebrandt," Striker said this out loud so we would all hear, then he directed his voice back into the phone. "Tell the teams it's a go."

I walked myself partially out from behind the Veil. "You will not be able to find Anushka — she's hiding. The rescue team will cause her more harm if they go in and try to get her. Anushka is ready to kill herself. She believes if anyone discovers her, either Naomi or Andrew will kill her baby. Can you surround the house to protect Anushka but wait for the baby to be in our custody? Then we'll walk through this carefully."

"Do you know where Naomi is right now?" Striker handed me the stack of pictures, careful not to touch me. I found her at a restaurant with the children, eating ice cream and laughing. "Down the street from her house — a place called Vito's." Striker held his phone to his ear, mobilizing a team.

My gaze fell on Andrew's picture. "Striker, Andrew is using a key to open a box in a vault room. He's putting three flash drives into his briefcase in a secret compartment in the bottom. Wires. The compartment is booby-trapped." I dropped the photo and kicked it away from me like it was a rattlesnake. Horror. Repulsion. I couldn't abide a psychic connection to evil. I gulped water from a bottle that Jack had set beside me and vomited. I aimed for the wastebasket, but I found it hard to hold my head up. Groaning, I collapsed on the floor. "I need to close my eyes."

Time passed.

My body ached, the burns screamed, the welts, covering me from the whiplashes, swelled, raw and angry. I cried and moaned from the pain.

My team hovered. Fists tight. Jaws clenched. Their distress

was tangible; I could taste it — thick and salty. It combined with the bile on the back of my throat and choked me.

Another phone call came in. Striker listened on speaker. "Sir, we're at the address of the Hildebrandt home. There's no one here."

I pulled myself painfully up into the chair and picked up the drawing of the baby; I asked her where she had gone. I put the pen on the map, starting at the Hildebrandt house, and traced a route. This time I got a clear picture in my mind. I wrote down the address.

"The woman who lives in this house is a good woman. She has no knowledge of any of the horror that her son helped to create by adopting Olivia. Please treat her with the utmost respect. She is so fragile. The shock will be difficult. Have medical support at the ready. This is the home of the paternal grandmother. The whole family is sitting down to her birthday dinner. The baby is sleeping in a crib, up the stairs, third door on the left."

The apprehension and extraction teams went out again, arrest warrants in hand, search warrants with the new address being faxed to the car. Iniquus got what it wanted when they wanted it; that was part of their success.

I laid myself back down on the floor. It felt better down there. The phone rang; Striker put it on speaker so I could hear. "Striker, sir, we've apprehended Naomi Brennon. Social Services is en route to help with the two children. Once they've arrived, we'll take her to the client for questioning," Clay said.

"Affirmative," Striker replied. "Make sure you're recording at all times."

"Yes, sir, Bonz had the camera on the entire capture."

Jack put another bottle of water down beside me. I struggled to sit up and drank some of it. It burned my throat, and I vomited it back into the wastebasket. I drank and vomited, drank and vomited. I needed to purge the toxins from me. I was panting from the exertion of sitting, and I dropped into a heap on the floor. I cried again. Softly, Anushka and I whimpered and moaned.

Striker lay down beside me. "Lynx... Chica," he called softly, careful not to touch me. I cracked my eyes open to see him. "They have the Hildebrandts in custody. The elderly Mrs. Hildebrandt is being taken to the hospital for observation. They have the baby. She's sleeping and healthy. Andrew's apprehension is in play. We need to get help to Anushka. Please tell me how to do this."

My voice squeaked from my raw throat. "They gave her poison. She wears it in a vial around her neck. She's supposed to swallow it if she thinks that she will be discovered. It will kill her, but in her mind, her death will save her child. I need to ask what to do."

I rolled onto my back. I breathed in slowly and sank deeper behind the Veil. I called for help — to what or whom I didn't know. I had never tried before. I was following my instincts. I waited, shivering now from the cold sweat covering me—lights and colors kaleidoscoped before my closed eyes. Then the answer played out for me in my mind's eyes like a movie. I heard Naomi's voice yelling down the stairs that she was going up to take a hot bath and relax. Anushka was to get herself covered up, and take the girls up to Vito's Pizzeria for dinner and keep them out of her hair because she had a sick headache. The girls were in the backyard playing. This was from a recording that was made of Naomi's voice being played on a computer by one of our operator s.

In the movie came an image of Anushka gathering herself up from her hiding place in the wall. She washed up in the bathroom, dressed, put on her coat, and limped outside to find the girls. As she looked around the jungle gym and in the playhouse for the children, the team raced in and restrained her before she could do herself harm. They were careful not to have any weapons on them. Anushka could not be asked to think or act rationally. She was immediately tranquilized for her own protection.

When she regained consciousness in the hospital, a uniformed woman was holding Anastasia out to her mother.

I whispered, "Thank you," and opened my eyes again.

Striker was still lying next to me.

"Did I say that out loud? Do you understand the plan?" I asked him.

"Jack is on the phone, arranging it. We're telling Naomi we know about the drug, and she will be charged with first-degree murder if anything happens to this girl. Naomi's been cooperating so far. I'm sure she'll do this. As soon as Bonz and Clay have the recording, they'll send it to the rescue team's computer. Medical is already in place. The tranquilizer is en route."

I nodded; nothing to do now but wait and hope for speed of action. I wanted my own meds. I wanted to go blissfully into the deep, deep sleep I knew awaited me when I came fully back out of the Veil.

I felt enormous pain as Anushka roused herself and pulled her clothes on to her body. I cried out and sobbed in distress, though I knew Anushka held her groans back behind clenched teeth. Her body swayed up the stairs as she forced her legs to bend and straighten, bend and straighten. She stood outside in the cold air, calling for the little girls — frantic when she didn't see or hear them, afraid they were lost or injured — not for the children's sake, but for her own, and that of her baby. Flashes of gray, as men sprang from nowhere; a scream of terror wrenched from our throats. In my office, my teammates jumped at the sound, their eyes wide with shock. Anushka and I were restrained by the extraction team, and a tranquilizer pricked into our vein.

I flung myself back toward reality…but the tranquilizer… Someone banged at the Puzzle Room door. Blaze stepped out into the hallway to reassure the men who had gathered there that everything was fine; they had just heard a portion of a surveillance tape we were reviewing.

The phone rang. Striker whispered to me, "Lynx, Anushka, and the baby are safe and heading to the hospital. Please, please come back out now."

I was trying, but the medication they gave Anushka made it hard for me to stay conscious. I was so dopey. I struggled away from Anushka toward myself.

"Jack?" I called.

"Here, Lynx." He crouched beside me.

"I'm back."

"We can help you now?"

"Please." And that's all I had in me.

Jack checked my vitals while Striker cut away my yoga pants and shirt. Blood had seeped into the fabric, dried, and adhered my clothes to my wounds. Striker tugged gently, painfully ripping off my scabs. I bled again, becoming a sticky mess.

Deep ran for the bathroom to vomit when he saw the burn marks on my inner thighs. They were oozing with chunks of flesh hanging off me. As my team worked on cleaning me up, they spoke minimally and in hushed tones.

Gator brought up medical supplies. He ran an IV with dextrose wide open. "Lynx," he spoke quietly in my ear, "your vitals show you're in a lot of pain. Can I please run some morphine in your drip?"

232 | FIONA QUINN

I nodded ever so slightly.

My body acted of its own accord. I shook with cold. I sweated. As the pain meds smoothed the edges of my agony, I felt my oxygen levels drop, my heart barely pumped. They put a mask over my nose and mouth.

After they cleaned me and dressed my wounds, Jack and Striker lifted me, ever so gently, on to a roll-away bed they'd somehow produced. They lowered the lights, so I could sleep. I heard them talking as they sat on the floor, their backs against the wall, watching me.

"Fucking A," Gator bit out. "What the hell was that? That was like living in some fucking sci-fi film. That was fucking insane."

"Sir, is that what happened to Lynx in the safe house?" Blaze asked softly.

"Lynx went through a similar experience when she saved Lynda and Cammy." Striker confirmed, his voice tightly controlled, masking his emotions. "Lynx trained with Miriam Laugherty, the psychic who does remote searches for the police."

"I've heard of her. Laugherty was one of Lynx's un-schooling teachers?" Deep asked.

"Yup." Out of the corner of my eye, I saw Striker stretch his long legs out in front of him. "Someone noticed along the way that Lynx is intuitive, so they hooked her up with Laugherty. Laugherty was training Lynx to be her protégé, but you see what happens to her. Lynx decided that doing these kinds of remote searches wasn't for her, and she walked away from all that."

"Until the safe house," Jack said.

"Right. She decided to help me when Lynda and Cammy went missing. Had I known then what she would go through, I never would have handed her my photographs. I'm not sure I understand why she went behind the Veil for this case. Jack?"

"Don't know, Striker. She took the photos from Gator and sucked air like she was shocked by what she saw. Her eyes got that look. You didn't see this part back at the safe house, but Lynx was in terrible shape before you got there with your photos. I can't describe it, but I will never forget it. I knew what she was about to do as soon as I saw her face change. I tried to get her to wait for you to get in — thinking maybe you could talk her out of it. Maybe it had something to do with the baby," Jack said, "You know how she is around dogs and babies. She just can't help herself, even to her own detriment. Damned brave."

"You know how she's always saying that she don't do no deeds of daring-do-or-die?" Gator asked. "Total crap. I ain't never seen no one ever face something like that." Gator's voice cracked on the last word.

Through slit eyes, I saw his gaze resting on me. "She's gonna be okay, though, right? Like at the safe house — there was all that blood and slime, looked like a chain saw murder happened in there. But after a week passed, she woke up fine. She weren't permanently damaged or scarred nor nothing."

"I'm hoping that's the case here, too." Striker came over to see me. "Hey, I thought you were supposed to be sleeping through this."

"Me, too. I want to. This is excruciating."

"What can we do? We'll do anything. Do you want meds to put you out?"

"No, no. I have to go on my own…" I panted as I waited for an answer to come to me. "It's Gator. He's taking this hard. He's holding me here. Let me talk to him."

"Hey, Gator?" Striker called softly. "Come here for a minute."

Gator crept over on silent feet, took a knee, and reached for my hand.

"Look at me and know I'm telling you the truth, okay?"

Gator forced his gaze to mine. "Yes, ma'am."

"I'm going to be fine. I need to sleep to gather myself back and heal. Your job, along with everyone else in this room, is to guard me and my secret. The mission is over. I'm not going to be hurt anymore. I'm not going behind the Veil when I sleep. Do you trust what I'm saying to you?"

"Yes, ma'am." His words were so soft I strained to hear them. But they brought a sigh of relief to my lips.

"Will you sit with me until I go under?"

He sat in a chair with my hand between both of his.

I knew this was where Striker wanted to be, but it was Gator who was holding me to this plane.

Maybe by holding my hand, he could let me go…

23

For six days, I drifted in blackness, unaware of anything happening around me. Finally, the world came into focus. A harsh light coming from my bathroom hit across my eyes — Striker stared at me from his place, leaning against the wall, arms crossed over his chest.

"Hi," I whispered.

"Hi." He worked his jaw. Tension tightened his eyes.

"What day is it?"

"Saturday." He pushed off the wall and came to stand next to my bed. "You've been gone for almost a week. How do you feel?" Striker brusquely flicked on a lamp sitting near my head. I pushed my covers off and checked my arms and legs. They had healed completely. I moved around a bit to see how everything was working.

I glanced over at the medic. "can you unhook me, please?"

He stepped forward and removed my catheter and IV line.

I sent him a smile of gratitude, then turned my attention back to Striker.

"How do you feel?" he asked again.

"I'm a little stiff — but that'll wear off. You look as bad as you did in the safe house. Your face is gray."

"Yeah?" He scratched his hand through his hair. "It's a pretty hellish thing to participate in. We're all pretty messed up about this. It's probably a conversation that needs to wait, but what in blazes did you think you were doing?" He glowered at me.

I sat cross-legged on the roll-away bed in a pair of panties and an over-sized T-shirt, my covers pulled up to my hips. "I don't know. This is something I would normally have refused." I furrowed my brow in thought. "This time, though, the call was strong, and I had the impression — and this is going to sound crazy, but I had the impression that your ladies from Africa were involved here."

"They wouldn't be. I don't have any personal connection to this case."

His tone shocked me. "No, no." I was off-kilter — my body, my thoughts, my emotions. "This wasn't about you. It was supposed to be a gift to me. There was something I was supposed to learn — uh-uh, that's the wrong word..." I sat for a minute and waited for the right word to bubble up. "...Discover. There was something I was supposed to discover that would help me — save me."

"And what did you discover?" He tilted his head to the side. Curiosity crept into his gaze.

"I have no idea." I shook my head in confusion. "Maybe when I need it most, it will come to me."

"Maybe, or maybe you're just trying to spin this in a direction that feels safe." He was back to angry.

What a slimy thing to say. I couldn't keep up with his yo-yo, un-Striker-like emotions. I had my own to deal with. "And you say this because you've known me to lie? Or stretch the truth with you before?"

He threw his hands in the air and then rested them, balled into fists, on his hips. "No, Lynx, your honesty is not in question. It's…" His voice broke, and he was pleading. "Chica, I don't want you to do this ever again. I mean, if you're trying to save yourself, or someone that you love or care about, someone directly connected to you, then maybe, maybe I would understand that, but, Lynx, this isn't to happen again."

"Is that an order?" Defiance painted my words scarlet. How dare he tell me what to do.

"I'm talking to you as Team Lead. I know you don't fall under my command. I'm not commanding you." His face had affected that impermeable mask. He wasn't open to debate. "You need our support and our resources to be effective, and I won't make those available to you if you go Veil walking on a whim."

"Veil walking?" My eyebrows shot up.

"Whatever. I don't even know what to call this. It's terrifying to watch." His nostrils flared with exasperation.

I was obviously taxing his patience, and Striker's patience always seemed ocean-deep.

When he looked at me again, his equilibrium was back in place. "Okay. Let me put this another way. You have the idea that this event was teaching you, preparing you for some challenge to come. Until then, can we leave this tool in your toolbox and only take it out on rare occasions? I mean, like never?" He was sitting beside me now, pulling me into his arms.

My voice lost its defensive timbre. "Believe me, that's my plan," I whispered back.

Striker shifted his hip to pull his phone out from his pocket, then punched a number on his speed dial. "She's awake," he said and disconnected.

"Who was that?" I asked.

"Gator. He's on his way." Striker pushed another button. "Jack, she's awake."

I excused myself to the bathroom for a minute to brush my teeth and run a comb through my hair. When I came back, my office was full.

I flashed them a big smile. "Hey, guys."

No one smiled back. They all looked exhausted and haunted. They sat and stared at me, and I let them.

"Men, normally after an assignment like this, we'd have already debriefed and been assessed. Obviously, that's not going to happen here. The best I can do is to let you talk to Lynx, ask her your questions."

No one said anything for a long time. I decided to start, "Can you tell me the status of the case? How is Anushka?"

"She's been moved off to middle America under a new name. They've got her at a mental care facility within a hospital. She's scheduled for surgery next week to repair…some things that were damaged by Brennon. Brennon is being held under high security." Striker answered in his normal debriefing voice— facts, not emotions.

More silence.

Gator started in slowly, carefully choosing his words. "Ma'am, I've seen a lot of things. A lot of them were heinous deeds no man should ever have to see. The thing about them was, I was there in the fight. I never had to sit on my hands before and watch a female take it on. It's not really in my make up to be able to do that… I know you're an operator, just like me, and if I could have done what you were doing, it would've been me doing it. Or, maybe even if I were fighting beside you, it might have been all right. This weren't all right."

The other men nodded their agreement.

"I know Jack and Striker have been through this with you

before. And I'm real grateful that you saved Lynda and Cammy. But this weren't family. I guess maybe if you could tell me why you did this, it might help some. To be honest, I don't ever want you to do it no more. Surely, we could have gotten Brennan some other way."

"I understand what you're saying, Gator," I said. "Let me try to tell you a little about what happened, okay? First, Striker probably told you that I was training to do remote searches and that going through the Veil is dangerous for me. So I stopped. I can do little things from time to time, like find someone's dog or even a lost child. But that's a completely different skillset from what I used for Lynda and Anushka."

"Lynx." Deep stepped forward. "Sometimes you say or do things out of the blue that seems like ESP, and it's got nothing to do with someone being lost. Like when I need a certain file, and you walk in with it. Or, I'm looking for a word when I'm writing a report, and you say the word I need out loud."

"Things come to me." I shrugged. "It's nothing like walking behind the Veil, which I trained to be able to do, and demands so much more of me."

I pulled my legs up to sit cross-legged on the roll-away bed and pulled the blanket back over me.

"So the Veil sort of sucks you in?" Blaze asked.

"No. It's not like that. I accept the opportunity to go. I'm beckoned. In the safe house, maybe you remember, Deep and Jack, you were on duty the day that Lynda was kidnapped. You saw me."

Both men nodded.

"I was being called to duty. I was glad to go. Like you said, Gator — that was family. In return, though, I was also given information. I was told about Wilson's proximity, and I was told how to get him into custody. We don't know how bad things might have gotten had we not known this information. We don't know if I would have been hurt worse, or killed, or if one of you would have been…"

Again the men nodded, acknowledging what I was saying. I could tell, though, that there was a clear distinction in their minds between my helping Striker, and my helping Anushka.

Maybe they forgot that Brennan was a terrorist and America was at risk.

Or maybe the alphabets had never planned to let Brennan on that plane, and so our involvement was merely to put a feather in our cap, which would have made my efforts seem foolish at best.

Except I hadn't really been thinking about America when I made my decision.

I was focused on the African women's call.

"So, here we are a few months later, and again the Veil was opened to me, un- bidden. It wasn't the same experience as with Striker. Like you said, it wasn't personal. This was a girl in a photo. All I can tell you is that…my instincts told me…I had a 'knowing' that this was important. And while I thought it was important to help the girl in the photo, I thought it was more important to my own survival. I don't know why. I can't explain it. When I have it figured out, though, you guys'll be the first to know." I searched the skeptical faces in front of me for forgiveness. "You have to understand, I did this for selfish, self-preserving reasons. And I'm sorry for the obviously horrible distress I put you all through." I ended in a whisper.

"This was your choice," Blaze said.

"That's right. I always have the choice to go beyond or not."

"And when you went, you were connecting to different people, and what they experienced is what you experienced?" Blaze continued.

"That's right. Though the physical damage done to me is a mere shadow of what is happening to the victim." I nodded.

"You don't have to connect with people. You can connect to objects. Like when you were searching for Lynda, you asked the car where it was going," Jack said. "Wouldn't it be safer to sit and observe through an inanimate object? Like, instead of connecting to Anushka, maybe you could have been a vase on the shelf?"

"Objects don't process sensory information. When I asked the car where it was going, my hand was moved on the map tracing the direction — no thoughts or insights were involved. In order for me to understand what's going on, I need to have sensations and thoughts. Being connected to Anushka gave me her story and the way to save her. We never could have guessed any of that. We were after Brennon for extortion, cyber-terrorism, and espionage. Anushka and Anastasia would never have been discovered."

I looked at the men's eyes. They hadn't softened. They still felt angry with me and my decision. I sighed loudly, a little defeated. "Anushka will eventually be able to testify. She heard and saw quite a bit. That's neither here nor there. To answer your question, Jack — no, the way I do it, the rules that I have asked you to follow, that's the best I can do to protect myself."

"Okay, well, what about it coming in from the other direction? Couldn't you get the information from the attacker instead of the victim? That way, you wouldn't be hurt." Blaze asked.

"Oh, no. I would much rather face the risks of being a victim than the risks of being in the head of someone like Brennon while he's committing an act of violence. No. That's much too dangerous."

I could tell that my team didn't understand what I was saying, and I had no good way of explaining the dangers of evil on the other side of the Veil. The seduction of it. How the evil seeped into my cells, sinking sharp talons into me. The few times I connected to evil, it was always a hard fight to extricate myself from its vice-like grasp. I remembered the brief brush I had when I saw Brennon's picture, and it took me to the vault with him, and I shuddered. That feeling was intolerable.

We sat for a minute in silence.

"And you're okay now?" Gator asked.

I pulled off the covers and stood there in my T-shirt and pink cotton panties. I lifted my shirt to expose my belly. I showed them my arms and legs had healed as if nothing had happened. "The real scars of my life, like the ones I got from Wilson's attacks, I keep those. The wounds and scars I get when I go behind the Veil are illusions of a sort. As I gather myself to me and separate from the person who sustained the real trauma, then I keep what's mine, and they keep what's theirs."

"When you were helping Cammy, were you taking on the same medication she was?" Striker's gaze pushed against me.

"Right. But she's a tiny little girl. What was too much for her body could be supported by mine."

"What about when Anushka was sedated?" Jack asked.

"Once they tranquilized her, I tried to come back quickly, before she went all the way under. It was hard for me to walk back through the Veil drugged."

"And that means if Anushka had swallowed the poison, then you…" Jack stopped mid-thought, obviously unwilling to voice the outcome.

"Then I would have reacted to the poison as if it were in my body, probably to a lesser degree, though. Again, what you saw happening to me was a shadow of what was happening to Anushka."

"Jeezus — that poor girl." Blaze rubbed his hands over his head.

"If the person you're connected to dies…if they had beaten Lynda to death while you were with her, then you would have died too?" Striker was standing now, hands on hips, face ashen.

"That's my theory, though hopefully, I'll never know how that really bears out. It could be that I would have nothing to connect to anymore, and I could walk back through the Veil. I don't know," I whispered, shocked by his question. I hadn't extrapolated it all the way out before.

Striker excused himself and walked quietly out of my office.

"Lynx, when you were connected, you could still talk to us, and you could ask us to confirm or refute something. How is that possible?" Blaze pulled me back to the Puzzle Room — my thoughts had gone through the door with Striker.

"Sometimes, I'm not sure if I'm talking out loud. I hope I am. Sometimes I try to put one foot on each side of the Veil, one here and one there, so that I can relay information. It's hard to do. It's not exactly painful. It's more… well, there isn't really a word for it…exhausting…uncomfortable. I struggle to be in both places." The men nodded. This part they seemed to get.

"As far as the confirmations go, they are incredibly important. That information is for my rational self and your rational selves. To me, it's like a horrible nightmare I'm living through." I pulled on a pair of yoga pants from my closet and reached for a sweatshirt. "How do I know it's not a nightmare? How do I know I'm not going crazy and telling you random crazy things? How do you have enough conviction to send teams of people out to follow up on my raving words? It is all so irrational. Having an outside source, who knows nothing about what's going on, confirm the validity of what I'm saying helps all of us stay sane. And you'll notice that I'm never refuted. I'm always confirmed.

That gives all of us a layer of confidence, which can help us get through."

"Could you do the Veil walking for cases that wouldn't put you in harm's way?" Deep asked.

"How do you mean, Deep?"

"Like this Consuela woman. Could you go and sit in her brain and figure out what's going on?"

"Like surveillance? Um, no. First of all, she doesn't have a shimmer."

"A 'shimmer'?" Deep asked.

"That's what I call the energy that radiates off of a person — like a ripple or a shiver in the air. It's where their aura is...um... jagged?" I looked around to see if that made any sense at all. Heads nodded, so I moved on. "A shimmer is rare and usually involves situations that are life-or-death. Hey, you guys look like shit, by the way."

"Yeah. It's been hard to sleep and eat lately," Gator said.

"Jack and Striker had the same problem last time. Remember, Jack?"

"All too well, Lynx."

"After I woke up, you were okay after that, right?"

"I guess. You aren't going to do this anymore, are you?" Jack asked.

"I promise you, I promise all of you, I will only walk behind the Veil for two reasons: to help myself or to help family. If one of you were in need, I wouldn't think twice. I would fly out of my body." I held up my hand against their protests. "Just like you'd walk in front of a bullet for me. You know you would, so that's going to have to be our understanding. Okay?"

24

I found Striker sitting at his desk, his elbows resting on the arms of his chair, steepling his fingers in front of his face. I slid onto his lap and waited for him to look me in the eye.

I cupped his chin in my palm. "It's over," I said.

"I don't think so. Were you telling me the truth about the women from Africa? They were trying to show you something to save you?"

"That was my 'knowing.' Yes." I curled up, so my head rested against his chest. His arms wrapped around me, his cheek brushed against my hair.

"I don't want you playing with Consuela anymore. You're done. I want you to come to the barracks and live at my place until she loses interest."

"You're about to leave on your mission next week."

"I tried to get this re-assigned or postponed, but Command says they need me now."

"Gator's got my back." I tilted my head so I could see his eyes.

"Don't get me wrong, Gator's as good as they come. He's the

guy I'd want next to me, no matter what the situation—him, Jack, the whole Strike Force Team. I like how we all work together. But walking away when there's crazy in your life is a hard thing to do, Chica."

"If you're going to love me, then you're going to have to get used to crazy. I'm a crazy magnet."

"I'm starting to understand how true that is." Striker's arms tightened around me as he stood up. He turned me into a tight hug and bent to kiss me. His mouth pressed against mine, warm and gentle; I could taste his exhaustion.

"Let's go to your place, so I can tuck you into bed," I said.

Striker collapsed onto his mattress, drained. He pulled me under the covers with him holding me tightly against his body. I figured he needed to feel I was safe so that he could sleep deeply. Though I wasn't tired at all, lying here with him was the least I could do after his week's vigil. And soon he'd be gone.

We gathered out on the Iniquus lawn after lunch. Axel, our team's explosives expert, manipulated the computerized robot, stalking Brennon's briefcase that lay out in the sun on the other side of the field. As Axel maneuvered the robot up to the case, the team was laughing and having a great time. Robots and explosives — might as well have been Christmas morning.

We all watched the monitor closely; the robot stood flush with the case. A pincer reached out to twirl the locking system, using the combination that I had uncovered while behind the

Veil. The mechanical arm moved with amazing dexterity, slowly releasing the catch and retrieving the papers and files.

Axel wiggled the toggles, and the robot zipped back to us with the booty. Again Axel maneuvered the machine to the case. The robot sent a video image to our laptop; I studied the screen until I could show Axel where the concealed latch protected the hidden compartment. We all held our breath while Axel maneuvered the motorized claw to release the hook.

Even though the authorities definitely had enough evidence and testimony to implicate Brennon on slavery, kidnapping, and torture charges, we really hoped to solve the cyber-terrorism case. Both because we wanted to make sure we had scooped up all of the accomplices, but also because Iniquus pride and prestige in having protected America hung in the balance.

The robot headed back with the flash drives to the sound of cheering. Axel sent the robot back in to detonate the explosives. A loud bang with an impressive fireball and shower of sparks made us all duck and cover. The men laughed and slapped each other on the back. Boys.

While Deep took the information to the computer lab for analysis, Striker and I headed to my house. I needed to pack my bags and tell my friends I was going on a business trip for a while and that I wasn't sure when I'd be back. We drove down Silver Lake Road and around a huge moving van parked in front of Maria's house.

"What the heck?" Striker swung into an open parking space in front of my house and pulled out his phone. We waited inside the Iniquus Hummer while Striker listened to Command. I could feel his frustration mounting.

"Understood." His clipped voice ended the conversation.

"You're not happy."

"Nope, not happy." Striker got out of the vehicle and came around just in time to catch me as I jumped down.

"Can you tell me what's going on?"

He waited until we were at my house before he answered. "Tactical failure. Apparently, Consuela figured out her computer was being remotely viewed. She swept the house and spent yesterday evening destroying all of our equipment. Now she's moving out."

"And you're upset because when she was here, we could keep an eye on her. Now that she's moving, she'll be in the mists?"

"Exactly." He held my curtain to the side as he watched out my front window. "I need you to talk to the neighbors. See if you can pick up any gossip

"Okay." I moved toward my stairs. "I'll throw some things in my bags. People should be coming home from work soon, and I can make the rounds. You still want me to move to the barracks now that she's gone?"

"Definitely." The tension under his eyes was a give-away. This was serious.

"And this is still for my safety's sake?" I looked up at him coyly.

Striker gave me a wink. "Yeah, I want to guard your body."

As soon as I spotted Manny and Justin gabbing on the sidewalk, I abandoned my packing and sauntered over.

"Hey, did you see Consuela moved out today?" I pointed toward her house.

"She got transferred. What a drag after just getting settled in," Justin said.

"Yeah? Where's she relocating?" I shoved my hands deep in my pockets.

"New York City," Manny said.

"And her house? Is that going back on the market?"

Justin looked back over his shoulder at Consuela's house. "She said she's going to rent it to her niece."

"Her niece?" Holy cow, now what?

"Kid's living in a bad situation. Boyfriend problems. Consuela was trying to get her to come and live with her, but the girl, Tammy, is young and didn't want to live under her aunt's thumb, so now that Consuela is leaving, she's going to rent the house and move in."

"Have you met her? Tammy, I mean," I pressed.

"Yeah, I know her. She's babysat for my boys a couple of times. Cute girl. Not the sharpest knife in the drawer, though, if you know what I mean," Manny said.

"Do you happen to know Tammy's last name?"

"Pineda. Why?" asked Manny.

"Curious about my new neighbor." Curious to know what the hell Consuela's got planned, that is. "She grow up in this area?"

"Consuela said she graduated from my old high school, Woodrow Wilson, so Tammy's been here for a while." Justin was twirling his keys and looking over at his car with a got-a-go stance.

"Any other gossip I should know about?" I asked.

"None that comes to mind," Manny said.

"Okay, then I need to give you guys hugs. I'm off to some computer training for my work. I'm not sure how long I'll be out of town. They said at the office that if things got busy, they'd have to call me back to Washington. Can you keep an eye on my house? Make sure it's not on fire or anything? I'll be reachable on my cell."

"Will do." Manny released me from a bear hug. "Hey, you be safe now."

"I'll try." I waved good-bye. Cowardly or not, I was thankful to be heading to Striker's to live far away from all this mess. As I strolled toward my porch, my mouth bowed with pleasure. The vibrations that tickled my nerves had nothing to do with my fear of leopard woman and everything to do with my thoughts of spending time with oh-so-delectable Commander Rheas.

25

"Chica, what kinds of things did you pack in your bag?" Striker asked. We were cozied up on the couch in his living room, watching the evening news.

"Um, I have workout clothes, regular work clothes, and a couple of dresses with heels."

"Fancy dresses?"

"No, regular dresses. Why?" My curiosity was piqued. A date?

"We're in the field on assignment tomorrow night, and we need you with us."

Not a date. Shoot. "What's up?"

"It's a delicate situation." He eased down the sofa to rest his head on the back. "We have a guy we need to run surveillance on. He's got bucks, and he's got a security team. A good one. He put a call in to Cachet for a girl for tomorrow night. The manager there has a working relationship with Iniquus, so he's going to let you take the job."

"I'm taking it that Cachet is a prostitution ring?"

"Escort service. They provide intelligent, well-mannered, beautiful women for out-of-town clientele. It's the girl's call whether she pursues extra-curricular activities. We need you to be scintillating company and make sure he takes you back to his hotel. Get him to have a little spiked drink, and let us in through the balcony. We'll do our work, and you'll leave the way you came in so as not to arouse suspicion. If at any time you think things aren't going well, you'll bail, okay?"

Striker had an odd glint in his eye.

I tilted my head as if that would help me read him better. "Yeah, okay. What's the mark's name?"

"Griffin Babcock. I'll get you all of the particulars later. Your name is going to be Gabriella Ricci."

There it was again, a brief shadow across the eyes. Huh. My guess was he was keeping something from me. "That's pretty. I like it. It's Italian, though."

"He requested an Italian girl."

Italian? I was of Irish descent, for heaven's sake. "Striker, how am I going to pull that off?"

"Don't know. I was hoping you had something in your bag of tricks."

"Okay. Where am I going?"

"Halston Ball."

I sat bolt upright. "No way! Are you kidding me? That's going to be full of politicians and celebrities. I don't have a gown suitable for that. I'll have to call Celia and ask her if she has something."

"Yeah — about those political types. We need you to plant a bug on Babcock as soon as he's in the car. You'll be wired, as well. We need to make his connections."

I waited for more, but Striker was suddenly very engrossed by a Tide commercial. I knew that was all I'd pull from him tonight.

The next day, I drove over to Celia's so I could look through her closet and try on a few of her gowns. Celia and I were the same size, and as the wife to a bajillionaire, her job was to look marvelous. What that meant to me was lots of free, beautiful clothes. Since Celia did red carpets and celebrity dinners all the time, I was sure she'd have the right thing for Gabriella Ricci to wear tonight hanging in her closet.

As I drove, I thought through my next move with my Maria problem. I needed to investigate this Tammy chick and see how involved she was with her auntie. I'd ask Iniquus to run surveillance equipment through the house again and Tammy's car. I wondered how long it would last. Would Maria come and do a sweep again? Well, even that would be information. It would mean that Maria was concerned about what we'd pick up. I'd do a background check on Tammy for sure. Casting a wide net, maybe I would catch a new lead.

Beyond that, I wanted to locate Maria's husband. See if he was on anyone's grid.

"Celia, you have wonderful taste. I love these gowns. They're beautiful. Are you sure it's okay for me to borrow one?" I held up a dress cut like a Grecian goddess's.

"More than okay. You know I can't wear them again, and they're just taking up my closet space. I don't like that one." Celia wrinkled her nose. "That bronze is too hard for a blond to wear — it looks harsh."

"Why do you have it? You're as fair as I am." I looked at my reflection in her floor to ceiling mirror.

"A designer friend gave it to me as a gift. I've never actually worn it, myself." Celia was sprawled across her bed with her head resting on her hands, kicking her bent legs like a schoolgirl.

"Do you mind if I try it on? See if it fits?"

"Knock yourself out." Celia flopped onto her back. "Do you have a Spanx with you? Grab one out of my drawer there."

I tried the dress on. Standing on my toes, I looked in the mirror. I thought it looked acceptably Italian.

"See?" Celia asked. "You look terrible. It's the wrong color for you. Try the indigo one I laid out. It's comfy and beautiful on."

"You know, I think I'm going to use this one if it's okay with you. I'm going to get a spray tan, so that should help."

Celia made a face. "Okay, if that's the one you want, you're welcome to it. Take the Spanx. Don't wear hose. Here." Celia crawled off her bed and went into her closet to draw out a shoebox with a pair of strappy sandals that matched the hue of the dress perfectly. She pawed through her jewelry closet and pulled out a snake arm-cuff that went above the elbow. The snake's eyes looked like rubies, and it stuck out a diamond-studded tongue.

"It's a fake," Celia said. "But it looks fun with that dress."

I gave Celia a quick kiss good-bye and left with my loot. My next stop was the day spa. I chose a dark garnet polish for my mani/pedi and went as dark as the technician dared with the spray-on-tan. In their salon, the stylist used a temporary hair color in deep chestnut to darken my hair and eyebrows. They dyed my eyelashes black. I stared at myself in the mirror. Wow, I looked creepy being so dark with my pale blue eyes, like a

Voodoo priestess. I left with my hair styled in big, soft, almost-black curls.

When I got back to the barracks, Striker wasn't home. I found my wire on the countertop with a note, "Wish I were there to help you get this in place. I'll be back to pick you up at six — Striker."

I checked my watch. I still had ten minutes until the Iniquus photographer would be here to get my picture for my fake ID.

———

I stared into the bathroom mirror and saw the shock on my face reflected back at me. My makeup brush dangled in my fingers. I had been thinking of Babcock and the mission when Hydra Marionette glowed before me. A "knowing."

Shoot.

Is Striker going to tell me at the briefing? I tapped my foot. Well, I'd soon find out.

With the tech gone to get my driver's license manufactured, I finished up the makeup job, trying to find the right balance between lovely lady and arm-candy-for-hire. My dark brown contact lenses really helped. I pulled on my Spanx, strapped on my heels, and lifted the soft, silky fabric up over my hips.

When I heard Striker at the door, I drifted out for inspection, pulling the snake up my left arm. Striker gave a start when he saw me.

"Striker? It's me." I laughed. I guess that meant I was pretty well disguised.

Striker walked around me, looking me over. "That's amazing." A wolfish grin spread over his lips.

My breath hitched. "Thank you." I managed. "Italian enough to make Babcock happy, you think?"

"Babcock's going to be happy. Maybe a little too happy." Striker narrowed his eyes. Was that jealousy I read there?

"We need to make sure he stays at the party," Striker said. "He can't be racing back to his hotel room with you." He paused for a beat. "Let me clarify: his hotel room is the most important part of the plan. That takes precedence. But the longer he stays at the party, the better. We'd like to see who he knows and what he talks about at the ball. You'll need to follow your instincts. We'll have eyes and ears on you the whole time, so whatever happens, we'll have your back."

Deep walked in, dressed in his perfectly tailored tuxedo. He nodded at Striker and shot a curious glance at me. "How do you do, ma'am," Deep said.

Striker bent over laughing. "This is Lynx."

"Lynx?" Deep took a step closer and scanned over me. He let out a low whistle. "Damn, woman."

Okay, so I knew my disguise was a good one.

Striker reviewed the plans for the evening with Deep and me. He checked to make sure my wire was functional and handed me my fake driver's license and credit cards, which I slid into my evening bag.

Striker drove me over to Cachet Mansion, where Babcock's limo was supposed to pick me up.

I broke the silence. "Is there anything you need to tell me about this mission?"

Striker turned his head to glance at me, then turned back to the road. "You're thoroughly briefed. Was there something you need to go over?" he asked.

I crossed my arms tightly under my breasts. Nope. No mention of the Sylanos connection. I sent a vehement look over to Striker.

He glanced my way again. "What?" he asked as he pulled to

an abrupt halt in front of the massive carved doors of the mansion.

"Nothing." I flounced out of the car. Bewilderment etched his face as I slammed the door shut. Well, that was mature and highly professional of me.

26

Babcock was an odd little man with a huge, shaggy, prematurely gray head. His body started with thin sloped shoulders from which his belly and hips swelled like a giant raindrop. His tiny feet were ensconced in beautiful leather dress shoes.

"*Sei molto bella stasera, mia cara,*" he whispered in my ear. His breath smelled of garlic and scotch.

"*Grazie non vedo l'ora di una serata favolosa con te.*"

"You speak Italian!" He vibrated when he said that. Maybe odd was an understatement.

"I call it kitchen Italian." I gave him a friendly smile. "My Nona was always busy cooking delicious things for us, and I liked to help her. She was from Sienna and never got around to learning English. And you? Where is your Italian from? Family?"

"No, no. I have a villa near Milan. Do you know Milan?"

"I've never been." I sighed my disappointment.

"If we get along as well as I think we will, perhaps I'll take you to my villa."

"Oh, I'd like that." I smiled. "Now, what shall I call you?"

"Babcock." He emphasized the last syllable.

I gave him a mischievous look. "Oh, you are a bad boy, Babcock." That sent him over the edge; he giggled madly. He didn't seem like he could be a Hydra Marionette, I mused.

Our driver pulled up to the hotel. The attendant opened my door and held out a hand to me. We started up the carpeted entrance, me in my heels towering over Babcock's five-foot-five frame. Inside, we stood in the receiving line. Babcock was regaling me with an explanation of how automatic windshield wipers knew when to turn on.

After giving the room a cursory scan — getting the lay of the land — I refocused my attention on Babcock, trying to take in what he was blathering about. I prepared myself for a long night of this. I smiled and nodded as if he were telling me the most interesting story in the world.

We rounded the corner, moving toward the head of the line. Security checked our invitation, then Babcock's and my identifications. *Thank you, Iniquus, for your attention to detail.* We lined up, ready to shake hands in the receiving line, and who should be the second hostess in line?

Celia.

I looked around, trying to figure a way around this debacle. Nope. Nothing. I'd have to move through with everyone else and shake Celia's hand if I were to get into the ball. My mind flew to all of the things I could say if she called me by my real name, or mentioned where I worked, or... dear God, this was a nightmare.

"Griffin Babcock escorting Miss Gabriella Ricci," Babcock said.

Celia stared at my dress. Her eyes moved to the snake on my arm, then up to my face. For just the quickest flash, just the smallest instant, I could see Celia's mind hard at work. Then her face became placid, if a little bored, and she said, "What a beautiful dress. It's perfect for your coloring, Miss Ricci. I hope you have a wonderful evening." She turned to the next person in line.

I loved Celia. I'd blown my cover — she'd know I wasn't an office worker the way I said I was — and I'd need to explain my job to her now, but at this moment, I was safe.

Griffin Babcock was a well-connected man with obvious intelligence. Men in designer tuxes and women in haute couture asked his opinions on everything from foreign affairs, to the stock market, to art collection. He was certainly not lonely. He seemed to enjoy saying my name as he introduced me to people, trilling the r in Ricci. He looked approvingly at me when I stood next to him, as if we belonged to one another, without my fawning or draping like a hooker.

A man approached — it was the one man whom Babcock did not introduce me to. They talked about mergers and acquisitions. This guy cast uncertain glances in my direction and breathed heavier than perhaps he should, shifting from foot to foot like he wanted to run. I looked impassively back at him, cradling my drink just below my breast-line, and I surreptitiously tap-tap-tapped my wire to give Control a heads up. The conversation sounded innocuous, but it looked and felt like something was being passed under the table. After the guy moved away, I asked Babcock who he was. Babcock changed the subject. Yup. I'd lay money that that was the unknown that Iniquus was trying to catch in their net. Hydra Marionette. I wondered how much Babcock knew or if he was being duped and used. He reminded me of an over-sized, very shaggy garden gnome — not someone who would be in bed with Sylanos.

After a yummy dinner, the band tuned up to play. Babcock danced hobgoblin jigs to the modern music, but he wasn't tone-deaf. When the music switched to waltzes and tangos, he was much more self-assured, though spinning under his arm gracefully was something of a trick. While I danced, I felt hard eyes on me and caught the mergers and acquisitions guy staring at me. Did something about my disguise shift? Was something off about me that made this guy's antennae go up? I caught a glimpse of Deep out of the corner of my eye. I turned my head, and he gave a discreet tap to his watch — it was time for the main event.

"Babcock, you're very popular." I smiled down at him.

He rewarded me with a wink and moved his hand from the small of my back to the curve of my bottom. Ugh.

I tilted my chin and cast what I hoped was a seductive smile his way. "I'm jealous. I'm done sharing you with everyone else. I want you all to myself. Now."

His smile dropped off, and his mouth hung open; he snapped it shut. Babcock took me by the elbow and purposefully steered me to the front entrance while he called his limo to collect us.

Into the car, and on top of me. Double ugh.

"Babcock." I giggled as I pushed him off. "Babcock, you're going to ruin my dress. If you muss me up, I'll look like a teenager coming home from the prom. And I want to be beautiful when you walk me through the lobby and onto the elevator. Don't you think everyone should be enviously imagining all of the wonderful things I'm going to do to you as soon as we're in private?"

"Yes." He nodded his lion's mane vigorously.

Quickly, I found myself on the elevator heading up to Babcock's penthouse suite. Two huge bodyguards paced at our heels. They'd been irritatingly within arm's reach all night, working hard at their jobs with their sunglasses and ear transmitters. Lots of show. They measured about the size of Jack. Jack was six-foot-five, probably 250 pounds of muscle. Big. I hoped I didn't end up going hand-to-hand with them, especially in this dress. My mind flitted to my Ruger strapped to my inner thigh.

Standing in the hall outside of the suite, Thing One said he wanted to pat me down. Oh, hell no. I snuggled closer to Babcock. "Baby, the only one who gets to pat me down is you. This isn't an orgy." My voice threatened that I'd leave if the guy laid hands on me.

Babcock looked indecisive.

I twirled in front of Thing Two. "Do you see any bulges on me? What exactly do you think your partner is feeling for? Does he always try to horn in on Babcock's dates?" I asked with derision.

Babcock took his cue from me. No one would touch me but him. Babcock keyed the room open and shooed the two away.

"I plan on giving you a very thorough body search." Babcock chuckled as he hitched off his jacket and tugged the ends of his bowtie.

"Champagne?" I smiled. "We need to toast this beautiful night and our meeting. I think it's fate. Don't you?"

"Absolutely." Babcock called down to room service for champagne and chocolate-covered strawberries.

We had come to make-it or break-it time. The mission was riding on me. No pressure, though. I took a steadying breath. "You're a wonderful dancer. I love how I feel in your arms. Could you find something romantic and slow on the stereo?" I asked.

Babcock headed over to the radio. Good glory, I hoped this kept him occupied until Deep could get here. I didn't think I could hold this guy off with small talk for much longer.

Come on, Deep! Where's that champagne?

Soon, a knock sounded at the door. Deep pushed a cart into the sitting room, popped the cork on the bottle, and poured a glass, assiduously averting his gaze from mine. Lifting the flute, I pressed my lips onto the rim to leave my lipstick mark. I needed to tell which glass was which. I moved to the other side of the room to draw Babcock's attention away from the powder packet that Deep was tapping into the second glass. Deep left, pocketing his tip with a slight bow.

"Oh, just leave it there, Babcock. I like that music. Come, let's make a toast." Our glasses clinked, and I pretended to sip.

"I have to tell you," I smiled over at him, "I'm not good at holding my alcohol. I'm fun with one, but you need to make sure I don't drink two, or I'll pass straight out."

"I'll keep you safe," Babcock told me gallantly. After we drank down our first glass — I dumped mine on the carpet when he wasn't looking — I poured more into our flutes.

"Hey, you said you should stop," Babcock protested mildly, but his pupils dilated, and his gaze skated down my dress.

"It's okay. I'm going to crawl into your bed with you. If I pass out?" I smiled what I hoped was a lascivious smile. "Well, you can do what you want with me."

Again, with the mouth gaping open — this time, he was sucking air.

"Babcock, baby. Are you okay? Was it something you ate? Should I call for a doctor? What's going on?" I colored my voice with quiet concern.

Babcock's eyes spread wide with fright. Eyes that trusted me.

"Come on, baby, let's get you in bed." I caught him by the arm and steered him toward the bedroom. Babcock didn't make it. He fell trying to reach for the credenza, hitting hard. He knocked over a lamp on his way down, and I knew his security would hear that.

"Ouch! Darn it, Babcock! That hurt," I shouted for the bodyguards to hear. "You'll have to pay extra if you want to play that rough." I ran to the door to listen and to be close to an exit if I wasn't convincing.

The guys in the hall laughed. "Holy shit! I didn't know the pip-squeak had it in him."

Babcock sprawled on the floor. I turned up the radio and ran back to check his vitals, then over to the balcony door in the bedroom. Blaze and Striker — crouched in black cat burglar outfits, right down to the ski masks and rappel harnesses — slunk in and lost no time getting to work.

I pulled the bed covers down and jumped around on the mattress to muss up the sheets. They stripped Babcock naked and threw him on the bed. Blaze went into the other room to do a search.

I looked over at naked Babcock. "That's the second hideous troll penis I've seen because of Iniquus," I whispered to no one in particular. Striker shot me a strange look.

"No, really, look at it, Striker. That looks like a tiny grotesque version of the dildo Chablis gave me to practice on when she was teaching me her techniques. Is it supposed to be purple?"

Striker laughed. "Lynx, focus. You have work to do."

"Gah! I need to Clorox my eye-balls. That's not happy. Who would want to have sex with something like that?" I asked as I applied fresh lipstick, then picked up Babcock's shirt and kissed it from top to bottom before draping it over the lamp. I took the back off of his phone and planted a monitor and GPS, then removed the transmitter I had planted in the breast pocket of his tux on the way to the ball. I pulled out his wallet to photograph the contents.

Blaze glanced up from the computer. "It's secure. We don't have time to crack the encryption. Plan B. I'll have to switch out the memory. Poor guy got a computer virus."

"Have you tried the usual? 123456, qwerty, password, Griffin, openup..."

"Yeah, none of those."

"Try '12161970,'" I read from his license.

"What's that?" Blaze looked up at me.

"Birthday."

"Nope."

"How about Muffin," I said.

"Bingo. Muffin it is. How'd you guess Muffin?"

"Cat's name." I held up the photo of Babcock and Muffin. On the back, he'd drawn a big heart around the name.

"Huh," Blaze grunted as he downloaded the information onto a flash drive, then planted the software so they could monitor his computer remotely.

I took Babcock's $520 in cash out of the wallet and put it in my handbag. I wrote a note on the hotel stationery. "Babcock, you're a wild man! Whenever you're in town, please give me a call. Remember you promised me a trip to Milan in exchange for my doing... what you wanted. XOXO, Ella." I folded the paper and put it where the cash used to be. Striker watched me curiously.

"Gabriella would have taken the money. I'll be donating it to the SPCA in Muffin's name unless you can think of something better."

My next task was to open up the room safe, so we could catalog the contents. It wasn't terribly high-tech, easy enough to crack with a stethoscope. Once that was done, I went through all of the rooms to stage them as if we'd had a night of sexual debauchery. My team couldn't leave any tell-tale signs that we had tampered with Babcock's belongings.

"Looks fine," I said to Striker. "Was there anything else on the to-do list?"

"Nope. I think we're done here. Deep's in the hall. He'll shadow you out. A limo is waiting for you downstairs."

When I got back to Striker's, he was sitting in his armchair, watching the city lights, and drinking a glass of port. My trip home in the limo was uncomfortable; my thoughts virulent red with anger. I planned to confront Striker as soon as we were together. But all of my rancor dissolved when he greeted me with that warm, slow smile.

I shook my head and focused on the ceiling. I could give in right now and go cuddle with Striker, or I could challenge him.

Neither seemed like the right thing to do.

I walked over, sat down, and looked him straight in the eye. "I had a 'knowing.'"

"And?" Striker shifted, leaning forward with his forearms balanced on his knees.

I stopped for a minute...picking out my next words. I thought maybe Deep's slip-up — when he assumed I knew about the Schumann/Sylanos connection — would get him in trouble. I needed to choose my words carefully. "I know many things," I said.

Striker's gaze became opaque, unreadable.

"Were you going to tell me that Schumann and Sylanos were linked?" I asked.

No response.

"Or tonight, for that matter. Didn't you think it would be important for me to know that Babcock was a Sylanos puppet?"

"How would that be important?" Striker tipped his head to the side.

"Let's see, maybe I would like to know when and why I'm spying on members of a group that thinks I am equally worthy of their in-kind attention? Maybe that?"

"Lynx, you are a paid Iniquus operator." His voice was deadly calm. "You were trained by Spyder, but let me review your job description with you. Your work is mission-specific — that means you will function within the confines of your orders. You will perform the duties required of you, and that is that. You don't get to know unless knowing will advance the cause. If you are not offered information, it's because the information is deemed unnecessary for you to know. Clear?"

Something tickled at the edge of my consciousness. "Brennon, too?" I whispered.

Striker's lips formed a long tight line. That was my confirmation.

"What about the FBI debacle?" I asked.

"No. Not every case. Not that one."

"Seph Richy?" I held my breath.

I watched the muscles in his jaw tighten. Yes, Seph Richy, too. Shit! Hydra on steroids. Three really high up, well-placed moguls. When I had some downtime to think…

"It shouldn't matter, Lynx."

I stalled, wide-eyed, breath coming in shallow pants. "But I'm Lexi, too. I was Lexi before all of this." My voice was small. I spread my hands wide. "It's Lexi they're interested in."

Something moved across Striker's face. Oh. I think I get it now. I knelt at his feet, gazing up into his eyes. "Striker, I can't live life in neatly compartmentalized boxes — that's your problem, isn't it? I'm supposed to be mission-specific, and I'm just not."

Striker watched me warily.

"I don't fit neatly into one of your boxes, do I? A box for Lexi, and a box for Lynx."

Striker waited a beat. "That is the understatement of the year, Chica. You're right, though. It's very hard for me to balance my personal feelings and my professionalism. Especially knowing what you're doing. It's not like we're accountants, working in the same office, and the worst that could happen would be a paper cut." He wanted me to smile, as usual, wanted to take some of the heaviness from the air.

"Do you think you'll ever be able to manage it?" I held my breath. My scalp prickled. I was suddenly very afraid I'd have to choose which box to live in. I manically twisted my rings back and forth on my finger.

Striker looked down at what I was doing with my hands. "We said we'd take it slow. I'm not the only one who needs to adjust."

I sat down, my legs curled underneath, the silken fabric of my gown puddled around me. We watched each other.

Striker broke the silence. "The mission went smoothly. I liked the little touches, the lipstick, and the note. Woman's perspective — very helpful."

Hmm, that felt like a cover-up. "Good," I answered and waited for what he really wanted to say.

"You ever do anything like that before for Spyder?"

"He'd never have let me do something like that. I was Alex remember?" I raised an eyebrow. "Why?"

"The whole evening seemed to come naturally to you, that's all."

"Did I make you jealous?"

"I knew you were doing your job. Did I particularly love this job? No. But Babcock isn't your type, so I let it go."

"Oh? You have me figured out, then. So, what is my type?" I pulled my legs around and hugged my knees.

"You like men with superpowers."

"Doesn't every little girl?"

"Not from my experience. Most are satisfied with your run of the mill boy-band singer or football hero." Striker offered me a lop-sided grin.

"And what's your type, Striker?"

"My type for dating and my type for a serious, committed relationship are pretty different."

"Different boxes, huh? Okay. For dating?"

"I dated for pleasure. I was looking for beauty, grace, good sex, and basic conversation."

I took note of the past tense he used, and happiness effervesced in my veins.

"When I think of a forever relationship, I want a diamond — multifaceted depth, beauty, fire, enjoyment, intellectual sparkle. I want to viscerally feel the connection." Striker spoke slowly, hypnotically, looking deep into my eyes, watching how his words affected me.

Boy, were they affecting me. I wanted to launch myself into his arms, feel his hands and mouth on me…

"Up until this point, I've been married to my job," he said.

My breath caught. "Like Gator?"

"I was like Gator, yes." He nodded slightly, eyes unwavering.

"No more?" I asked.

A slow dimpled smile, warm eyes — *oh, yum.*

He tipped his head. "I'm evolving."

"I'm not sure I understand what that means," I said.

"I'm not sure I do either."

That was quite the statement. I focused on my hands as I let the information sink in. I was thrilled and terrified at the same time. When I looked back up at Striker, he had that assessing look again.

"One little thing bothered me. Could you please explain your comment in Babcock's bedroom?"

"Which one?" My mind scanned the bedroom scene and came up empty.

"The one that went, 'That's the second hideous, troll penis I've seen because of Iniquus'."

I sat with this for a minute. He was holding his breath. Apprehension? I waited to figure out what it was, and when it dawned on me, I started laughing a deep-down, belly-grabbing, open-throated, tear-streaming laugh. When I was at the safe house, I had accidentally walked in on Striker when he was getting out of the shower. Believe me when I say Striker has nothing to do with hideous troll penises.

"You think this is funny?" Striker asked.

"Totally." I gasped for air and tried to compose my face. "You're afraid that I was making reference to your family jewels."

Striker didn't move a muscle. He didn't blink an eye. Oh, the poor boy, and his male ego. It wasn't particularly kind of me, but every once in a while, I liked to see cracks in Striker's perfection. They were so rare.

"Yes, tonight was the second hideous troll penis," I said. "You saw Babcock. You have to agree, that was unpleasant." No reaction. "And, there was the one I saw the day of the bank robbery." I told Striker the story of Seph's lady friend getting into his briefs when I was trying to get into his briefcase. "Shall I tell you how I would describe you?" I asked, innocently, kneeling up, so we were eye to eye.

"No, thanks. I was just wondering why you were looking at penises when you were on duty. Normally, we don't pay for that kind of work."

"Right, and if I have to look at troll penises in the line of duty, I think I should get combat pay." I smiled as I slipped onto Striker's lap and took a sip of his port. "What happens now with the Babcock case? Do I need to do some puzzling?"

"Not yet. He gets watched for a while. We'll see if he leads us anywhere. We're fishing."

That night, I dreamt I lived in a small cage… eating food like a little rodent, nibble, nibble, nibble. The leopard sat on the other side of the bars, watching me and licking her teeth.

When I woke up, I felt grubby, hungry, despairing, and terrified.

I took a long hot shower and tried to wash the memory of my dream down the drain.

27

Iniquus installed surveillance on Tammy's house and car. Central Command had found Tammy's link to Maria through Maria's brother, Carlos. Carlos was married to Tammy's mom for about a nanosecond before he was put in prison for life for shooting a police officer.

Tammy was an easy study. She'd written a blog since she was a freshman in high school. Blog might be a stretch. It was more like an on-line, open-kimono journal. She shared everything about her life, and I mean everything. She friend-ed me, as Pete Sake, on Facebook. What's one more friend when you had thousands, right?

Manny knew what he was talking about; Tammy definitely wasn't the sharpest knife in the drawer. Naïve. Easily wounded. Easily taken advantage of. Easily manipulated. Desperately wanting to be seen as loving and loveable. Tammy didn't present the face of an enemy. I'd keep close track, though, to see how much auntie influenced her.

My task now was finding Maria's husband, Julio Rodriguez. I put his name through the national criminal background check. I wanted to see if he got caught playing ball and what court he liked to play on…and there he was: Julio Philippe Rodriguez, Honduran National. He lived in Nelson Federal Correction Complex in Florida. Maximum security. That was pretty naughty.

According to records, Julio said nothing to anyone throughout his trial, including his lawyers. They couldn't determine if his crime was gun-running or terrorism, so they went with terrorism. I wasn't sure I understood how such different crimes could be confused. I'd have to get Legal to explain this to me. Another thing to put on my to-do list. That was only last September. Julio has been in Nelson for about four months now. Two months ago, Maria, as Consuela Hervas, was buying the house here on Silver Lake. Hmm. Hmm. Hmm. So Julio was locked-down in maximum security in Florida; his wife was up here watching me in DC. What was the connection? Was there a connection?

I wrote down my thoughts. Spyder had shown me that if you write something out, you use more areas of your brain: see it, hear it, feel it, speak it…the more brain parts in action, the better the chances you can connect the dots and puzzle something out. Okay, what did I know? I knew Spyder had been working on a case I'd puzzled for him that lead to the king-pin, Marcos Sylanos. Sylanos was still at large. The piece of the puzzle I worked on had to do with gun-running into Colombia with a stop off in Honduras.

But now, we had Schumann, Richy, Brennon, and Babcock involved. That was quite a metamorphosis.

Another tack: I knew there was a player that distantly connected me to Marcos Sylanos, and that was Beth Sylanos, aka Mrs. Agnew. She was married to Marcos' cousin, Amando.

Looked like Amando got himself killed in a federal raid

about seven years ago. At that time, Beth turned informant and was hiding in my apartment complex, as Mrs. Agnew, where I babysat for her two children. She knew that Spyder and I were connected, but probably not how. . . I tapped my fingers on my desk — curioser and curioser. Beth left the country when I was sixteen to go live under yet another assumed name. She wasn't traceable — unless Command started sharing.

If I followed this connection — boy did this feel tenuous — Maria was friends with Beth way back when. Could Beth have told her about Spyder and about me? Would Maria remember something as mundane as that all these years later? Yeah, that thread felt weak. Maybe Maria didn't have any clue that we had Beth in common...

I couldn't find any direct association between Maria and me, or me and Julio Rodriguez. From reading the file, I didn't think that Spyder had any direct association with them either. What did Maria want with me? Did she think I knew something? Was she trying to help her husband? Some kind of exchange of information for a lesser sentence? The time for negotiating and bargaining was over. Julio was sentenced to a hundred years in maximum with no chance of parole. Post 9-11, our courts weren't messing around with would-be terrorists.

My mind needed some time to let the information marinate. I marked the file and put it in my bottom desk drawer rather than my file cabinet, hiding it among some other tickler files I had in there, and locked it up. I didn't want someone coming upon this information by accident. I needed more time, and I didn't want Striker or Command to take away my candy.

My girls and I went for a jog and then went back to the barracks to make a light supper for Striker and me. This was going to be our last night together before he left on his classified mission.

In the kitchen, I moved the mail and newspaper off the counter where Striker had stacked them as he ran in and out earlier today. Underneath was an artist pad with four graceful hands drawn in colored pencils. Each hand wore a ring. As I looked at them, I realized that these were the designs that Striker had offered at the New Year's Eve party.

They were stunning. Absolutely my aesthetic and delicate enough for my small fingers. I looked them over closely and imagined each one on my hand. I decided that I liked the first one. It spiraled gently, giving the feel of a yin yang or an infinity figure. Striker had been able to give the impression of these timeless symbols without being overt about it. It was more of a suggestion. Yes, lovely.

I was holding the sketchbook up when Striker came in.

He paused. "I hope it's okay I did that."

"Striker, you are so talented. Really, wonderfully talented. What a special gift you've given me."

He walked over to stand close enough that I had to tilt my head back to see him. "When you're ready. At your own pace."

I slipped my wedding and engagement rings off of my hand. "I'm ready. I like the first one you drew." I placed my rings into Striker's open hand.

"I'll take good care of them."

"And me?" My voice warbled uncertainly. "You'll take good care of me?"

"Of course." His eyebrows came together.

"You won't break my heart? You won't go off and get yourself killed?" As soon as the words left my mouth, I wished I could suck them back in. How selfish of me.

Striker folded me into him, his arms strong and capable around me. His hand cradled my head as he pressed my cheek into his chest. "Chica, I promise, I'll do everything in my power to come home to you safely. I love you. I only want good things for you."

The evening felt tense, though we acted as if it didn't. It was time for me to tell Striker how I felt about him — maybe even define our relationship. Why was it so hard to acknowledge the obvious? *I love you, Striker.* It was there in my head. It was definitely in my body. I was confused by the barricade I had thrown between us. Why did I do that?

After sitting in miserable silence, eating our dinner, I tried to at least broach the subject of my living arrangements. "Consuela looks like she's really gone. I've been researching her niece, Tammy. She's innocuous. There's nothing on the surveillance that indicates Consuela has any contact with her right now. I was wondering how you'd feel about me moving back home."

"You don't want to be here?" Striker asked.

"I love it here, but only when you're here with me."

That made him smile. He reached for my hand.

"This is your place — not mine. I don't know how well I fit here without you. I miss my neighborhood — my neighbors are my family. I'm going to have to distract myself to keep from worrying about you constantly."

He laughed softly. "That's a switch."

"Yeah, I guess it is. So I can go?"

"Are you asking my permission?"

"More like your approval."

I could see his cogs whirring. "And are you asking me from an Iniquus point of view, or personal?" Boxes again.

"Both. I want to make sure you think this is a safe move strategically. I also don't want to have you worrying about me unnecessarily. I'll stay here if it helps you."

"Because I love you?" His gaze became intense.

I was silent for a long minute, trying to get my mouth to say the words, "No, because I love you, Striker."

But I couldn't do it.

Instead, I said, "Because it's costly to repair a transmission."

28

At the break of dawn, Striker rubbed my back to wake me. "Lexi, I have to leave."

"No." I moaned into my pillow, rolling toward him, arms outstretched. He gathered me up and hugged me tightly.

"I'll be back as soon as I can," he whispered into my ear.

"Be safe, okay?" I clung to him, trying to tamp down the sensation of foreboding that made my stomach clench. *Please don't go,* I wanted to beg. I didn't want to jinx the mission, though, so I bit my tongue. Nothing I said would stop him from heading out anyway.

"You be safe, Chica. I love you." He brushed the hair out of my face and gave me a kiss that made me know, right down to my toes, how much he meant his words.

After he left, I dragged myself up, into the shower, over to work, and through the morning.

At noon, Gator went home with me. I made something for lunch. Gator wolfed his food down; I made circles with mine on my plate. We washed up together, and Gator hauled the trash outside. When he came in, he found me staring vacantly out my living room window.

"Hey, you okay?"

I was moping, feeling a kindred spirit in the gray day, watching the rain drizzling down. "Yeah." I sighed. "The weather's a real bummer."

"Yeah, that's what I thought you were bummed about," Gator said with a grin.

"Don't." I held up a scolding finger.

"Don't what?" Gator's grin widened.

"Just don't go there with me. I can't help that I'm worried." I rested my forehead on the cool windowpane and drew designs in the condensation. "I wish one of our team was with Striker. I don't know the guys who're with him, and you're only as good as the guys behind you."

"Ma'am, if it makes you feel any better, I know the men that are out there. They're all capable and honorable."

I turned back to Gator. "Thanks. I'll tell you what, let's distract me. The floors are cured in the duplex now, and we can move you in next door."

"Yes, ma'am."

"Gator, I'm not your client anymore. I have no rank over you, and I'm younger than you are. Why do you still 'ma'am' me?"

My question seemed to catch Gator by surprise. I could see his mind searching for a reason. "I don't know, maybe habit? Naw. I don't think it were out of habit. I guess maybe I like to say it because I feel kind of like it's affectionate to say 'ma'am' without being disrespectful. You know, like Striker calling you Chica…well no, you know I ain't saying that I feel affectionate about you like Striker feels affectionate about you. I feel different affectionate about you like you're a special-person-to-me kind of affectionate."

Poor Gator. I don't think he had a lot of practice discussing his feelings. It was an honor that he was willing to stumble, red-faced, and shuffling, through all that.

"I feel special-person-to-me kind of affection toward you too, Gator. You are dear to my heart."

"Thank you, ma'am."

Aw, that was a little ray of sunshine breaking through my emotional storm clouds.

Iniquus maintained a storehouse full of furniture and all of the household-y kinds of things people would need: plates, linens, cleaning supplies…they were ready for the taking. Sometimes an operator needed to do covert work, and they'd have to stage their operation with the right furniture to play their role. A junkie, for instance, wouldn't move in with a matching bedroom suite, and an executive wouldn't move in with crate furniture.

Gator got to choose furniture for a working-class neighborhood — fairly new, matchy-matchy, medium quality that all but screamed, "I'm a single male." Okay, it screamed, "I'm a single male on the make," but out of deference to his relationship with Amy, I was going to leave that last part alone. The men loaded up a truck and had Gator all moved in and set up by nightfall. Luckily, the rain had stopped.

Gator and I quickly fell into a rhythm. We drove to the office and worked regular hours there — or mostly regular hours — based on what puzzles landed on my desk. Since Striker was out, our team wasn't doing any fieldwork. On a few occasions, we needed to stay in the barracks; but for the most part, we were home by six. I cooked dinner; Gator did KP.

The rhythm broke when Striker called to tell me he was heading home. I did a little happy dance right there on the phone with him. Apparently, a puzzle I'd recently solved showed there were a lot of players at risk on the case he was working. Too many good guys were in the way for him to take down the bad guys successfully. The agencies were going to have to put a different plan into place, get some of the hands out of the cookie jar. Turned out that one agency was using us to play another agency. It made no sense. We were all supposed to be on the same team, right? Turf wars. Well, Iniquus was handing the case back; we don't play bully on the playground.

"So, I'll be home very late tonight, maybe around two? I miss you. I want to see you bad." His voice was softly urgent and made me think...Well, what I thought was that Striker Rheas would be getting a well-deserved hero's welcome that would make us both very happy.

"Me too," I said. Yes, Little Miss Webster was ready for her relationship to be defined now, thank you very much. I hugged myself in anticipation.

"You're smiling," he said.

"Absolutely. I'm impatient to see you."

"Oh, really? Are you at your house?"

"Yes, at my place. Do you want to head right here?" Smiling was an understatement; I thought my face might split — my grin was so wide. Oh, I was excited.

Now that I'd made my decision, I wanted Striker here in my arms. Waiting sucked. I busied myself with primping, then I invited Blaze and his girl, Faith, Gator and Amy, Jack and Suz over for the evening to hang out in my backyard. I desperately needed a distraction, and today had been one of those rare winter days when the air suddenly warms and smells of hope and the possibility of spring.

Circled around the crackling fire pit, we drank hot cider — with Beetle and Bella warming our feet. We laughed as Gator told us stories about growing up in the swamps when his momma used to call him Mud-Pie.

Suddenly, my skin prickled. I heard the scream of a wild cat in my head. I swung around, startled, and found myself hunkering with a gun in hand.

My dogs growled low in their throats, flanking me. The men had leaped instantly out of their chairs, and crouched, vigilantly scanning the walls, guns drawn. Blaze hustled Faith, Suz, and Amy into the house and told them to go down into my basement until he came for them.

Gator placed a hand on my back and whispered in my ear, "What's happening, Lynx?"

"I don't know. Instinct." That's all I had. Something terrible was about to happen. Adrenaline shined my skin, every nerve ending strained for information. For survival.

Blaze and Jack left the walled garden to search for anything unusual. My girls growled their warning.

"Your dogs are picking up something, too — can we let 'em loose? Will they take us to it?"

"Beetle. Bella. Find it."

Off they sprinted as soon as the command left my mouth. They ran to Consuela's old house then up to Sarah's house, where they howled until Tammy came to the door. Tammy? What was she doing there?

I peeked past Tammy's form to see inside Sarah's house.

Everything looked normal. "Hey, I'm Lexi. I live across the street there." I turned and pointed toward my house. "Is everything all right here? Where are Mike and Ruby?"

"Yes, ma'am, everything's fine." She seemed perplexed. "I'm babysitting. Ruby's down for the night, and Mike's playing video games."

"Do you know when Sarah and Bob will be home?"

"Tomorrow morning. They went to a wedding in Richmond."

"And, you're sure everything's okay?" I stalled, hoping for divine inspiration — a "knowing." Something. Anything.

Tammy pulled her brows together. "Yes, ma'am, everything's fine." She was guileless, obviously telling the truth, but the quiver in my gut told me that this was where the danger lay.

I fake smiled and retreated. Beetle and Bella trotted beside me, sniffing the air.

Gator and I headed back to my house, where I found Blaze at the front door. Jack was out back. We gathered in my living room — their dates still sequestered in my basement. The men sat and waited for me to talk. I didn't really have anything to say; I gave them a shrug and pinched my lower lip to keep it from trembling.

"Okay, Lynx, you obviously felt something, and we all know to pay attention when you do. Your dogs sure picked up on the same thing, and they tapped Consuela's house and then Tammy," said Blaze.

"Don't know what to do with that." I bit at the inside of my cheek.

"Do you think Consuela might be in the neighborhood?" Blaze asked.

I shrugged and shook my head. I didn't know.

"What are you feeling?" Jack asked.

"The heebie-jeebies."

"I think you should pack a bag and stay at the barracks until we can review the surveillance tapes," Jack said.

I shook my head.

"No?" Jack's voice held his surprise.

"Tammy's staying with Ruby and Mike. Their parents aren't going to be back in town until tomorrow. If there's something that's going to go down — I need to be here to make sure the children are safe."

"You could look at it that way, Lynx, or you could look at it that your being here makes things more dangerous for them," said Blaze.

Dilemma. Conundrum. What should I do? Which was the bigger risk? I pursed my lips. "If I knew what the danger was if I knew it had something to do with me…that's not a given at all. It could be…anything. I don't have enough information — just heebie-jeebies." Wow, that should take my professional image to the next level. Could I sound like a bigger moron?

They sat quietly; no one offered an opinion.

"I can't leave the neighborhood while I think the kids are in danger. And Striker is supposed to come back into town tonight. He's coming straight to my house around two this morning." I took a quick peek at my watch. Eleven. Three more hours and Striker would be here. The thought of him calmed me. "I'll pack a bag and go back to the barracks as soon as Sarah and Bob get back into town tomorrow."

The guys nodded.

"I'm sorry, but I think it would be best if you guys took your girls home."

"Jack, can you take Amy for me? I'm not leaving," Gator said.

. . .

Gator watched sports on TV. I paced. I sat in the dark and tapped frustrated, anxious fingers on the dining room table. The dogs lay calmly at my feet, and I wondered if my own shot of adrenaline was what made them react earlier. Maybe I was just so tightly wound from…well, everything…that knowing Striker was headed home, and that I had made the decision to take the plunge. Maybe I just started unwinding too quickly and overloaded my synapses. I remembered the sense of foreboding I had before he left and jumped up again to resume my pacing, wringing my hands. I wanted Striker to be home already.

I decided to go lie down. Gator said he wouldn't leave until Striker ordered him out. I pursed my lips. Fine. But I wasn't planning on sleeping, and my being up would keep Gator up; that felt like overkill on a case of heebie-jeebies. As time passed with no issues, I felt downright embarrassed. Jack called in to say that they had reviewed the surveillance, no one suspicious had contacted Tammy. He and Blaze had come back and swept the neighborhood. They found nothing suspicious there either. Yup. I was feeling more ridiculous by the minute.

Still, Gator refused to leave. When Gator entrenched himself, it would take a bulldozer to move him. I set the alarms on my house and went to bed fully clothed, leaving Gator to do whatever.

I heard the back door open, Gator letting the girls out in the back yard.

At one in the morning, my phone rang. Gator filled my bedroom doorframe, his gaze intense as I answered. I was hoping it was Striker coming in ahead of schedule.

"Lexi?" A soft voice faltered. "This is Tammy across the way. Sarah left your number with me in case of an emergency."

I was instantly upright. I had the phone trapped between my

shoulder and ear as I grabbed my cross-trainers, pulling them on while I listened.

"It's Ruby. There's something wrong." Her voice hitched. "She's making funny gurgling noises, and her skin is blue."

"I'm on the way. Go open the door." I pushed past Gator and thundered down the stairs, yelling back at him that Ruby wasn't breathing. As I reached for my front doorknob, Gator lifted me off my feet and threw me bodily onto the couch.

He pointed a commanding finger. "You stay put. Call the team. Call 911," he ordered.

Gator sprinted out the door and down the street.

I punched three into my speed dial. "Jack. Here. Now," I screamed and disconnected. I dialed 911 with a shaking finger. Every second counted; her brain needed oxygen. I had to get to Ruby. I ran out my door. I paused for a split-second when I saw Gator crouched, gun in hand, behind Manny's Camry, scanning Sarah's house. What was he doing? Ruby needed air. She was blue. He turned as my feet stampeded down the stairs. I had 911 on the phone and told them the address as I ran past him.

"SHIT," he hollered, grabbing my hand and yanking me to the ground. I went down hard, scraping my hands and taking out the knees on my jeans.

"I said, stay back," he yelled over his shoulder at me as he ran up the lawn to the house, his long legs propelling him forward.

But, Ruby! I bolted up the stairs behind him and straight into Sarah's house, where I slammed to a stop. My mind reeled as I tried to grasp what I saw. Gator twitched on the ground.

Two probes stabbed into his chest and bicep.

I followed the long wires up to the Taser held by a man with a ski mask over his face. Sparks flew from the probes. Gator made guttural reverberations from down deep in his chest as he jolted on the ground. Ski-Mask held a gun in his right hand — it pointed at Gator's head. Gator's gun lay at Maria's feet.

Everything moved in slow motion. I'm sure only a moment had passed, but in my mind, everything was cold molasses. I focused on Tammy. She was on the sofa, sobbing uncontrollably, the phone still in her hand. Maria stood with Ruby in her arms. Sleeping? Dead? Unconscious? A hunting knife was poised over Ruby's heart. I raised my hands in the air in submission.

"STOP IT. STOP IT. I'll do whatever you want, Maria. Tell him to stop Tasering Gator." I jerked my head toward Ski-Mask.

Maria threw a bag at Tammy. "Take out the cuffs and leg irons and put them on him."

Tammy fell from the sofa onto her knees — I saw her phone bounce on the floor — she pulled out a pile of cuffs. Maria pointed at the leg irons with her toe. Tammy picked them up along with a pair of handcuffs and crab-walked over to Gator. Crazily, my mind willed Tammy to hurry and get Gator secured so Ski-Mask would stop torturing him.

Tammy tilted her head up at Ski-Mask, who took his finger off the trigger, and the electrical current stopped sparking. With hands that trembled to the point of being useless, Tammy worked to get the cuffs on. Gator was panting and drooling on the rug. My mind was stuck in neutral, and no matter how hard I pushed on the gas, it wouldn't move forward.

"Now, you. Facedown," Maria barked at me.

Gator was still attached to the probes, gun to his head; Ruby's heart was still under the knife. I went back to my training scenarios. What should I do? A trained operator would abandon the scene. Should abandon the scene. Escape and get help. The chance of Maria actually plunging that knife into Ruby's heart as I fled was almost zero. I knew that. Cerebrally, I knew that. But this was Ruby. Maybe I could gather the wherewithal to run if this were an unknown. But I could not, would not, risk Ruby.

Stall. That's what I should do. Help was coming. "What do you want from me, Consuela?" My heart ricocheted around my ribcage like a pinball.

"I need you as leverage."

"For what? I'll do anything you want me to. Just put Ruby down." It was my sweet, fluffy voice. My trademark disguise. Trained into me by the best.

Get here, Jack.

"She's safe, as long as you're a good girl and do what you're told, Lexi. You're going to be going on a little trip with me."

Oh? "You're kidnapping me?" My eyebrows jumped to my hairline. I stood there like a scarecrow, pinioned to this one spot by fear. Any of the Kung Fu moves that played in my mind were useless. Maria and Ski-Mask were physically too far apart for me to take them down together. I would have to sacrifice either Ruby or Gator.

"I don't really know if it can be called kidnapping if you're going voluntarily. Lie down on your stomach. Hands behind your back. Ankles crossed."

"Don't do it, Lexi. Run," Gator roared. Ski-Mask sent another jolt of electricity through Gator's central nervous system.

I complied instantly, throwing myself prostrate at her feet. Stop torturing Gator!

Tammy clamped the cuffs around my wrists; the cold metal bit into my skin. I hoped she would leave them loose enough that I could wiggle my hands free. She wasn't thinking, though; she had snapped them down tight. When the leg irons were on my ankles, Ski-Mask came over and lifted me to my feet. He put a bag over my head.

Jack, I screamed in my head.

Claustrophobia gripped at me. *"Panic will kill you, Lexicon. It makes you unable in mind and body."* I heard Spyder's voice in my head. I hyperventilated and swayed with dizziness; he would be so disappointed in me.

Maria and the man spoke briefly in Spanish. She left to get a van parked down the road, out of sight. Moments later, I heard the rumbling of an engine, and Maria came back into the house. The sirens from the EMS screamed toward us. I knew that Iniquus would be out in full force seconds away. I just needed something — anything — to stall, to give me those few moments until salvation. Like the seconds counted off before the parachute could be pulled. Stop and think. Maybe my pulling that ripcord would save me — but what about my Ruby — my Gator? You or them, Lexi? Them. Obviously. Without a single doubt.

Ski-Mask reached around me under my arms; Maria took my feet by the shackles, and they rushed me, without a fight, down to a vehicle waiting in the driveway and threw me in the back like a bag of garbage.

29

I was stunned — in shock. I needed to keep my head together. I needed to figure out where they were taking me, count off minutes, pay attention to turns, get a plan together. Now I'd only be protecting myself; I wouldn't be endangering anyone. Those were my thoughts when the sharp hypodermic needle pricked my arm. My muscle burned from the liquid being plunged into my tissue. Little by little, my world went foggy.

Time passed. The drugs made lucid nightmares that I could taste with my hands and hear with my eyes. Like a trip down the rabbit hole, my senses were on a wild teacup ride, spinning uncontrollably. I rumbled and bounced in the back of the van. It was hard to breathe through the bag. Coming out of the medicated-fog, with my mind starting to function again, terror consumed me. I needed to keep myself distracted — needed to visualize good outcomes.

Help had been moments away. They would free Gator. Gator would have Iniquus fully mobilized. Striker would be there by now.

My phone was shoved into my bra. Iniquus could follow me

through the GPS. No, wait. I didn't have my smartphone. Tammy had called me on my personal phone, which was an older phone that would need a phone call to ping off a tower to get a very generalized location — nothing specific and nothing immediate. With no GPS, Iniquus would be triangulating pings from the cell towers. And then I remembered my phone ringer was on. If someone tried to call me, Maria would find my phone on me. Right now, my cell phone seemed like my only hope. Had she patted me down when I was unconscious? I rolled onto my belly and felt the hard case of the phone press into the flesh of my breast. No. I still had it. Surely, Iniquus would ask the phone company to do something. Forward my calls. Something. . .

I needed to get a grip already — and trust in my team.

It turned out that I was right to speak only English around Maria. She felt comfortable talking openly with the man, Hector, in Spanish. He sounded like a paid thug — not invested in the mission. Maybe I could work with that at some point.

"Stop worrying, already," Maria ordered. "No one saw your face. No one knows anything about you. Just take us to the airport, and help me to get her on the plane. She won't even be in the States. She won't be a threat."

What the…not in the States? A plane?

"What about now? You keep using my name. Stop calling me by my name."

"She's drugged. She can't hear us. Besides, she doesn't know Spanish. She won't be able to distinguish your name from any other word I'm saying, so stop making issues."

"What about my van? Surely someone saw it. What about

that guy who came out on the porch when we drove away? He looked at us pretty hard."

"Who? Manny? He's an idiot. Don't worry about him. Look, if you're really concerned, call the police in the morning and report the van stolen, then ditch it somewhere. It's not your damned van anyway — you said it was your girlfriend's. Tell her it was stolen and put it in the woods."

Manny was on the porch? Manny wasn't an idiot. He was hyperaware of the comings and goings of our neighborhood. He has an ex who disappeared, and he was always afraid she might resurface and take his boys.

Our street was pretty protected. There was no reason for through traffic. If you were on Silver Lake, it was because you lived there, or you were visiting, not driving through.

Hope. A bright light.

Manny would notice a van at one in the morning. That was what I told myself at any rate. Maybe the police had issued a BOLO already. Maybe they'd find us before we reached the airport.

I took the clasp of my handcuffs and started scratching as best I could, unseeing, and behind my back, into the paint on the floor: "skylinks." Hopefully, this would be legible and cryptic enough that Hector and Maria still wouldn't realize I understood them. I knew it was a long shot, but if the van had been in the neighborhood long enough, then the license would be in a log that Blaze and Jack kept while running a sweep of the area. If they could find the van, they would do a thorough search; they might find my name and know to look for me…far away. Shit. Even if all the "mights" came true, would this help? No.

It seemed like we'd been driving a long time. That dimmed my hopes. We'd stopped for gas. Surely if they'd planned to drive any kind of distance, they would have started with a full

tank. Okay, say fifteen miles to the gallon, twenty-gallon tank —
we had gone about 300 miles. Are you kidding me? If that were
true, then I had been out for hours.

It sounded like Hector was paying at the pump. That was
good. Very good. If Manny had the van plate, or Tammy or
Iniquus did, then they could trace the owner. If they looked for
the owner, she could name the boyfriend, and they could get the
credit reports and have his card numbers. The computers would
pick up his transactions. Iniquus would know I was — well,
wherever the heck I was. Help could be on its way right now.
Yes, right this minute, a police alert could be going out. My
friends from my police department would be calling in favors —
they'd be searching for me as if I were one of their own.
Someone would find me before I got to the airport.

Again we drove. Again we stopped for gas. Again we drove.
I had been playing as if I were still drugged. I thought that was
safest and also put Maria and Hector at ease, so they'd speak
freely to each other.

I was too uncomfortable; I had to go to the bathroom. I
needed something to drink. My hands and feet had swollen in the
tight restraints.

I moaned loudly. "Consuela? Are you there, Consuela?"

"What?" she asked in English.

"I need to go to the bathroom badly. I need some water."

She conferred with Hector in Spanish. I guess this was the
part they hadn't figured out. We stopped. Hector took the bag off
my head. I could see out the front window that we were at an old
mom-and-pop station with the bathrooms on the side. Maria
went in for the key. She brought back some bottled water and
two packages of peanuts. Hector swung the van around, pulling
up next to the girls' bathroom. Maria opened her van door and

then opened the bathroom door — effectively screening me from view.

"Make a sound, and I'll cut your tongue out of your head." Leopard eyes sliced at me, hard and glittery.

Hector had to help me; he half carried me out of the back of the van. I reflexively looked down at the license plate: SNK OIL.

My legs were numb from lack of circulation. Maria unlocked my hands, and I quickly considered my options. If I had any use of my legs, I knew I could have made a good try for freedom. I was still woozy; my knees buckled under me. Hector ended up having to take me into the bathroom; I couldn't manage it on my own.

I would like to say that Hector was a gentleman and turned his face to the door while I lowered my jeans, but that wasn't the case. He gawked, and smirked, and watched everything I did with a leer. I took a chance and used my sleight-of-hand skills to take out my phone and turn the ringer sound off. Hector was pretty much focused on other parts of me as I lowered my hand beside the toilet. I turned my phone on and dialed 911, then quickly disconnected before a voice could come out of the receiver. I prayed that it was long enough to ping over the cell tower, that Iniquus would know about where I was and was now sending the Calvary.

I set my phone on silent mode and stuck it back in my bra. I yanked a clump of hair out of my head to leave in the van as DNA evidence. I wouldn't be able to reach my head once I had the cuffs back on. As I finished up in the bathroom, Hector stared at me, glassy-eyed.

He licked his lips, making me nervous for my immediate safety.

I depended on Maria's authority, whatever that was, to keep Hector's lascivious hands off me.

As Hector put me back in the van, I looked around to see what I could see.

The sun was almost directly overhead. It was close to noon. That meant we had been driving for about eleven hours. The cars parked across the back of the station all had Florida plates. We must be on 95 heading south. There was nothing else to see, and no one around to see me. No one would be making a sheepish call to the police to say they saw something unusual; a shackled woman was being thrown in the back of a van.

We sat for a few minutes while I ate my peanuts and drank a bottle of water, then they cuffed me behind my back, and we took off. The bag was back on my head. I lay on the cold, dirty, metal floor and prayed.

30

I woke up to hard hands on me. They pulled me from the back of the van by my ankles. I could smell pine trees. A flock of geese honked in the distance. I was hoisted up like a bag of potatoes and slung over someone's shoulder. Hector's? I had seen his face when I was in the bathroom. I was afraid he would want to kill me, but he seemed satisfied to dump me unceremoniously into an airplane seat and buckle a belt around me.

Another door opened, and I heard Maria talking to the pilot in Spanish, "The package is tightly wrapped. You won't have any problems with her. There will be a guard from the prison at the airport to pick her up. Remember — you want your money? You get her there on time and in good condition."

"Done," came a man's voice in front of me.

As we flew, I couldn't talk to the pilot to get information. I tried a few words, and he told me clearly, "No English." I listened to the radio instead, trying to get a grasp on where we were headed.

My pilot wasn't staying in contact with a tower. He didn't call in when we took off, and he never reported our position.

I had no sense of time and no sense of direction. I slumped in the seat, dazed and confused, struggling to get enough air through my bag. The plane bucked across the uneven ground — this was not a normal runway landing. This was a field landing, rough, and nauseating. I knew we were in a prop, not a jet, by the sound of the engine.

If we left from Florida, how far could we possibly get? It depended on how big this plane was. It felt substantial. I was sitting behind the pilot, so it wasn't a two-seater. It might have been reconfigured with extra fuel bladders; still, we wouldn't have the fuel range to fly far. Four, five-hundred miles? Maria said I was leaving the States. The best they could do was to get out into the Caribbean to an island somewhere.

I heard the pilot make noises on the side of the plane. Refueling. It sounded like he was using a hand pump. After some time, the pilot opened the door. He touched me, and I keeled over. I wanted to see how much this guy wanted to deliver his package in good condition. I made choking noises and went silent. Sure enough, Pilot panicked. He grabbed the bag off my head and unfastened my hands from behind my back. He rubbed the circulation back into my arms.

I listened to the radio. I could hear pilots talking to a control tower. Isla de la Juventud. I was in Cuban territory. That preempted any thoughts of escaping. The last thing I wanted was to get stuck in Cuban territory with the possibility of being charged with espionage. With my Iniquus credentials...well, things were looking dim. I was going to have to try my escape at our next stop — if there was a next stop.

Pilot worked hard at bringing me back around. Now that an escape wasn't on the table, I was done playing with him. I blinked my eyes open. The pilot let out a sigh of relief, hand-cuffed me again — thankfully in front of my body — and put me back in my chair, this time without the bag.

We didn't take off. We sat on the runway. I wondered if we were waiting for someone here. I desperately hoped this wasn't our final destination and that he was waiting to do a transfer. Day turned to night. There was the sound of an engine, and lights bounced toward the plane. My heart stammered in my chest. Now what? The pilot got out and spoke with someone. They weren't talking about me. They were talking about boxes. The pilot didn't want the man to approach our plane. He would transfer the boxes himself. I counted twenty, not that it mattered to me. I guessed I needed something to do with my mind. Terror was an insidious emotion. Even this little distraction was helpful.

Come morning, the pilot opened a brown paper bag and ate breakfast. He had bread, cheese, and a couple of juice boxes. I had been more than 36 hours with only a bag of peanuts, but he didn't offer me anything. I was faint from the heat. I asked for some water, pretending to painfully search for and finally come up with the word *agua*. The pilot pulled out a plastic bottle and handed it to me. It wasn't particularly clean, yet I couldn't have cared less. My throat was parched.

The pilot jumped out and made a check of his plane. We took off again. Now I could see some of the instrumentation; we were heading southwest. Not good.

We were in the air for hours. As we descended, I scanned the terrain for clues, for possibilities. This time we landed at an actual airport, not some drug smuggler's secret grass strip. The airport was small, though, and not in the best of shape.

The door opened to a uniformed guard. He unbuckled me. I had been dozing with my head down. Damp and limp, the effects of Maria's drugs still hadn't fully worn off. He brushed my hair

300 | FIONA QUINN

from my face and took a good look at me. I was obviously not a threat. He released my cuffs and the shackles on my feet. The guy's partner protested.

"Are you kidding?" the guard asked in Spanish, "You're worried about this little thing? Look at her. She's half-dead, and it will be easier for us to get her out of here if she can walk out on her own."

Well, that was optimistic. I couldn't walk at all. My legs had lost all feeling hours and hours ago. It took the two of them, on either side of me, to half-carry, half-drag me to their truck and push me in, to sit between them. They handed the pilot a fat envelope. He saluted and took off again. I never heard the pilot's name.

No one talked while we drove. I begged my body to cooperate — to focus and stay lucid; I needed to know how to get back to this airport. We drove for about half an hour, never making a turn. 20 kilometers — that's about twelve miles — less than a two-hour run. Hah. There was my optimism again.

Our truck slowly rolled through the middle of a huge forest with nothing, absolutely nothing, but trees. Suddenly, a break exposed cleared land and a prison. A third world hell hole. The menacing razor wire... Oh, I definitely didn't want the car to turn in there.

The prison was composed of three large rectangular buildings, three stories high, made of cinder block. There were guard towers at each corner of the compound and a large open space, making a dash for the chain-link fence and freedom, pretty much a suicide run. We slowed, and the driver steered through the front gate, passed through a checkpoint, and drove to a large gray building, where I was unloaded and dragged inside.

I wasn't trying to be uncooperative, though maybe I was

being a little histrionic. I thought weak, sweet, and innocent was the way to go. I wanted their guard down, literally.

The interior looked economy model. Industrial green paint, old metal furniture bolted to the floor, dust. I scanned for anything that would tell me where I was — even just the country.

The intake officers shifted quickly from sheer boredom to elation. Here was a new show to entertain them. They jeered at me, calling me names, making lewd suggestions. I looked confusedly at them and then at the guards holding me up. "English, please?" I asked with my scared, little girl voice. I can't say I was acting any more.

A uniformed man stepped forward. His fat gray mustache twitched. "I speak English."

"Where am I? Why was I brought here? Can I call home? Or a lawyer?"

Gray Mustache translated back to the men, and I focused on my blank look while they laughed. Gray Mustache told me to take off all of my clothes. I did as I was told, as best I could, swaying on rubbery legs and trying not to collapse.

I unzipped my hoodie and laid it on the desk. One of the guards pulled it over and searched it. The phone. The phone. I looked for options as I tugged off my cross trainers and socks, and then came my T-shirt. As I pulled the shirt over my head, I got my cell phone out of my bra and slipped it into Gray Mustache's pocket — standing in the middle of the room, all eyes on me, I couldn't find any other options. And this was a dangerous one, but I took it.

I pulled off my jeans and saw blood caked on my knees from when Gator tried to stop me — to save me — had I only listened. I unclasped my bra and let it fall; Gray Mustache stopped me from taking off my panties. The other men were disappointed and yelled at him. They wanted the whole show.

Gray Mustache fixed his eyes on my torso, where Psychopath Wilson etched my souvenir scars. He lifted my right arm and traced the line of the knife wound that ran from under my arm to over my hip. He turned me into the light to look closer at the red spider web of scars that crisscrossed my torso and hadn't yet faded. He brushed my hair back from my forehead to see the three-inch scar along my hairline, still pink and new.

"Someone hurt you badly," he said in a fatherly voice. I couldn't tell if this was an interrogation tactic or if he was genuine. Maybe a bit of both.

"Yes, sir," I said, lowering my lashes.

"How did this happen?"

"There was this crazy man who thought that I needed to suffer."

"And did you need to suffer?" He crossed his arms and scowled at me.

"I thought I already was suffering."

"Why do you say this? You look like a nice girl."

Why did I say this? Hell, I didn't know. Words bubbled from my mouth; for a moment, the connection between brain and tongue seemed to be severed. He picked up the gold cross that Nona Sophia had given me before she moved to New York.

"Are you Catholic?"

"Yes, sir, Catholic." That seemed the safest thing to say.

"And why were you already suffering?"

"My mom had just died, and then there was a fire in my apartment building — my home burned down with everything in it. Then a crazy man attacked me." I desperately wanted him to feel pity, that I was victimized, traumatized, maybe he would help me.

Gray Mustache picked up my left hand. "No rings. You are not married?"

"I don't have a husband, no."

"Your father, you are living with your father?"

Was this guy trying to determine if I had anyone looking for me? Better let this one play as a great big "no," so they don't take extra security measures with me. "No, sir, my father died when I was seventeen."

"And how old are you now?"

"I'm twenty."

"Twenty? What do you do for a living?"

Uh-oh. My mind scrambled. What did they know? "I'm a student."

"Where is this? At a university?"

"Yes, sir." Fluffy. Innocent. Watch your facial reactions. Watch your tone.

"And you are studying…"

"I haven't declared a major yet, sir. I'm still trying to make up my mind. I thought maybe I might like to be a nurse."

"I see, and you have no job?"

"I sometimes have a little job singing at a neighborhood restaurant." Damn. I'm going to have to tell them about Iniquus — Gray Mustache probably already knew and was seeing how honest I was. The more harmless and stupid I seemed, the better.

"Right now, I have a job at a place called Iniquus." The other men in the room had been mostly ogling me since they didn't seem to understand what was being said. I had an arm over my breasts, trying to look as modest and demure as possible. Their attention changed when they heard the word "Iniquus." Holy hell

— they all recognized the name. I was no longer a victim. I was a what? Soldier? Spy?

"What is it you do for Iniquus?" Grey Mustache asked.

"I deliver mail to the offices. I run errands — you know, to the dry cleaners or to get birthday gifts for the wives. I pour coffee, whatever they need me to do."

"Iniquus will be looking for you."

God, I hoped so. But could they get me out of a prison? They'd be in terrible danger. Would I ask them to? Should I hope for this? I let my face brighten for a minute, and then I let it look crestfallen. "No."

"And why is this?" Gray Mustache peered closely at me. I could see the plaque on his teeth. His clothes smelled of long unbathed days. I hid my revulsion.

"My boss is out of the country, and I don't know when he's expected back…weeks, maybe months. No one else really keeps track of me. If I'm not there to fill their coffee cups, they'll ask some other low-level person to do it. No one will notice I'm gone."

Then I let myself cry silently. Tears dripped down my face. Nothing feigned here. I looked around for a tissue. Gray Mustache pulled a hankie from his pocket. My heart caught in my throat for a minute until I realized my phone was on the other side of his pants.

Gray Mustache pointed at my clothes, laying crumpled on the table. "Get dressed."

Then he walked me upstairs, down a long hall, to a metal door with a window and a chute. I retrieved my phone from his pocket, repositioning it in my bra, as he took a massive set of keys from his belt and unlocked the door. Gray Mustache gestured me in.

As the door clanged shut behind me. I stood in the middle of a small room. Mouth agape. Eyes wide.

I'm in a cell. My mind whispered in disbelief. I was in a cell! I sagged, my skeleton failing to hold me upright. Holy FucKING HELL! What?... How the...? But why...? Cell? I tilted my head back and let the banshee-scream rip from my throat.

31

I perched on the edge of the sleeping-shelf, bewildered. My feet barely brushed the floor. My focus scraped from my knotted hands held tightly in my lap to the holes in the knees of my jeans, dark where the cotton absorbed my blood when I fell. Gator, I'm so sorry — my defiance landed me in this cell. Holy crap. My brain still stuttered on the words — reeled with shock.

I couldn't believe I was alone in this grimy, stark, cement-walled, eight-by-eight box. The smell of decaying flesh filled my nostrils. My gaze flickered across to the puddle stain on the floor by the wall. Blood? My body convulsed at the thought.

I blinked vacantly in the bright light of the sun that shone through an opening on the wall and imagined a Cyclops staring at me. An empty track surrounded the hole. Thick, rusted, unyielding bars created stripes in the sun's rays that fell across the shelf. No glass, I registered. Right now, it let in fresh air and light, but what about nights? Or when it rained?

My focus traveled to the stainless-steel toilet with a tiny sink at the top and a tin cup hanging from a chain, and I blew out the breath I had trapped in my lungs.

Next to me on the shelf-bed lay a mattress stuffed with straw, folded in half. Beside it, piled haphazardly, I found a set of threadbare sheets, a moth-eaten, musty wool blanket, and a misshapen thing that I guessed would pass as a pillow.

I opened my phone to call home, and I had no bars. No tower? No ping. No triangulation. No one knowing where the hell I was holed up.

I walked to the window and gripped the bars. Standing on my toes, I could see the flat, dirt-and-weeds stretch of the security yard, the fence line, and beyond that, the tantalizing tree-tops of freedom. So close… I reached my hand out to the sunlight. Why am I here? What are they going to do with me? I pulled my hand back inside and angled my head to watch a lazy cloud roaming, listless, and alone in the blue sky.

I turned my attention to the door, testing the latch to see if it locked behind Gray Mustache. It wouldn't budge even though I shook the handle and pulled with all my strength and weight. I pounded my fists until they were bruised, screaming bloody murder the whole time, to no avail.

Crouched on my heels, my chest heaving after the tirade, I tried to rebalance both body and mind. "Open Sesame," I muttered with my head against the cold metal. But unlike Ali Baba, I was all out of magic.

Standing, I peeked out the door's window, trying to see what was in the corridor. I had a small visual field, and it was empty.

Bleak. And eerily silent.

I used the bathroom, washed my hands and face, made the bed, and then I was out of things to do. Terror seeped from my gut out through my pores. I could smell the fear on my skin and on my breath. How do people survive like this? Sitting on the shelf, I rolled myself into the fetal position. For a long time, I couldn't move. Couldn't think. I was inanimate, falling asleep crunched up like wadded paper.

Like discarded waste.

As I woke and stretched my stiffened limbs, my mind drifted to Master Wang. He was the only person I knew who had been imprisoned. When I was a teen, he told me stories about the time he was held as a political prisoner in China. In an attempt to re-educate him, Master Wang had been put in a box too small for him to straighten his legs or even sit up straight. The guards would leave him there for as many as twelve days at a time. When they finally dragged Master Wang out, he was crippled for weeks. He spent years in that prison before someone helped him escape.

Years? Holy shit. Will I be here for years? I don't think I can do this. Yeah, right, like you have a choice? I scoffed. Furious. Volcanic. How did I let myself get into this mess? I paced and kicked at the wall, trying to burn off the rage.

Finally, reason edged around my anger, poking a nervous head out into the fray to whisper, "Castigation is probably the wrong direction." I plopped down. Okay. I had to be focused and proactive. Taking in a deep breath, I looked around the all but empty cell. My mind remained an unrelenting blank. I had no idea what to do. Prison never came up as part of my training, even on Spyder's computer programs. I guessed he thought he prepared me better than this, and I should never have ended up in Maria's clutches. Shame glazed over me. If only I had listened to Striker and my team and not been so damned hard-headed.

Stop!

How did Master Wang survive? I willed myself to recall his

words. Sitting very still, I pushed my mind back in time and place to listen again to his stories. Perhaps he had given me a resource, a roadmap. His tales about imprisonment were rare. He hated remembering and only offered up his memories as object lessons.

Master Wang told me that he had kept his sanity in two ways. First, he had a schedule of things to do during the day, and second, he varied the schedule, so his mind didn't numb. And he stuck to his program. I could do that.

I also knew that he credited his martial arts training for keeping his mind and body prepared for his escape. "Your mind is your best friend or your worst enemy." That refrain constituted a ubiquitous part of my daily Kung Fu lessons, right along with the kicks and punches. I could see how that would be true. My mind wanted me to be claustrophobic and panicky, but how would that serve me?

Singing filtered under my door. "Ave Maria." Church bells chimed four o'clock at a distance, barely audible. From the little port-hole in my door, I couldn't see who was in the hall, but I heard the chutes squeaking open on rusty hinges, swoosh, clanging shut.

A young woman — late teens? Early twenties? — shifted into my view. She moved bird-like on a slight frame. Her raven hair coiled in a tight bun at the nape of her neck. Perspiration dotted her forehead and stained her blouse. She pushed a cart in front of her, picking up a tray from underneath, plopping a spoon from one bucket, a scoop from another.

When she approached my door, I peered at her through the window. Her eyes were obsidian and feverish, too big for her face. The dark circles ringing her eyes made her look haunted — from ill-health? No sleep? I wondered if she might be a prisoner, too. She shoved a tray toward me, and I caught her eye. I said

"Gracias" with a heavy American accent. She startled and moved quickly to the next door. Squeak. Swoosh. Clang.

Sitting on the shelf, I balanced my tray on my knees. The food looked unhealthy and gray, like the cinderblocks that surrounded me. I looked over at the open window, where I found my only source of color, then swirled my spoon in the food. Anxiety and revulsion took my appetite. My stomach hurt badly

The memory of a story I read as a young girl bubbled up. A Polish woman in Auschwitz had dug up worms for breakfast every morning and ate the bugs that nested on the barracks walls in order to survive. Even though I was worried that the food would make things even worse for my cramping intestines, I choked down the mess. The rice was sticky, cold, and tasteless, and so were the beans, but at least it wasn't worms and bugs.

At the five o'clock chime, the same raven-haired woman came back to collect the trays. I stood at the door.

"Give me the tray," she said in Spanish.

"*No hablo espanol*," I said in my best bad accent.

She held up a tray and pointed to me.

I smiled with an "Oh, oh!" sound. As I pushed the tray through, I held it for a second, making her look at me again. "Catholic," I said, showing her my crucifix.

She nodded and made the sign of the cross. Success? Could I make friends with this woman?

I needed information.

I needed to know where I was.

Not that it would help me escape — but it was really frustrating my brain not knowing where my feet touched the planet. It made me feel… obscure.

A bath, that was what I'd do next. The water from the single spigot only came out as cold. It was tricky to twist the handle to the on-position and wash one-handed. I took off the clothes that I had worn for three days now. Hanging up my jeans on the window ledge so they could air, I rinsed my shirt, bra, and panties and hung them to dry. I dressed in my hoodie and scrambled under the covers in a tight ball.

It was time to make a plan for my day. Maybe it wouldn't be long until I was free again. Perhaps one of the welcoming-band of guards downstairs called Iniquus wanting a reward, and soon my team would come, bribe money would cross palms, and I'd be heading home. But until then, I needed a plan.

My thoughts alighted on my Kitchen Grandmothers. My grandmothers didn't just teach me cooking skills; they taught me about their ways of doing and being. The families were very much alike and yet very different. The continuity and change of my Kitchen Grandmother habits could be useful in following Master Wang's example for surviving imprisonment. I gripped the edge of my shelf with anxious fingers.

Each day I was here, I could make that day about a Kitchen Grandmother. Thursday, I could try to think in Italian all day, and on Friday think in Spanish all day. I could sing their songs, say their prayers...yes, this would be good. This would make each day different.

Things probably ran on some kind of a schedule here. As soon as I knew more about what a day entailed, I would work that in. So far, I had a four o'clock meal delivery and a five o'clock tray collection. Hmmm. Language, prayers...what else would take time?

Well, I could separate the day into hours since I had the church bells, and I could give myself a specified task to do in each hour: meditate, exercise, martial arts. Eating would take up some time. Stories. I could tell myself about books that I've read, or make some up — write books in my mind. I walked to the door and tried to see down the hall. I wondered if they would give me writing materials? Or reading materials? Yeah, but I would have to give reading materials back. They would be in Spanish, and no one could know that I understood Spanish.

What else? I laid on the straw pallet; it was prickly and unpalatable. I giggled maniacally at my play on words. And so it starts; I was going to lose my freaking mind in here. I wasn't made to fly solo. I shook my head at myself in disgust.

Okay, I read about a guy once who was a prisoner of war, and every day of the ten years that he was imprisoned, he played eighteen holes of golf in his mind. When he was released, the first thing he wanted to do was to hit the links. After not swinging a club for a decade, he actually improved his handicap. Now, I don't know how to play golf, but I'm sure there's something in there that I can use. I have to figure out something that I can practice…

Had I been home, I'd be with Striker right now. If this was Sunday, then it was Valentine's Day. I had anticipated having a roller-coaster of a day. Valentine's Day last year, Angel had proposed, and I had accepted him. Thinking about Angel made me feel empty and sad. I knew that Striker had planned something special for me today; he had said as much the last time I talked to him. I had made some plans for him too — I certainly hadn't planned on this.

Oh my God, I felt so sick. Terrible cramps had me pulling my knees to my chest. My mind went to the pilot's water bottle. Then it went to words like cholera and dysentery.

Coiled up on my hard wooden shelf that first night, I dreamt of an African priestess. It was this woman's commanding mind that had reached out over the ocean to me and asked for my help to protect Striker's family. She had sparse gray hair, braided tightly against her head, and held in a shell-studded bun on the very top. Her face was deeply wrinkled. She looked fragile and light as if her bones had given up their solidity. When she smiled, her mouth was dotted with a few remaining teeth. She was beautiful and majestic as she walked with me through the village.

"It has been many years now since the time of great weeping. Did your man ever tell you our story?"

"No, Grandmother," I replied, as we came to a large, flat rock by the muddy river.

"Come and sit. We are living through a very dark time, a very dangerous time. But we are now finding some peace. Not very long ago, four years, I think, the guerrilla soldiers ran through the jungles. They came to our village and made us leave our huts. The guerrillas lived in our homes and ate our food — used our women, young and old. They wanted our men to leave the fields and come with them to fight. Our men said no. They did not believe in this warring. This angered the guerrillas, and they killed our men — all of them. Our husbands, our fathers, our babies. They only left the women. Each night they slept with us, and they beat us. We became pregnant with their children."

I was lying on the rock curled up like a small child with my head in her lap. I had decided to call her Grandmother Sibyl after a Sudanese story I had read as a child. She stroked my hair. And in this image, I was perfectly clean, wearing a pristine white dress, barefooted.

"One night, a man with white skin came to my hut and spoke with me. He was called Gavin Rheas, and he dressed in war clothes with a big gun by his side. He asked me why the women were wailing so loudly, where were our men? I told him about our kin and our treatment, and about Namou, who had just died giving birth to a guerrilla's baby girl. The baby girl survived, and we named her Bitter. Gavin Rheas said that his sister had just given birth to a baby girl named Cammy. He said that he would stay and help. I remember laughing. He was a big man, but with so many guerrillas, what could he do?"

I stretched and turned so I could watch Grandmother's face, hungry to hear about Striker-the-hero. *My* hero.

"I was wrong to doubt him," she said. "By morning, all of the guerrillas who slept in our village had their throats slit. He loaded the bodies onto one of their trucks and drove them far away, leaving their corpses in the jungle to be food for the animals and to rot.

"We were afraid for the time when the second patrol returned. We believed that the guerrillas would kill us all when they discovered their friends missing. Gavin Rheas said no that we were under his protection.

"The guerrilla patrol came back to our village drunk. They wanted to lay with women and go to sleep. Again, that night, Gavin came. Again, he loaded up the bodies in the trucks and drove them away. And there were no more guerillas. We told him Gavin Rheas was not a good name for a man such as he. He needed a war name. We called him 'The Striker,' like a deadly bush viper."

Oh. Now I knew how he got his call name. Why wouldn't he tell me this story before?

"We are safe here until another band of men finds us. We honor Striker, and our release from enslavement, by remembering him every night in our prayers for protection against evil."

A leopard scream in the distance made me jump. I pulled myself up to look Grandmother Sibyl in the eye, suddenly afraid. "Why did you tell me this story?" I whispered.

"So you would know that you are loved by a worthy man. A man who searches for you." She reached out and brushed my hair from my face and caught my chin in her fingers; her gaze held mine, making sure I focused on her. "You know, as things are written now, he cannot find you, my child. You will have to find your way to him, one way or another."

My heart faltered. I bowed my head to hide my tears. "Yes, Grandmother, I guess I know that —, but still, I had hoped." I lay back down and tried to assimilate this news about being on my own.

My lungs wouldn't fill.

My cells begged then screamed for relief.

Grandmother Sibyl blew lightly over my face, and I gasped the air in.

"You have much power. Do you forget your power? You may still help him to help you. If you sit on a rock, you will have no food. You must hunt, and you will find something to fill your belly."

"Yes, Grandmother." And suddenly I remembered. "I helped the girl, Anushka."

"You were brave. Do you know what gift you received for this?"

"No. I understood you were there watching as I walked back through the Veil. I paid attention like you said I should, but I didn't recognize the gift."

"It will come to you, child. Striker calls you his woman."

"Yes. I am his. I love him."

"Without a doubt. And so our prayers will be for you as well…"

32

I woke up feeling peaceful, connected, and cared for. My dream was tangible; I could still feel Grandmother Sybil's fingers in my hair. So, Striker wouldn't find me. I suspected that already. How could he? Grandmother told me I was powerful. What powers would she be talking about?

I lie still on my shelf, counting off the chimes. Sudden cramps had me racing for my toilet. The cramps were sharper than yesterday's. I was afraid to drink the water from my spigot, though I knew, without it, I would die very quickly.

Six o'clock, I heard the chutes opening and closing.

An old woman, stooped and potato-shaped, waddled to my door. She was too short to see into my window as she shoved a tray with a splat of gray, gelatinous oatmeal toward me.

My stomach flip-flopped, and I worked hard to still my gag reflex.

If the schedule was like yesterday, I'd have an hour before my tray was collected. I'd try to take up the whole hour eating. I folded the pallet and sat cross-legged on the shelf. I said a long prayer of thanksgiving and started on my first nibble.

My mind went to Master Wang's wife, Snow Bird, and my East Indian Kitchen Grandmother, Biji, who had taught me to eat meditatively. Using every sense, I took small, thoughtful bites of my food. They told me to listen for any sound, even if the sound was silence, and breathe deeply and gratefully. Each bite of food was a gift from the sun, which provided the energy for growth; the rain that provided the moisture; the earth that provided stability and nutrients for the roots. When I ate, I was one with the universe: the sun, the rain, the soil. It was a beautiful senti-ment, I thought ruefully, and gloriously true when I ate a ripe mango and felt the sweet, sticky juices drip from my chin. But not so much as I spooned the gray gloop into my mouth. Why didn't they use salt? How could they possibly get oatmeal to be so slimy — like okra, or mucus, or garden slugs? I shuddered and forced another spoonful between my unwilling lips.

Today was probably Monday. Monday was Jada's day. Jada, my Kitchen Grandmother from Turkey, was of the Muslim faith. So Mondays, I had performed Salat, the ritual prayers, with her five times a day. That was good; it would break my day into segments. Time — stretching bleakly out in front of me — was so damned daunting—my enemy.

At noon, I waited expectantly for the rattle of the food cart and the sound of "Ave Maria." It never came.

That was okay.

I didn't think my stomach could handle any more distress.

I watched out the windows where the guards walked their dogs back and forth across the yard — beautiful German shep-herds. I missed Beetle and Bella.

When the bells chimed two, a male guard came to my cell and unlocked my door. Holy hell, what now? I cowered into the corner, blinking at him.

He seemed confused and then said in Spanish, "Why won't

you come with me? I'm going to take you to the yard for exercise."

Oh, what a relief.

Of course, I couldn't let him see that I understood. "Ejercicio?" I repeated timidly.

The guard did a couple of jumping jacks. "*Ejercicio*."

"Oh, *gracias*." I walked toward him.

The exercise yard was a flat space with baked mud that cracked in jagged lines, sprinkled with a few determined weeds. I was glad to be outside, though, away from my four walls. I glanced around at the few women who were with me in the yard and wondered who they were and if any of them spoke English.

The guard seemed to read my mind and pointed at them. "No," he said, wagging an authoritative finger.

I wondered why. Was it for my protection? Theirs? I didn't want to go back to my cell, so I turned my back on them obediently.

How could I best spend this time? I wanted to know the size and shape of the buildings, how many guards they posted, how many dogs... I wanted to discover everything I could discover that might help me in making my getaway. If I wasn't going to be rescued, it was up to me to escape. I wondered why the hell I was here in the first place. What were they going to do with me? To me? I scuffed a foot into the dirt and felt fear climb my vertebrae.

The bells chimed three times, and I arrived back in my cell. I washed my hands and face and stared vacantly out my window until the bells rang out four o'clock. Sure enough, here came Ave Maria with dinner. Tonight she didn't sing. Rice and beans, blah. I sat down on the shelf and ate meditatively. This time I tried to conjure up spices and aromas — garlic, and fresh cilantro, lime, and salt. Dinner was much better in my imagination. After I sent my tray back through the chute, I did the ritual washing and chanted *Asr*, the third of the five daily prayers of *Salat*. I thought about Jada and her garden full of butterflies and felt a moment of peace.

I made it through my first day, and that's about all I could say. How was it possible for prisoners to stay sane day after day, month after month, year after year? I paced my small cell and thought about the books I had read — The Man in the Iron Mask and The Count of Monte Cristo. Their plights were unfathomable.

I compelled myself to drink from my tin cup; the water tasted metallic and tangy. I was glad the toilet was handy. My body held on to nothing. I cramped terribly. My fever spiked.

Now what?

I forced my mind away from my physical distress. If breakfast came at six, then I could get up at five. I could do an hour of meditation, and at seven, I could do an hour of yoga…if I got up at five, and I gave myself eight hours of sleep, then I should go to bed at nine o'clock.

How do I spend the last three hours today? I decided I would try to tell myself stories for an hour after dinner, and then I'd send Reiki energy to those I loved and was thinking about. I could do this for two hours each night.

When the bells tolled nine, I hung my clothes to freshen in the air and laid naked on the shelf sandwiched between the lumpy mattress and the old wool blanket. I pulled out my memories of the captives, prisoners, and cast-aways that I had read about as a child.

I tried to cull through the ideas for strategies that might help me. I remembered reading in some diaries written by early-American settlers captured by Native Americans that there were tribes who would sing until they fell asleep. This sounded like a worthwhile plan. It would keep my mind in check from the wayward scary thoughts and feelings that I tried to push aside. And so I decided to sing myself to sleep, too. Watching the brilliant stars twinkling against a black velvet sky, I tried to sing, but the notes dried up in my throat and came out as fever colored moans.

33

The sun slanted through my Cyclops window. Bird calls brought my thoughts back to the surface. I was damp with sweat. I counted the church bells — five o'clock. I bathed in the ice-cold water from the sink and dressed. My body wanted nothing more than to curl back up in a ball, but I was determined to get on a schedule. I was calling today Tuesday.

If this were Tuesday, it was Biji's day. She came from Punjab in northwestern India. This morning I used the mantra, *"Satnam Waheguru"* — God, wonderful teacher — from the Sikh tradition for my meditation hour. Then came the oatmeal. Sigh. After yoga, I attempted cardio, but my body revolted in the worst possible way.

My head was heavy. My stomach ached. I lay on my shelf, miserable. I thought about my medicine cabinet at home and how lucky I had been to have ibuprofen and Imodium. Three more hours to kill until the exercise yard.

Laying here wasn't helping. I wandered over to my window and watched the German shepherds patrol.

Last night I sent Reiki to Beetle and Bella. They felt anxious to me, but I think the Reiki calmed them. While I was working on Beetle and Bella, I remembered Mr. Miller training me to handle dogs.

"Dogs," he had said, "will read your mind far more easily than your gestures or your words. You have to think clear thoughts, and the dog will follow."

Now, of course, my dogs were trained to follow hand and voice commands, but Mr. Miller was right. If I was thinking with a clear focus, commands weren't necessary.

Then came the flash of inspiration — a two-fold idea.

First of all, it had occurred to me that the only true obstacles standing between me and freedom were the guard dogs. I could probably sleight-of-hand a set of keys from one of the guards and shadow walk myself out of here, at some point, but the dogs wouldn't be fooled. They needed to be under my command. What if I sent them Reiki and worked them energetically until I was accepted in their pack? Was it possible to bring them under my command with thoughts alone? If it just took up some of this god-awful time, then it would be worth the effort.

My mind went to a story I read about a man who worked in a canning factory. How did it go? He'd choose one person to focus kindness on… Something. No, I didn't remember. But the gist of the story clung to my consciousness. He would send out his happy thoughts, and the person in his focus that day became joyful.

And that led to the second part of my idea. If sending thoughts could theoretically work on dogs, could it also work on people? Like the man in the factory, spreading joy. What if I created Reiki energy in my cell, filling it with love and light? If I manipulated the Reiki energy to form a ball, and when someone opened my chute or door, they would be engulfed with kindness. What would that do for the person? Over time, would we develop a relationship? Could I make a connection and get some help — even though I couldn't speak to them? Well, that too was a worthy, time-consuming experiment.

In my head, my words sounded as desperate as my feelings. Right then, I just wanted to make connections enough to get a toothbrush or some soap. I wasn't sure how to maintain my hygiene or how I'd get healthy again under these conditions. I went over and dunked my head under the faucet; the frigid cold exploded my blazing headache. I scrunched my eyes tight against the pain.

It was approaching two. I had been gathering energy with the thought that it was a gift for whoever took me out for exercise. I filled my thoughts with kindness and friendship, and as the door swung open, I let the energy flow like a tidal wave.

The guard from yesterday stood with a look of stunned surprise.

I stood with a smile. "*Ejercicio*?"

"Si, *ejercicio*." And he gestured me out with an unfathomable look on his face.

My hair was still wet from my sad attempt at getting myself clean. The guard pointed at my head. I grimaced and pointed at the sink and gave him a shrug, and then mimed brushing my teeth and gave another shrug. He frowned and gestured for me to go down the hall.

The day was warm. The bright sunshine soon dried my hair. I combed it as best I could with my fingers, but it was matted and well on its way toward dreadlocks.

As I walked around the yard, I tried to get a feel for each of the dogs that I could see. Which one was the alpha? And I recalled what I had read about the "Hundred Monkey Phenomenon" in a book by a guy named Keye. In 1950's Japan, some macaque monkeys lived on the island of Koshima. Scientists taught a couple of them to wash their sweet potatoes in the water before they ate them. Other monkeys on Koshima would watch the first couple, learn, and soon they imitated the behavior. After a hundred monkeys learned to wash their sweet potatoes on Koshima, all of a sudden, monkeys on neighboring islands started washing their sweet potatoes. Yum, sweet potatoes. I kicked at the hardened ground. I'd like to eat a sweet potato — steaming hot with lime and pepper…oh, or cinnamon and butter… Anyway, the point of the story was that monkeys on the other islands had not observed the washing — they just up and started washing their sweet potatoes out of the blue.

I wondered what the critical number of dogs would be that I would need to train to be part of my pack before all of the prison guard dogs simply got it and understood. Or if they'd even behave like macaques.

In theory, if I could train the alpha, then all of the dogs should learn. I thought that I'd found him, too. He was a massive dog — a Belgian Malinois. He stood as high as my waist. I sent pictures to him of me, petting him calmly.

All I did the rest of my exercise time was pet Alpha in my mind.

The guard startled me when he came over. He had an odd look in his eye, and I rubbed nervous fingers up and down my thighs as I walked behind him. Back in my cell, he slipped a toothbrush into my hand. My eyes flew open; a grin stretched across my face. Amazing the gratitude that swelled in my heart over a freaking toothbrush.

The five o'clock bells rang on Wednesday. This was Nana Kate's day. She was a Lutheran who thought that idle hands were the tools of the devil. Nana Kate wouldn't have made it 24 hours in here. It was going to be a challenge to figure out how to use Nana Kate's tools to make the day go by.

I meditated, but only for a half-hour, then I gathered energy for the breakfast lady. She must be over a hundred. I was glad to send healing energy to her poor arthritic body. Grandma Oatmeal opened the chute, and I sent her the energy I had been gathering. She stood with the little door open for a long time after I had pulled my tray through. Finally, I heard her sigh, and the chute closed.

"Mmm. Yum. Gray slime," I said sarcastically. Shit. I was talking to myself. Crazy train, here I come. I took a bite of oatmeal and started to cry.

After forcing down my last bite, I gathered energy for Ave Maria when she came to collect my dirty plate. She, too, held the door of the chute open for a long time after I passed her my tray. Then her hand came back through the opening with a tiny, pink, plastic rosary.

"*Catolica,*" she said.

"*Gracias,*" I replied as the chute closed.

Outside my window, I saw Alpha patrolling the eastern fence with his handler. I decided to spend the afternoon with him. I sent pictures of me to him, and in my mind's eye, I sat down to scratch behind his ears and rub his belly. Soon, I received the impression that Alpha had been in a fight with another dog, and he was wounded. His skin had been pierced by the other dog's fangs, and his shoulders were sore. I watched carefully, and yes, he limped slightly. His handler seemed oblivious. I sat down on my shelf, making the hand gestures and saying the phrases that allowed me to remotely connect to Alpha and send him Reiki.

It took a long time and patience. As I worked, the sun set behind the trees, and my cell dimmed. In my own body, I felt my intestines unknot a little, making the cramps less intense. As for Alpha, he was unsure of the energy. Then I felt a shift, and the energy flowed smoothly; he seemed to welcome it, to drink it in. When I was finished, I walked over to my Cyclops, and in my imagination, I petted him some more, sending him the image of me in my window.

I swear he looked up at me as he walked by.

That night, I picked my six people to send Reiki; I'd focus on each one for twenty minutes. I made sure to start with Nana Kate since it was Wednesday; Spyder, of course; and Mrs. Nelson, since I was worried about her; and as always, I ended with Striker.

Tonight's songs were American folk tunes, not that I'd ever heard Nana Kate so much as hum a note, but it seemed to fit with a Wednesday.

And so went my week. Awful. Grandmother Sibyl came and sat with me in my dreams last night. As she walked over to my rock, I looked down and saw that there were enormous paw prints from a wild cat circling round and round me. The cat must have come while I slept in the sun. I scanned the horizon but couldn't see the leopard. Out of sight, yes, but always on my mind. A shiver ran through me.

Grandmother Sibyl handed me a bowl of tea and told me to drink it down. It tasted strongly of bitter herbs. I felt my gut untwist and the fever lift. As I rested my head on Grandmother's lap, she calmly stroked my hair.

"You are a good girl," she told me. "Thank you for sending me healing light. It was unexpected and most welcomed."

I nodded. I was too comfortable to talk.

"You know, little one, you have many skills. I see that you are trying to use them. But I also see that you are afraid to unsheathe your knife. If you are to fill your belly, you must hunt. You must be brave."

Brave. I thought I was probably all out of brave. And still, for the life of me, I couldn't figure out why the hell Maria wanted me down here in prison. The best I could figure, they planned to use me to get to Spyder.

God, I hoped that wasn't so.

Spyder...are you okay?

34

Grandmother Oatmeal brought me a comb yesterday and tweezers. I didn't have a mirror, so I couldn't pluck my eyebrows, but
weeding the hair from my legs was a time-consuming blessing.
And untangling these rats' nests from my long hair would take
hours, and hours, and hours.

Thank you, Grandma Oatmeal.

As I ate my gray-glue breakfast, trying to think nutritious
thoughts. I remembered stories of the holy men who traveled
throughout India with their begging bowls and nothing else.
They would probably feel very grateful for a bowl of slimy
oatmeal. I couldn't bring myself to a place of gratitude. I could
barely bring myself to swallow this crap.

I tried to do yoga this morning. But my fever had returned,
making my head clang. Making me greasy with sweat. I stank.
What would they do with my body if I were to die? Would they
let my friends know so they'd stop searching for me? I needed a
way to get safe water. Maybe with time, I'd build up immunities.

There was a depressing thought.

I forced my mind onto last night's dream. I knew what

Grandmother Sibyl was asking me to do; she wanted me to walk behind the Veil. I wasn't sure how in the world that would help... Possibly I could gather some information, but I didn't have any photographs. I had never tried to just pull up a vivid image in my mind. I stood at the window, my fingers wrapped around the bars as I stared at the cloudless blue sky. Maybe I could go behind the Veil with someone, like Ave Maria, if I was looking at her. Ave Maria did have a shimmer — there must be something horrible happening in her life. I still thought she might be a prisoner, too. Okay, think practically. If I went, I would have no support; I've always had support before. What if someone touched me? Very, very bad consequences, but then no one has touched me since Gray Mustache on the first day. And after I went behind the Veil, I'd need to sleep for a long time. Well, that wasn't necessarily true. I slept for days after I'd been injured; I slept for hours if I just gathered information. So, what was the problem there? Sleeping offered me respite from my reality.

All right, say I went with Ave Maria. What could I hope to gain? Maybe she'd go to her own cement cell and sit on her own wooden shelf — that was the worst-case. Best case? I'd get the name of the country and maybe even the town. So what? What would I do with that information? Maybe...maybe... I'd discover a way to escape.

I closed my eyes and sighed. "I'll go." As soon as the thought whispered through my mind, I swear a hand patted my shoulder.

That night, after I sent my tray back through the chute with Ave Maria, I looked her in the eye and asked the Veil to open to me, to let me go with this woman. Quickly, I felt the tug from my center as I was pulled from this plane. I draped myself over my sleeping shelf and left my body.

We pushed the cart down the corridor together, opening the chutes to collect the trays. At the end of the corridor, we put the trays and empty food buckets on a dumbwaiter and sent them down — I assumed to the kitchen. At the bottom of the stairs, we pulled a key tied to a piece of rope from her skirt pocket and let ourselves into a small room. After washing the filth and sweat from her hands and face, we hung her soiled apron on a hook and sank onto the bench. The cold cinderblock wall felt good against her throbbing head. We closed her eyes and rested — bone-weary, drained, and numb.

Warm lips brushed her cheek. "Are you okay, Elicia?" Oh, Ave Maria's name was really Elicia. My exercise guard crouched in front of us with a worried frown.

"Yes, Franco." She felt happy to see him; he was her balm. Elicia twisted a slender silver wedding band around her finger, then placed her hand in his. We left the building together.

At an interior checkpoint, they signed a timesheet. We moved to the guardhouse at the gate; I could feel the hard-baked yard through the holes in her shoes. Elicia moved her head, and I was able to see the other prison workers. They all looked exhausted and unhealthy. Alpha sat at his handler's feet, looking keenly at Elicia. His nose went up in the air, sniffing, making Elicia nervous, and we moved to hide behind her husband. Franco responded by wrapping a protective arm around us.

Once the gate opened and the workers swarmed free, Elicia and Franco walked hand in hand, silently up the road. We moved south, closer to the bells as they chimed out a fresh hour. A rusty blue pickup truck slowed; we clambered onto the back bed.

Franco yelled, "Gracias" to the driver. Franco and Elicia traveled in silence, Elicia from sheer exhaustion. She didn't feel sick to me; she felt worried. Worn down by anxiety. The truck pulled up to an unpainted cinderblock cottage, with a metal roof, the edges made lacey with rust. The door and windows opened to the warm evening air.

We slogged through the rickety wooden door. Elicia gave an old woman — her mother, I thought — a kiss and moved into the only other room, where a child lay in the middle of a rumpled bed.

"Pablo, Mommy, and Daddy are home, my love. How was your day today? Were you in much pain?" A tiny black-haired boy, his eyes huge in his little face, felt heated to our touch. Pablo didn't answer; he crawled into Elicia's lap and wept.

The feel of Pablo in her arms was tragic.

My heart told me that this little boy was dying.

Elicia lifted her legs so that she could cradle Pablo with her whole body. Wrapped together, they fell asleep. When she slept, I returned to my body. I learned nothing about where I was except there was a village to the south.

Supplies?

Discovery more like. I'd need to stay north when I escaped. So Elicia, Franco, and a very sick Pablo...

35

Come morning, I postponed my morning meditations until after yoga, so I could do healing work for Grandma Oatmeal and Elicia. I was rewarded for my efforts when Elicia passed me a bar of soap. I still hadn't been given a shower, and I had to use toilet paper to take care of my monthly needs. I gratefully used the soap to wash the stickiness and black filth off my skin under the trickle of cold water. This made me feel human again. Almost human. While my fever seemed less of a problem, keeping food down was still a big issue. I don't remember ever being this physically weak. If the opportunity came for escape, I wasn't sure I could take it.

When Franco saw me cleaner, he smiled. I walked quietly to the exercise yard, not sure whether my next move was a good idea or not. But I decided what the heck. It couldn't hurt. With a great deal of theater, I struggled to say, "*Bebe...es...enfermos, si?*" Baby is sick, yes?

Franco went rigid. "How do you know this?" he demanded in Spanish.

I molded my expression to portray confusion and shrugged my shoulders. Those seemed like the right reactions to express confronted in a language that wasn't understood. I made the sign of the cross, then I mimed and said in English, "I will pray for your baby."

Franco grabbed me by both arms. I wasn't sure if he would shake me or hug me; he did neither. He just looked deep into my eyes, with grief and pain. He released me, saying, "*Gracias.*"

I walked out and turned my face to the sunshine.

Alpha stood in the exercise yard today. He stared hard.

I plunked down on a little clump of grass and calmly pet Alpha in my mind's eye. I asked him about his wounds and sent him some Reiki.

Alpha sent pictures of Elicia leaving last night, and I tried to convey that I had sent my thoughts with her.

Alpha seemed to understand this.

I wasn't sure how much of this I was making up. Was I really communicating with Alpha? I needed confirmation. I spotted an empty plastic water bottle near the guard's station and asked him to go get it and return to his spot.

Alpha got up and moseyed over to the bottle and brought it back. Laying down, he rested his paw on the prize. He checked to see if his handler had noticed and gotten upset.

The handler was busy smoking a cigarette and thinking far away thoughts.

When Franco came to collect me, I picked up the bottle that Alpha had abandoned when he went on patrol.

Franco saw it in my hand but didn't take it from me.

Up in my cell, I washed it thoroughly with soap and water, then filled it full and put on the cap. Very carefully, I set the bottle on the window sill where it would get the most sun. On a cloudless day, ultraviolet light can kill bacteria in just six hours. It wouldn't make the water pristine, but my morale was bolstered by this one small proactive achievement.

I paced the floor of my tiny cell, four steps on the diagonal. I contemplated my experiences behind the Veil. The memory that kept poking at me was of Cammy's birthday party in Miami. I went through all of it, from when she saw me sitting in the orange chair — until we drove away. What was it that I should notice here? And then it sprung at me. Cammy had felt me with her. She knew how I wore my hair on the night she was attacked. And Cammy identified me the instant she saw me. Wow. I had to sit with that for a minute. I hadn't recognized this for the important piece of information that it was. When I was in Miami, I was so wrapped up in my head and my emotions that I almost missed vital clues.

Let's extrapolate this out, Lexi. Cammy was nowhere near me at the time she was kidnapped, but if Cammy saw me and knew what I said to her, maybe someone else could. Maybe even someone with developed skills could talk to me. Like Miriam Laugherty. Tonight. Yes, tonight I'd try to contact Miriam. Oh, awesome, Lexi, can you imagine if this works? Oh, holy hell. I have to stop talking to myself like I'm another person, or I really would go nutso.

That afternoon, I went behind the Veil and connected with Elicia. I wanted to watch the details of how they left the prison more carefully. I needed to know what was around once she walked out of the gates.

"Elicia," Franco said as they walked down the road. "Today, I was given a promotion."

"You were, Franco? That's wonderful. What will this mean?"

"A little more money, not much more, two hundred lempiras a week. We can maybe pay for the doctor to see Pablo again."

"And what will he say differently this time, that he hasn't said each time before? There is nothing he can do. Pablo must have an operation in the city. We will never be able to afford this. All we can do is pray." She wore her grief and resignation like a second skin.

"I had something unusual happen today," Franco continued. He seemed to weigh his words carefully.

"Besides the promotion?" Elicia braced herself for bad news.

"Besides the promotion, yes. I went in the cell to take the American woman out to the exercise yard. She is growing thinner already. Can you put more food onto her tray?" Franco paused momentarily to look down at Elicia.

Elicia read deep concern in his black eyes. We pulled her eyebrows together. "I will. Did she ask you for more food?"

We walked on. "She doesn't speak Spanish. But today, she took my arm, and where she touched me, my skin became hot and sparkly. There is something strange about her. Every time I open her cell, it feels like I'm in church. It's like…" Franco gestured his inability to find the right words.

"I know." Elicia nodded. "It's prayerful. This is what I feel when I pass the tray in and out to her. Sometimes I just stand there for a minute, and I gather strength from her. I try to show her that I am grateful — today, I passed her some soap."

"Yes, she smelled much better when I went in. Are they not going to let her shower or have clean clothes?"

"She's scheduled for the shower at the end of the week. She gets a shower once a month, like the other women. They will give her fresh sheets and wash her clothes then. I just thought about how miserable she must feel. I wanted to give her something to help. But you said something odd happened?" We reached out for Franco's hand and stopped walking so he would turn and look at us.

"We were at the door of the exercise yard when she took my arm and looked at me as if she was trying to tell me something. She came up with a few words that I could understand. She knows our baby is sick. She is praying for him." Franco's eyes were wide and unblinking.

Elicia read this as awe. "How could she possibly know this?" she asked.

"I am curious, too. Have you spoken to her? You could lose your job, Elicia."

"No, no. I haven't. How could I with no English? When she first came, she held up the cross on her necklace, and she said 'Catholic.' The next day, when I opened the chute to give her her tray, the air filled with love and healing. I wanted to give her something in return, so I gave her the rosary that I kept in my pocket. That's it. Nothing else."

"She's a saint," Franco announced.

They walked along in silence for some time.

"No one knows her name. She came in from a different burro, not the same man as usual. No one has touched her — she is not beaten like the others. They keep no file on her. I tried to find out why she was brought here. There is no record of her anywhere. No family contacts are documented."

"No information on how she ended up here in Honduras?" Elicia asked.

"Nothing. She might be connected with a drug family or

daughter to a wealthy businessman. I think she's been kidnapped. That's what I think."

"Shhh, Franco! Don't say that out loud. If it's true, you'll get us killed."

"No one's here to hear us, Elicia. I won't say anything to anyone else. What do you think about this? Why do you think she's here with no papers?"

"I think she's here for the same reason you do. We need to stop talking about it. Tell me about your job. What will you be doing now?"

"I'll start training tomorrow to drive the delivery trucks to bring supplies up to the prison."

"I won't see you anymore during the day?"

"No." And then they were silent.

A passing car picked us up and drove us to the cottage. The old woman held Pablo in her lap, rocking his damp, sleeping body back and forth. We gathered him in Elicia's arms and carried the little boy back to the bed, where we collapsed and fell asleep.

Wow. Okay. I was in Honduras? Well, that made sense. This was where Maria and Julio would have their connections and influence. When I escaped, I would have to make my way toward the airport. Even if I didn't know Honduran geography, I figured heading north would get me back to the US. Loved my optimism there.

And what else? Someone besides Franco would be taking me to the exercise yard. Franco would be driving a supply truck. Hmm, that was interesting. They thought that I had been kidnapped. If they helped me, they wouldn't be helping a prisoner escape; they'd be helping a victim escape. And their baby was ill. He needed help — an operation. I sighed. *Poor little guy.* They felt the Reiki. Wasn't that cool? I hoped it was helping.

But me a saint?

I laughed out loud for the first time since Maria's attack.

I took a short nap to recover. It was much easier to walk behind the Veil with people who were not being physically abused and drugged. It wasn't taking me days of sleep to recover myself, like it had before, just hours.

I still wanted to travel to Miriam Laugherty and see if she could communicate with me. Another first. My main concern was that I would walk behind the Veil to find Miriam, and she would be out of her body doing police work. What would that do?

Turns out it didn't matter. I was wholly unsuccessful. I found Miriam, but she had a strong field of protection around her — no one was getting in. But of course, she'd done that. It was the first lesson I learned from Miriam — always protect yourself from other people's energies.

I laid perfectly still — downcast and exhausted from trying to work with Miriam. I thought I'd landed on such an easy solution, too. I let my fingers trace the shadows that the prison bars cast across my stomach.

"Hi Miriam, it's me, Lexi. Hey, I need a big favor. Could you tell Striker Rheas, over at Iniquus, that I'm being held captive in a Honduran prison, and I need a little help, please?" Yeah, right.

I watched a spider building her web in the corner… *Spyder? What would you do if you were me? Are you alive? Do you know why I'm here?*

36

Gathering love and light for my new exercise guard was a complete and total waste of my time. The new guy was a drunk.

The mean kind of drunk that liked to show off power.

Today, he caught me by the arm and slammed me into the wall because I wasn't moving fast enough for him. I guessed in this man's life, the only dominion he had was over us prisoners, so he made the most of it — screaming cuss words at me and spitting on me as if I weren't disgusting enough already.

No Reiki love session was going to touch this guy. All I could do was try not to provoke him. I scrambled after him, cowering against the wall to stay out of arms' reach. I tried to block all of the crap he yelled at me in Spanish. How ugly and horrible I was... I didn't need him to take me down a peg. I was already rock bottom.

Yup. Pretty much every day I had contact with him was a day my loathing grew. And even though he revolted me, I had decided to attach to him briefly. I wanted to see if he went anywhere interesting in the prison.

I wanted to try to gather more intel.

Turns out that besides harassing the other prisoners and me, this man did very little. He went into an office where he sat and took swigs from a bottle he had hidden there. Fortunately for me, he sat facing in, away from the window. There was a Honduran map that came into focus every time his head swung left. Push-pins dotted the image, and on the East Coast was a big red dot. That must be us.

If my assumptions were correct, then I needed to leave the country by plane or boat. On foot, it would be too treacherous, and I wouldn't survive the trek — especially standing out the way I did — all blonde and fair-skinned. I didn't know about the web-of-intrigue I had caught myself in here. All I really knew was that Maria took me from point A to point B.

Was it just Maria, for God-knows-what reason?

Or Sylanos?

Or some unknown?

I didn't know if *any*one would come looking for me or if *every*one would come looking for me. If they would spend tons of time and money? Or if they would shrug their shoulders and eat some beans.

Why was I here?

Knowing that would make my decision making so much easier. I served someone's purpose...but what?

Since I'd landed in this hell hole, I had tried to puzzle through every crumb of my knowledge to get the answers I needed. And still, I had nothing. What if Sylanos found out that I was the one who solved the crime and busted his opera-tions? He'd be furious with me, but then, why wasn't I already dead?

A Honduran freaking prison?

Drunk got up and headed back to my corridor. I slipped back into my body. I still felt tipsy from his booze when Drunk opened my cell door. Why was he here? I had already exercised. Fear washed over me.

"*Es el tiempo por la ducha*," he snarled.

"Huh?" I shook my head, trying to be coherent — his alcohol tolerance was far superior to mine.

"*Ducha*," he yelled.

Shower time, yay!

I still had to play confused.

We walked down the hall in the opposite direction of the exercise yard. We moved through a thick metal door to the outside. Drunk held my arm in a tourniquet-tight grip. A guard with his dog stood under the roofline. It was the one I call Socks. Socks laid his ears back and growled viciously, warning Drunk to let me go. Afraid Socks was going to try to protect me, I sent images of calm, and I asked Socks to stay quiet and sit, and sure enough, he did. That was a close call. I didn't want to show my hand — I didn't want anyone to know that Socks played on my team.

"That's right, you nasty mutt. You shut your mouth and sit your ass down when you see me," Drunk snarled.

I sent love and thanks to Socks.

I'd like to say that washing up was a wonderful experience, but the best I could say was I got clean. I was ushered unceremoniously into the shower room, where I was provided with shampoo, a washcloth, and a towel. I was told to undress in front of Drunk and the male shower attendant. They took my clothes away, including my shoes. This made me nervous. If they gave me prison garb and flip flops like some of the other prisoners wore, that was going to add another element of difficulty to my escape plans…whatever they were.

I stood under the warm water and imagined myself away from the ogling. I scrubbed myself over and over again. I had kept clean as best I could, with my scrap of soap and ice-cold water, but this was so much more. After a while, I guess the guards got bored with me. They told me to stop. I wrapped up in a towel, and they escorted me to a windowless room, where I sat by myself. I was there a long time. When Drunk finally opened the door, he handed me a pile of laundry. All of my clothes had been cleaned, including my shoes, and I was given a fresh blanket and linens.

Drunk took me to yet another room. This one had a chair and nothing else. I was made to sit in the chair with yesterday's paper in front of me, *Diario de Mexico*, a Mexican City local paper. A video camera was set up with a guard crouched behind the tripod, adjusting the focus.

"You are okay?" asked a man with a horribly pock-marked face. He spoke in heavily accented English and stood to the side of the guy with the video equipment.

I said nothing. What do I do? What do I do? This is my chance...

"You will answer me when I ask you questions. You will be polite, and you will say 'Yes, sir.'"

"Yes, sir." I tried to think of a way to pass information to whoever would be seeing this. I flashed back to a story I read about the Vietnam prisoner of war who had trained himself to blink 'torture' in Morse code while he spoke. His wife saw that something was off with his eyes. They finally figured it out, and America knew of his heroism. It didn't help his lot, though. He wasn't rescued.

I hadn't thought of the possibility of a video. I hadn't practiced blinking in Morse code. I didn't know what information I would send if I had. All I had was the sliver-thin possibility that I was in a prison on the East Coast of Honduras. How helpful was that? Not very. I sighed loudly and drooped in my chair, defeated and deflated from the outset.

"What is your name?"

"Lexi Sobado," I mumbled, still trying to come up with a plan.

"You eat every day?"

I nodded.

Pock-mark glared at me.

"Yes, sir."

"You are not abused?"

Was I? Well, they weren't beating and torturing me. I turned my head to the side and looked down at the floor. Just my being here was abusive. "No, sir."

"You have time to exercise every day?"

"Yes, sir."

"You are well?"

I sat with my lips pursed tightly, eyes glaring straight ahead. Hell no, I wasn't "well."

"You are well?" he repeated with emphasis.

"I am coping," I managed to spit out through clenched teeth. Beating myself up for not having a plan in place to surreptitiously pass information to Strike Force.

"Good, good. You are well."

I said nothing. We sat there in silence. I guessed the guy had run out of questions or English phrases. The red light on the camera blinked off, and the guard stood up and stretched his back. I picked up my linens and plodded off behind Drunk, back to my cell, thoroughly depressed.

Lying on my shelf, I thought about Striker and the team. Seeing this video was going to be hard on them. Elicia had been giving me almost twice the food she had before. I knew she gave me everything she could.

Beyond my share.

Surely this meant there was less for the others. That made me feel guilty. Very guilty. But there was nothing I could do about it.

Each day, I was doing an hour of yoga, an hour of calisthenics, and an hour of martial arts. I was losing a lot of weight. Even fresh from the drying line, my once tight jeans hung from my hips. My bra was loose to the point of being ineffectual. My skin looked gray and dry. I had thought maybe I should cut down on exercising, but I needed my strength, needed to waste time, and I needed to shed some of the stress that had rooted itself deeply in my psyche. The physicality helped me maintain my sanity. So I would continue.

If I were calculating correctly, then I'd been gone over four weeks. I'd missed my twenty-first birthday; it was about two weeks ago. I had imagined a fun cocktail party with all of my friends, lots of music and dancing. All I had was solitary and gray-glue oatmeal. It sucked.

Today had been too much for me.

Thinking about my team and how frantic they must be to get me back. Homesickness thrummed in my veins.

Right now, I needed to sleep, but tonight I would try to use the Veil to visit home...if I could manage it somehow.

37

Eight o'clock, the church bells clanged from south of the prison. The sunset painted the sky fire-opal, and a flock of birds chirruped to each other as they flew toward the tree line to roost for the night. It must be ten o'clock in Washington. I worked on reasoning out a strategy for my attempted Veil walk — the best route to successfully make contact with my team.

In my imagination, they had someone in place at my house in case anything interesting happened in my neighborhood. If positions were reversed and I had drawn up the plans, I'd have chosen Gator for the assignment. Striker would want to be at Command, and Gator had already established a presence in my neighborhood — the neighbors all knew him; he'd cared for their children. Yes, they'd feel most comfortable going to Gator if they had anything at all to share. I tapped thoughtful fingers on the sleeping shelf where I sat cross-legged in my holey jeans and bare feet. Yup, Gator would make the most sense — the person I'd probably find at my house. I'd bet I could find him at my kitchen table.

I lay down on my cot and breathed deeply, conjuring a

picture of Gator. Focusing hard, I willed myself to go behind the Veil. There... Oh, I felt the pull...it was easier than I expected. Strangely simple. Unnerving. I was actually frightened by how effortlessly my consciousness separated from my body, how tenuous my hold was to this plane.

Gator and I sat at my kitchen table, chewing pizza. I could taste the hot cheese and grease. Oh yum. Flavor. Texture. We swigged a bottle of beer. The yeasty liquid bubbled, cold and relaxing, down his throat.

Gator hung warm, familiar, and huge on my small frame as I wore him like my father's winter coat when I ran downstairs for the mail as a child. Gator also weighed heavily in spirit. It was hard to support him in my weakened state. He was deep down-tired, as if he had gone for a long time with endless days and nights.

Unbearable guilt consumed him.

A phone vibrated against his hip. "Gator here."

I heard a sugar-sweet, wheedling voice. "Hey, baby, where are you?" It must be Amy.

"Lexi's house." Our answer was monotone, numb.

"Any word?"

"Yeah." Gator cleared his throat.

Her voice dropped to a whisper. "What's happening?"

"I can't tell you."

"Not good?"

"Classified." They must have gotten the video already.

"Oh. Okay. Do you want me to come over and take your mind off her for a little while?" She purred her invitation. Sex? Was she offering to come over and screw around with Gator? What? That was a scenario I had never envisaged. Imagine going behind the Veil to find...Oh. No, no, no. Say no, Gator; I can't be around for that.

"Amy, look. I'm just... I'm not gonna be able to do this right now, I'm sorry."

"Do what, Gator?" Her voice hitched. "What are you saying?"

"I'm saying I gotta hang up. I'll call you when things get better."

As he was talking, Beetle and Bella had trotted into the room and stared hard at us — unnerving Gator. Beetle whined and sniffed the air, and Bella followed. I knew they could sense me, but they couldn't see me or smell me. Poor girls. But they gave me an idea.

Using the same mind techniques I'd practiced with the guard dogs, I commanded Bella to go into the living room and get the picture of me and Angel that sat on my side table. She brought it back and laid it in Gator's lap, and then sat and whined again, stomping her paw emphatically.

"I'm here," I said. "I'm here. I'm here."

Gator froze. We focused first on the dogs and then on the photo. He held his breath. Muscles taut. Nerves strained. He moved only his eyes as we looked slowly around.

"I'm here, Gator. I'm here."

Gator stilled his search. Not even blinking. His scalp prickled. His heart raced, making his blood drum in his ears. He pulled out his phone and pressed two on his speed dial for Striker.

"Hey, man, get over here. Now," he said, pressing end before Striker responded.

The dogs whined and tapped at the floor insistently, jacking up Gator's tension.

"You feel her, too, don't you? She's here, ain't she? This is damned creepy."

Gator and I breathed and waited.

Striker must have broken the speed of sound getting to my house; that, or he was already close by. It wasn't long until we heard a knock at the front door, the key in the lock, and heavy foot-steps moving toward the kitchen.

"What's going on?" Striker asked, walking in on the strange scene.

Gator turned his head and…Striker. Oh. He was so beautiful. I wanted to fling myself into his arms. Feel him against me.

"Striker, man, she's here. She's here in the room with us."

"Lexi?" Striker looked wildly around at nothing.

"Yeah." We swallowed; Gator's spit caught on the lump in his throat.

"Can you tell me how you know?" Striker stood in the middle of my kitchen, hands on hips, legs wide, eyes narrowed, looking too big for such a small space.

"Well, I sat here on the phone when Beetle and Bella started looking at me that there way." We pointed the finger at the girls. "Bella, she run out of the room, and brought me this here photo and slipped it in my lap, and now they're crying."

"And you think she's made contact with you?"

"I thought I heard her. Well, no. I didn't hear her. You know how she says, 'I had a knowing?' If I could describe it, that there's the way I'd say it. I have a knowing that she's here." Sparks of anticipation lit Gator's nerves.

"Okay, okay, let's think this through for a minute. If she is here, and she walked behind the Veil, then she gets snatches of information and puts them together. She said it's like tiles on a mosaic. She reads the thoughts and sensations of the person she's connected to… Have you ever heard her say anything about passing information to someone from her side?"

Gator shook his head and worked his jaw.

"We have to communicate with her. I don't know how she

gets information best, so let's try some different ways." Striker pinched at his lower lip — a sure sign that his mind was working on over-drive. "We need Laugherty," he announced.

Striker got on his phone and told someone to bring Miriam Laugherty to my house now. He didn't care if she needed to be hogtied and brought in at gunpoint.

Striker looked right into Gator's eyes. He embodied everything that was good and right in this world...in my world.

Gator said out loud, "Lynx, we're looking for you. Your phone pinged from southern Florida. A contact down there says the word is you were taken out of the country by a drug mule. Can you tell us anything about how or where they took you?"

I breathed in and asked for help sending information to Gator. I pictured an airplane, and as I spoke the word, I willed Gator to understand. But he didn't. He got nothing but a stress headache. Then Striker repeated Gator's words. Then Gator said them in his head — all right, he screamed them in his head. Yow!

They got nothing from me.

Striker looked directly into Gator's eyes and spoke clearly. "Lexi, Iniquus has told us that finding you is a priority. We have every resource to find you, and we're using them, believe me. Gator said that you had pulled out some of the files from Spyder's storage area — that you had made a link to one of the men in Sylanos's network. We can't find that file, so we don't know what connection you made." Striker scrubbed an exasperated hand over his face. "We don't have any way to contact Spyder. He was taken off-grid by our client. They're refusing to let us contact him or show us the Sylanos information. Only you and Spyder know what's going on with this Marcos Sylanos guy." Striker squatted in front of Gator and looked deeply into our eyes. "And, Lexi, I don't think this has anything to do with

Sylanos. Two weeks before your kidnapping, he was shot and killed accidentally by one of his men." Striker cleared his throat and shifted to a chair. I could tell this was awkward for him — like he was acting in a play…or I was playing with his paradigms.

"We got a video of you today." Striker stopped. Violent emotions stormed behind his eyes. God, this was painful to watch — for Gator and for me.

"You looked like you're holding up as best you can," he finally said, his voice was raw. "There was little we could get from it…just you in an empty room with a newspaper. A Mexican paper. If they're smart — and they have been acting smart up until now — then they brought in the paper to throw off our search. My guess is you're not in Mexico." Striker stopped and gave me time to try to convey…something.

I tried. I tried to say it, to picture it, to visualize a traffic signal with red and green lights…

Gator felt me struggle to communicate. He was overrun with the feeling of powerlessness — flashes of the time I was tortured as Anushka crossed his memory. Guilt for not being able to help me then, guilt for not stopping the kidnapping, guilt for not helping me now, guilt upon guilt until he could hardly stand it — he dammed his emotions behind a stoic face.

Jeezus.

I'm so sorry to do this to you, Gator.

"I'll wait for Miriam to get here to ask you questions," Striker said. "Your pups are doing fine. They miss you — we all do. We need you to stay strong." He paused, then whispered, "I need you to stay strong."

Striker told me random things about my neighbors and work — the kinds of things people would ask about if they had been away for a long time. It was nice to hear him talking to me. To see him through Gator's eyes. He was balm for my heart.

Blaze burst through the backdoor, propelling Miriam forward with a tight grip on her arm. Miriam — dressed in her pajamas and tennis shoes — didn't look happy.

"What in Heaven's name is going on?" Miriam demanded.

"Ms. Laugherty, I'm so sorry to meet you this way, but this is an unusual set of circumstances. I'm about to brief you on highly classified information. I need your professional word that this is all to remain in your confidence."

"And this pertains to?" Miriam had her arms crossed tightly over her chest and tapped a ticked-off foot on the ceramic tile.

"Lexi Rueben now Lexi Sobado," Striker replied.

"Lexi?" Miriam stopped and looked around. "She's here in the ether now, isn't she?"

"We believe so, yes, ma'am," Striker said.

Miriam's face tensed, pulling her nostrils wide. "That girl's in bad trouble."

"Yes, ma'am," Striker said. He took a few minutes to lay out what had happened to me to the best of his ability. Then, Gator told her how he came to be aware of my presence.

Miriam looked right into Gator's eyes and said, "Lexi-girl, it's up to you. You're going to have to try out different ways and try on different people. Start with me." Then she sat down and waited.

I pulled away from Gator's body.

"She's left me," Gator said. Beetle and Bella went over and stared at Miriam. Miriam had opened herself to me; I slid easily into her skin. I tried again to send messages. I begged for her to help me. She sat there with her eyes closed, and her palms open.

Finally, she said out loud, "Lexi, I feel you tickling at the edges of my consciousness. Your dogs seem to think you're here with me now. Like I said, I can sense you, but I can't read you. I think you should go back into your body before you wear your-self out. I'll make a remote recovery from my end. Here's the plan, if you can travel at this time, we'll be back in this kitchen tomorrow night."

I dejectedly slipped back into my body — that had laid empty on the wooden shelf in my Honduran prison cell — and fell immediately into an exhausted sleep.

38

Outside, the night shifted to dawn. I dreamed of an African fire circle. I sat in front of Grandmother Sybil as she braided my hair, humming a comforting tune.

"Grandmother, I'm trying so hard. I want to go home. I want to be with Striker. I miss him," I whined.

"You are becoming a good hunter — following the right tracks. You must continue this path. Do you remember when you helped the young girl and her baby?" There was a rustle in the bush nearby — a form crouched. I thought I caught the glitter of leopard eyes watching me.

"Do you see that, child?" Grandmother whispered under her breath.

"Yes, ma'am."

"Remember that while you hunt, you too are being hunted. Be wise. Be careful."

How could this get much worse? I wondered, almost thankful for the depression that muffled and muted my anxiety.

Grandmother must have heard my thoughts. "No! You will

not fall prey to your emotions. You are a fighter! A warrior! Now focus. What did you discover? What gift were you given?"

"That's a good question." I thought as I woke up. What was the gift? I gave up my regular rituals for the day, except for sending Reiki to Grandma Oatmeal and Elicia. Instead, I sat on my shelf with my tweezers and plucked the hairs off my legs. What did I learn? I went over the Brennon/Anushka case, again and again, trying to focus on the finer points, trying to sift through the various details, searching for unintended consequences. I was surprised when Drunk showed up to take me to exercise. I had lost track of time as I often did when I puzzled a case.

A storm blew green and purple to the east, swelling as it moved in.

The dogs fretted nervously. As thunder shook the sky, they lunged, barking, and snarling at some of the prisoners.

The guards laughed. I imagined these men would think it a great sport if the dogs pulled away from them and attacked.

I decided to test my relationship with the dogs that I'd diligently built day after day.

"Calm. Leave it," I commanded in my mind. The dogs swung their heads to look at me and paced at their handlers' feet, dropping their heads and panting.

The handlers tried to rile them back up to no avail — even with another crash of thunder. I pushed harder. "Sit," I thought.

They sat.

I turned to hide my grin, thrilled. In my mind, I praised the dogs and rewarded them with soothing energy.

Suddenly, the rain hit with such velocity that each drop stung and bruised. We prisoners stood exposed in the yard, pummeled by the onslaught while the guards relaxed under an overhang, smoking. My sopping wet clothes offered no protection; I crossed my arms over my head and screwed my eyes tightly closed. The men laughed at our misery. As the church bells chimed three o'clock, Drunk hailed me to the door. As I ran to reach him, the mud sucked at my shoes and splattered my jeans.

Up in my cell, the floor had flooded from the rain pouring through my open window—the wind wolf-howled.

Stripping myself naked, I hung my clothes on the sink and dried myself on one of my sheets. Chilled to the bone, I wrapped myself, shivering violently, in the scratchy wool blanket and balled up on the far end of the shelf where the rain couldn't reach me.

When dinner came, I didn't budge.

Elicia looked in the window. "Saint Blanca, come and eat," she called to me. I looked at her with feverish eyes and dropped my throbbing head back on the pillow.

"Saint Blanca, you must eat. You will not get better if you do not eat."

I didn't respond. My head clanged, my sore muscles felt like I had been beaten violently, fever diffused off my skin, making me broil and shiver. Elicia sighed and left. Left without the healing energy that I offered her each day, to walk back home through this horrible storm. And what would she find there for all of her work and compassion? An empty cupboard, an ailing mother, and a dying son.

Life sucked.

Several days passed before my head stopped pounding. I had a deep bronchial cough, and I saved all of my healing work for myself. It was Sunday. I only knew that by the church bells calling the believers to prayer. I washed as best I could with cold water and my ever-dwindling soap. I dressed in my clothes and accepted the gray glue from Grandma Oatmeal.

My pants were enormous on me. I had to hold them up to walk. Elicia tried to give me huge amounts of rice and beans, but I was having trouble forcing any food past my lips. I was deeply depressed. I knew I needed to fight this, but my depression was sapping my energy and will.

I thought about Master Wang and his wife, Snow Bird. I always thought that Snow Bird's mom must have sensed her baby's spirit before she was even born in order to have bestowed such a perfect name on her daughter. Snow Bird Wang had been small and delicate. She had a vulnerability about her that reminded me of an unsheltered bird in a winter's storm, perched on an icicle-laden branch, feathers puffed out to insulate against the assault. The little I knew about the Wangs' story — what they were willing to share — made me wonder how such a vulnerable creature could possibly have survived the storms of her life. One thing I did know was that when Master Wang was by her side, Snow Bird was at peace.

Peace... I decided to go and spend the day with Striker. I needed a little peace. I would leave my body and just be with him. It might exhaust me, but it might just be the best medicine.

I found Striker in his office. It was lunchtime, and Gator came in with a tray of sandwiches. He had my girls with him. They plopped down at the men's feet and closed their eyes. The sandwiches were delicious — roasted vegetables and grilled chicken with melted cheese. The act of biting into something that needed to be chewed...

So many tastes on Striker's tongue...

Oh, so good.

He swallowed way too soon. I wanted the experience to last.

Instead, he put the sandwich aside and gulped from his mug. Striker drank his coffee black — which I detested.

Gator stared at Striker and me.

Disconcerted, Striker shot Gator a warning glance. "What the hell, Gator? Cut it out."

"Yes, sir," Gator replied. He kept staring.

"Stop!" Striker barked. Wow. His nerves were wound tight. I didn't like this — Peace? What was I thinking? Striker was antithetical to peace.

"Sir, do you remember last week when the dogs brought me Lexi's picture, and I thought I could feel her with me?"

"Is she here? Can you feel her?" Striker jumped to his feet. Hope radiated through him.

"I think she's with you. Can you feel her?"

Striker stilled. He scanned his body and his emotions, straining to feel me. "No. I can't," he muttered.

We looked at the dogs, lolling on the ground. "You said that the dogs had come over and whined at you when you felt her with you. Wouldn't they do that now if Lexi were here with me?" Striker asked.

"I don't know, sir. I don't think it were wishful thinking. I'm pretty sure she's here right now. I can see a shimmer on you. I know what Lexi was talking about now. You look like you're standing in a heat mirage — sort of pulsing and blurred."

Striker's frustration levels were through the roof.

It was hard to be in his body. Too hard. Too painful.

I left him and slid into Gator.

Gator froze.

Beetle and Bella lifted their heads and locked their focus on us.

It was an "ah-ha" moment. Striker didn't feel me. Miriam, with all her expertise, barely felt me. But Gator...my mind sprang back to the Brennon case when I couldn't go into my recuperative trance. The gift that I had been given from helping Anushka had come when I needed to heal. Gator had held me in place; he had power.

We had a psychic connection.

"Sir," Gator whispered, "she's with me now. She moved from you to me."

Beetle and Bella sat at attention. Striker yanked his phone out, calling Miriam. He quickly explained what had happened.

"Lexi, sweetheart." I heard Miriam's voice over the speakerphone. "If you're here, you know how worried everyone is. You know that everything that can be done is being done. Every night we've been going to your kitchen in case you tried to make contact — none of us could feel you. I've been doing remote searches to get any information possible that might help your team, but you know that I work with the imprints of things that have happened, and all I could get from you was 'red van,' a jumble of letters — maybe 'OIL?' And 'airplane.' My thought is that you probably weren't conscious during your extraction. Or maybe you were unclear about what was going on. I'm told you had a bag over your head." Miriam's voice stumbled. "So there weren't many imprints for me to find. I'll keep looking, though. I'm not giving up. I'm sorry I haven't been much help." Miriam cleared her throat. "Striker thinks you've been taken out of the country. We need to know where you've gone. You must find a way to communicate that to us."

Striker pulled down a huge wall map of the world. And the men waited. I tried everything I could think of to communicate. Miriam had hung up — she was heading over to Iniquus to be there in the office with me. Gator sat there, still as a statue, barely breathing, waiting for some sign. Maybe even my voice booming out, "I'm in Honduras!"

Bella must have felt my frustration. She stuck her nose in the air and, as if reaching back to her ancestral wolf-spirit, she howled a song of lament.

The men tried in vain to get her to stop.

The sound raked across Gator's and my nerves. "Hush," I commanded, and Bella did.

The dogs.

Of course!

I commanded Bella to stand up and paw at the office door. Gator and Striker jumped to their feet to follow her. Bella trotted to my Puzzle Room and over to my desk, where she stuck her nose against the drawer.

Striker used my keychain to open it.

How could I get Bella to retrieve the correct file? I had buried the Sylanos information so it wouldn't be found. I tutted at myself. Hindsight. What a damned fool.

I asked Bella to tap the desk drawer with her paw.

Striker sat on the floor, and Gator followed suit, Striker held up a file for Gator to see; Gator read off the name out loud.

They waited.

Bella did nothing.

Striker moved on to the next one. When he finally got down to the information about Maria Castillo, I asked Bella to bark.

Striker flipped the cover open.

"Holy crap," he yelled.

My energy dwindled. I knew I had to leave...They had the file. It was something. For the first time in a long time, I felt the flutter of hope.

39

Days were followed by weeks. Drunk has escorted me to four showers, so this must be June. Now the sunlight blazed through my window each day, turning my cell into an oven. I soaked my sheet in cold water from my sink and draped it over me. My clothes hung from my jutting bones, gray and threadbare. The mosquitoes that came through my window made me nervous about malaria — even with medicine, I wouldn't survive an illness. I thought about Spyder. Was he alive? Better? Was he back at Iniquus? Did he know I was gone?

If there was a Pablo, the images I got from him told me that he was growing thinner and weaker too. He didn't have much more time. Something had to be done for him — for me. I was having a really hard time of it. I questioned everything. My thoughts about craziness were self-fulfilling — they rattled my brain.

From my walks behind the Veil, I believed that Iniquus received a package from Maria — my ransom was a prisoner exchange. Her husband for me. Her husband. That was laughable. The US government thought he was a terrorist. They weren't going to expose hundreds or thousands of innocent people to this man in exchange for a twenty-one-year-old Iniquus Puzzler. Absurd. Maria was obviously desperate and dim. It wasn't going to happen. This left me with two options: one, my team finds and rescues me — or two, I escape.

No one would find me. Sure, Grandmother Sibyl had said that all along in my dreams. I had even unsheathed my big knife and walked behind the Veil — but that turned into an enormous leap toward crazy. I had taken a magnificent dive off the cliff of rationality. And the leopard. The damned leopard has been growling and screaming at me day and night for a week now, giving me no rest. My nerves were stripped of their myelin sheathe, leaving me painfully exposed and raw.

Last night I dreamt of Grandmother Sybil.

"Run!" she screamed at me. "Run! Run!"

Where the hell am I supposed to run? What am I supposed to do? I paced like a caged animal in my cell, rattling the metal bars that held me in place. My carefully formed plans for sustaining myself went to hell. Hell. Yes, this was fucking hell.

Losing it.

I am losing it.

My intellectual mind knew all along that people in solitary confinement for long periods of time with no one to speak to and nothing to do predictably go crazy.

"Did you think you could beat the odds, Lexi?" Ha. I stood in front of my Cyclops window, staring past the razor-wire out into the trees. "Yeah. I thought I was that special — that strong. I've been living in Delusion-land."

I can do Reiki, and I see the good effects. I slunk over to my sleeping shelf and lay down on my pallet, staring up at the ceiling where the moss grew like continents on a gray globe.

And there are the dogs. That works, too. But, my applying simple animal communication techniques? So what?

I swung my legs off the shelf and returned to pacing. Back and forth. Back and forth. So I thought that I could get Bella to find a file? I told my team the East Coast of Honduras? *Ha.* And what about the other stories I told myself? There was no little Pablo dying and depending on me to sustain him. He was simply the creation of my hallucinations, the mad mirages conjured by my bored mind.

In my fantasy world, I told myself the fairy tale of what was happening up in the States. Striker had read the file exposing Consuela Hervas as Maria Castillo Rodrigues. In that same file, Striker found out that Julio was her husband and was in the federal pen down in Florida. It only took a quick phone call to find out that Julio was getting regular visits from his wife. It was only a short plane ride down to Florida to find Maria with the hopes that she would lead the team to me. And of course, if that were true, logic would say that Iniquus then put her under surveillance until they received my ransom note, offering a prisoner exchange for Julio. Once Iniquus received the ransom note, they'd realize Maria could no longer visit her husband. Surely, then they'd arrest her.

I imagined Maria as a prisoner — just like me. Only in an American prison, she'd get food, clothes, showers, health care…

And then Iniquus would interrogate her, make her crack. Soon. Soon they would be coming to set me free.

I knew this wasn't true. If it were, then Grandma Sybil's warnings wouldn't sound so frantic. "RUN."

I doubled over, laughing hysterically.

Hysteria — I lived there now.

I moved to my window and stared blankly out. Shit.

Going behind the Veil was a lovely piece of fiction I had told myself that never happened, though it made these months tolerable. And now I didn't even have that.

When I walked behind the Veil back in DC, I always had people confirming my every detail. 'Yes, that's right.' 'Yes, confirmed'... 'Confirmed'... 'Confirmed'... 'Confirmed.' Nothing was confirmed. Therefore, I could trust nothing was real. If nothing was real, then I was a crazy loon. If I were basing my survival on my vivid imagination, I was dead. I was dead and gone, and Iniquus would never find my body.

The leopard screamed, and I jumped.

Holy shit, that was close.

I grabbed the bars on my Cyclops and tried to shake them. Then slid down to squat against the damp wall.

Yesterday, I let myself wallow in mental instability. This morning, I was determined to get myself back together. To pull myself off the ledge.

Elicia was here before Grandma Oatmeal had made her breakfast rounds. She stood at my door and sobbed. Just stood there and let grief pour out of her. She was moaning, "Pablo."

I had continued to send Reiki to Pablo, even though I doubted his existence. I thought that I was probably sending Reiki to some child named Pablo, somewhere, that had no connection to Elicia and Franco — if those were even their names, and if their connection wasn't created in my imagination. Emotions flooded me as I heard her. She said, Pablo.

Hope glimmered — maybe I hadn't lost my mind entirely.

But what was wrong? Was Pablo worse? Did he die?

I couldn't talk to Elicia. I needed another solution; I needed to think. While she sobbed, I sang "Ave Maria" to her and hoped she felt some solace.

Every day I had watched for the rhythm of the compound. Things worked on a dependable schedule. From my window, around one each afternoon, I saw Franco drive his truck over to the buildings and park near the showers. At two o'clock, when I was in the exercise yard, I couldn't see the back of the truck, but I could hear the men unloading. Franco would stroll to the front of the truck, which was in my line of vision. He smoked a cigarette while he waited for the church bells to sound three, and then he drove away. I decided to talk to Franco today.

I stood staring out my window at the woods beyond, preparing myself for my coming interaction with Franco, feeling disjointed.

Run. I still felt the force from Grandmother Sybil's command, yet again. "Run. Run." Her plea cycled through my brain.

Today, Grandmother? Now?

A pouf of dust rose into the air at the far reaches of my visual field. A car must be charging up the road fast.

Danger is moving in.

My "knowing" blazed mottled-red behind my eyes. My breath caught. Maria! Oh, holy hell.

The keys rattled in my door, making me jump.

The church bells rang two.

Drunk had come to take me out to the yard. Thank God.

I trotted beside him down the stairs, glad for the first time that he had such a fast gate. Get me out of here.

As usual, he used my exercise hour to go sit in the shade and smoke a cigarette with his eyes closed. This time, he sat down without his keys on his belt loop. I shadow walked back to the building. The guard dogs' ears perked; they stared unwaveringly at me. I could hide from human eyes, but not a canine's. I commanded them to "leave it" when they looked at me and asked them to turn their attention to a uniformed guard walking toward the front gate and bark. They did, giving me enough cover to unlock the door and slip back into the prison.

I worked as quickly and quietly as I could, moving through the building to the main entrance. I watched as Maria, dressed in a baggy, green sweatsuit, hugged Gray Mustache.

"What are you doing here?" he asked, his voice filled with tension. He searched up and down the hallway to see if anyone was listening. I froze in the shadows.

"Well, I…"

"In here." Gray Mustache interrupted. He grabbed Maria by the arm and jerked her through the door to an office. I slunk up the corridor and rolled under the bench that sat to the side of the door. It wasn't the best of covers — it was all I could do.

"Is she still alive?" Maria's voice drifted under the crack at the bottom of the door.

"Barely." Came Gray Mustaches grim answer.

Me? I'm barely alive?

"She does us no good dead, *Tío*," Maria scolded.

"Believe me, I am very aware of this. You knew before you sent her here what a dangerous little game this was for both of us. I have to treat the girl the same as any other prisoner, or it would attract even more attention."

"Bad then?"

"I don't know that she can survive the summer. Are you making any progress with Julio and the money?"

"No. I came to get some incentive."

"You don't mean…" Gray Mustache stopped mid-sentence. My skin prickled with fear.

"Why not?" Maria asked.

Why not what? What the hell are they talking about?

"Because she won't survive it, and without her, you've got Iniquus, the US government, and maybe even Sylanos's people coming after you. It was a brash plan at best. Did you hear Sylanos is dead?"

"Does that change anything?" Maria asked. "Julio's still alive, and he's still locked up — so, that tells me there is still someone pulling the strings. Someone who cares about being exposed when the computer dumps those files into every in-box in America."

What were they talking about? I wasn't following this conversation at all; it made no sense to me. I was still stuck on the incentive.

"…that means gangrene. And probably death. You won't have anything to bring to the trade," Gray Mustache said.

"I'll have to take my chances — right now, I'm about out of options. I made a bad mistake, *Tío*. I thought Spyder McGraw cared for Lexi like his own child. That's what Beth Sylanos told me. But if McGraw loved her, she would be home by now. Either he would have pulled out one of his many chits, or he would have broken Julio out of the prison."

"Maybe he doesn't know she's in danger," Grey Mustache said.

"Lexi worked for Iniquus, for Heaven's sake. Surely, they contacted McGraw. Of course, he knows. He must have decided she's not worth the trouble. I should never have trusted Beth." I heard things slamming around the office as Maria threw a tirade. "I can't think of anything else to do. I need Julio out of prison, so we can access the money he hid away. Something has to make

Spyder McGraw act. I need to send Iniquus her fingers. Maybe then we can stop playing games."

WHAT?

Silence followed. I wondered if they stopped talking because they could hear my heart pounding like a kettle drum — my raspy breath hitching and sucking air erratically.

"Nobody from Sylanos's cartel knows she's here?" Maria finally asked.

"So far, we've been extremely lucky. They haven't sent us any new packages since Sylanos's death, so no one has been here sniffing around. Once you do this? Well, I'll end up dumping her body in the ditch with the others. After a week in the sun, no one will be able to identify her. Sylanos's cartel would only care if they figured out how you worked to outsmart them."

Maria murmured something I couldn't catch.

"Yes, well, I figured we'd have to kill her eventually anyway," Gray Mustache said with a ho-hum voice. "Especially if things turned out well, and Julio was released. Come. It's been a long trip for you. Take a shower, eat something, maybe a nap? I have a man that I think will greatly enjoy this project."

The door opened, and the two of them walked out arm-in-arm, moving toward the front entrance.

He changed from Spanish to English, I guessed, so no one could understand. "Tomorrow morning, the three of us will go visit your little Lexi. I suggest you video the whole thing. Her begging and screaming and all the blood will have a bigger impact on those all-American-heroes at Iniquus than a couple of fingers in a box." The front door squeaked open. I lie petrified.

As soon as Gray Mustache and Maria left the building, I rolled from my hiding place and ran for the door to the side yard and Franco's truck.

There, I waited for him to smoke his cigarette; my emotions exploding.

Emerging from the shadows — just enough so that he knew I was there — I shrank back again and spoke quietly. "Franco, don't move. Don't show any signs that I'm here with you," I said in fluent Spanish, with a decidedly Puerto Rican accent. Franco froze. I was surprised I was able to get my lips to work properly.

"I am worried about your son Pablo. Tell me what's happening."

Franco visibly shook; his cigarette dropped to the ground. "You are speaking Spanish. How do you know our names? How did you get over here? They will shoot you," his whisper was fierce with alarm.

"Franco, I'm supposed to answer your prayers. You have prayed that a miracle would come to your family and that Pablo would get the medical attention he needs to survive. Yes?" Confirm me, Franco, oh please, confirm me.

"We have prayed hard. But Pablo grows weaker in this heat. Without surgery, the doctor has no hope for him."

"Yes, that's what I feel to be true. So much so that I need to escape and help him, Franco. I am risking my life to escape. I am your hope — your only hope for your son's survival. I'm an American and have a great deal of power where I come from. That's why they have imprisoned me here, to offer me in exchange for a terrorist being held in America. But, Franco, look at me. I'm too weak, and it's too dangerous for me to take Pablo with me now. Once I get home, I will send a team to take your family to the United States, where Pablo will get the medical help he needs."

Franco was beyond frightened. I could see the shine of it coming off his skin. He would be shot if they found out he'd helped me. I was putting him in terrible danger by asking him to trust me, and more, to trust in his prayers.

What if God had sent me to be their miracle, and he turned me down?

How could he survive knowing that when offered a chance to save his little boy, he was too cowardly to grab it?

His face hardened as he made his decision. "What am I to do?"

"Nothing. Forget I was here. Forget I said anything about your son. Breathe deeply and know that all will go well."

The bells rang, and Franco moved toward the cab. I shadow walked to the back of the truck, climbed in, and lay down against the tailgate so anyone looking in would see past me into the emptiness. Franco cranked the engine. We drove over the grassy field to the front gate. I heard the guard's heavy boots on the gravel. He stopped to talk to Franco. Another guard walked over with his dog; it was Alpha. Alpha wanted to know why I was in the truck. He sent pictures telling me I should be in my window. I sent pictures back, saying I needed to go home and feed my dogs, but I would visit him. Alpha walked around the truck without alerting anyone I was inside.

The bells that rang to mark Franco's time to leave were the same bells that signaled Drunk that his break was over, and he needed to take me in. By now, he had discovered that his keys were gone, and I was, too. Since there was no commotion, I assumed that Drunk went into self-protection mode. He would have found that I had left the door ever so slightly open for him. He probably let himself in, and tried to go on about his tasks as if I were still there. Buying himself a little time to find an alibi, an excuse, or an escape plan of his own.

40

Elicia would discover that I was not in my cell when she brought my food at four. I wasn't sure what she'd do. I didn't think that she'd send up an alarm, but she might ask questions. She was the wild card. Would she bring attention to me? How much time did I have? If I were lucky, I wouldn't be discovered until Grandma Oatmeal in the morning. Possibly longer. If Grandma Oatmeal didn't notice, then maybe I'd have until Maria and Gray Mustache came to remove my fingers. I convulsed. If any of that were true, I had to get to the airport and away tonight.

As we drove down the road, Franco stopped and jogged to the back of the truck. "Now, what should I do?"

"What do you usually do, Franco?"

"I drive by my house and check on things, then I drive the truck over to the supply center and walk home."

"I need some things. I need a set of Elicia's clothes, some food and water, a map, a blanket, a plastic ground cover, and a gun."

"I have no gun."

"Okay, a knife then. Where is the supply center?" We whispered even though we were out in the middle of freaking-nowhere with no one to hear us.

"Ten kilometers to the south of my house."

"That's fine. Just stop as soon as you can when there's no one around, and I can get out of the truck. You will continue on." Franco pulled a rag from his pocket and wiped at the sweat that dripped in his eyes.

"There's a tunnel a short distance down the road from my home. It would be a good place to get out, and you can hide in the forest. They will have the dogs out looking for you, but they won't look to the south, and they won't look that far away."

"Where will they look?"

"To the north, where there's an airport, or to the east, where there are boats on the coast. They wouldn't think south because of the forests. Do you have a plan?"

"Yes, but it's better for you that you know nothing."

Franco looked over his shoulder. I could hear a truck rumbling toward us. He ran and climbed into the cab and headed back down the road.

Our truck stopped. The cab opened and shut. I heard Franco ask about Pablo.

The door hinges screeched.

The grandmother said she needed to go down the street for a minute; Franco told her to go ahead.

Time passed, then Franco told the old woman goodbye.

We were off down the road. We had only driven a short way when everything was thrown into darkness, and the truck stopped.

"Hurry, hurry, the coast is clear." Franco thrust a backpack into my arms.

"And here is the map. I have circled our village, so you can find us again, the airport, and a fishing village. The fishing village is twenty kilometers away. The airport is not quite thirty kilometers. I have thought about it — overland, you will fail. Even though they will watch the boats and planes carefully, you seem to know what you're doing. I depend on you for my son's life. May you be blessed in all you do. We will pray hard. I know it will take you time to get to America — please, please hurry. Pablo hasn't got much more time to wait."

Franco jumped into the cab and drove away. I slunk from the tunnel and eased into the trees, walking a ways off, then pulled off the pack to see what Franco had gathered for me.

The heavy camping pack held a compass, a sharp hunting knife in a side holster, and a belt. I attached those to me right away. I needed the belt to hold my jeans up. There were no other clothes - probably Elicia had no others. That or Franco was afraid that what he'd packed would implicate his family if I were captured. He had wrapped a ratty wool blanket in a plastic ground cover. Underneath, I found a two-liter bottle of water, some soap, and lots of food in old plastic margarine tubs. I pulled out the packet of tamales wrapped in waxed paper and ate them right away. They were still hot; the pork juices dribbled down my chin. I ate until I was full. I needed the energy. It would be too burdensome to carry all of this weight.

Church bells sounded nearby; it was four o'clock.

I would make the best progress while it was still light enough to see. I'd have to push hard with eighteen miles to cover — daunting under the best of circumstances. If I could keep a pace of four miles an hour, I could make it to the airport by dark — maybe get a chance to look over the planes. I checked the map, checked the compass, and kept the road vaguely in sight, on my left, as I made my way through the trees and underbrush at a slow jog.

A little over an hour and a half had gone by when I had to cross the road. I was approaching the jail. I had sent thoughts to Alpha, asking how things were at the prison. He sent back pictures of calm: lazy guards, heat, thirst, boredom. I told him that soon they would discover that I had left my window to go home to feed my dogs, and please lead the guards, away from my scent, to the west. He said he would. I slowed to a walk as I connected with each of the dogs that I had gotten to know over the past months, asking them for their help. That might buy me time. And the exercise helped divert my attention away from my screaming body.

Exhausted and panting, I leaned against a tree. Eighteen miles had been too much. Too hard, especially in this heat.

I thought of Striker at SEAL training. He had pushed his body beyond what he thought was physically possible and had not just survived but thrived. I focused on that, pretending this was my BUDs training. If Blaze and Striker could get through their hell week, I'd be *damned* if I was going to ring the brass bell. I pretended I was in training with them beside me — anything to get away from the voice that said 'lie down,' even when my muscles, enfeebled from months in prison and lack of food, bunched into cramped knots, and my heart knocked on my rib bones.

The stitch in my side doubled me over.

I gasped and spat into the dust at my feet.

I will *not* lie down.

As the sun tilted past the horizon, the evening sky was painted indigo and filled with bats. I crouched beside a pine tree, feeling the rough bark under my fingertips. The forest vibrated with evening sounds.

I spent time getting a feel for the airport — trying to sense any guards, dogs, or people. The SEALs have a saying, "slow is smooth and smooth is fast." I needed to apply a little smooth to this operation.

I slunk from plane to plane to figure out which one I would take. I settled on a Cessna C500 Citation. It was the largest plane out there. I was looking for fuel capacity. I had a long way to go. The others were little Cessna 150s and the like; their tanks were tiny, 200 maybe 300 miles.

I shadow walked to the C500. Its fuel gauge showed full. As I peeked into the back, I saw everything unnecessary had been stripped out. Most likely, this one was used for carrying drugs and other contraband. There was nothing in it now to balance the weight from front to back. That might be a problem, but I didn't see another viable choice.

I made my way to the hangar and tried the handle on the locked door. I slithered around, peeping in windows. No one seemed to be here. On the far side, one of the bays hadn't been completely closed. I squeezed under, dragging the backpack after me.

My first task was getting my cell phone operational. I found a five-volt cord and a couple of paperclips to make a you're-in-deep-shit charger. As the battery charged, I went to the bathroom and took a quick shower. I was desperate to clean myself. I was sure to wipe the moisture out of the stall and take the wet towel with me. I changed my clothes into some man's jeans and T-shirt

I found in one of the lockers, stuffing my clothes into my pack. I refilled my water bottle and filled another bottle that I found under the kitchen sink. I ate a bite or two out of each of the open containers in the fridge — not wanting to give a heads up that I'd been here. And I studied the maps in the control room, jotting down coordinates.

This was the scary part. My survival came down to the decisions I was about to make. I needed to figure out what in the world I was going to do from this point. I could try flying to a different country, Belize or Mexico — but I still had no idea about the role I was playing in the kidnap-Lexi show. Would the prison guards just ignore the fact that I was gone? Would they launch an international manhunt? Who was the puppet master here? If it wasn't Sylanos himself, were there others from the cartel in on Maria's scheme? I didn't understand the conversation between Maria and Gray Mustache. They seemed afraid of Sylanos knowing where I was. Was he actively looking for me? Were they holding me away from Sylanos' group because they wanted me, and Maria wanted a pay-off? If the cartel was searching for me, then I couldn't land anywhere in the Caribbean, Central or South America; their players would snatch me as soon as the door opened. The Sylanos machine's power and connections were omnipresent, and they would not like it if a little chicklet from Iniquus outwitted them. I would die.

What if it were just Maria and her tio? Then I could safely land at any airport and ask for help.

Since I didn't know, I had to assume a worst-case scenario and act as if there was an international manhunt that I needed to thwart. So, the only direction I could go was to the US. Texas was about a thousand miles away. Miami looked like around 800 miles. I was going to aim for Miami. I didn't know how far a single tank would take me. I'd have to plan on refueling.

I'd retrace my original flight and set down on that grass landing strip on Isla de Juventude to refuel. Oh, holy hell, Maria would probably know about this strip. I'd have to make the stop darned fast. Up and out, and back to the States before morning when my escape would certainly be discovered. I shook my head at the map, hands resting on my protruding hip bones. My teeth chattered together, rattling my thoughts.

It had been many months since I had been at that landing strip. Hopefully, it was someone's job to come in and refill those fuel bladders regularly. I sucked in a deep breath and tried to focus, moving my shaking finger over the map. There were little red lines all over the Caribbean, and all of them were in remote locations. Secret landing strips. I found a red line drawn on Isla de Juventude. I would bet anything this one was the strip that I was looking for. Probably a drug lord paid the government graft to ignore it.

I heard a jeep motoring up the road. I crouched by the window and watched it go by. They didn't even glance over at the airport.

So far, so good.

I wiped my sweaty palms down the stolen pants. Okay, I had a plan.

I grabbed a set of keys from the flight room and retrieved my cell phone. Making my way carefully to the plane. I did a pre-flight check. If I was going to leave, it had better be sooner rather than later. The wind bent the treetops, and the air hung heavy with moisture—a storm boiled in the distance. I needed to get going while I still had a chance. "Stupid as hell flying in this weather," I muttered.

Whoever owned this plane was serious about what they did. I checked for an ELT, the emergency tracking device, and found that it had already been disconnected. The owner didn't like to be tracked any more than I did. The plane had a Garmin system for navigation. I put in the coordinates for the grass strip.

Time to go.

The engine roared.

I taxied to the runway, and the plane raced upward.

41

When I turned twelve-years-old, I joined the Civil Air Patrol with my dad. C.A.P. was like the aviator version of scouts. We learned how to fly and practiced our skills by doing orienteering runs and search and rescue missions. I won a scholarship to do ground school, which I loved. My dad taught me how to fly, and I'd go up with him on practice missions all the time.

I'd flown a lot of different kinds of planes — jets and props — not just the little two-seaters like the ones I had left behind at the airport, but I'd never flown a C500 before, especially one that had been stripped down. I couldn't wrap my brain around just how mind-bogglingly dangerous this was. With nothing in the back to balance the plane, I ended up front-end heavy. Now when I made adjustments with my flaps — the only way I had to adjust for my height and orientation in the sky — the plane responded erratically. My plane acted like a drunken sailor listing from side to side, sliding up and down in the sky.

And if that wasn't enough, the turbulent air bobbled me around. My stomach lurched — not good. Eating food rich with fat for the first time in months made my stomach volcanic. It roiled — wanting to spew everything back up as red hot lava. I found a pile of airsick bags in a side pocket of my chair, and I used them one after the other until I had nothing left in me but dry heaves and a trickle of bile.

A two-hour flight, I cajoled myself. But faced into an enormous headwind, I knew it would take much longer. The squall slowed my progress and sucked my fuel. My palms sweat, my knees trembled — I never once thought that it would've been better to have stayed back at the prison with Maria.

I shouted Blaze's motto out loud every time the plane dipped and dropped through the sky, "If I'm going out, it's going to be in a blaze of glory!" Somehow this fit Blaze so much better than me. But I needed to borrow some of his bravado.

The storm expanded on the Garmin screen; most of the Caribbean fell under its enormous reach. Expletives zipped up and burst like fireworks on the surface of my consciousness. I heard men talking over the radio about Tropical Storm Ivan, out in the Atlantic. As it approached the Gulf, Ivan was organizing into a category one hurricane. Holy hell! I needed to get down. NOW.

Please, God. I don't want to die. Please let me get home.

I inched closer to my goal. My nerves were frayed and misfiring. Desperately, I grappled with my panic — "Head in the game, Lynx." I heard Striker's words coming back to me from the bank robbery debacle.

"I can do this!" screamed my inner cheerleader over the roar of the wind and the engine. Gusts tossed me like a rag doll. The wind shear could break my wings off at any given moment.

Insanity.

I forced my eyes to blink, my lungs to expand then contract.

I didn't hear the voices of any other pilots coming over the radio. I did see some boats below me being pitched on the waves. I wondered if they had looked up, and having seen me, thought, at least I have a chance.

———————

I approached my coordinates with thanksgiving. But boy, would landing take all of my skills and then some. I could only see by the strobe lightning. Well, I had that to be thankful for, I guessed. I had landed a few times in pastures and on country roads to get a feel for making emergency landings. Everything I knew was from my dad; he was the best. God, I wished he were piloting now.

"Dad, help me. Help me get down," I prayed. Landing in this albatross was going to take fine-tuned skill. I needed the hands of a surgeon, or I would wreck in the jungle.

I took every inch of the landing strip. I skidded toward the tree line then jerked to a stop. The storm winds picked up in velocity. I took a deep breath, opened my door, and fell thankfully to the ground.

I stumbled to my feet — my legs rubbery beneath me.

Okay, Lexi, think. The storm was too big. I'd have to wait it out. Maria shouldn't find out I've gone until morning. Then they'd form a search party. Possibly, she'd make a call to someone to check this place out if and when she figured out I had a plane. I should be safe here until the storm calms — from Maria at least. I looked at the sky and the trees. This was bad.

If I were to park the plane by the trees and a tree fell on it, and if I survived, I'd be stuck in Cuba. If I parked on the runway, the plane would take the brunt of the wind. The wind could get under the wings and toss me around some more. I could lose the plane that way. I had no idea what to do here, and I was well aware that my decisions were forming in a panic-stricken brain. I blew out a long-held breath and climbed back up behind the steering column. I taxi-ed around to the bladders to refuel and make my plane as heavy as possible.

I peeked under the reservoir cap. Yes, full. I did a happy dance. As I grabbed up the hand pump and filled my reservoirs, the wind whipped up debris that stung my exposed flesh. I had to lean against the plane for support.

Lying flat on my back in the belly of the plane, I tried to be reasonable. Okay, my situation sucked, but it sucked a lot less than twelve hours ago. Anything was better than rotting with gangrene, waiting for death in prison without my fingers.

Oh, Maria, this isn't over by a long shot. When I'm strong again, I'm coming for you.

I kept my cell phone turned off. I was afraid to call any attention to myself. If I checked for bars on my phone, I could ping on some cell tower, and that just might be the thing that would put a spotlight on me. Even if people weren't looking for me because of my prison break, the guy I stole this plane from wouldn't be happy. I'd guessed that this type of plane costs about a half-million — used. And again, I had no information. The plane's owner could be working solo, or he could be in a show with a big-time puppet master. That wouldn't be pretty. I may have two drug kingpins looking for me now.

With my plane at the top of the runway full of fuel, I rested. I ate from my backpack and drank from my water bottles. I only exited to urinate, and I didn't walk away from the plane.

Even though the location was somewhat protected by the hills on either side of the runway and from the pine trees that grew thick and tall, the plane still rocked and creaked ominously.

It didn't rain where I was, but the wind was terrifying. I thought it might catch under the wings and roll me like a wave breaking on the shore. The lightning strobed like a disco laser show. It was stunning and nightmare-inducing. Thunder was a constant. The storm wasn't letting up. I listened to the radio, and it seemed that the weather system had stalled in the Gulf, causing catastrophic flooding to the islands. I portioned my food and water to last me through the storm.

I had thought I might be stuck here for a day or two, and then once I was in the air again, I was only a short flight to freedom — the US. But I was sadly, very sadly, mistaken.

My body wasn't doing well. I was in dire straits. I probably weighed less than a hundred pounds once I left the prison. Jogging eighteen miles had taxed my last reserves. The food that Franco gave me was far too rich for my system — after living on only beans and rice for so long. I couldn't keep any of it down, and now I was out of food and on my last half bottle of water. I made the decision to fly to Guantanamo, on a wing and a prayer, as it were. My life wasn't the only one at stake. Every day that went by was a day that Pablo suffered and drew closer to death. I needed to save him.

I found some paper and a pen and wrote my goodbye letters. I wasn't giving up; I was just being prepared. Stories don't always have the hoped-for ending, no matter how hard the person fights for their happily-ever-after. No guarantees in this life. Nope. None.

The first letter I wrote to Striker. I told him how I'd tried to save myself; I'd never given up trying to get back to him. I asked him — as a gift to my memory — to help Pablo. I told him the story, vaguely, leaving out the part of how I knew about this little boy and the part about Franco's help with my escape, in case my letter landed in the wrong hands.

I told Striker how much I was in love with him. It was my great shame to have been too fragile and self-protective to be able to say that out loud to him. I told him that I knew how painful it was to experience the loss he was going to be experiencing, how ironic I found it that I had begged him not to go away and die and hurt me. And here, I was the one to go away and die and leave him alone to mourn my memory. I would never have chosen to cause him this kind of pain.

As I worked on my letters, I realized I had no will, so I wrote one out. I left my wedding rings to Striker that and the gold brooch he had given me as my Christmas gift with my mistletoe kiss the morning this whole fiasco started, and Spyder came into town. These were my symbols of love and commitment. I knew he'd understand their meaning.

I left my duplex and everything in it to my neighbor Missy. That would give her a safe place to live and the income from the rental side. I left my girls, Beetle and Bella, to Gator the Great, with thanks for his affection. I left my motorcycle to Jack, with the hope that he would never be ambushed again. My car went to Blaze. And to Deep, I left my guns and my gym equipment, with thanks for all of our times training together. I asked that my money be put into educational accounts for all of my neighborhood kiddos. It wouldn't be much, split up among them; it was more a gesture of hope for their future and my joy in having known them.

I wrote what I knew about Maria — hopefully, someone would go after her if…well if worst came to worst. My final note was to Spyder. Maria was wrong. I was his daughter. We loved each other. He was just off-grid — incommunicado, or too sick, still. Something. There was a reason, a good one, that Spyder didn't help me.

I fell asleep in the back of the plane, wrapped in the moth-eaten wool blanket. I woke up to nothing.

Nothing?

I peeked out. The trees still swayed, but gently now. Debris stippled the clearing. I had to go. I had to go! Guantanamo wasn't far away. They'd feed me and get me medical attention. I cleared off the runway as best I could. I started the engine and looked down at my instrument panel. Fried.

A direct lightning strike? I sat in stunned disbelief. I could still fly, but I had no navigation and no communication systems. A chill ran through me. I leaned over the yoke as a sob broke free—no Guantanamo.

I couldn't announce myself and surely flying — unidentified and unannounced — into a military area on high alert was certain death. I would have to navigate off the sun and aim for the US coastline. Ah, there were my expletives again. The familiar refrain of cuss words sang through my head in three-part-cacophony.

I took off. While the wind seemed calmer on the ground, these were still near-impossible flying conditions. As I climbed higher, things got worse. I didn't stand a chance heading for Miami under these circumstances. I put the wind at my back, which pointed me north-west. That gave the body of my plane some relief. Where would that land me? Northern Mexico? Texas? Did I have enough fuel to get that far? For a girl who announces, constantly, that she didn't do daring deeds of do or die, I sure as hell ended up in a lot of situations that required daring deeds of freaking do or die.

I was getting disoriented and faint — mentally and physi-cally desperate. After flying for hours with the bright sunlight glaring into my right eye, I spotted a coast line up ahead, and I came in low. I had been trying to decide which I was more afraid of, getting picked up on radar and not being able to hear or respond by radio or coming in without being spotted?

I didn't know what the FAA did about aircraft that didn't respond.

I'd never not responded before, and it never occurred to me to ask.

I guessed it depended a little bit on where I was flying and what was near me. I thought southeast Texas was probably riddled with oil rigs and military installations. I decided to try to fly in low enough to avert radar and see if I could get a cell phone connection.

I still had a trickle of battery left on my phone. I kept it turned off until I was pretty darned sure that I would succeed. I turned my cell phone on and off. As soon as the first bars blipped onto my screen, I called.

"9-1-1. What's your emergency?"

"Mayday. Mayday. Mayday. This is India Alexis Sobado from Iniquus. I am flying a Cessna C500. I was hit by lightning and have lost electricity. I have no navigation equipment or communication equipment. Please advise." I spoke as clearly as I could, but my voice quivered like the strings on a harp.

Nerves.

I waited for a response, but none came. I looked down. My call had dropped. I waited again for a bar to show up.

"9-1-1. What is your emergency?"

"Mayday. Mayday. Mayday. This is India Sobado. Iniquus. Cessna C500. No fuel. No navigation or communication. I'm going down. HELP ME."

"Ma'am, we are in contact with the FAA. Can you…"

Dropped.

Dropped?

No more battery.

My plane sputtered. I glided low over the desert. The wind buffeted me left and right. Not a single thought ran through my head. I flew by instinct alone, doing what I had been taught to do —step one…two…then three.

I hit down hard. The sand didn't let my plane lose its forward momentum by taxi-ing properly. Basically, I thunked down, rolled a bit, then went plane's nose into the sand, my chest to the yoke, head to the dash, blackness. . .

It was nighttime when I came to. I tried to breathe deeply, but my ribs were broken — each shallow gulp was excruciating. Under exploring fingers, I found blood caking my face. I lifted my head... Dizzy. Blurred vision. God, I had a monster headache. Concussion? Whiplash? Both? No way to help myself but to lie still. I wrapped my neck in my hoodie to protect my spine. I wished for ace bandages to support my ribs, but I knew from my time caught on the island that there was no first aid kit.

I pulled myself to the back of the plane to lie down. I said prayers of thanksgiving that I had made it back to America. This must be America; 911 picked up my call. I knew they heard my first distress call because the second person knew that the FAA had been contacted.

I felt the plane shivering and shaking as the storm picked up again. It followed me from the east. With a sinking heart, I knew no one would look for me until the winds died down. Might as well get comfortable — no point in setting out signals.

I slept. How many days had gone by? I think maybe two. During the day, the plane heated up like a furnace. On the first day, when the temperatures were so unbearable, I tried to lie in the shade under a wing. But there was no good place to go. Inside, I broiled. Outside, the wind wicked what little moisture I had out of my body; the sand abraded my skin. I put the smallest amounts of water into my mouth. I tried to stretch out the few drops I had left. I stopped sweating. That was a bad thing. I was vomiting again, which was even worse. Looked like dehydration had kicked in…heat stroke. Simple things — seeing, breathing, and staying upright — felt like a marathon run. The weather conditions exacerbated my impact injuries.

I focused on a steely will to win.

Today, the wind died down considerably. Probably this was the first day when anyone could even think about getting off the ground for a search. I figured it was getting close to being my "last chance for hope" day. If no one comes and finds me? Well, I didn't really want to go there in my mind. Survival was my focus.

I pulled myself outside the plane to look around with an eye to signaling. All I saw was desert — as austere and forlorn on the ground as it had been from the sky. Coming in, I scanned the horizon for rivers, houses, anything that would help me. All I had seen was dirt. Some cacti dotted the landscape. I'd never been to this part of the US; this terrain was foreign to me. I didn't know which plants were edible and which were poisonous. I knew, in theory, how to test them, but my mind was so untrustworthy right now that I wasn't willing to try.

I realized my landing gear had broken off when I hit down. Just as well. It saved me a lot of problems. I dragged myself about, positioning the tires in a huge triangle around the plane. A rattlesnake slithered past. That made me laugh. Of course. Why not? Add rattlesnakes to my list of how to botch my own rescue mission. I took the flight books from the cockpit and lit them on fire with the book of matches Franco had put in my pack. I set the flame against the rubber tires. Black smoke plumed into the air. I sat under the wing and watched the sky as best I could, waiting to use the mirror to signal.

Hallucinations. Faces swirled in front of me: Pablo crying; Franco and Elicia in frantic prayer, begging.

"I'm sorry. I'm so sorry. I failed you. Forgive me," I prayed.

Grandmother Sybil threw herbs into the fire and called to the sky.

I saw Striker and Gator, Blaze, Jack, and Deep; they were doing a lot of yelling in my head and cussing.

I thought I would see my mom and dad and Angel. Surely, Angel would come and help me cross over. Where were my loved ones? Why wouldn't they be offering me solace and support as I left this terrestrial world to join them? I thought about trying to go behind the Veil again. I wanted to see if I couldn't get help for myself, but I was afraid that I'd never find my way back to my body.

Buzzards circled overhead. Hysterical. They had actually found me and were circling. Who knew that really happened? I thought that was the stuff of Saturday morning cartoons. I guessed the black smoke helped to keep them away. When I really thought that I didn't have another breath, I'd try to get in the plane so the birds wouldn't gouge out my eyeballs and peck my flesh from my bones. I shuddered at the image.

My thoughts were raging, crazy. Sometimes I floated in beautiful peace. Other times, I fought monsters in my brain. I was end-stage. My time had come. I crawled into the plane up to the pilot's seat and laid back.

In my head, I heard Gator calling to me. "We're trying. We're trying, Lynx! Where are you?"

I thought about Striker, and Bayard Taylor's beautiful words sang in my ears:

· · ·

From the Desert, I come to thee,
  On a stallion shod with fire;
  And the winds are left behind,
  In the speed of my desire.
  Under thy window, I stand,
  And the midnight hears my cry:
  I love thee, I love but thee,
  With a love that shall not die.

Ironic as hell how much I have always loved this poem, "Bedouin's Song," and it was turning out to be my dirge.

I had lost my grip on reality. My brain responded to the toxic poisons circulating in my body. Fear wrapped me in a tight embrace, holding me back as I tried to push death away. That felt futile.

Exhaustion. Pain. Turbulence. That was how my end was coming to me. In my mind's eye, a helicopter landed in the desert. I saw the faces of those I love: Gator, Deep, Blaze, Jack… Striker. I wanted to say goodbye to them, to thank them for all they had been to me — for trying so hard to help. Sand swirled around my plane, making it impossible for me to see anything beyond my closed eyes. And, oh, just to see my friends' faces…

In my hallucinations, Striker ran, shouting. He jerked the door open, and I fell into his arms. My last thought, I hope you know how much I love you, Striker. You can stop searching now.

I was pretty sure I was dead.

The End

Thank you for reading Missing Lynx, book two of the Lynx series.

Please follow Lexi Sobado and the Iniquus family
as they continue their fight for the greater good in the next Lynx Series novel.

Please turn the page to read chapter one of Chain Lynx, so you know how Lynx is saved from the plane crash.

Readers, I hope you enjoyed getting to know Lexi and her Iniquus team. If you had fun reading Missing Lynx, I'd appreciate it if you'd help others enjoy it too.

Recommend it: Just a few words to your friends, your book groups, and your social networks would be wonderful.

Review it: Please tell your fellow readers what you liked about my book by reviewing Missing Lynx. If you do write a review, please send me a note Hello@FionaQuinnBooks.com so I can thank you with a personal e-mail. Or stop by my website www. FionaQuinnBooks.com to keep up with my news and chat through my contact form.

Please follow Lexi Sobado and the Iniquus family as they continue their fight for the greater good in the next Lynx Series novel, CHAIN LYNX.

Please turn the page to read chapter one of Chain Lynx, so you know how Lynx is saved from the plane crash.

CHAIN

Lynx

FIONA QUINN

1

Death was louder than I expected. I didn't think there would be any noise at all, only a bright light to guide me. Where were my loved ones who had passed on? Shouldn't they be here to lead me — to help me transition from the corporeal life to life ever-lasting? Mom and Dad should be here. My husband, Angel. My dear friend, Snow Bird. . . but I was alone with the sound of thundering wind and yelling.

My body jolted. Liquid fire saturated my skin. I lay smol-dering at the edge of a wide abyss. If I slid an inch to my left, I'd fall straight to the Devil's door. What did I do to find myself at Hell's Gate? My mind scrambled. I had indeed committed the worst possible of sins. I'd killed four people in my lifetime. Once in self-defense — a psychopath, Travis Wilson, had stalked me and tried to skin me alive. Surely, God would forgive me my will to live.

The other three were bank robbers. They'd taken twenty-two people hostage. A bullet tore through an elderly lady's brain. The robber was pressing his Glock to a pregnant woman's temple, making a show of his ruthlessness for the SWAT team outside.

I'd been in the building, armed, on an operation for Iniquus. Protecting innocents was just an extension of my job, and killing those men were not sins in my mind. But they must have been, and this must be the road to Perdition.

Something in my soul clung to the idea of justice. Damnation was not the path I would voluntarily roam for eternity. I sensed the Devil, red-faced and gloating, reaching out his craggy hand, laughing as he tried to drag me over the edge. "No!" my mind screamed as I desperately tried to scuttle away from the chasm, the smell, the heat, and the sound. "God, help me. God, please help me."

As if on cue, peace quenched the inferno that raged through my veins. With the flames from Hell's threshold extinguished, I floated away from evil into nothingness.

Time danced inevitably forward. I felt solid again. A bright light assaulted my pupils. Not the light of Heaven's beauty, but a penlight, checking for dilation.

"She's coming around," the man in a lab coat said.

Striker's face came into view. "Lynx? Lynx, can you hear me?"

I tried to work my jaw muscles to respond. I couldn't. Something large and hard filled my mouth. The trickle of tears sliding down my cheek was the only signal I could muster. The salt stung my cuts and abrasions and burned my face.

"Lynx, if you can understand me, squeeze my hand." Striker used his commander voice, even and authoritative.

I was loopy. Heavily drugged. But that much I could do.

"Chica, you're safe. We're taking good care of you. I need you to keep fighting. Don't leave me now."

Unable to move, unable to speak, I closed my eyes and let

myself drift back into the peace of the drugs flowing through my IV.

I knew that minutes and hours slid by. But it was an awareness that sat in an armchair, reading a book, muttering over the pages from time to time – not an awareness that actually held my attention or made me think. I lay stupefied on my bed. Slowly, I realized that Striker was rubbing a finger up and down my arm, trying to rouse me.

"Lynx? I need you to open your eyes. Look at me."

I worked hard to comply, squinting up at his face through a morphine haze. I felt the sturdiness and strength of his body beside me. I wasn't hallucinating him. He was real. Real? Yes, solid. Here. The relief I felt rushed through my body like a tidal wave, floated my emotions to the surface, and overwhelmed me. My body shivered under the light cotton blanket.

As I focused on his face, Striker gave me a slightly crooked smile with a hint of dimples. His gaze, steady and warm, held mine, though worry made tire tracks between his green eyes. I breathed in deeply to form a happy sigh until pain exploded my chest into bright colors, freezing me in place.

Striker's thumb stroked over my jawline. As I exhaled, the pain receded into the background.

"They've taken out your breathing tube. Can you say something?" He tried to hide the hitch in his voice behind a cough.

I licked my swollen lips. They were crusty and dry under a thick layer of what tasted like Vaseline. It took me a minute and a few false tries to coordinate my tongue and teeth into intelligible words.

"Chest hurts," I croaked, toad-like.

"I'm sure it does, Chica." His grip tightened around my hand, pinching my fingers together. "We had to defibrillate you."

His vowels and consonants leaped like a gymnast doing floor exercises, swirling and spinning. It was hard to form them into understandable words. Defibrillate. I let the word condense into a thought. "I was dead?"

"When we pulled you from the plane wreck, you had no vitals. You must have just gone into cardiac arrest because we were able to bring you back right away."

I tried to shift, but my body only moved centimeters. I couldn't turn my head. I was fastened by some kind of restraint. I let my gaze take in what I could. Plain, green walls. Fluorescent lighting. An IV stand. I wasn't in the desert anymore. I wasn't alone anymore.

"We flew you here to Lackland Air Force Base. You're in their hospital," Striker said.

"Texas, then. Not Honduras."

"You're on US soil." His eyes hardened into his assessing look. "That was one hell of an escape plan."

I tried to screw my expression into a wry smile, but my skin wouldn't oblige. "My face. . . can I see a mirror?" I hadn't seen my reflection in a mirror since mid-February when Maria Rodriguez kidnapped me and hid me in a Honduran prison. It was what — sometime in late June? July?

Striker locked down his emotions. His facial muscles froze into combat stoicism. What made him brace? I lifted my hands to my face, where my fingers explored the unfamiliar terrain. Bandages and tape crisscrossed over my forehead and down my nose. Scabs, like chickenpox, dotted my cheeks. Everything felt scaly and tight.

Striker eased my hands away, moving them gently down to rest on my stomach. "Lynx, I'd rather you wait a little while before you look in the mirror. You don't look like yourself right now." His combat mask slipped a little, and I saw the shadow of sadness and concern written in his eyes. No pity, thank goodness. Pity made me weak.

"You've lost a lot of weight," he said. "You were just over eighty pounds when we brought you in yesterday. Your skin's pretty badly sunburned. Those sores you're feeling are from the toxins trying to get out of your system when you were dehydrated."

"What else?" My voice cracked. I'd love a sip of water—some ice chips. I wondered if they'd allow that. Somehow, it felt like too much effort to ask.

"Broken nose. Broken ribs and sternum. Trauma to your head and spinal column. The head trauma is worrisome because it's your second traumatic brain injury in the same year. The doctors are stabilizing you for surgery. Hopefully, that'll happen in the morning if you continue to improve."

"Because?" When I squeezed his hand for support, the tubing and tape from the IV pulled at my elbow.

"They need to rebuild your sternum and re-attach your ribs. You're strapped to a board right now." He reached out and rapped on the surface beneath me so I could hear its solidity. "But when you wake up, they're going to have you in traction for your spine and neck." His words became gruff when he drew my hand to his lips for a kiss. "Chica, it was a near thing." Emotions under his skin and behind his eyes fought for expression, but Striker's steely will held out, and he maintained his control. As always.

That didn't mean I couldn't feel his distress empathically. His energy entwined with mine until I couldn't tell us apart or tell his pain from mine—one of the many things I hated about ESP.

"I'm sorry. I'm so sorry." I couldn't handle the guilt. This whole fiasco was my own damned fault. Poor decisions. Impulsive behavior. Secrecy. I offered Striker the closest thing to a contrite smile as I could form on my inflexible face. I felt like I was treading water - my head lifting just above the black swirl of morphine. It was exhausting to struggle, so I tried to float for a minute. To rest. My words slurred together. "You know, it's going to feel so good to get home again. We can—"

"No." Striker's voice slammed into my thoughts, bringing them to a screeching halt like a brake stopping a barreling car. My eyelids stretched wide.

"You aren't going home," He softened his tone. "It isn't safe. You still have people out there trying to get you."

Monumentally confused, I played his words over again in my mind. I wanted answers, but the pain had turned into a raging monster, clawing at my chest. I gasped at the shock of it. It pulled all of my attention away from here and now, and my questions of what? Why? And, who in the world? Striker pressed the call button. A nurse appeared next to me. That was all I remembered.

GRAB YOUR COPY OF CHAIN LYNX AND LET'S GO!

CHAIN LYNX IS AVAILABLE IN DIGITAL, PRINT, AUDIO & AUDIO CD FORMATS.

THE WORLD of INIQUUS

Chronological Order

Ubicumque, Quoties. Quidquid

Weakest Lynx (Lynx Series)

Missing Lynx (Lynx Series)

Chain Lynx (Lynx Series)

Cuff Lynx (Lynx Series)

WASP (Uncommon Enemies)

In Too DEEP (Strike Force)

Relic (Uncommon Enemies)

Mine (Kate Hamilton Mystery)

Jack Be Quick (Strike Force

Deadlock (Uncommon Enemies)

Instigator (Strike Force)

Yours (Kate Hamilton Mystery)

Gulf Lynx (Lynx Series)

Open Secret (FBI Joint Task Force)

Thorn (Uncommon Enemies)
Ours (Kate Hamilton Mysteries
Cold Red (FBI Joint Task Force)
Even Odds (FBI Joint Task Force)
Survival Instinct - Cerberus Tactical K9
Protective Instinct - Cerberus Tactical K9
Defender's Instinct - Cerberus Tactical K9
Danger Signs - Delta Force Echo
Hyper Lynx - Lynx Series
Danger Zone - Delta Force Echo
Danger Close - Delta Force Echo
Cerberus Tactical K9 Team Bravo
Marriage Lynx - Lynx Series

FOR MORE INFORMATION VISIT
WWW.FIONAQUINNBOOKS.COM

ACKNOWLEDGMENTS

My great appreciation ~

To my editors, Lindsay Smith and Kathleen Payne

To my cover artist, Melody Simmons

To my publicist, Margaret Daly

To my Street Force, who support me and my writing with such enthusiasm.

To my Beta Force, who are always honest and kind at the same time.

To H. Russell for creating the Iniquus Bible—so I can keep all the details correct

To all the wonderful professionals whom I called on to get the details right.

Please note: this is a work of fiction, and while I always try my best to get all the details correct, there are times when it serves the story to go slightly to the left or right of perfection. Please understand that any mistakes or discrepancies are my authorial decision making alone and sit squarely on my shoulders.

Thank you to my family.

I send my love to my husband and my great appreciation. T, you live in my heart. You live in my characters. You are my hero.

And of course, thank YOU for reading my stories. I'm smiling joyfully as I type this. I so appreciate you!

ABOUT THE AUTHOR

Fiona Quinn is a six-time USA Today bestselling author, a Kindle Scout winner, and an Amazon All-Star.

Quinn writes action-adventure in her Iniquus World of books, including Lynx, Strike Force, Uncommon Enemies, Kate Hamilton Mysteries, FBI Joint Task Force, Cerberus Tactical K9, and Delta Force Echo series.

She writes urban fantasy as Fiona Angelica Quinn for her Elemental Witches Series.

And, just for fun, she writes the Badge Bunny Booze Mystery Collection with her dear friend, Tina Glasneck.

Quinn is rooted in the Old Dominion, where she lives with her husband. There, she pops chocolates, devours books, and taps continuously on her laptop.

Visit www.FionaQuinnBooks.com

COPYRIGHT